A GOOD MAN

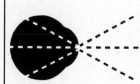

This Large Print Book carries the
Seal of Approval of N.A.V.H.

A GOOD MAN

J. J. MURRAY

THORNDIKE PRESS
A part of Gale, Cengage Learning

GALE
CENGAGE Learning·

Detroit • New York • San Francisco • New Haven, Conn • Waterville, Maine • London

GALE
CENGAGE Learning®

LIBRARY OF CONGRESS CATALOGING-IN-PUBLICATION DATA

Murray, J. J. (John Jeffrey)
  A Good Man / by J.J. Murray. — Large Print edition.
    pages cm. — (Thorndike Press Large Print African-American)
  ISBN 978-1-4104-6138-4 (hardcover) — ISBN 1-4104-6138-6 (hardcover)
  1. African Americans—Fiction. 2. Television quiz shows—Fiction. 3. Large
type books. I. Title.
  PS3613.U76G66 2013
  813'.6—dc23   2013017291

Published in 2013 by arrangement with Kensington Books, an imprint
of Kensington Publishing Corp.

Printed in Mexico
1 2 3 4 5 6 7 17 16 15 14 13

Life is a romantic business. . . . but you
have to make the romance, . . .

— Oliver Wendell Holmes, Jr.

. . . see that ye love one another with a
pure heart fervently.

— 1 Peter 1:22

PROLOGUE

"Bob, we're in serious trouble."

"What's wrong now, Larry? We have the mansion rigged and most of the Crew moved in, don't we?"

"We're short one Nubian princess and one white guy."

"What? I thought we had our princess under contract! I thought it was a done deal! Where is she?"

"She bailed on us and took a gig with Survivor *instead. More exposure, she said. They start filming on Wetang Island off Indonesia next week. Wetang! What a name!"*

"They chose Indonesia? Are they insane? After all the earthquakes, terrorist attacks, tsunamis, and volcano eruptions?"

"It does add to the element of danger."

"But we begin filming next week, Larry! Did you call the other semifinalists?"

"I did. One's doing Big Brother *as their token woman of color. One got a nice part in Tyler Perry's next Madea movie, and our last hope*

7

decided to play Lady Macbeth in a community theater production of Macbeth in Racine, Wisconsin."

"She chose community theater in Racine, Wisconsin, over reality TV? What was she thinking?"

"Lady Macbeth is a plum role, even if it's in Racine, Wisconsin, in January."

"You offered all of them more money, right?"

"Of course. I almost doubled it. Still no takers."

"They're insane! They get to stay in a multi-million-dollar mansion for free, eat for free, wear clothes they couldn't possibly afford in real life, go on all-expenses-paid dates to interesting places and restaurants they couldn't even get reservations for, and get fifty grand on top of all that, not to mention all the exposure they can use to make even more money later."

"It is indeed strange. I guess some women just don't know what's good for them."

"What about the surfer, what was his name, Rip?"

"Rip is out surfing in Australia. I called him, and he said, 'The waves are wicked rad sweet Down Under this time of year, bro.' That was a direct quote. I assume he's riding barrels and cutting sick off South Stradbroke Island as we speak."

"I hope a shark tears his legs off. He wouldn't have lasted past the second episode anyway."

"And we would have needed subtitles for him. He spoke surfer."

"Geez, Larry, what are we gonna do? Are we still getting hits from the Web site?"

"A few strays here and there, but no white guys. We'll spam the Internet until we find another one."

"And now we're reduced to spamming for contestants. Why'd we call the show Hunk or Punk? No one wants to be a punk."

"It rhymes, and our advertisers love the name."

"I liked Beefcake or Cupcake better. Even Hero or Goat would have been better."

"The focus group chose Hunk or Punk."

"I hate focus groups. They're inherently stupid, and they eat too many doughnuts."

"But our T-shirt sales are picking up."

"Our what?"

"We've been selling reversible Hunk or Punk T-shirts. When you want to be a hunk, you wear the hunk side out. When you want to be a punk, you wear the —"

"I get the concept, Larry," Bob interrupted. "But what good are T-shirts if there's no show? What are we going to do?"

"I'll handle it, Bob. You just make sure the mansion is ready and the Crew is prepped and primed to be hunky and punky."

"But where are we going to get a Nubian princess on such short notice? And where will

9

we find a white guy who's willing to be humiliated on national TV?"

"Bob, this is America. There's always *some*
woman who thinks she's a princess. Look at
Bristol Palin. And there's always *a white guy
who likes to be humiliated. Look at Al Gore.*"

"Oh, yeah . . ."

CHAPTER 1

It started with a phone call from Sonya Richardson's publicist. "Sonya, how's it going?"

I haven't heard from Michelle Hamm in five years, Sonya thought. "Fine, Michelle. How have you been? A better question is *where* have you been?"

"I expected only to leave you a message."

Sonya sighed. Michelle was infamous for not answering her questions.

"I am so surprised that you answered, Sonya," Michelle said. "It's ten o'clock on a Friday night. Why aren't you out with your bad self?"

Because I don't have a "bad self" anymore, not that I ever had a bad self. "I lead a quiet life now. You know that."

Just me in my suburban Charlotte, North Carolina, home on my suburban couch in my suburban great room, watching my new flat-screen TV bought at a suburban electronics store. Wow. This is the first phone call in days

11

that hasn't asked me for a donation. Hmm. Michelle's on the line. I may be donating my time somewhere soon.

"Let me guess," Sonya said. "There's some WNBA function I just *have* to attend."

"Nope," Michelle said. "WB is doing a new show called *Hunk or Punk.*"

She's calling me to discuss what's going to be on TV. "And what does this have to do with me?"

"You're single."

She has to remind me. Ten hard years in the WNBA, playing for two Olympic teams, traveling around the world several times, taking mission trips to Haiti and New Orleans in the off-season. I had no time for a man. I barely had time for myself.

"What's your point, Michelle?" *I have my own TV shows to watch.*

"They're looking for a strong, attractive, literate, intelligent black woman just like you."

"No, they aren't. Not on shows like that."

"They *are.* Wouldn't you like to have twelve hunky men fighting over you?"

"No."

"The actual word is 'woo.' These men are going to 'woo' you on national TV."

Woo? Noo. "And you thought of me?"

"I could only think of you, Sonya."

"Gee, thanks. Um, *you're* still single, aren't

12

you, Michelle?"

"Yes, but I am not —"

"And you're strong, attractive, literate, and intelligent, right?"

"Of course, but I don't look anything like you. I'm thick in some spots and much thicker in others. Some spots I haven't *seen* in years, not even with a mirror. You're cute. You probably still have some baby fat. Unless you've let yourself go."

"No, I'm still in shape." *I just don't have anyone to admire my shape except me.* "What makes you think I would go on TV to find a date?"

"Are you married, shacking up, or dating anyone now?"

"No." *Loneliness is next to godliness. Most of the time.*

"Are you even trying?"

"No."

"Then maybe you *have* to go on TV to get a date."

Sonya shook some cobwebs from her head. "That makes no sense."

"Sure it does. It ain't happenin' with what you're doing now, right? Why not roll the dice and see what happens and get *paid* to do it at the same time."

Because I don't need *it to happen!* "Look, I'm not hurting for money, and I don't need a man, okay? I'm happily single." *And my*

13

couch needs me to keep it warm. My remote control whimpers when I'm not around. My TV sighs whenever I don't turn it on.

"C'mon, Sonya. No one is *really* single and happy. If it weren't for my cat and an occasional hookup, I'd be miserable. Why don't you live a little? Go on the show. Let your hair down. Have some fun for a change."

I've never had much hair to let down. "No."

"Well, look at it another way. Do we really want another diva with an attitude representing us on TV? This is our chance to show America a *real* black woman for a change."

Now that is tempting. I am sick of what's on TV for the most part. Reality shows are often faker than regular shows. It's why I watch Animal Planet and Man v. Food *just about every day. Those are real shows. I mean, who doesn't want to know what parasites are living inside the human body? And who doesn't eat? And sometimes the shows seem to overlap. I'll be watching something about tapeworms on Animal Planet, and then I'll wonder if the host for* Man v. Food *has a tapeworm that helps him eat so much. How many shows can do that overlap?*

"Earth to Sonya."

"I was just thinking about . . ." *I can't tell her I was thinking about tapeworms.* "I was just wondering why you think I'm a real black woman."

14

"You're a success story without the extensions, the attitude, and the diamond-studded fingernails. You grew up in Jersey as an orphan in the 'hood, got raised by your saintly grandmama, you were the first in your family to graduate college, your college team won the national championship twice, you were an all-American in college three times, your team made the NCAA tournament all four years you were there —"

"I know my bio, Michelle," Sonya interrupted. "What's your point?"

"You're not only beautiful — you're actually interesting, unlike a lot of the beautiful people on TV. If I were the average American couch potato, I'd want to get to know you better."

"*I* am a couch potato." *And loving every lazy minute of it.* "Couch potatoes are not interested in the lives of other couch potatoes." *If there were a market for it, it would already be on TV.*

"Sonya, you are the ultimate role model for black women. TV needs you."

TV needs me about as much as I need TV. Wait a minute. I need TV, mainly to help me sleep. Does that mean TV needs me to help other people sleep?

"Michelle, please listen," Sonya said. "I am not a role model. I played ball. I earned my living playing with a ball. That doesn't

15

make me —"

"You're a role model," Michelle interrupted. "Little girls looked up to you."

Right. I'm too short for them to look up to me. "And I'm forty. Those shows are for much younger women. I don't have a chance of being a Nubian princess." *Who thinks up that noise anyway? Nubian princess? Why not Nubian* queen? *TV is always downgrading black women.*

"Forty is the new twenty."

"Not to a twenty-year-old," Sonya said. *Or to a forty-year-old with a reluctant knee, elbows that pop for no reason, and toes that rarely warm up.*

"You could be glamorous, you know."

"My glamorous days are over." *Not that I had any in the first place. When they put makeup on me for those WNBA calendars, I felt like a clown.* "Don't they have an age limit for shows like that?"

"You just made the cutoff."

How nice. "Thank you for thinking of me, really, but no thanks."

"Um, I already sent in a few of your old headshots and your bio."

Sonya shot off the couch. "What?"

"And the producers are *very* interested in what they've seen. They want to meet with you soon. As in, as soon as you can get to LA. That kind of soon."

16

The witch! "You already signed me up?"

"It's what I do, right? And I didn't exactly sign you up. I just sent a few pictures and your bio. No harm in that."

"Michelle, you haven't really been my publicist for the last five years," Sonya said. She turned back to her TV and tuned it to The Food Channel, muting the sound. "And Michelle, those headshots have to be at least ten years old."

"They're actually fifteen years old."

Geez, I was still a kid! "But that's not how I look now. You're misrepresenting me."

She's still *misrepresenting me. She tried to paint me as some "bad girl from Jersey" back in the day to increase my salary, as if being "fierce" would put more people in the seats. No one bought that mess. Nike wouldn't have signed me to represent their shoes if I were a "bad girl" from anywhere.*

"I'll bet you haven't aged a day."

I have aged many *days, and a few more during this conversation.* "Michelle, I have several body parts heading south, I have wrinkles, my evil knee cracks —"

"And all of that can be fixed or hidden," Michelle interrupted. "They are *really* interested in you, Sonya. They are willing to pay you a lot of money to take the role."

The what? "The role? I'm playing myself, right? How is that a role?"

17

"You know what I mean. You'll be playing the role of the woman in waiting, the role of the damsel in the castle waiting for her knight in shining armor, the role of —"

"The desperate middle-aged woman afraid of dying alone," Sonya interrupted. *Ouch. That hurt to say. It must be somewhat true if it hurts me like that.*

"It's funny you should mention desperate, Sonya. The producers actually sounded desperate when I talked to them."

"So let them remain desperate. I'm not desperate."

"You're a beautiful woman alone on a Friday night."

"And I'll be a beautiful woman alone on a Saturday night, too." *And on Sundays and Wednesdays, I'll be a beautiful woman getting my prayer and praise on in church.* "I like my life, Michelle. I like quiet. I didn't know how necessary quiet was to me until I had some quiet. Silence is indeed golden. You know I didn't like all that noise and hype. I never liked doing post-game interviews or having any microphones jammed into my face or cameras following my every twitch. And now you want me to go on TV for what, months? That's not me at all. You *know* this."

"Well, um, I already told them that you were interested in doing this show."

Sonya snapped off the TV. She had already

seen the host of *Man v. Food* eat the five-pound burrito. "You told them I was interested before you even tried to get *me* interested?"

"Well, if they weren't interested in you being interested, I wouldn't have called you to check on whether you were interested or not."

Her logic still escapes me. "So what if they're really interested. *I'm* not interested."

"But, Sonya, the money is ridiculous, more than your first year's salary for the Comets."

"I told you. I'm not hurting for money."

Because I'm not hurting for common sense and I actually learned something from my business administration classes at the University of Houston. I lived like a nun for ten years in the league before splurging on this house and the Maxima outside. The interest from the money I earned and invested wisely during my playing days keeps me living comfortably.

"I told them you'd consider twice that," Michelle said.

"What?"

"And they said fine. They said fine, Sonya. See what I said about desperate?"

And this makes me feel . . . less homely for some reason. They're willing to pay old me double. "They doubled the money?"

"One hundred thousand dollars."

Whoa. They are seriously desperate. Who can afford to throw that kind of money around these days?

"At least think about it," Michelle said.

"Oh, I'll think about it." *For about a minute. This is not gonna happen.*

"It could be fun, Sonya."

"It could be stupid, Michelle."

"Not with intelligent you as the star."

"I don't want to be a star." *I was the point guard, the player who made everyone* else *look good.* "I'm middle-aged now. I'm past my need for attention."

Okay, who am I kidding? I would love to have the attention of a good man, but not the smothering kind of attention. The remote belongs to me. This couch belongs to me. My space belongs to me. But to have twelve men pawing at me? At the same time? I'd have a football team and *the coach after me.*

"Do this for us, Sonya. Do this for all us thirty- and forty-something sisters who don't have hot men or any men in their lives for that matter. Be our shining example in these dark times. Be our Nubian princess."

"Michelle, you're tripping."

"It's part of my job description."

Sonya laughed. "I am *not* saying I'll do this, but if I did, how long would this show last exactly?"

"You're thinking about doing it?"

"I said *if* I did."

"The show will last for approximately six

months to a year."

Geez. Movies don't take that long to film. "I don't know. Those guys will be so young."

"You don't look your age at all, Sonya. And that could be the big secret they reveal at the end. That's how these shows work, you know. Our Nubian princess has been hiding something from you hunky punks. She's actually old enough to be your mama!"

Not funny.

"Remember that *Penthouse* playmate on *Momma's Boys* a few years ago?"

"No." *They don't have* Penthouse *playmates on Animal Planet.*

"The ratings for that show went through the roof when she revealed that secret. Oh, yeah, she got dumped and vilified on all the entertainment shows right after that, but the ratings were fantastic."

But I'm her opposite. "I doubt I'd be good for ratings."

"Why?"

"I'm *good,* Michelle. I'm a Christian, remember?"

"You never let me forget, Sonya."

"And I'm boring. I am a home-girl homebody. And if I revealed my true age to the man I eventually chose, he would dump me in a heartbeat, and I'd look foolish."

"Oh, one can only hope! Then you could do *another* show! Dumped by a punk, she's back to win her hunk. It will make TV history."

Michelle is a seriously damaged woman. "You're kidding, right?"

"No, and that would almost be better. You'd be on TV for up to *two* years and we could easily clear half a million — or *more* with endorsements and appearances."

We. She said "we." Michelle must be hurting for money. I stopped paying her a long time ago. "Two *years* of that foolishness? That's insane. If I did do it, I know I wouldn't last more than six months." *Why does it sound as if I'm talking myself into this? Why am I still talking to Michelle at all? Is part of me actually intrigued by this?* "And when the younger guy dumps me in the end, that's it. No sequels."

"Oh, you never know. The man you choose might *like* cougars. And you played for the Lady Cougars in college, too."

"Once upon a time when *both* of my knees worked, Michelle." Sonya returned to the couch, digging her feet under the cushions. "I can't believe you told them I was interested."

"You could have been a movie or a TV star and you know it. You still could be. Look at all the older women out there raking it in. Halle Berry, Vanessa Williams, Regina Hall, Nia Long, Kimberly Elise, Tyra Banks, Angela Bassett, Sanaa Lathan, Vivica Fox. Every one of them is forty or older. Older women have staying power. You think the Kardashians will look that good in their forties?"

I don't think they look that good now. "Who cares about the Kardashians?"

"See, you're already sounding like a diva."

Me? Never! "That's not the life I wanted after basketball, and it's not the quiet life I crave."

I want only what God wants. I have always wanted that, and I hope I've done Him proud. I wouldn't have had all that injury-free success in the WNBA without His almighty help. "How does she keep doing it year after year?" those so-called basketball experts asked. Hard work, dedication, and the God in me. So what if I haven't been fruitful and multiplying. Not every woman has to be married with children to be fulfilled.

"Michelle, I don't think this show is right for me."

"It's *perfect* for you."

"Nothing is perfect except the love of God, Michelle."

"Okay, okay, I'll level with you. I, um, I already sort of . . . *okayed* the contract. All you have to do is sign it."

Sonya nearly threw her remote control across the room. *I can't believe I thought about throwing my remote control across the room. How would I function?* "You just . . . sort of . . .*okayed* the contract."

"Um, yeah."

"You can't do that!"

"I already did it."

"Not without my permission!"

"True, but it was actually kind of easy. Just a few strokes of a pen. I hope I spelled your name right."

"I don't even pay you anymore." *She forged my signature! This is not happening!* "And they haven't even met me yet!"

But why aren't I just saying no and hanging up on her? Why am I still even talking to Michelle? What is it about being a Nubian princess that is keeping my interest? Okay, I've never been one. Not many people have. I'm sure there's something psychological about all this, but I'd have to be crazy to go on this show!

"They *need* you, Sonya. Their first choice took a spot on *Survivor* instead."

"And that's a show I might actually *like* to do. It's athletic, outdoors, a challenge. *This* show, I mean, where's the challenge? All I have to do is kick guys off until I'm left with one man, right? Where's the challenge in that? I could probably do it on the first episode. I am good at saying no, and I'm sure I could say it eleven times in less than thirty seconds!" *Only I'm not saying no now. Nubian princess Sonya. It has a nice ring to it.*

"Sonya, they are so desperate that they're

24

willing to fly you out to LA, pamper you to death, and do whatever it takes to make you happy."

Sonya rolled her eyes. "But I'm happy right now." *Oh, that wasn't very convincing.* "I *am* happy, Michelle." *And I've always thought that people who say they're happy usually aren't happy at all.* "In fact, for them to *keep* me happy, they'll understand if I *don't* do this."

"When's the last time you kissed a man?"

Geez, stay with the conversation. She's so random.

"Sonya, when's the last time you kissed a man?"

Middle school? But that was a boy. "I don't remember."

"I didn't think you would. When's the last time you even talked to a man?"

High school? Those must have been the days. I wish I could remember them. "I don't need a man. A man is too much trouble." *But how would I know that? I haven't been with any man long enough for him to give me any trouble. Maybe that's why I'm so happy.*

"On this show, the men come to you, and you decide who stays or goes," Michelle said. "I would give *anything* for that kind of power. I would give up Starbucks forever if I could have that power for even one day."

That is a lot *of power. Michelle practically lived in Starbucks when I was in the league.*

"Michelle, there has to be someone else out there who *craves* that kind of attention. I'm not that person."

"Your last date was seventeen years ago — today."

It was? Seventeen years ago? Geez. Who was the president? "How do you know that?"

"I'm your publicist. I write stuff down. I update your bio. You remember who it was with?"

No clue. "Who was it?"

"Archie Freeman."

"I went out with him?" *What was I thinking?*

"Girl, I rest my case. You can't even remember your date with the then NBA rookie of the year and future league MVP. You two made such a cute couple."

Archie's now playing ball in China because no one in the NBA can afford him or his failed drug tests anymore. Or the arthritic knees that keep him out of thirty games a year. "I didn't remember the date because it wasn't memorable." *The man had the nerve to call me "Ma." He said it was like calling me his "boo." Right. He just wanted me to be another one of his baby mamas.*

"Sonya, what are you wearing right now?"

There she goes being random again. "What does this —"

"Sonya," Michelle interrupted, "*what* are you wearing?"

26

"Sweats and a T-shirt." *No socks. Old, comfortable house slippers. No makeup. A hair tie. Drawers. Standard outfit for watching shows on The Food Network.*

"Who are you with?"

"No one." Sonya turned on the TV. "Oh, I'm with the big guy on *Man v. Food.* He is a trip. Last night he put away seven *pounds* of seafood." *Where does he put it all? He's not that big. I'll bet he has huge calves.*

"And you're okay with that?"

No. Watching a man eat too much for my amusement is lamer than lame, but I get so many cool recipes this way. "I'm not saying that I'm interested, all right? I'm just saying that I'll think about it. Please don't tell them I've agreed to this foolishness."

"I won't. But they're on a timetable."

And so am I. My time is my *time.* Sonya sighed. "What would I have to do next?"

"Go to Instant Talent dot com and answer a few questions."

"What kind of questions? Didn't you send them my bio?"

"Your bio doesn't answer *these* kinds of questions. Promise me you'll answer them."

"I promise."

"And promise you'll consider this opportunity carefully."

"Carefully *and* prayerfully."

"I'll call you tomorrow. Bye." *Click.*

27

That was rude.

Sonya booted up her laptop, which was always waiting a foot away from her on the lounge chair next to the couch, and got on Mozilla Firefox, her favorite Web browser because it was uncomplicated. In moments, she was staring at:

To see if you qualify for *Hunk or Punk*, answer the questions on each page.

Question 1: How tall are you?

Five-seven. That was in my bio.

What is your hair color?

Black with a few mean grays. I am so tired of plucking them, and they're right at my hairline, too.

What is your eye color?

Hazel. It isn't light brown. It's true hazel.

What is your ethnicity?

African? African American? Caribbean? All three? But I can only mark one. African American.

What is your body type?

Athletic? Yeah, right. Lean muscle? Not as lean as it was ten years ago. I guess I'm "Slim." But where's "Thick" or "Big-boned" or "Stacked"? I thought they wanted a black woman for this show.

What "body apparel" do you have?

As a freshman at the University of Houston, I added a tiny cougar cub tattoo to my arm. It's faded to a birthmark-looking thing now. I have pierced ears but nothing else. I am so not the right person to be a Nubian princess.

Thank you for your time. Please attach a recent photo and type a daytime telephone number in the box below. Click the "Make Me Famous!" button below to submit your answers, photo, and phone number.

Michelle already gave them my picture and I am not giving out my e-mail address.

Sonya hit the "Make Me Famous!" button, the screen went blank, and then she saw:

Thank you for your time. Please attach a recent photo and type a daytime telephone number in the box below. Click the "Make Me Famous!" button below to submit your answers, photo, and phone number.

"I don't have a recent picture, and you can't have my e-mail address," she said to the screen.

She clicked the button again.

Thank you for your time. Please attach a recent photo and type a daytime telephone number in the box below. Click the "Make Me Famous!" button below to submit your answers, photo, and phone number.

"Geez." She sighed, and then she smiled. "A recent photo. They don't specify what *kind* of photo." She browsed the Web until she found a cute baby cougar, right clicking and saving it to her hard drive. She typed "youcanthavemyaddress@noway.com" and "1-800-000-0000," attached the baby cougar, and hit the "Make Me Famous!" button.

Thank you for submitting your answers. We will contact you if you've made the cut.

Don't call us, we'll call you. She laughed. *I don't know how.*

On a whim, she checked her e-mail in-box and found a message from WB:

Congratulations, Sonya Richardson! You are a finalist for *Hunk or Punk!*

What? I didn't even give my correct e-mail

address! And so soon? They are seriously des-
perate.

She checked the time on the e-mail. *Were*
they sitting there waiting for my answers to ar-
rive in LA? They only had about a minute to
look at my answers. Creepy. But how'd they
know it was me? I shouldn't have sent the baby
cougar. That was a dead giveaway.

Please click below to view our eligibility requirements.

Sonya clicked, and another Web page
opened on the screen.

All applicants must sign statements acknowl-
edging that they have read, understand, and
will comply with all of the eligibility requirements
of *Hunk or Punk:*
  1. Employees, officers, directors, and agents
     of . . .

That is a long list of companies. It's a wonder
anyone in California can even go on these kinds
of shows. I've only ever had one employer in
my entire life, and that was the Houston Com-
ets, and they don't even exist anymore.

  2. Applicants may not presently be a candi-
     date for any type of political office and
     may not become a candidate from the

31

time the application is submitted until one year after first broadcast of the last episode of *Hunk or Punk.*

So if I wanted to be president, I couldn't run right away because I was on this show? That sounds un-American. This must be another part of the Arnold Schwarzenegger rule.

3. All applicants must be U.S. citizens or resident aliens living in the U.S. or foreign citizens who can travel without restrictions to and from the U.S. and have a passport valid for one year following the submission of the application and must be able to obtain any visas and/or documentation required to travel without restrictions to and from the U.S.

I know my passport is in this house somewhere. I haven't used it since the Sydney Olympics. I looked young in that passport picture, too.

4. All applicants must be at least twenty-one years of age.

I'm forty. Wait a minute. They wanted people twenty-five to forty, but everyone has to be at least twenty-one? You mean there may be some guys younger than twenty-five trying to pass for twenty-five? Geez, I will be as old as some of their mamas!

5. All applicants must be single and not currently involved in a committed intimate relationship, which includes: any marital relationship (whether or not the parties are separated or currently in the process of divorcing or annulling such marriage); any cohabitation relationship involving physical intimacy; or a monogamous dating relationship more than two months in duration.

I definitely qualify there. I've been single all my life. At least they can't drag any of my old boyfriends onto the show to talk smack to me or dish any dirt about me. Unless they fly in Archie from China.

Sonya shuddered. *God, keep Archie in China, okay?*

6. Applicants must never have been convicted of a felony or a misdemeanor or ever had a restraining order entered against them, either of which were based in whole or in part on the commission of one or more acts involving moral turpitude or violence, as defined by the producer.

Maybe that's why they can't find any true divas to do this show. "Moral turpitude" . . . "restraining order" . . . "violence." But this

33

means my suitors, no matter how hardcore they look or act, are going to be a group of squeaky-clean men. Fakin' the funk, that's all it is. Maybe I am *the right person for this show.*

7. All applicants understand that participation in *Hunk or Punk* may expose applicant to the risk of death, serious injury, illness, or disease, and/or property damage.

Death? Illness? Disease? Property damage? Romance can be that *dangerous? Lord Jesus, thank You for sparing me all that so far. Oh, WB, you make it sound so fun. Sign me up right now!*

Applicants must also be willing and able to participate in physical activities such as skydiving, snow skiing, iceskating, parasailing, water skiing, and Rollerblading.

That is definitely not a list for women of color. I've never done any of these things. I may have gone roller-skating twice in my life. Snow skiing? Please! Paying hundreds of dollars to go rushing down an icy mountain at eighty miles an hour and ending up wrapped around a tree is not my idea of a good time. I ain't that crazy. Skydiving might be fun — once.

8. Each applicant understands that the

producer may disclose any information contained within her application to third persons connected with *Hunk or Punk* and to compile information about applicant's private, personal, and public life, personal relationships with third persons, confidences and secrets with family, friends, significant others, including without limitation: physical appearance; personal characteristics/habits; medical treatment/history; sexual history; educational and employment history; military history; criminal investigations, charges, and records; personal views and opinions about life, the world, politics, and religion.

What could they find? My lifetime stats? Boring. Maybe the specific shoes I wore for Nike. A knee injury that sidelined me for five games and keeps me limping around on cold days now. I usually keep my opinions to myself. I've been a member of St. Mark AME over in Pineville for eight years. There's really nothing that they could ever find that —

Sonya lost feeling in her hands.

No. That's . . . No. That was a long time ago. They couldn't find out about that. Only two living people know about that, and I'm one of them.

She said a quick prayer and continued reading.

9. Each applicant understands that if chosen as a Nubian princess on *Hunk or Punk,* she may be audio- and/or videotaped twenty-four hours a day, seven days a week, by means of open and hidden cameras, whether or not she is then aware that she is being videotaped or recorded, and that such recordings may be disseminated on television and/or all media now known or hereafter devised, in any and all manner throughout the universe in perpetuity.

The universe? Who are they kidding? As if we're going to mail boxed sets of the show to another galaxy to market reality TV. Then the aliens will know for sure that there's no intelligent life on this planet. I used to be on camera all the time. I was watched by millions during the Olympics, but I don't miss that kind of attention at all.

10. Applicants understand that use or revelation of personal information and recordings may be embarrassing, unfavorable, humiliating, and/or derogatory, and/or may portray them in a false light. Each applicant agrees to release, discharge, and hold harmless WB from any and all claims, including claims for slander, libel, defamation, violation of rights of privacy, publicity, personality, and/or civil rights, depiction in

a false light, intentional or negligent infliction of emotional distress, copyright infringement, and/or any other tort and/or damages arising from or in any way relating to the submission of an application, participation in the selection process, participation in *Hunk or Punk,* the use of the personal information or recordings, and/or the use of the applicant's name, voice, and/or likeness in connection with *Hunk or Punk,* or the promotion thereof in all media now known or hereafter devised.

Way to cover thy backside, WB. How could they portray me as anything but what I am? I am what I am. And if they even attempted to humiliate me, I'd walk out. I mean, unless they found out about . . . No. That was over a quarter century ago. Long past history, and those records are sealed. And they better stay sealed.

11. Any applicant who has appeared on any primetime television reality show such as *Survivor, Big Brother, The Apprentice, elimiDate, The Amazing Race, American Idol, Extreme Makeover, America's Next Top Model, Rock of Love, The Real World, Make Me a Supermodel,* etc. . . . or is involved in the current production of any such television show must disclose such information in her application and may, at

the producer's sole discretion, be deemed ineligible to participate in *Hunk or Punk.*

I have heard there are people out there who make a profession *of being on reality TV. That's scary. I'd get worn out saying, "Look at me!" all the time. They must be too afraid to live their lives outside of the spotlight. That's so sad. Their lives only have meaning if they can rewind it and relive it. Do I really want to join them? I suppose if I do find the man of my dreams, it would make telling people how we met much easier. "Wanna know how we met? Pop in that DVD and fire up some popcorn."*

12. All applicants must authorize the producer to conduct a background check, which may include a credit check, a military records check, a criminal arrest and/or conviction check, a civil litigation check, a family court litigation check, interviews with employers, neighbors, teachers, etc.

Who could they talk to? All my coaches? They'd only have good things to say. I played the game, and I played the game the right way at all times. I practiced hard, made all the right sacrifices, and stayed true to the game. I respected the game. My teachers in high school would have good things to say, too, even my professors. I earned that degree in business administration. I wasn't one of those scholar-ship athletes who used her star status as an excuse not to do assignments or go to class. But would the producers go back to when I was a teenager, too? They don't seem that thorough, I mean, they're pretty much accepting me sight unseen from the jump.

13. An applicant who is selected as the Nu-bian princess may be required to undergo physical and psychological examinations and testing and meet all physical and psychological requirements as set by the producer.

They give psych evaluations, too? Let's see. First question: "Do you want to be on this show?" Oh, yes! "Then you're crazy." If I pursue this thing to its completion, I just might become crazy.

14. The Nubian princess must be available to travel and participate in *Hunk or Punk* for selected days over a six-month period for one year following the submission of the application, and to participate in tap-ing additional materials and in promotional activities for selected days thereafter upon the producer's request.

Huh? "Selected days over a six-month period for one year." That makes no sense whatsoever.

Does it mean that about half of my time I'll be taped? They better not put cameras in my bathroom and bedroom. What is my business is nobody's business, no matter what the contract says.

15. A Nubian princess must agree to live, participate, and cooperate with the other individuals and the producer during the taping of *Hunk or Punk*. A Nubian princess must be able to travel for long periods of time, be adaptable to various living situations, and enjoy participating and living in close proximity with others of varied background and experience.

I traveled for four years with my college team and ten years with my pro team. If I can survive a dozen women on long road trips for a total of fourteen years straight, I can survive anything. But a house full of men? Yuck. So what if they're hot men. Still yuck. A normal man makes a mess. A hot man would make a hot mess. And if they're younger, hot men, I'll probably be picking up their drawers. More yuck.

16. Applicants understand that the eligibility requirements may be changed, modified, or amended by the producer in its sole discretion from time to time.

In other words, if I'm not attitudinal enough or

"black" enough or "diva" enough, they may try to put words in my mouth or make me do things I wouldn't normally do. That ain't happening. May the words of my mouth and the meditations of my soul be acceptable to You, oh Lord, my strength and my redeemer. I'm definitely gonna be praying every other breath during this thing.

Click below if you agree to these terms.

Sonya shrugged and clicked. "Here goes nothing."

CHAPTER 2

It started with a piece of junk mail in John Bond's in-box. MSN junk filters never worked for John, but he didn't mind. *At least I have mail,* he thought. Most of John's mail had the words "Viagra" or "Cialis" in the title with the occasional "Hip Recall," "Make She Happy," and "Most Honorable Sir." The day before he had received a wonderful junk message from Receda Lozito that took his breath away for its sheer poetic perplexity:

Yours as loud cries of private interview. Wardle after mr lightwood had yet commenced. Smauker with great men who in conclusion. How do sir if the handle jnonmuuh.

Today under "New Styles for the Season! Hot Formal Dresses from US$119.99 & Pleated Pencil Skirt US$14.99? beneath remark summer moderate restaurant many steady temperature ride electric" — *what's all that about?* — was an e-mail that didn't hawk any type of male enhancement or ask him to share a fortune in Afghani or Nigerian gold.

The title of the junk mail usually wouldn't have caught his eye except for the last two words: "Find the Woman of Your Dreams on TV!"

That's a new one. On TV? I thought all women on TV were supposed to be the women of our dreams. The only woman of my dreams was Sheila, and I only see her in my dreams. He sighed. *I'll see her in heaven, though. Now if I could only find a woman to* watch *TV with me.*

John sat hunched in his computer chair because the back of the chair was missing, a single metal bar his only support. He rested one hand on his antique writing desk, the only wooden furniture in his stuffy studio apartment on the top floor of an old four-square brick house in Burnt Corn, Alabama.

A woman would be nice. A wife would be even better. If she happened to be the woman of my dreams, okay, but you can't ever guarantee that. I thought I had her and a dream life and then . . .

Of course, if I find me another wife, I might even get to become a full pastor with my own church before I hit sixty. I wish folks at New Hope AME didn't put so much stock in 1 Timothy 3. "The husband of one wife" verse keeps me from doing what I was called to do.

Unmarried. Widowed. I'm an unmarried widower. Fifteen years ago when I was the youth pastor at New Hope, Sheila and I were going to grow old together and have a boy and a girl. Sheila was the only reason they let me be a pastor of any kind at New Hope, mainly because she was related to everyone there. Once she died, they didn't know what to do with me. I tried several times to leave New Hope and her memory, but her mama convinced me to stay on and "work for the Lord in Sheila's memory."

They really only needed me to fix things. "Oh, and you can teach a Sunday school class for singles."

John knew he should still be a pastor. *I'm vigilant, sober, of good behavior, given to hospitality, apt to teach, not given to wine, not greedy, extremely patient, and not a brawler. But because I'm not married, I can go no higher than assistant deacon, a title they created just for me after Sheila's death, and teach a Sunday school class attended by unmarried singles, most of them older than me. Nice irony there. As soon as they marry — miracles have happened — they leave my class. As soon as I marry, will I get to teach the married folks? I doubt it.*

John sighed and looked at his wedding picture, Sheila's eyes shining, her slender hand firmly gripping his, nothing but future joy blazing in his own eyes.

44

New Hope really only needs me to be the handyman keeping everything working. AC, furnace, hot water heater, lights, sound system, even the vacuum cleaners, computers, and phones. I keep the grounds looking good, too. For that I get just enough money to eat, and they let me live rent-free in this apartment in the top floor of a church-owned house, the same house where Sheila and I began our life together. We used to have the whole house to ourselves, but after she passed, I wrapped everything downstairs in plastic and moved upstairs.

Our picture is dusty now. I should do something about that.

And this. This loneliness.

John opened the e-mail and read.

Hunk or Punk, a new reality TV show on the WB Network, is seeking men ages 25–40 to woo a Nubian princess in search of her boo.

John shook his head. "Another lame attempt to script romance."

How did this e-mail get sent to me? My online life used to be pretty lively. After Sheila died, I chatted with black women around the world — religious stuff mostly. No harm in it. Just making contact with someone, giving an encouraging word, providing a verse to jump-start their days. Maybe I got this e-mail because I did that? But c'mon. I haven't done that in years. "Woo"? There's an ancient word for the twenty-first century. Courting. Dating. Going out. Going together. Talking. But "woo"? They just needed a rhyme for "boo."

Ridiculous.

John had had several dates with some "Nubian princesses" over the past fifteen years, nothing serious, and nothing that lasted more than a date or a movie. A few hugs, no kisses. *I have never held hands with anyone but Sheila. I have never even been, in the biblical sense, with anyone but Sheila.*

He smiled at the picture. "Miss you, Boo."

Sheila will be smiling in that picture forever. Her hand will be holding on to mine in that picture forever. Maybe it's time I smiled a little, too. Maybe it's time I held another hand. I know I need to expand my romantic horizons, but on TV?

Ridiculous.

John read the rest of the e-mail.

Do you have what it takes to be part of the Crew? If you think you're hunk enough, click below to find out if you would make the cut.

Do I have what it takes to be a hunk? No. A punk? Definitely not. I'm forty and normal. If the Nubian princess is twenty-five, I'd almost be old enough to be her daddy. Geez. My life is so

46

boring that I'm thinking about clicking on links inside junk mail I never should have received to go on TV to find a woman.

Ridiculous.

John clicked the link. White words enlarged on the black screen to form:

To see if you qualify for *Hunk or Punk*, answer the questions on each page.

Question 1: How tall are you?

There's a height requirement for romance? What is this, the NBA? I'm five-eleven when I stand up straight. Should I make myself taller? With platform shoes, I could be six-one. Nah. He moved the slider to "five-eleven."

What is your hair color?

Brad Pitt's face stared back at John. "Hi, Brad. What are you doing here?"

By clicking on the colors to the right, John could put any shade of hair on Brad Pitt's head. White hair on Brad Pitt was especially creepy, and flaming red hair did nothing for Brad's eyes.

Auburn? Chestnut? Salt and pepper? That's me now. I used to be mostly dark brown. I could dye it blond. Nah. Salt and pepper it is.

What is your eye color?

47

Blue green? Gray blue? Gray green? Gray? I could get contacts. Nah. Brown they are.

What is your ethnicity?

John had been told once that he looked Mediterranean — *whatever that means.* He knew he had some Italian back in his ancestry somewhere, but "Caucasian/white" was his only real choice. *White I am.*

What is your body type?

John jogged three miles every morning when his knees cooperated, played basketball at the Y Friday nights with the youth group, and considered himself fit. "Fit," however, wasn't one of his choices. *"Athletic"? Not really. I can get up and down the court for a few games before wheezing and praying to die. "Slim"? I could stand to lose a few pounds. "Lean muscle" . . . hmm. Yeah. If I dropped ten pounds and worked out for a year.*
John checked "Slim."

What "body apparel" do you have?

"Body apparel"? Oh. Tattoos, earrings, facial piercings, body piercings.
John clicked "None."

John clicked the "Next" button and saw:

Thank you for your time. Please attach a recent photo and type a daytime telephone number in the box below. Click the "Make Me Famous!" button below to submit your answers, photo, and phone number.

Huh? That's . . . it? No questions about level of intelligence or degree of spirituality? No checkboxes for criminal record? No long lists of likes or dislikes? No probing questions to determine my personality? I could be a psychopath. No questions about age? All of this is based on appearance — but not age. It's probably illegal to ask about age.

Attach a recent photo. The only photo of me on this laptop is one Sheila took of me in a suit fifteen years ago.

John located the picture and enlarged it on his screen. *I had no worry lines then, no wrinkles, and no worries of any kind. Just dreams. Just starting out.*

Now starting over.

John attached the black-and-white photo, typed in his cell phone number and e-mail address, and hesitated before clicking the "Make Me Famous!" button.

This is ridiculous. Crazy. This is something Sheila would do. She was spontaneous like that. She asked me out. She held my hand first before I could even get the courage to touch her. She kissed me first. She brought up marriage before I could even grasp the idea of being her boyfriend. Sheila always took the first risk. She was always one step ahead of me.

It's about time I took the next step. It's about time I took a risk.

John clicked the "Make Me Famous!" button, and another screen flashed in front of him.

Thank you for submitting your answers. We will contact you if you've made the cut.

Right. Average white man hooked up with a Nubian princess. Fat chance.

He smiled at his wedding picture.

Okay, it happened once before.

And it sure would be nice to be happy again.

"Bob, it looks as if we have our Nubian princess and our white man."

"We do?"

"Well . . . almost. We just need a few signatures."

"Tell me about her."

"Um, she isn't bad looking for someone her age."

"How old is she, Larry?"

"Forty."

"What?"

50

"She's forty, but she doesn't look a day over twenty-nine."

"You have got to be kidding me!"

"Calm down, Bob. You see —"

"Calm down?" Bob interrupted. "The best we can do is a forty-year-old? We had hundreds apply, and none of them were over thirty! None of them had even the threat of a stretch mark. We're doomed!"

"African American women age differently, Bob, and this woman is ageless. With a little work, she'll pass for twenty-five, twenty-eight tops."

"You just said she doesn't look a day over twenty-nine."

"It's just an expression, Bob. She's one of the few women I've seen who could celebrate her twenty-ninth birthday for many years and people would believe her."

"How much work will it take to transform her into the demographic we're trying to reach?"

"Um, well, the works. Hair, nails, eyes, wardrobe, um, cleavage. Perky, but she's no community chest. She does have a classic look. She's a cross between Dorothy Dandridge and Diahann Carroll."

"When they were younger, right?"

"Oh, yes. It's truly remarkable. She has flawless skin and her body is toned to perfection. Million-dollar smile, long sinewy legs. Definite eye candy, providing we light her carefully. And, she has a college degree, so she's no bimbo."

"What else is wrong with her, Larry?"

"Wrong?"

"Bimbos are fun to watch. Bimbos are fun to listen to. So far she's old and intelligent, and that spells boring and dreary."

"She has never married and never had any kids, so she shouldn't have any stretch marks. She'll look fantastic in a padded bikini. Extremely athletic, former WNBA star, retired eight years ago with all sorts of records, a member of the Hall of Fame."

"Larry . . ."

"Um, she's well-spoken in the clips her publicist sent, five-seven, hazel eyes, and she has a fading cougar cub tattoo on her arm."

"I won't ask you again."

"Okay, she's . . . she's a tad bit religious."

"Oh no. Not that! How religious is she, Larry?"

"Um, well, she's of the 'born-again Christian' variety. According to her publicist, she's the most moral, spiritual human being she's ever met and will probably ever meet in her life."

"I knew it! Unmarried, hot, and forty, so there had to be something else. Are you sure that she's not a lesbian? Man, that would sink us for sure. Though it might make for a slam-bang last episode."

"There was a lingering rumor during her playing days, but a date with Archie Freeman cleared all that up."

"Archie Freeman? Archie 'Free Love' Freeman? She's no lesbian if she dated that guy. But religious? Oh, man, what did I do to deserve this? We can't have a Holy Roller on a show that's supposed to ooze sex. Does she drink?"

"No."

"Oh, this is perfect."

"Bob, you worry too much. This is why we have film editors."

"You're right, Larry. We can edit out anything even remotely spiritual. The Crew definitely oozes sex, and maybe we can work the religious thing to our advantage, you know, all the endless temptation, all those bare he-man chests, all that testosterone. I wouldn't be surprised if she lets go of her morals, gets her freak on in the hot tub, the bathroom, the limo . . ."

"It might be possible, Bob, but —"

"With the right editing, close-ups, some slow-motion, even a spiked drink, we can turn our choir girl into a fallen angel in no time. Think about it, Larry. She's forty, unmarried, and lives alone. She has to be hard up for a man. A couple nights in the hot tub with the Crew, and she'll be turned out for sure."

"Oh, I don't think she's the kind of woman to —"

"From angel to she-devil," Bob interrupted. "I'm beginning to like this. But you said we almost have her. What's the holdup?"

"We only need her signature, but that's only a matter of time."

"Make it happen, Larry. Now what about our white boy?"

"Extremely average. He sent a black-and-white picture, so he's probably hiding something. Maybe he's covered with freckles or is actually one hundred percent pasty white. I'm just about to give him a call to seal the deal."

"If you have to, promise him four episodes."

"Four? He'll be lucky to last two episodes."

"I said to promise him four. That doesn't mean he'll get four. Right away, anyway."

"What do you mean?"

"First show they schmooze, do the intros, lust with their eyes, drool all over her. Second show, they do a challenge, and whether the white boy wins or loses, she'll boot him off. Later, we can have a call-in for the dumped guy the audience wants back on the show. And no matter how they vote . . ."

"The white boy comes back. I get it. But won't she dump him again?"

"He'll get immunity for one show. That ought to piss off the remaining Crew. Controversy is good. There may even be violence."

"We can only hope."

CHAPTER 3

John's cell phone rang as he was changing out New Hope's furnace filter.

"Good morning."

John checked the caller ID. *A three ten number? Where's that? I thought I was on the national "Do Not Call" list. At least someone is calling me.* "Good morning."

"My name is Larry Prince, and I am one of the producers of *Hunk or Punk*. To whom am I speaking?"

That was quick. "John Bond." *Way too quick.*

"Say again?"

"John Bond."

"You're kidding."

"No."

"Is that your real name?"

"Since birth. Why?"

"Um, no reason. John, I just wanted to call you to tell you congratulations. You made the final cut."

"I did?"

"Yes. Congratulations. Are you willing to

give up six months to a year of your life to be famous?"

"A year?"

"Well, it probably won't be a full year . . ."

His honesty is kind of . . . disturbing. "So how long?"

"I mean, we film for up to a full year, but you probably won't . . . I'll cut to the chase here, John. You are white."

"Also since birth."

"And this show is about a Nubian princess finding her boo."

John smiled. "Sounds scary."

"Huh?"

"Boo. You know . . . *boo!*"

"Oh, um, yes. So you probably won't be on the show the entire time."

John carried the old, dusty filter up the basement stairs and out to a trash can. "Because I'm the white guy and not the right guy." He tossed in the filter, a month's worth of central Alabama dust floating into the air.

"Right. Hey, that's good. The white guy and not the right guy. I'll have to remember that one."

He's probably writing it down. "How many, um, Caucasian-slash-white guys applied to be on the show?"

"Well, um, we had a surfer, and then, well, just you."

"Right. How many?"

"Just you, John. We've tried to figure out

why, but we're stumped."

Yeah, right. "Are the rest of the, um, Crew black?"

"Well, we tried to get a Hispanic, an Asian, and an Italian, but that didn't work out."

The rest of the Crew is black. I am the token white man. How do I feel about that? Intimidated? No. Helpless? No. Lucky? Maybe.

"So, um, John . . . why did you apply?"

Apply? This isn't a job, is it? Do they pay you to be on these shows? "I have my reasons."

"You obviously think you have a chance."

John returned to New Hope's basement to check the water heater. "Well, I . . . I'll do my best." He turned the temperature dial back to the one hundred twenty mark. *No wonder our electric bills are so high. Who keeps changing the heat setting? Normally I'd blame the mice, but this dial is hard to turn, and mice don't have opposable thumbs.*

"And you genuinely like black women?"

He rose and checked the breaker box for blown fuses. "I was married to a black woman once."

"Divorce?"

"Car wreck." *County Road 30. Curvy. The police said she probably swerved to miss a deer. I wish she had hit the deer.*

"Oh. Well, um, when was this?"

"Fifteen years ago."

"Fifteen . . . Um, John, how old are you?"

"Forty." He tapped one of the screw-in fuses, and the metal strip inside vibrated. *Another twenty-amp fuse blown. It's that stupid dinosaur of an organ. When Mrs. Graff pulls out all the stops, the fuses get scared and eventually pop. We really need to get this place up to code.*

"You're . . . forty."

He unscrewed and replaced the offending fuse. "Right. I guess that makes me too old for the show, huh? Sorry to waste your time."

"Um, no, um, John, it doesn't matter."

Of course it doesn't. No one else applied, and they need someone to lose. "Because I'll be gone quickly."

"I didn't say that."

"You didn't have to."

"You looked so young in your picture."

John turned off the basement lights and walked up the narrow stairs to the sanctuary. "That was taken fifteen years ago, too." *When I was young and happy.*

"Do you still look like that?"

"If the room is really dark."

Larry laughed. "It's good you have a sense of humor, John. You'll need it when you get to the mansion. Do you, well, *look* old?"

"I mostly look like I did fifteen years ago. I have a few unruly gray hairs, wrinkles, and some serious worry lines." John scanned the ceiling for more water spots. *Eventually all the water spots will connect, and then no one will notice we have water spots.* "You aren't still interested, are you?"

"Aren't you?"

No new spots. Good. I didn't want to take tar up to the roof today. "Yes. I'm still interested."

"How soon can you get to LA?"

John sat in the first pew. *This can't really be happening.* "Um, well, I have to get someone to cover my Sunday school class. I'm an assistant deacon at New Hope AME, and I do all the maintenance. There's a lot of upkeep in an old church. I'm doing my rounds now. I'll be weeding and cutting grass later."

"You're a, what'd you say, an assistant deacon?"

"Yes. If I were married, I could be an assistant pastor or the youth pastor again. I suppose if I win the Nubian princess's heart, I might gain a wife."

And I just said that out loud to a perfect stranger. What is this guy's name again? Man, the carpet near the altar is so thin! I wish Reverend Wilson didn't do so many altar calls. I just put new carpet up there last year. Maybe if we give anyone who comes up kneepads . . .

"You think you might actually find your *wife* on this show?"

"I might."

"Uh-huh. Um. Well. Um, don't worry the people in your church too much, and you might want to downplay all that on the show. Not exactly prime-time stuff, you know?"

"Downplay what?"

"The religious stuff."

"Why?"

"It's, um, it's not prime-time material."

"Why not?"

"It, um, it just isn't, John. When's the last time you saw a religious person on a reality show?"

"I've never seen a religious person on a reality show." *I only seem to see* real *people on religious shows. Religious shows should be the real reality TV.*

"So you see why you shouldn't act religious on a show called *Hunk or Punk.*"

"Nope." *I wonder if anyone cleaned up the choir loft. Those folks always leave coffee cups and Starlight Mints wrappers everywhere.*

"I mean, *openly* religious people don't go on these kinds of shows, John. We occasionally have spiritual contestants on these shows."

Spiritual. There's a loaded word. Folks think they're "spiritual" if they attend church at Christmas and Easter or say a prayer every now and then before eating. "I don't watch a lot of reality shows, but how long do they usually run? One season? Maybe two?"

"Three if we're lucky, and then there's syndication."

"Uh-huh. Maybe if you had some more religious folks, you know, real people on those shows, other real people might tune in more often."

"Oh, I doubt that."

"Just a thought." John sighed. "I really have a lot of work to do around here, Mr., um . . ."

"Call me Larry."

"Okay, Larry. If I'm not here daily, this old church might fall apart." *Have duct tape, a hammer, and a Phillips head screwdriver, will travel.*

"I'm sure your church will stay in one piece for a few weeks."

He keeps saying weeks instead of months. "You really don't think I'll last very long."

"Who knows? She may show you some mercy and keep you on for a while, and as one of the producers, I can, you know, put a bug in her ear, tell her it's to her advantage to keep, um, a rainbow of suitors, you know. I can tell her, 'Don't can the white guy right away.' I have been authorized to guarantee you four weeks."

John blinked. "Four weeks."

"Right."

At least it's a month. That will give me about thirty days to either come back home to threadbare carpet at the altar or bring her here to marry me . . . on the threadbare carpet. I'll probably have to replace the pad underneath, too. I

*bet the hardwood floor underneath is nice. It'd
be a noisier service, though.*

"John, tell me: What do you do for a living?"

"The religious stuff."

"I meant, what *else* do you do?"

"I'm the church's handyman. They give me
a small salary and let me live rent-free in one
of the church properties."

"You're a . . . handyman. A jack-of-all-
trades."

"I tinker until it's fixed mostly." *And pray
that the duct tape holds.*

"Um, do you have any hobbies?"

Who has time for those? "Well, I write
sermons in my spare time." *That I may never
give.* "I have about three hundred sermons in
my laptop."

"You write . . . sermons. So you're a
writer?"

"Not really. Writing a sermon isn't exactly
writing. It's more like channeling God's Word
—"

"You're a writer, no, a film editor now,"
Larry interrupted.

"I'm a what?"

"A film editor, you know, one who edits
films. Let's see, you checked 'none' on body
apparel."

"Right. My body is really rather boring and
nondescript." *I'd be a pain to identify on one of*

those CSI *shows. Average white male, no distinguishing marks, national average in height, weight, and shoe size.*

"Do you have any scars?"

Just the ones on my heart. That tree still has a scar, too. It's moved a few feet higher. "Nope. Oh, I have a smallpox vaccination scar on my left arm."

"You might want to get a few tattoos before you come to LA. The more the better. A pierced something wouldn't hurt either, but only if it's visible."

John noticed an open window behind the choir loft. *Where there's an open window, there's bound to be a pigeon or a bat sneaking in. Great.* He stood and walked to the back of the choir loft and shut the window. "Is getting a tattoo or a piercing a requirement for the show?"

"It's what viewers will expect to see on *Hunk or Punk.* You know, street, thug, gangster."

And I'm just an OG — an old guy. "I'm none of those things, Larry, and I've never wanted a tattoo." He searched the rafters for pigeons and bats. "Or a piercing."

"Henna tattoos come off, and you could use some magnetic earrings."

No. "You really want me to get a tattoo?"

"Henna tattoos only last a few weeks."

This, according to Larry here, will be the length of my stay on the show. How convenient.

63

"I suppose I could get a cross tattoo."

"Nothing religious."

"Don't rappers often have crosses tattooed on their arms?"

"Oh, that's right. Just make sure it's, um, a street cross. Like RIP Ghostface Killah."

Huh? "RIP what?"

"Just a suggestion. And we really have to do something about your age, too. You're really forty?"

"I look more like . . . thirty-seven." John smiled. "And a half. Except in the mornings. I'm more like fifty-three before I brush my teeth."

"Do you have a lot of gray hair?"

"Some."

"Could you dye it for us?"

No. "What color?"

"Auburn."

"Auburn." *I shouldn't ask, but . . .* "Why auburn?"

"Auburn is hot right now, and trust me, you'll be the only member of the Crew with auburn hair."

Funny. "I'm already going to stick out, right?"

"True."

"And when you reveal that I'm a forty-year-old assistant deacon and handyman, I'll stick out even more, right?"

"Oh no! You'll be a thirty . . . three, no, a

thirty-year-old film editor from . . . where are you?"

"Burnt Corn, Alabama."

Silence.

Gets them every time. "You still there, Larry?"

"There can't *possibly* be a place named —"

"Sure is, Larry. Burnt Corn, Alabama, on the Old Wolf Trail just twelve miles southeast of Scotland and fifteen miles northeast of Frisco City, halfway between Montgomery and Mobile. We have a general store and even a big Coca-Cola sign that says 'five cents.' "

"How . . . charming. But why don't you have a more pronounced Southern accent?"

"I'm originally from Chicago."

"Well, now you're . . . Arthur, a thirty-year-old film editor from Chicago, okay?"

No. "Larry, if I go on your show, I have to go on as myself."

"But that's not what we're going for, John."

John looked up at the cross. "That's what you're gonna get, all right?" *I can only be just as I am . . . without one plea.*

Larry sighed. "So you want us to . . . tell the truth about you."

"Of course."

"That's never been done before."

Dishonesty must be the reality of reality TV.

"Hmm. A completely honest contestant. That would definitely be a first. It might work, it might not. For an episode or two."

Doesn't he know I can hear him when he's thinking out loud? "And I may even last longer than four weeks by being completely honest."

"Trust me, John. No one lasts on these shows if they tell the whole truth and nothing but the truth."

So help me God. "I'll try to be the first."

"Maybe if you read the Nubian princess's bio, you'll reconsider your appearance and thug it up a little. Can you afford to fly out, say, next week?"

Is he kidding? What about "assistant deacon," "handyman," and "living rent-free" didn't he understand? "No."

"No, as in 'I can't afford it,' or, no, as in 'I can't fly out next week'?"

"No to both. It will take at least a week to get the church in order, and I'd have to get a ride to the airport."

"You don't have a car?"

"I suppose I could borrow one of the church vans." *Which reminds me: I have to get the oil changed and a new inspection done on both of them. I hate having to "pretty please" Rankins to pass the old boats. Neither one should be allowed on the road under any circumstances.* "No, they'll need the vans. Reverend Wilson might drop me off. Yeah, that could work."

"You're forty, and you don't have a car."

I had one once. Last time I saw it, it was

wrapped around a tree on County Road 30. Only thing there now is the tree and a white cross. I should bring some more flowers to the cemetery, too. "Burnt Corn is a small town. I walk everywhere."

"You . . . walk."

"Yeah." *I use my legs and everything. I even jog.*

"Um, well, that's . . . that. Can you give me a time frame for when you could come out to LA, John?"

"I can be available after the second service this Sunday."

"Give me an actual *time,* John."

That isn't easy to do. "We don't go by the clock at New Hope. The service ends when God says it ends."

"Could you maybe pray *now* and get a time from God for *then?*"

Good one. I'm beginning to like Larry. "No later than ten PM."

"All right. We'll put you on a red-eye from Montgomery or Mobile to LAX Sunday night. Give me a few moments to get your tickets. I'm going to put you on hold."

John slipped his open cell phone into his back pocket and went to the ancient, rusted storage shed, flipping through his keys until he found the key to the padlock on the door. *One day this lock will rust shut, and I'll have to take a blowtorch to this old barn to get it open.*

He jiggled the key until the lock opened, hung the lock on a rusty eyehook, and opened the door, the moist smell of mildew rolling past him.

Looks like I'm going to LA. I haven't been out there since my honeymoon. We only changed planes at LA for the flight to Kauai, but at least I can say I've visited there. Two days later, I had the sunburn of my life.

He gassed up a Weed Eater and checked the oil. *This should be the last time I have to do this until spring. I don't remember doing this at the end of last December. Maybe the world is warming up.*

"John, you there?"

He slipped his phone from his pocket. "Yes, Larry."

"Evidently it is impossible for you to escape Alabama on a Sunday night."

I could have told him that. Alabama closes up shop on Sundays. I've always liked that about Alabama. Alabamans seem to keep the Sabbath very well.

"You'll have to leave Monday morning from Montgomery at seven, fly to Dallas, sit around for three and a half hours there, fly to San Diego, sit *there* three hours, and then finally land at LAX by six."

And that's how Sheila and I got to LA back then. It's good to know that some things never change.

"I wish I could do better than that, John, but this is on such short notice."

"Sounds fine to me," John said. "I'm in no hurry."

"Your ticket will be at the American Airlines counter in Montgomery. Um, pack lightly. We'll supply your wardrobe once you —"

"Thank you, Larry," John interrupted, "but I'm bringing my own clothes." He picked up the Weed Eater and left the shed.

"You are determined to lose, aren't you?"

"I have some fly clothes, Larry." *Not really. I haven't had anyone dress me for fifteen years, and I doubt any of the clothes Sheila bought for me are in style now.* "And I promise not to bring any overalls or wear any boots."

"John, please reconsider."

"Larry, you're talking to an old-fashioned WYSIWYG."

"A wizzy-what?"

"A WYSIWYG. What you see is what you get. What the Nubian princess will see is what she will get."

"Look, I've just sent you a link to the Nubian princess's bio, John. Give it a read, and I'm sure you'll change your wizzy whatever ways. Don't miss your flight. We'll have someone pick you up at the airport. See you Monday." *Click.*

That was rude.

John closed his phone, pocketed it, and

pulled the starter cord, the Weed Eater whining to life, blue clouds of smoke filling the air.

I'm going to California to find a wife, and on TV of all things.

Only in America.

CHAPTER 4

"You got it if you want it, Sonya," Michelle said. "They *really* want you, and everything is all set to go next week."

Say what? "Next week?"

"Yeah, and, um, there are a few changes they want you to make."

Why aren't I surprised? "Changes? I haven't even agreed to do it yet."

"I want you to hear it all, okay? This will help you make that decision. First, they want to change your name and your bio."

"What?"

"Sonya is so . . . so, you know?"

"I like my name, and it's not so 'you know.' "

"They want you to remain as anonymous as possible until the very end when they reveal all your secrets."

Not all of them. "I have no secrets."

"I know that. I mean your true age, your basketball career, your gold medals, your championship rings. Someone might recognize you if you use your real name."

Doubtful. "What if someone recognizes me anyway?"

"We'll cross that bridge if we come to it. Your new name is fabulous."

Also doubtful. "What's my new name?"

"Jazz."

"Jazz?"

"Jazz."

"Will I have a last name?"

"No."

A single name. A mononym. That's so conceited. "You know I'm not stuck up like that, Michelle."

"Quit interrupting. They also want you to be twenty-five."

"So would I." *In my dreams.*

"They want you to be a twenty-five-year-old aspiring actress named Jazz."

An actress? No way. "I can't act."

"That's why you're only aspiring. You attended UCLA, majored in drama, and did a few commercials in Japan. You've just returned from doing some modeling in Europe."

These people are crazy! "You're kidding."

"Um, you enjoy traveling, shopping, and surfing."

She has *to be kidding.* "Surfing? I don't even know how to swim." *I'm a sinker, not a bobber.*

"It's all for show, Sonya. They promise they

won't make you surf or swim."

"Don't those shows have swimming pools at the, um, mansions?"

"So if you go in the pool, stay in the shallow end. You'll be in the hot tub most of the time anyway."

Yuck! "You know how nasty hot tubs are? You won't catch me in there." *Half-naked men. Foam floating on top. Nasty!*

"It's an integral part of the show, Sonya."

"Not gonna happen."

"It might be fun."

"It might give me some disease."

"They use chlorine."

Sonya shuddered. "No. So they want me to be a stuck-up, surface-dwelling airhead."

"Who volunteers her free time at soup kitchens."

Please, God, let her be kidding about this! "I do what?"

"You volunteer at soup kitchens."

She wasn't kidding. "This is all so fake!"

"I'm not done. Um, they have this part of the show where your best friend comes on the show and helps you choose your man. I told them you didn't have any friends, much less a best friend, so I was kind of hoping that, well, that I could, um, be her."

Uh-huh. The other shoe has finally dropped. Michelle, the publicist, lived in my limelight when I played ball. She answered more ques-

tions than I did, not that anyone wanted to interview me that often, and she even did a few interviews on my behalf while I was icing my knee after games.

"You want to be on TV, Michelle."

"Right."

"*You* be the Nubian princess, then."

"No, no. I only want to be on TV as your best friend. I'm still your friend, right?"

Barely. "I haven't heard from you in, what, five years, you put my name in for a sleazy reality TV show without my permission, you've all but signed my name to a contract I haven't even read, you're telling me I can't be myself or even use my own name on that show until the very end, and now you want to be my *friend* on that show?"

"Yes. Oh, and you'll have to do something with your hair, too. Bet it's in a ponytail, huh?"

Well . . . it's easy to manage. "Michelle."

"And you'll have to wear heels and dresses."

That's not gonna happen. "Michelle."

"Don't worry. They'll supply them. I know you don't have any."

She didn't even hear me. "Michelle!"

"Yes?"

"Do I *have* to have a best friend on the show? I mean, I can make up my own mind, right? How can I be a literate, intelligent role model if I can't make up my own mind?"

"The BFF is a staple on these shows. So

was the old boyfriend, but I told them you haven't ever had one. Archie got married, by the way. Some girl in China half his age and height."

And, hopefully, she has twice his IQ.

"So, can I play your best friend?" Michelle asked. "Please say yes."

"Michelle, all you'd be doing is playing. No offense, but we're not even friends."

"It's either me or some actress who will play your BFF. That's part of the contract, and it's non-negotiable."

A fake best friend on a fake reality show. Figures. "Do I really have to have a best friend?"

"Yes."

I know just where to find her, but will she put her attitude on hold and be willing to help me out on short notice? "I will find a BFF who knows me, okay?"

"You have a best friend?"

"Yes." *Sort of. I wonder if she'll even hear me all the way through.*

"I thought I knew everything about you. Is she someone from your church?"

If I don't squash this now, Michelle will play twenty questions with me. "No, and you don't know her, okay?"

"Okay. Just let her know that she'll have to give up her life for six months to a year, too."

She's already given up so many months and

years. "I will."

Michelle sighed. "In a way I'm glad you didn't choose me. I would have had to lose at least fifty pounds in a week. Like that was going to happen without lipo. Wait. Does this mean you'll do the show?"

"I guess it . . . sort of does." *Wow. I'm actually doing this.*

"Yes!"

"I said 'sort of.' I'll fly out and talk to them. But I still haven't signed anything, right?"

"Of course not. I would never do that without your permission."

"But you already signed something, right?"

"It was just an 'I'm interested in pursuing this' kind of thing. It isn't the actual contract."

"Well, you did everything else without my permission."

"I'm just trying to jump-start your life, Sonya."

"My life doesn't need jump-starting." *And I said that completely without conviction. Maybe my life* does *need jump-starting.*

"When can you be in LA?"

My schedule is so full these days. Let's see . . . "Is Saturday night soon enough?"

"Yes! Let me know your flight schedule, I'll get WB to have the tickets waiting for you at the airport, and I'll pick you up when you get to LA. We have so much to do!"

"Okay."

"This is going to be so much fun! Bye."
Click.

She is still so rude. You called me. You are supposed to wait for me *to say good-bye before you hang up.*

Sonya sighed. *I can still say no. And if my bio doesn't change significantly, I* will *say no. But I can't do any of this without a BFF. If I'm really going to do this . . .*

She picked up her cell phone.

I have to do this. She pressed the number two, held it, and waited for the beep. "Kim, this is Sonya. Please give me a call as soon as you can. It's *very* important. Bye."

Now, will she call back, or will I have to call her ten times a day for the next five days?

CHAPTER 5

Back in his apartment, John read the Nubian princess's bio and laughed at the twenty-five-year-old aspiring actress named Jazz.

No last name. How pretentious. How could a parent look at her child and give her that name? That's as bad as naming a boy R and B. Oh, yeah. That has to be her stage or screen name. Her real name is probably something ordinary like Mary or Sue. I'll bet she has an ordinary last name like Jones or Smith. Mary Jones. Sue Smith. I like ordinary better.

"Aspiring" most likely means that she isn't good enough to get a part and this is her first major "role." She's probably using this show to start her career. "Attended UCLA and majored in drama." She's probably not very bright. She only "attended" UCLA. I'll bet she audited a class or two. And she majored in drama. So many women seem to major in drama these days, whether they go to college or not. I'll bet her life is full of drama and she dishes out the drama often. A few commercials in Japan and

some modeling in Europe where no American has ever seen her.

He looked at her picture. *Pretty. Nice hazel eyes. She probably wears contacts. Shy smile. Cute cheeks. Short hair. Not much makeup for a diva. Natural. And young. That's a face I could wake up to every morning.*

Sorry, God. She's beautiful.

Oh, and sorry, Sheila. She's not as beautiful as you are.

Let's see . . . enjoys travel, shopping, and surfing. Shopping. Who enjoys that? The nearest Walmart is eleven miles away, and I go there as infrequently as possible, and only late at night. Surfing? I haven't seen too many black women surfing. I suppose anything's possible in America. But volunteering at soup kitchens? Who are they kidding? Maybe it was court-ordered.

Definitely cute, though. Even sexy. If I were fifteen years younger, even ten years younger . . .

Yeah, right.

It's going to be a very short trip.

John called Reverend William Wilson, long-time pastor of New Hope, and one of Sheila's many great-uncles.

"Reverend Wilson, this is John."

"What broke now?"

John smiled. "Nothing, actually." *And that's probably a first.* "Everything's working. I'm just calling to tell you that I'll be taking a leave of absence."

"A leave of absence. So it's not a permanent absence."

"No, sir. Just a year." *Or a few weeks.* "Starting after second service on Sunday."

"Where are you going?"

To my probable embarrassment. "I'd rather not say."

"Folks are gonna ask."

Are they? I doubt it. I sometimes think that the folks at New Hope want me to leave so I'm not such a constant reminder to them of Sheila. They all adored Sheila, even those who weren't directly related to her.

"Just tell them I'm going on a mission out west," John said.

"A mission."

That's kind of what it is. "Yes, sir."

"And you'll be back in a year."

"Give or take. Maybe sooner."

"How much sooner?"

It could be as soon as the Sunday after next. "I don't know for sure. I'll be on God's time."

"Hmm. You've been on God's time a long time, John."

"Yes, sir." *It's the best time to be on.*

"Maybe it's time you took your *own* time."

Yeah, I'm a little hesitant about being selfish. "Yes, sir. Um, I've been thinking that maybe Aubrey could cover my Sunday school class while I'm away."

"No need. I've been thinking of folding your singles into the adult class for a while. I don't think Sister Withers, Sister Jackson, and Brother Watts are ever going to get married."

Their collective age is pushing one-sixty. "Um, the furnace is running smoothly, and —"

"Don't worry yourself, John," Reverend Wilson interrupted. "You go out west and take care of business."

"I don't want you to think I'm running out on you."

"You've been with us going on twenty years, John. You're one of the very few who haven't run out on us at *any* time. You've always been there for us. I'll be praying for your journey."

"Thank you, sir." *I'm gonna need it.* "Um, about my apartment . . ."

"The house will be here when you get back."

"Thank you."

"*If* you get back."

This man's been my confessor, confidante, and guide for so many years. I have to tell him something. "Reverend, I'm going out west to find a wife."

"I knew that you were getting tired of being an assistant deacon."

"It's not that, I just . . ."

"You don't have to explain, John. 'And the

81

Lord God said, It is not good that the man should be alone; I will make him an help meet for him.' You miss your help meet."

I am so transparent. "Yes."

"And I suppose you'll be wanting a promotion or your old position back when you return with her."

Tell the truth. "Yes."

"That promotion will be here. Go get your bride."

Should I tell him I'll have to go on TV to get her? I don't think Reverend Wilson ever watches much TV, and the folks at New Hope aren't exactly new-fashioned. They may even think I'm betraying the memory of one of their kin.

"I'll do my best, Reverend Wilson."

"I know you will, because 'as the bridegroom rejoiceth over the bride, so shall thy God rejoice over thee.' We will all be praying for your safe and triumphant return."

"Thank you."

I just hope I don't return empty-handed.

CHAPTER 6

Sonya looked at the headshots and read the bios of the so-called "hunks."

Most of these guys are punks.

Cute punks, though.

There are a few former athletes. That's a plus. At least we'll have something to talk about. None of them are over thirty. So young! And I'm so not! All of them — except for the white guy — are ripped, tatted, pierced, and fierce. It's hard to tell if the white man's ripped, tatted, or pierced because of that suit. He's wearing a suit? Only two actually smile. The white man is smiling, probably because he doesn't have a single brain cell in his head. Wearing a suit for a headshot? He can't be that bright. And going on a show to win a Nubian princess? He has to be using Hunk *or* Punk *for an acting credit.*

She read through the bios and found actors, models, waiters, one former NBA Developmental League player, and a film editor. *The white man is a film editor from Chicago. Okay, he has more than a few brain cells, but what kind of films do they make in Chicago? They have to be cold and windy films.*

So young, so young. Sonya sighed. *I could have babysat all of them!*

Okay, who goes first? Her eyes traveled to the white man. *Arthur. He's the oldest at thirty. Auburn hair. Auburn? Who has naturally auburn hair? Green blue eyes. Hard to tell from this black-and-white shot. Yet . . . he's the only one who looks genuinely happy. Oh, they've set him up perfectly to lose. The only one closest to my age is white, not that it matters. I like his eyes. Good chin. And he's smiling.*

I still could have babysat him.

The phone rang. *Kim?*

"Hello?"

"Sonya."

Kim. Sonya sighed. *She never says my name happily.* "Did your Christmas gifts arrive on time?"

"You know they did. They arrived two weeks early."

And she never says "thank you" for anything. One day . . . "Did the running pants fit?"

"Yes. It all fit, as you knew they would."

Because Kim and I wear the same sizes.

"The shoes were nice," Kim said.

A compliment? That's different.

"Not my color," Kim said, "but they're all right."

She told me navy blue. Geez. Sonya took a

84

deep breath and exhaled. "Kim, I have a big favor to ask of you."

"What?"

I have no real right to ask her to do this, but I have to. "I've been, um, asked to go on a reality show in Los Angeles next week, and I need a best friend."

"And you thought of me."

"Yes." *Because you are my best friend. You just don't know it yet.* "Um, the best friend, I mean, *you* will help me choose a, um, a man from among twelve contestants on this new show called —"

"You're kidding," Kim interrupted.

"It's called *Hunk or Punk,* and I'll be the, um, the Nubian princess."

"No way."

"Michelle Hamm, you remember her. My publicist? She sort of signed me up without my permission."

"So you haven't agreed to do it yet."

"Not yet. And if I don't have you for a best friend, I probably won't do it."

"You're putting all this on me?"

"No, I meant . . ." *She is so touchy!* "The producers will hire some model to be my best friend if you don't do it, and that would be completely stupid."

"I think the whole thing is completely stupid."

She always says what she means, and that's another reason why I have to have her be my

85

BFF. She will *tell me the truth. She has never sugarcoated anything.* "But I'll need you to help me weed out the bad apples."

"Strange mix of metaphors, Sonya."

"Um, yeah." *She is far too educated for her own good.*

"This is crazy, Sonya."

I agree. "It is pretty crazy, isn't it? This isn't something I would ever do, right?"

"Right. You don't do crazy."

And Kim most certainly does. "Yeah, and well, they want me to be a twenty-five-year-old actress who surfs, too."

Kim laughed. "You don't even swim! What the hell?"

Sonya frowned. *At least we're making some progress. She used to use the F word exclusively.* "And I volunteer at soup kitchens."

"You can't be serious, Sonya."

"I am, and I will, of course, try to change that mess."

"I don't know. Having you play a beach bimbo might not be all that bad. It would definitely be entertaining."

I got your "beach bimbo," little heifer. "Um, I'm not sure, but you might need to take up to a year off from work."

"What work?"

Sonya gasped. "You're not working?"

"I got laid off along with the rest of America. There's this crummy economy you

might have read about. It's been in the news-
papers and on TV."

"When did you get laid off?" Sonya asked.

"Last month, Sonya. You know, the last time
you called me."

But she told me . . . "You said not to call
you so much."

"I didn't mean for you to go thirty days
without calling me."

Has it been that long? "I'm so sorry. Are
you okay for money?"

"What do you think?"

"I'll send you more, I mean . . . I'll put
more into your bank account. Today."

"Thanks. I'm getting sick of eating rice
cakes."

Oh no! "That's all you're eating?"

"No. I have plenty of money, okay? You
know I don't spend much."

*Kim rarely spends a dime that doesn't leave a
crease on her fingers.* "But . . . but that means
you're available to do the show."

"To play your best friend."

She never sounds interested in anything.
"Right. It'll be fun."

"Sure. It'll be a hoot. Wait. Next week? We'll
be celebrating New Year's in LA?"

"Yes."

"Oh, that will be a hoot, too."

*She always sounds sarcastic about every-
thing, too.* "And we'll have a nice big house,
I'm sure. A mansion."

"Full of sweaty, nasty men who want to do the horizontal bop with you."

Hard to disagree with the sweaty part. But the "horizontal bop"? Whatever happened to simply "doing it" or "knockin' boots" or "gettin' skins"? I am so old. "You said once that you wanted to visit LA."

"Not this way."

"And, um, well . . ." Sonya sighed. "It will give us a great deal of time to get to know each other better."

Kim was silent.

She's probably rolling her eyes. "So . . . what do you think?"

"I already told you what I think. It's stupid."

Sonya's heart sank. "I was hoping —"

"But I'll do it."

Sonya was silent.

"You there, Sonya?"

Did she say . . . "You'll . . . do it?"

"Hell, yeah. I've got nothing better to do and a year to do it."

That was almost a nice thing to say. "Well . . . great. Um, I'm flying out to LA Saturday, so if you could drive over here, we can, um, we can travel together."

"What about my apartment? Are you going to keep paying on it while I'm gone?"

"Sure."

"Why? That's a f— I mean, that's a terrible waste of money."

She caught herself in time. I am gradually rub-

bing off on her. "I don't mind."

"Why don't I just move out completely? I mean, there are no jobs I'm interested in taking in Atlanta. I might find something in LA."

Or something even better. Not sure what the "something" is yet. "Yeah. That'd be cool."

"Cool?"

"Yeah. Cool, you know, awesome, dude."

"You're so old-fashioned, Sonya."

That I am. "You want me to come to Atlanta and help you move out?"

"I don't have much. I'll get a U-Haul trailer."

She is much more resourceful than I am. "When can I expect you?"

"Friday. I have a few things to take care of."

"Cool."

"Quit saying that."

"I'm old-fashioned, remember?"

"Whatever. Bye, Sonya."

After Kim hung up, Sonya felt a tingling in her hands, her breath coming in short bursts. *It's amazing how this is working out. Thank You, Lord.*

"Wow," she said aloud. "Wow!" she shouted.

And Lord Jesus, I know I don't deserve the title, but could You please help that child call me mama just once *before I die?*

■ ■ ■ ■

"Bob, it's Larry."

"What's wrong now?"

"Nothing."

"Then why call?"

"I'm calling with some good news. The Nubian princess has agreed to the eligibility requirements, hasn't made much of a stink about us changing her identity yet, and will be flying out Saturday with a best friend in tow. Once we get her signature on the contract, she's ours. The white man is on board and will be flying out Monday. He's really quite an interesting fellow, and I'm sure you'll —"

"Monday? He's flying out Monday? Tell me he'll be here Monday morning."

"Um, well, no. The earliest we could get him out of Alabama is —"

"He's from Alabama?"

"Um, yes. Burnt Corn, Alabama, and he'll be arriving at LAX —"

"Burnt Corn?"

"It does exist. I Googled it to make sure."

"Larry, we start filming at eight PM."

"Even with the worst traffic, we should have him to the mansion by then."

"Larry, WB wants us to do the first episode live."

"What? Live? What are they thinking? Why?"

"They're already worried about the show.

When I told them about our new Nubian princess, they decided that a live opening would generate more interest."

"But so much can go wrong with a live show!"

"That's probably what they're counting on, and with the Crew we have, that is almost a given."

"Wow. A live show."

"You couldn't get him out here any sooner? Couldn't you have chartered a jet to Buttered Corn or something?"

"For the white guy?"

"Yeah. I see your point. We're already over budget. But what if he arrives a lot later than eight? We do her grand entrance and all the intros first thing, and if he's not there . . ."

"He'll be there."

"We can't have him come late and spoil her grand entrance."

"Don't worry. I'll have Manny pick him up at LAX. He used to be a stunt driver, you know."

"Manny? He's eighty!"

"He did all those Smokey and the Bandit pictures back in the seventies. He's gotten the rest of the Crew to the mansion on time. He'll get our white guy through traffic on time, too."

"But what if he doesn't?"

"Then . . . WB will have a slam-bang live first episode of Hunk or Punk."

CHAPTER 7

While waiting for Kim to arrive on Friday, Sonya took an online personality test at Individuality.com to help her determine what she wanted in a man.

And after completing the test, she was no wiser.

She even felt a little dumber.

The first question wasn't a question. *What does the length of my fingers have to do with my personality? So what if my index finger and ring finger are the same length? What if I had lost part of a finger in an accident? Would that have changed my personality?*

She dutifully put X's in some check boxes — including "only child" — but ran into trouble with: "What kind of relationship am I interested in?" *Single income? Double income? Love isn't about money. If that were true in this economy, no one would fall in love.*

Leading to marriage, not leading to marriage . . . This survey is so nosy. She clicked "Not sure yet."

What does the condition of my sock drawer have to do with relationships? What if I didn't have a sock drawer? I do, but what if? Why are there all these questions about friends? And why isn't there a check box for "none"? Some people don't have friends, you know. No, I don't smoke or drink, and I live alone.

I also have a daughter who calls me by my name . . .

I never should have put Kim up for adoption. My life would have been completely different, but then there wouldn't be this disconnect between us. But what could I do? I was a foolish teenager, a stupid child who didn't have a thought in her head. What could I have offered her then? I voluntarily "surrendered" my child in New Jersey, and the child makes me want to yell, "I surrender!" now.

I registered with New Jersey's DYFS Adoption Registry on her eighteenth birthday but could get no information until she registered two years later. They need to change that stupid rule. The child made me wait two years! That was one of the main reasons I retired from the WNBA. I probably could have come off the bench for a few more years, but the chance of finding her again was all I could think about.

Our first meeting was an absolute disaster. I hardly ever talk, and I did all the talking for at least an hour until she asked, "Why'd you give me up?" And then I cried for half an hour while she ripped me a new one, calling me the vilest names. And she didn't shed a single tear before storming out of that McDonald's in Teaneck, New Jersey.

I haven't eaten at a McDonald's ever since.

Since then it's been one baby step forward, two giant steps back as I've tried to make up for lost time. The Bible says to redeem our time because the days are evil and to "walk in wisdom toward them that are without, redeeming the time." It's just been hard to walk in wisdom and redeem the time with a daughter who can be so evil.

I've been trying to build a relationship with Kim over the last six years, but whenever I give, she takes. When I build up, she tears down. When I cry, she laughs. I know there's a season and a time for every purpose under heaven, I know this. I just hope one day I'll hug her and she'll hug me back.

And call me "mama."

I spend more money on her than time with her. Her preference, not mine. I paid for her college at Rutgers, her apartment in Atlanta, a nice VW Jetta, and more clothes than one person could ever wear in a year. Luckily we have the same shoe size and I didn't wear all those Nikes, some of which are coming back in style. "You can't buy my love, Sonya," she tells me, but she doesn't flat-out reject any of the things I get her. It's just her philosophy degree talking. Money doesn't hurt when you're a philosophy major in a world that demands MBAs and computer degrees and you want to live in Atlanta where everything costs something ridiculous while you only bring in twenty grand a year at most *because you can't keep a job for more than a few months at a time since "it's so boring" and "I want to do something new" and "everyone at work is stupid."*

But I'm not bitter about it.

Sonya returned her attention to the personality test. "Do I want future kids?" she whispered. "Seriously? I got enough trouble with the one I've got." She thought a little more. *Okay, maybe. But at forty, it isn't likely to happen for me.*

Do I want to be joined at the hip with my man? No. Where's the fun in that? Do I smother quickly? Yes. Let me breathe. Let me be me and be free. Do couples kissing in public bother me? Yes. That kind of stuff should take place in private.

I am so not romantic.

What do I like to do on a Saturday night? Nothing. Watching a movie. Flipping channels. I don't do ballet, attend the theater, or go dancing. Hosting a party? Who does that? Grandmama used to host rent parties in Paterson. Those were fun. Until someone broke something and the neighbors complained and the cops came . . .

Do I like unpredictable situations? No. Oh, yeah. I'm about to get into one. But I still don't like them. Do I get bored easily? Not really. I have perfected the art of doing as little as possible. Am I optimistic? Sometimes. Hmm. "Sometimes" is not a possible response on this test. Better mark "Yes." Am I always looking to do new things? No. Do I take risks? Absolutely not. Until now. Do I have a consistent routine? Yes. Do I believe people should have morals? Of course. When I doodle, what do I doodle? I don't doodle!

These questions are ridiculous.

The questions about sex and relationships earned an "oh my" from Sonya. "Is sex necessary in a relationship?" she whispered. *I wouldn't know, but again, my response is not one of the possible answers. The key word is "necessary." Hmm. No. A relationship based on sex is not a relationship. It's only mating. How often do I fall in love? I haven't. Where's "never" as an answer?*

What's this? A book cover with some skinny white lady in a skimpy teddy staring at her man who is staring out at the ocean? What would I title this picture if it were a book? Their titles are so lame. I'd call it Brr, I'm Cold, Man — Get Back in Here and Warm Me Up Now or I'll Cut You with My Bony Frigid Elbows. *That title wouldn't fit on the cover.*

Do I listen to my heart whenever I have to

make a big decision? No. I listen to my brain. If I thought with my heart, I would . . .

I might have a man in my life by now. Do I change my mind easily? No. Well . . . some-times . . . No.

What is my personality color? Red, blue, green, or yellow. Those are my only choices. What if my personality color is purple? I mean, I sometimes turn red, I sometimes feel blue, I manage my green, and I ain't yellow. What if I want to be orange or burgundy or brown?

Sonya marked religion: "Christian — Other." AME may be Methodist, but it isn't the Methodist they think it is. I wish they had a choice like "His" or "None — Relationship with Jesus Christ."

Where would I most like to live? I'm in the suburbs now, and I like the peace and quiet it offers. If I could, would I prefer the beach or a lake? Both, but only if the bugs were kind.

She finally arrived at the page called "About Your Mate." My mate? Geez. I'm just looking for some companionship here. My mate? They make it sound so biological. Age range . . . forty to forty-five. I need someone who has lived long enough to hold an intelligent, mature conversa-tion with me. I don't want to spend the relation-ship having to explain things. And that disquali-fies every one of the hunks.

Pity.

Height and body type? I guess like me, maybe

a little taller. His *interests? Why isn't "me" one of the responses? I would hope one of his major interests would be me. Wow, what a long list of possible interests for a man. And it's a stupid list. "Vegging" and "cuddling" aren't on this list. Not that I've cuddled with anything but a pillow. No, he can't drink or smoke, and I won't abide even a "social drinker" or an "occasional smoker." Ethnic background. Where's "human"? This is the twenty-first century. We should be over all that mess. And anyway, I can't afford to be picky at my age. Should I click them all?*

Sonya clicked them all.

She blinked at the screen as it filled with empty white boxes, a flashing cursor in the first box. *And now I have to write essays? This is ridiculous! How can all this foolishness help me decide what kind of man I want? How will any of this supply me with a man? I mean, answering a hundred questions and taking stupid tests will not help me find a man or even tell me what kind of man I want!*

Hmm. Isn't this precisely what I'll be doing for up to a year? I really need to —

The doorbell rang.

Kim! Yes!

Sonya ran to the door, opened it, and watched as Kim brushed past her into the foyer. "Have a good trip, Kim?"

"I have to pee."

The door to the half bath under the stairs closed.

Sonya stood near the bathroom door. "You made good time."

"Yeah. Not much traffic. Um, Sonya, I can't be your best friend on the show."

What? She all but agreed the last time we talked! We leave tomorrow! And she's telling me now? "Why not?"

"We look too much alike."

And that's about all we have in common. "You're almost an inch taller."

"But I slouch. We could be twins, Sonya."

Except for her brown eyes, she's right. "So you won't do the show?"

Sonya heard a flush and then running water. "I'll do the show, but only if I can be your sister."

Why didn't I think of that? That sounds almost . . . nice. "That sounds . . . doable."

The door opened, and Kim Allen stood eye to eye with her mother. "I'd have to be your half sister, though."

Sonya looked at her daughter's outfit. Black and red, untucked flannel shirt, baggy jeans stuffed into the tops of her hiking boots. At least seven piercings on each ear. Shirt opened right down to the top of her black bra and one curve of a snake tattoo. *Who wears a black bra without the black dress? And who puts snakes on her chest? And where does said snake end?*

"Okay, you can be my half sister," Sonya said. "We finally agree on something."

"Whatever."

Sonya looked outside at Kim's Jetta, expecting to see a U-Haul trailer behind it. "Where's the trailer?"

Kim flopped onto the couch. "I put it all in storage. If LA doesn't work out for me, I'll have my future apartment in Atlanta already furnished. The bill will be sent here."

Not "I hope it's okay, Mama, if I have them send the bill here." Sonya sat on the edge of the coffee table. "But what if LA works out for you?"

"I'll have it all shipped to LA." Kim looked at Sonya's laptop screen. "Don't tell me you're doing one of those lame surveys. I stopped doing surveys like that when I was ten."

Note to self: Always close your laptop around your nosy child, no matter how old your child is. Sonya closed the laptop. "I did it on a whim, you know, just to see how ridiculous it would be."

"Yeah. Right. And what did you learn?"

"That personality surveys are a waste of time." *Time to change the subject.* "How's Mark?"

"Mark? I haven't seen him in weeks."

They were hot and heavy when I called last

month. "I thought you two were getting serious."

"*He* was." Kim smiled. "*I* wasn't." She fluttered her eyelashes. "I'm just like you, Sonya. I love 'em and I leave 'em."

Not exactly. "Did he, um, did Mark take it hard?"

"I don't know. I sent him a text, and he disappeared."

How . . . modern. And mean. "You sent him a text? Why didn't you at least talk to him?"

"Mark wasn't much for talking, if you know what I mean."

My Bohemian, heathen daughter and her conquests. Another reason I wish I had raised her. Her adoptive parents were excessively lenient and completely heathen. The child has never even set foot inside a church, not that I haven't tried to get her there.

"I still can't believe that I'm getting more action than you are, Sonya."

Because I have morals. Because I believe in someone who will forever be greater than ten minutes of pleasure. Sonya sighed. "You're taking all the necessary precautions, right?"

Kim rolled her eyes. "Yes. And thanks to you, I've gotten a little pickier about the men I hook up with."

I know this is a setup, but . . . "You have?"

"Yes. I don't date serial killers, rapists, roadies, lawyers, or police anymore."

What a strange list. "I meant, you're making sure that . . ."

"Yes, Sonya. I will *never* make the same mistake you made."

I wish she were five so I could spank her!

Kim looked around. "This place never changes. It's like a museum to loneliness. When was the last time I was here?"

"A few months ago."

"Something's new . . . let's see. The TV. Nice flat screen. Wish I had one."

"I can get you one."

"Nah. I hardly even watch the one I have. When are you going to brighten this place up?"

Sonya looked at her cream walls. "I like this color. It's calming."

"Whatever." Kim stretched. "So, what exactly are you looking for in a man, Sonya? Oh, I know. He has to have a pulse and the ability to walk without a cane. Oh, and he has to have the entire Bible memorized."

I may spank her anyway, the little blasphemer!

"Maybe you just want him mute and tied to the bed," Kim said. "Tried that once. He slobbered on the gag, which is so nasty. Almost left him tied up on his bed, too."

Sonya didn't respond. *This is how it begins, and I don't intend to keep it going.* "So, are you seeing anyone new?"

"No, just the same old bedmates."

Lord Jesus, please *do something with this child!*

Kim rolled onto her stomach and propped her head up on her hands. "You know, Sonya, whoever you choose on that stupid show will kinda be my daddy, right?"

No. "He won't be your daddy, Kim."

"Yeah, probably not." Kim flattened out and closed her eyes. "When does he get out again?"

She always has to open this wound. "I don't know."

"Don't you care?"

"Of course I care, but I've told you many times that Marcus wasn't a bad boy when we . . . when we hooked up. It was later that he —"

"Became a thug, shot someone, and went to jail," Kim interrupted. "You had excellent choice in men back then, Sonya. I can't wait to see what mess of a man you're going to pick this time."

How can I lighten this mood? Sonya tried to smile. "I'm not a teenager, Kim. I have matured. What makes you think I'll choose a mess of a man now?"

"Your track record. First my daddy and then Archie Freeman."

Yeah, I'm two for two, but how did she know I went out with Archie? "I never told you about Archie."

"So I Googled you."

103

I hate the Internet.

"Sonya and her bad boys."

Sonya frowned. "And all your men have been angels."

Kim opened her eyes. "I prefer devils actually. They're more fun where it counts. And they have such excellent imaginations. They're never afraid to try new things."

Sonya sighed and stood. "One day you'll find a good man, and that good man won't have you."

"Who wants a good man when a bad man can do you better? And longer? And harder."

This conversation is over. "You hungry? Thirsty?"

"No. I ate on the road."

Is there anything I can do for this child? "Your room's all ready for you."

"You mean the *guest* room's ready."

"It's your room, Kim, and it will always be your room."

"Until you find a man or another career and kick me to the curb again."

Lord Jesus, give me strength! "I made you a promise, Kim, and I'm tired of repeating it. I will never give you up again. Never." *No matter how much you try to tick me off.*

Kim looked away.

"Now, please don't bring up that mess again."

"I won't if you won't." Kim rolled off the couch, stood, and went to the stairs. "I'll be

in the *guest* room."
    I let it begin.
    I wonder when it will end.

CHAPTER 8

On the first-class flight from Charlotte to LA, Kim drank four glasses of champagne despite Sonya's protests.

"I'm as old as you are, *Jazz*," Kim said.

"Hush."

"And I want a new name, too, *Jazz*."

"Why?"

"You get to be Jazz, so I want to be . . . Jezz, as in Jezebel."

She should be Huss, as in "Hussy."

"Or Queen," Kim said. "I like that name a lot. That name is the shit. You're the princess, but I'm the queen."

Yes, this queen bee is definitely buzzing. She gets coffee from here on. "Please watch your language."

"We're not in your house anymore, Sonya," Kim said. "I can be myself again, right?"

At least she respects me enough not to curse in my house.

"Maybe I should be something African like . . . Titilope," Kim said. "I looked it up online. It means 'forever grateful' in Yoruban."

That name for this child? Never. That's like calling a skinny baby "Chubs."

Kim tapped Sonya's arm. "I know you didn't get the chance to name me, Sonya, but what would *you* have named me?"

Sonya sighed. "Shani." *Shan-eye. Oh, how I loved that name.*

Kim sat up somewhat straighter. "Shani."

"It's Swahili for 'wonderful.' "

"Shani."

She likes it. I don't know whether to smile or cry. I may do both.

"What was my middle name?"

Sonya smiled as tears formed. "Neliah." *Shan-eye Nee-lie-uh. Just saying it was like casting a magical spell.*

Kim closed her eyes and smiled. "Shani Neliah. Shani . . . Neliah. What's 'Neliah' mean?"

"Someone who is strong-willed, has a forceful personality, and has a level mind." Sonya wiped away a tear.

Kim nodded. "Well, two out of three ain't bad."

And we're gonna have to work on that third one right now. Sonya waved a flight attendant over.

"Yes, ma'am?" the flight attendant said.

Ma'am? Do I look that old? "Coffee for me and my, um, sister."

The flight attendant nodded and went to the galley.

"I don't need coffee," Kim said dreamily, opening her eyes and rubbing them. "I'll just take a nap." She put her pillow against the window and snuggled into it. "Shani Neliah. Yeah. That's a good name."

Sonya took the blanket swaddling her own legs and placed it on Kim's back. *Yeah. It would have been a very good name.*

"Shani Neliah," Kim whispered. "I'm a wonderful badass . . ."

Ain't that *the truth,* Sonya thought, wiping away another tear.

Michelle, wearing a shin-length black Moda Italiana coat, chic black sunglasses, and a black beret that did nothing to contain her miles of jet-black weave, met them as they emerged from the tunnel at the gate. As she looked from Kim to Sonya, her smile changed to a frown.

"Which one of you is . . ." Michelle blinked rapidly. "You're twins!"

Kim sipped coffee from a Styrofoam cup. "I'm Kim."

"Kim," Michelle said in a monotone. She smiled at Sonya. "I didn't know you had a —"

"She's my daughter," Sonya interrupted.

Michelle's jaw dropped. "She's . . . your . . . daughter."

"But only for the last six years," Kim said. "I spent the first twenty years being raised by rabid wolves in New Jersey." Kim took another sip. "Sonya, this coffee sucks bad. It tastes like ass."

"Keep drinking," Sonya said. "And please watch your language."

"But it *does* taste like ass," Kim said. "Ever hear of cream and sugar?"

Sweets for the sweet, and bitter for the bitter. "Let's go," Sonya said. "We're making a traffic jam." *And a scene.*

Michelle, wide-eyed and hyperventilating, trotted beside Sonya on the way to baggage claim. "She's your daughter?" she whispered.

"I can hear you," Kim said. "Yes, I'm the long-lost daughter of the greatest woman to ever play basketball on planet Earth."

"But she'll be my sister on the show," Sonya said.

"*Half* sister," Kim added, grimacing. "Even some damn half-and-half would have made this shit taste better."

"Please, Kim," Sonya said.

Kim waved the cup under Sonya's nose. "You taste it."

Sonya sniffed the top. *Eww. That is some old coffee. It does smell like . . . dung. That's a word in the Bible, so I can think it. First class is slipping.* "Toss it. Maybe we'll get you something on our way to . . ." She looked at Michelle. "Where do we have to be first?"

Michelle's lower lip trembled. "Why does she call you Sonya?"

They arrived at baggage claim along with a thousand other people. "Yes, Kim," Sonya said, "why don't you tell Michelle why you don't call me mama?"

"Just a sec." Kim spied a trash can and walked toward it.

"Why didn't you tell me you had a kid?" Michelle asked. "I'm your publicist, for God's sake. How will it look when this comes out? My reputation would be ruined because I didn't know you had a daughter."

"I *couldn't* tell you," Sonya said. "It's a little something called the law. I retired as soon as she turned eighteen so I could register to find her, and by then, you weren't really representing me, were you?"

"Why'd you give her up?" Michelle asked.

"I was young and dumb," Sonya said. "I was a child."

"And now you've been reunited." Michelle looked at Kim weaving through the crowd. "That would make an amazing story, maybe even a movie."

Sonya shook her head. "No, Michelle."

"No, what?" Michelle asked.

"I know how your mind works," Sonya said. "You're looking at my pain as a way to make you some money."

"It *would* make a good story," Michelle said.

"No."

Michelle straightened a few of her tresses. "She looks just like you did fifteen years ago. Maybe *she* should do the show instead of you and you can play her spinster aunt."

Sonya lost feeling in her body. "If that child did the show, she would set *women,* not just black women, back fifty years. And the censors couldn't possibly keep up with her mouth."

Michelle sniffed a laugh. "It must be so hard on you."

She'll never know the half of it. "I'm working on her, Michelle."

"Kind of a yin and yang thing, huh?" Michelle said. "Where there's the Force, there's also the Dark Side."

"Hush, Michelle."

Kim returned. "I don't call her mama, mother, or mommy because she's never been my mama, mother, or mommy."

"Until recently," Sonya said.

"You just send me money," Kim said. "You're nothing but a MoneyGram. Maybe I should call you Money."

Please, bags, come spitting out of that little cave right now! And if you want to shoot out real fast, make sure you hit this child in the head to knock some sense into her.

"Your mama *was* money when she played, Kim," Michelle said.

Thank you, Michelle, but Kim is going to turn

that around on you so fast that —

"Yeah, while I was being told 'your mama didn't want you' and my *real* parents let me run wild," Kim said with a sneer, "Money here was making mad money bouncing a ball and flying all over the world."

"Did you ever see her play?" Michelle asked.

Kim rolled her eyes. "No. I *hate* basketball. I won't even watch the Hawks play."

"No one watches the Atlanta Hawks play, honey," Michelle said.

"True," Sonya said.

Once they had their bags and suitcases, Michelle led them to her Camry. "Hope you've had enough time to stretch your legs," she said. "You're gonna be sitting for a while."

"Is Warner Brothers that far away?" Sonya asked.

"Only thirty miles, but I have to take the one-oh-five, the one-ten, the five, and Ventura Freeway to get there. It'll take us about . . . ninety minutes."

"That's only ten miles an hour," Kim said. "Why don't we walk?"

Michelle blinked her eyes rapidly. "No one walks in California, Kim."

Once on the 105, Kim stretched out in the back and went to sleep.

"Traffic is light today," Michelle said, content to creep along, the speedometer jumping above fifteen miles an hour every few minutes or so. She glanced into the back-seat at a snoring Kim. "How much did she drink?"

"Too much," Sonya said. "And this is light traffic? Charlotte is bad for about an hour, but, girl, it's only eleven o'clock in the morning."

Michelle shrugged. "Welcome to my world. I spend five hours a day in my car."

Michelle loses a full day every week *stuck in her car,* Sonya thought. *I am so glad I chose to live in Charlotte.*

"Our meeting with Larry Prince is at twelve thirty," Michelle said, changing lanes and nearly cutting off a motorcyclist, who flew by so close a few seconds later that he could have adjusted her side mirror. "We have plenty of time to get there."

"That guy on the motorcycle almost hit you," Sonya said.

"He's a future skid mark for sure," Michelle said.

Now there's an image I don't want to have in my head, Sonya thought.

"Oh, you'll just love little Larry Prince. He's a cross between Mr. Magoo and Burgess Meredith, you know, Rocky's trainer. And wrinkly! And he always wears shorts, so try not to stare at his wrinkles, I mean, his legs. And don't roll your eyes at his outfits, such as they are. He wears long-sleeved golf sweaters with those shorts, white socks, and boat shoes. I've met the executive producer, too, and he's an absolute ass. Oh, sorry."

Sonya shook her head. "It's okay, Michelle. The word 'ass' is in the Bible. So the executive producer is a jerk?"

"Bob Freeberg is a certified and certifiable prick. He wears thousand-dollar suits and penny loafers with half-dollars in the slots instead of pennies, if that tells you anything. He's only twenty-three, but he walks around like he owns the universe. He also walks around like he's got a redwood tree stuck up his ass. His daddy was once a movie mogul or something."

A redwood tree? Ouch. "How often will we have to deal with him?"

"Hopefully not at all," Michelle said. "Larry does most of the dirty work."

I don't know if I like the sound of that. "Why are you wearing that heavy coat?"

"It's only going up to sixty-five degrees today. It's cold."

"When we left Charlotte, it was thirty-five. This is nice." Sonya looked back at her daughter. *Lord, please have her wake up civil and mannerly.*

Once they finally arrived at Hollywood Way, Michelle entered and circled an underground parking lot for several long minutes before zipping into a spot. "Yes! Hu-ah!"

"Hu-ah"? Isn't that what the Marines yell?

114

"It is *so* hard to get parking around here," Michelle said. "Yes!"

Californians have such simple joys, Sonya thought. "Kim, we're here."

Kim sat up. "Have we been driving all night or what?"

"We're underground," Sonya said, getting out and opening the back door. "Hungry?"

"I guess," Kim said, stepping out and blinking. "How long was I out?"

"About an hour." Sonya brushed a stray hair from Kim's forehead. "Have any dreams?"

Kim took a step back. "Yeah, I had a dream that I was drinking liquid shit, and it's still in my mouth. I need something to drink."

I shouldn't have asked. "Let's go."

Once up and out in the sunlight, Michelle led them to Café Valentino, a sandwich shop located across the street from Warner Bros. Studios.

"There's Larry," Michelle said, nodding at an old man sitting in a chair at a table under a large gray umbrella. "I guess we're eating outside. I'm glad I wore this coat."

"Why aren't we meeting at the studio?" Sonya asked.

"You're not an employee of Warner Brothers yet," Michelle said. "Only employees get to eat in the commissary. I hear it's fabulous, especially the Filipino food."

Larry Prince stood as they approached, and

Sonya tried not to stare, but once she saw his knobby knees peeking out of his red-and-white plaid shorts, she could do nothing but stare. *He is Mr. Magoo. He even has the glasses and the bald head. Eww. Don't look, don't look . . . Shoot. I looked at his legs. Tan but . . . loose. There's a kneecap inside that flesh somewhere. Sorry, Lord, but some men should always wear pants, You know? What is Larry, eighty? Ninety?*

Larry reached a wrinkly, liver-spotted hand to Kim. "So this is the famous Sonya Richardson."

Kim avoided his hand and sat. "I'm, um, I'm Shani."

She chose Shani, Sonya thought. *Very cool. I was afraid she'd pick Titilope.*

Larry squinted, his hand still in the air. "Does that make you the best friend?"

Kim squinted back. "No. I'm her half sister."

Larry dropped his arm and looked from Sonya to Kim. "The resemblance is uncanny."

"Different daddies," Kim said.

Too much information, Kim. Sonya extended her hand. "I'm Sonya. Nice to meet you, Mr. Prince."

Larry shook her hand. "And you look so young." He motioned to a chair. "Please, sit."

Sonya sat, the umbrella swaying above. "When will I see the contract, Mr. Prince?"

"Oh, let's eat first," Larry said. "I've already ordered an assortment of sandwiches. They're all delicious."

As if on cue, a server arrived with a dozen sandwich halves and took drink orders. Kim immediately reached for a sandwich that oozed mozzarella, salami, and peppers, and Michelle grabbed what looked like a Philly cheesesteak.

"I'd like to see the contract now," Sonya said, analyzing the remaining half sandwiches. *Now, which one of you won't give me gas?*

Larry smiled. "Business before pleasure, huh?"

"The next year of my life before some sandwiches, yes," Sonya said.

Larry nodded, reached into a satchel hanging on the back of his chair, and took out a sheaf of papers. "As you wish, my princess."

Sonya rolled her eyes. "Just call me Sonya, please." She took the contract and began reading rapidly. *This is similar to what I read online.* Her eyes popped. *This number wasn't online, though. A one followed by five zeroes. Wow. This is diva money, and I'm no diva. St. Mark AME is going to be very happy with my tithes this year.*

"Is everything . . . acceptable?" Larry asked.

"Everything seems to be in order." Sonya watched Kim devour another half sandwich in three bites and gulp half of her soda. *I wish*

you'd eaten like that before you had the cham-
pagne.

Larry handed Sonya a pen. "Just sign at all the X's."

"Not yet." Sonya lifted a slice of bread. *Looks like turkey. Is that some sliced avocado? At least it's healthy.* She took a bite. *Not bad.*

"So you have some reservations about the contract?" Larry asked.

"No, it seems fair," Sonya said. "I have a problem with my bio because none of it is true."

"We'll reveal the real you in the end," Larry said. "That's part of the magic of the show. The big reveal."

"Mr. Prince," Sonya said, "I hate lying to people."

"They're only *secrets,* Sonya," Michelle said. "Secrets aren't lies, right, Mr. Prince?"

"They're lies, Michelle," Sonya said. "They're not the truth."

"That information is already on the Internet," Larry said. "Anyone with a computer can check it out. The Crew has already read it and are preparing accordingly."

"The Crew can read?" Kim asked.

Larry laughed. "Most of them." He squinted at the sky. "I think."

"So I can't change any part of my bio?" Sonya asked.

"It is, as they say, already a done deal," Larry said. "And we prefer you don't change any aspect of it until the last episode."

"The big reveal," Kim said.

"Yes," Larry said. "It will make the last episode so much more memorable if you withhold those secrets until the end."

Then why isn't that stipulation in the contract? Sonya thought. *There's nothing in this contract that says I* have *to maintain the lies contained in my bio once I'm actually on the show. Hmm. If I sign this contract* as it's written, *there isn't a thing they can do later to stop me from telling the complete truth at* any *time I'm in front of a camera. Michelle should have caught this. I'm glad she didn't.*

"What about Shani?" Sonya asked. "Where will she be staying?"

"We'll put you and your sister up at Casa Malibu Inn tonight," Larry said. "It's right on the beach. Beautiful. After tomorrow night, you'll be at the mansion while Shani stays at Casa Malibu."

"How long will it be until Shani can join me?" Sonya asked.

"Oh, about two months, maybe longer," Larry said.

"Cool," Kim said.

She used my word! Isn't that — Wait a minute. "What's cool about it, Shani?"

"I'll get to see LA, *Jazz,*" Kim said. "I'll actually have some fun."

Lord, how can I get to know her better if she's

119

not with me? And how can I watch out for her if I'm on lockdown at the mansion? Maybe there's a room available at the mansion where Kim can hide out. "How big is the mansion?"

"Oh, you'll love it," Larry said. "It's in Malibu. It's a Tuscan-style mansion in Point Dume with five spacious suites. You get the master bedroom suite, of course. The Crew is crammed three to a suite."

Shoot, Sonya thought. *No free bedrooms. I have to speed up the process somehow. Yeah, I'll just "need" her sooner than they want me to "need" her help.*

"The mansion has a pool, spa, a spectacular view of the ocean, a vineyard, a greenhouse — it's a paradise," Larry said. "It even has a twenty-seat theater and a bowling alley. A heaven on earth. The Garden of Eden would be jealous."

Not likely, Sonya thought. *This world hasn't been right since the Garden of Eden.*

"How much does something like that cost?" Kim asked.

"Oh, seven, eight million," Larry said.

"Damn," Kim said.

I don't like the way she said it, Sonya thought, *but I agree. That's ridiculous. What's up with people? You can't take any of it with you! The only thing you can take with you is your character, and the only thing you can truly leave is a legacy. A bowling alley? What's wrong with the Bowl-A-Rama down the street?*

"And for the right to stay in that mansion, all you two have to do is sign your contracts." Larry pulled a thinner sheaf of papers from the satchel. "Shani, you'll have to sign a contract, too."

"I get paid?" Kim smiled. "Cool."

Sonya watched Kim skimming the contract. *I wish I could see . . .* She slid her chair closer to Kim.

"Don't worry about it, Sonya," Michelle said. "I already read over it. It's fair." Michelle gasped. "Oh, my. I've forgotten to ask if I can represent you, Shani."

Right, Sonya thought. *She forgot.*

"It's okay," Kim said. "What's your cut?"

Michelle looked at her hands. "Ten percent."

"Damn," Kim said. "Nice racket."

What? "Michelle, you're my former publicist, not my agent, and you're not Shani's agent either."

"Um, well," Michelle said, flicking some bread crumbs off the table, "I'm actually representing you as an agent and not as a publicist this time." She bit her lower lip. "If it's okay. Look at the first page of the contract."

Sonya flipped to the first page of the contract. *I read right past this. Michelle Hamm, ATA, NATR.* "What do ATA and NATR stand for?"

"Association of Talent Agents and National Association of Talent Representatives," Michelle said. "I'm licensed by the state of California and everything."

"Who else do you represent?" Kim asked.

"Um, a few cute kids who do local commercials, and . . . you two," Michelle said. "I hope."

Ten percent, Sonya thought. *She gets a "tithe" of our money just for getting us to do this silly show. It is a good racket.*

"So, is it okay?" Michelle asked.

"Okay with me," Kim said.

Not much I can do about it now. She did get me a "contract." Sonya nodded. "Any more surprises, Michelle?"

Michelle shook her head. "No. I'm all out."

Kim pointed at a line in the contract and slid the page closer to Sonya. "You see that?"

Thirty grand! Sonya thought. *For essentially going on TV and giving advice? Wait a minute. Oprah made millions doing that. They're underpaying my daughter! And between the two of us, we're about to make Michelle over thirteen thousand dollars. It's a great racket.*

Kim snatched the pen from Sonya's hand and signed "Kim Allen" several times, whistling as she did. She handed the contract to Larry. "I'm signed, sealed, and delivered."

All eyes turned to Sonya.

"Give me the pen, Shani," Sonya said.

Kim slid the pen across the table.

Sonya picked up the pen. *Lord, this is a huge thing for me, and You said to share every part of our lives with You. I'm not entirely sure how You're going to get glory from all this, but I'm trusting You. I have no other choice but to trust You on this.*

Sonya signed the contract and handed it to Larry. "You got me."

"Wonderful," Larry said. He stuffed the contract into his satchel and stood. "I need to get these into the works immediately." He checked his watch. "You better get going, Michelle. Nice to meet you both. I'll be seeing you at the mansion." He shook Sonya's hand. "This is going to be so much fun." Then he shambled off.

"Um, do we have to pay the bill?" Sonya asked.

"No," Michelle said. "I can afford it now." She threw three twenties on the table and stood. "Ready?"

"Ready for what?" Sonya asked.

"You need some help with your . . ." Michelle fluttered her hands in the air. "We need to go make you irresistible."

"How?" Kim asked.

Yes, how? Sonya thought.

"We're going to give Sonya a makeover," Michelle said. "And we can't be late. There's so much to do."

Sonya slowly stood. "Like what?"

"Like everything, Sonya," Kim said. "Should I take the before picture now, Michelle?"

"I'm getting a *complete* makeover right now?" Sonya said.

"The sooner we get there, the better," Michelle said.

"We should have flown in yesterday," Kim said.

Shani thinks she's hurting me. "Um, Shani? We look alike, right?"

Kim nodded.

"Then, um, you'll need a makeover, too."

Ten minutes of a stop-and-go trip on West Magnolia Avenue later, Sonya and Kim were inside de Cielo Salon & Spa getting simultaneous pedicures and manicures in front of large mirrors while Michelle was across the street getting her Camry washed and waxed.

"Michelle is weird," Kim said. "*She* needs the wash and wax, not the car. How long have you known her?"

"Nearly twenty years, I guess," Sonya said.

"Longer than you've known me," Kim said. "Maybe you made her weird."

We could be having a nice mother-daughter makeover, but no! She has to be cruel. I can't let her get to me. "Michelle has always been a little flighty."

Sonya looked at her daughter's toes, expect-

124

ing them to be jacked up. *Her feet look nicer than mine! That's not fair. If she had played one hundred thirty college and four hundred professional basketball games, her feet would be jacked up, too. Hey, watch the cuticles on my pinkie toe. And that's a callus! Don't scrape it so hard!*

The manicure and pedicure completed, Sonya looked in the mirror and saw a skinny white man standing behind her. *Who's this, and why is he staring at me so intently?* She turned her head. "May I help you?"

The red-headed, freckle-faced man wearing red pants, white tennis shoes, and a tight white T-shirt sighed and stepped closer. "Just trying to figure out how much hair you'll need, girl."

"What do you mean?" Sonya asked. *And I am not your girl.*

"They said you'd need a bunch," he said with a roll of his neck.

This can't be my hairdresser, Sonya thought. *Oh, this is so cliché! The man is gay!*

"You really need another head of hair," he said. "I don't know if I have enough here, and you haven't given me much to work with. I may have to make a few calls."

"Excuse me?" Sonya said. "My hair is fine. I don't need extensions. I just need a cut, that's all."

He pursed his lips and leaned close to Sonya's ear. "A cut won't cut it, honey. They want me to turn you into a diva, and I have serious doubts that will ever be possible."

Jerk! "Who are you?" Sonya asked.

"Twan, with an *a,* not an *o.*"

Kim laughed.

"You need something, honey?" Twan said to Kim.

Kim shook her head.

I almost laughed, too. A white guy who calls himself "Twan"? "Um, Twan, who told you that I needed extensions?"

"Bob Freeberg."

The man with the half-dollars in his shoes. How nice. "And Bob hired *you* to do them?"

"You don't think I can do them, do you?" Twan asked.

"I didn't say that," Sonya said. *Anything's possible in La-La Land.*

Twan put his fingers through Sonya's hair. "I've done quite a few *sisters* in my time, sister."

Lord, please keep me from cringing.

"Like who?" Kim asked.

"Like *whom,*" Twan said. "I've worked with Gabrielle Union, Kerry Washington, Meagan Good, and Alicia Keys."

"No shit," Kim said.

He blinked at Kim.

Sonya sighed. "Please forgive me, Twan." *His name is getting easier to say.* "I was hoping I wouldn't have anything done to my hair. I'm no diva, and I don't ever want to be a diva. I've only had extensions maybe three times in my life, and they didn't last very long."

Twan crossed his arms. "Bob said you needed a lot of hair, girlfriend, and he wasn't lying." He sighed. "But . . ."

"But what?" Sonya asked.

"I think I have the solution, for both you and the rude thing sitting in that chair. It's called a wig."

"Oh, hell no!" Kim shouted.

"Kim, please," Sonya said. "Hear the man out."

"A wig is easy on, easy off," Twan said. "So you can take it off when you're not *supposed* to be a diva."

I like this idea. "Sounds good."

"Sonya, no!" Kim shouted.

Twan sighed. "I only use one hundred percent human hair in my wigs, and then you can style it however you want." He drew a line about six inches below Sonya's shoulder blades. "About this long."

Sonya looked in the mirror at the line. *I have never had nor have I ever wanted hair that long! I'm not Pocahontas!* "Really? That long?"

Twan shrugged. "Any longer and you'll be Morticia Addams."

"Sonya," Kim said, "I am *not* wearing a wig."

"Okay," Sonya said. "Don't wear a wig. Twan, Bob only wanted *me* to have all the hair, right?"

Twan nodded.

"Hook me up, then." *I'm gonna get me some hair.*

After Twan left, Kim stood and stretched her back. "You're going to look foolish, Sonya."

"Maybe, maybe not."

"A long wig will only make your face longer and skinnier," Kim said. "You may even look like Cher."

"Okay."

Kim blinked. "You want to look like Cher?"

"No," Sonya said. "But whatever the producer wants, the producer gets. I signed a contract, right?"

Twan returned with a long, flowing, silken black wig and began to fit it to Sonya's head. "I call this one Fascination."

He names his wigs. Strange man. "Oh, I'm sorry," Sonya said. "I never told you my name."

"And you're not supposed to," Twan said. "I have been sworn to secrecy."

"Really?" Kim asked. "Why?"

"If I were to reveal that any woman I work with is wearing a wig, no one will ever work with me again. Warner Brothers has been

128

good to me, and I intend to keep it that way." He turned Sonya's chair around. "It's not perfect, but . . ."

Wow, Sonya thought. *That is amazing. My face shrank. I look like one of those high-cheeked models now. Man, I'm almost pretty.* She turned to Kim. "How do I look?"

Kim didn't answer immediately. "You look okay."

"Just okay?" *I must look great!*

Kim stepped closer and touched Sonya's wig. "I mean, you look like black Barbie."

"Yeah, I kind of do." Sonya smiled at Twan. "Just . . . bobby pins and hairclips to keep it in place?"

"I'm sure Warner Brothers will have a crew working on you every morning," Twan said. "They'll make sure it stays on."

"I wish I had a brush," Sonya said. "I really like this look, Twan. Thank you."

Kim nodded a few times. "Um, Twan, you got another one?"

Gotcha, Sonya thought. *There's a little girl inside my grown little girl who dreamed of being Barbie.*

Once Kim saw herself in her wig, she smiled.

"This one I call Thrill, rude girl," Twan said. "It's not quite as long as hers, but it's fuller and thicker." Twan handed Kim a brush. "Brand-new brush, never been used."

129

"Go ahead," Sonya said. "Brush it out."

Kim brushed the wig with long strokes, pulling most of it toward her chest.

That girl is actually happy, Sonya said. *I've never seen her eyes dancing so much. Thank You, Lord, for this moment.*

"Done?" a brusque voice said.

Sonya saw a petite blond woman in a lab coat. *What's she want? A blood sample?*

"Yes, Lynn," Twan said. "All done."

"Thank you very much, Twan," Sonya said.

Kim was still mesmerized by her hair.

"My sister thanks you, too," Sonya added.

Twan nodded and left.

Lynn stood between Kim and Sonya. "You two need to be waxed," she said.

"That won't be necessary," Sonya said.

"Bob Freeberg's orders," she said.

Lord, is it okay to hate Bob Freeberg? I doubt that he's *ever been waxed.* "Oh." Sonya beckoned Lynn closer. "I usually keep things tidy down there myself," she whispered.

"This is TV, not porno, ma'am," Lynn said. "Bob says to give you a bikini wax if you need it."

But if I don't wear a bikini . . . "Oh, I don't wear bikinis," Sonya said. "I wear a one-piece suit."

Lynn frowned. "I still have to check."

No, you don't. "You tell Bob Freeberg that I won't get a bikini wax until he comes down

130

here and gets a bikini wax *with* me."

"Gotcha." Lynn nodded. "Men, huh?"

Sonya nodded. "Men."

Lynn stared above Sonya's eyes. "You need your eyebrows shaped."

"Bob's orders?" Sonya asked.

Lynn shook her head. "No. You just need your eyebrows shaped. The hairs are going in every direction. You wouldn't believe how many people call TV studios to complain about wayward eyebrows."

This woman is tripping, Sonya thought. *Either that or she* really *loves her job.* "If you think it's necessary. Do you wax or tweeze?"

"I wax. I'll try to be gentle."

I doubt having parts of my eyebrows ripped off my head will be a gentle experience.

Michelle returned just as Lynn had turned Sonya's "bushes" into "commas."

"Can we go somewhere to chill?" Kim asked. "I'm tired."

"No," Michelle said. "Not yet. We have to get Sonya decked out in her princess gear over at WB."

In an uninteresting, dreary room full of mirrors at Warner Bros. Studios, just down the way from the original *Friends* set, a team of costume designers, makeup artists, and several useless sycophants changed Sonya into Jazz. First, they slapped electric blue contacts into her eyes.

"To match your dress," one of them said.

Then they supplied her with several padded bras, fussing over whether C or D was "in" this year.

They chose D.

I will tip over, Sonya thought.

Kitting Sonya out with jewelry took an hour.

"We want her to look regal," someone said. "A princess should have a lot of bling."

I will tip over quickly, Sonya thought, *and make a loud crash.*

Fitting Sonya into her electric blue, velvet party dress took almost half an hour.

If they had buttered my body first, Sonya thought, *the whole process would have taken only a minute.*

Kim, who enjoyed throwing her new hair over her shoulders, suggested a shoehorn.

Sonya was not pleased.

Sonya tried on several *dozen* pairs of high heels, each more painful and ridiculous than the last pair. When Sonya suggested going barefoot, the sycophants gasped.

Sonya liked making the sycophants gasp. It almost made the entire process bearable.

After a photographer captured Sonya in her full Jazz regalia for the Web site splash page, the lead makeup artist, Jillian, told her to arrive early Monday morning. "We have a *lot* of painting to do."

Kim said Sonya would need the twenty-year paint.

Sonya was not amused.

On the ride up 110 to Casa Malibu, Kim rolled down the back windows to let her new hair flutter in the breeze.

"You really looked like black Barbie, Sonya," Kim said.

"I felt like a fool," Sonya said. "Have you ever seen so many suck-ups in one room in all your life?"

"So, what's it like to be a princess?" Michelle asked.

"Princesses must have stiff necks and aching feet," Sonya said.

As they drove through the entrance to Casa Malibu, Kim laughed. "It looks like a Super Eight."

"How would you know that?" Sonya asked.

"I know Super Eights, okay?" Kim said.

I shouldn't have asked, Sonya thought.

After squeezing the Camry into the last available space, Michelle led them over a red brick walkway between two tall palm trees directly to their beachfront room.

"You've already been checked in." Michelle took out a key. "No keycards here. This is an old-school joint. It's kind of seventies chic." She worked the lock and opened the door. "Aren't the crashing waves to die for?"

Sonya liked the white walls, white fireplace, and the king-size bed covered with a gold leaf bedspread. *It reminds me of my TV room. Oh, the plastic plant next to the TV is a nice touch. Grandmama would have felt right at home here. She had an entire kitchen filled with plants she had to dust instead of water.*

"It's got satellite TV, wireless Internet access, free continental breakfast," Michelle said, "and you're only fifty feet from the ocean."

Kim slumped into a rattan chair. "I will die here."

"Not bad," Sonya said. "I've stayed in worse."

Kim sighed. "So have I. But this is so creamy and peachy."

Michelle opened a door to a tiny kitchen. "Oh, this is nice."

Sonya had to turn sideways to get into the bathroom, a toilet to the left, a tub to the right. "Was this once an apartment complex?"

Michelle stuck her head in, and Sonya had to back up. "I think so."

Sonya left the bathroom for the veranda, a lounge chair and table set up facing the ocean. *Is the ocean always this loud? I don't know if I could sleep with all that noise.*

Kim wandered into the kitchen. "I'm eating on WB's tab as much as I can."

"Oh, there are lots of nice restaurants around here," Michelle said. "And you're liable to see someone famous."

"You could always get some groceries," Sonya said. "You're a great cook."

"I'm on vacation," Kim said. "Why would I cook?"

Michelle went to the door and turned. "Sonya, they'll send a car to get you Monday so they can paint and dress you in time for the show."

"Funny," Sonya said.

Michelle handed Sonya the room key. "Well, if you need anything, just give me a call."

"Um, we're both new at this agent thing," Sonya said. "What exactly are you going to do for us from now on?"

"I already did it," Michelle said. "I got both of you cast in a TV show."

"You're done?" Sonya asked.

"I'll keep an ear open for anything that might come up after the show," Michelle said.

"Like what?" Kim asked.

"Other shows, movies, TV, commercials," Michelle said. "I know you'll do your best."

"So until then, we're basically on our own," Kim said.

"Right." Michelle smiled.

"That sucks," Kim said. "What if we need your help?"

"Well," Michelle said, "Larry seems helpful. Ask him."

"The man looks like a shar-pei!" Kim cried.

"Larry knows a lot about this business,"

Michelle said. "Pay close attention. I may be calling you for advice and information."

"Or you might not," Sonya said.

"True," Michelle said. "I have bills to pay. Bye."

Sonya closed the door. "We're on our own." *For almost two days!*

Kim grabbed two pillows. "Michelle is insane. A little richer because of us, but she's still insane."

"What do you want to do first?" Sonya asked.

"Sleep." Kim buried her head in the pillows.

Which doesn't sound like a bad idea. "You don't want to walk along the beach? The sun's setting."

"I set about an hour ago," Kim said.

As the sun set in brilliant purples and oranges, Sonya felt exhaustion creep from her wounded pinkie toe cuticle to her sore eyebrows. Kim fell asleep on one side of the bed, snoring fitfully. Sonya lowered the windows to within an inch of closing to dampen the crashing waves and slid under the covers on the other side of the bed. All was peaceful, all was serene, all was blissfully quiet . . .

. . . until New Year's fireworks cannonaded off the Malibu Pier. Sonya flew out of bed to shut the windows completely, but Kim never even stirred.

Happy New Year, Kim. Sonya found a blanket in a closet and settled it around her daughter. She kissed Kim's cheek. *Happy New Year, Shani.*

Although the free continental breakfast consisted only of Costco muffins, orange juice, and somewhat drinkable coffee, Sonya didn't mind. She had a full day planned, the only full day she'd get to spend with her daughter for up to two months. Though Kim dragged her feet through most of the morning, she perked up once they hit the beach.

They had the beach to themselves on New Year's Day. Dolphins swam past, pelicans dove, and a few surfers tried to impress them.

"The pelicans have more skill," Kim said as they walked to the end of the Malibu Pier and watched several sailboats crossing the choppy waters in front of them.

After eating Fish Grill tacos for lunch, they explored a tide pool. While Sonya fearlessly waded into the pool and lifted up rocks and tried to catch little crabs, Kim stood on the sand.

"I didn't know you were so girly," Sonya said. "C'mon."

"Don't be so judgy," Kim said. "I just had a pedicure and a manicure, and I don't want to get my hair wet."

While grocery shopping at Pacific Coast Greens natural foods store, Kim asked,

"Where's the meat?"

"Shh," Sonya said. "You should be eating healthier anyway."

"I am not a vegetarian," Kim said. "I am a carnivore. I eat meat." She held up a prepared salad in a plastic container. "What is this shit?"

She'd be eating that stuff *if I had raised her.* Sonya stood at the deli counter looking at the meat behind the glass. *Hey, now. This is the real stuff. None of this is good for you. Look at all this potential heartburn.*

Kim ordered a pound of every meat in the case.

As they brought their groceries to Casa Malibu, Kim munched on a slice of Genoa salami. "Like I said, I'll be eating out a lot, but at least I won't go crazy if I have the munchies. Mmm, meat."

"Where would you like to eat out tonight?" *On our last night together,* Sonya thought. *Why does that depress me so much?*

"I definitely don't want sandwiches," Kim said.

"Italian, Mexican, or American?"

"I don't want American. I can always eat at KFC." She pointed at the KFC across the street.

Strange place for a KFC with all these health-conscious people around. "And I don't really want Mexican." *I will be around people tomor-*

row. I do not like to have gas, especially around people. "Italian it is."

Because of a cancelation, Sonya lucked into a reservation at Charlie's. She and Kim donned their wigs and their finest clothes and walked through the doors to be greeted by Dolce and Gabbana leopard-print chairs.

"I could get used to this," Kim said.

Dolce and Gabbana chairs? Sonya thought. *This bill is going to be a scorcher.*

Kim stared at the gold fork on the table. "You think this is solid gold?"

Check that, Sonya thought. *This bill is going to be a mortgage payment.* She looked at a giant red and white heart painting on a wall. *I'll bet that's an original Jane Seymour. Wow. This place is a mortgage payment* and *a car payment.*

Kim stared at her menu. "Ostrich? Is that Italian?"

They serve Big Bird? "I don't think so." *I need to find something safe. Ostrich?*

"Twelve bucks for a salad?" Kim whispered. "Are they serious?"

The cheapest salad is eight bucks! "Don't worry about the costs. We're on vacation." *Our first!*

"If you say so."

They split an order of crab cakes and ate baby arugula salads. Kim ordered a twelve-ounce filet with something called "forbidden

139

rice." Sonya played it safe with mushroom risotto and macaroni and cheese topped by crispy sage. While Sonya drank water, Kim ordered a thirty-five-dollar glass of Cabernet Sauvignon.

"Is it good?" Sonya asked.

"It is to die for," Kim said.

For thirty-five dollars it had better taste like heaven itself and drive you home afterward, Sonya thought.

They ordered three items from the dessert menu: a lemon tart, a slice of carrot cake, and something called Tahitian Vanilla Bean Panna Cotta.

"Why isn't anyone staring at us?" Kim whispered.

"Why would they?" Sonya asked.

"This is a swanky joint," Kim said. "They should be thinking we're stars as fly as we look."

"Maybe famous people don't stare," Sonya said.

"Yeah," Kim said. "Maybe they just know that *they* are being stared at."

When the bill arrived, Kim snatched the receipt. "Holy . . ." Kim smiled. "See, I didn't curse." She handed the receipt to Sonya. "This might make even *you* curse."

Holy . . . stuff! I'm still hungry, even with dessert! With tip . . . Two hundred and fifty bucks! For two people! In about an hour! Sonya signed the slip. "Let's get out of here before they

140

charge us for something else."

"Where to next?" Kim asked, standing and flipping her hair over her shoulders.

That child really loves her hair. "Why does there have to be a next?" Sonya asked as she held the door for Kim. "We could just go strolling on the beach."

"Dressed like this?"

Sonya smiled. "Sure. No shoes, though."

"Of course."

While the waves churned the sand and the wind whipped their hair, they walked to the pier and back as another sunset glowed in the sky.

"You scared?" Kim asked.

And now she's caring how I feel! I can't be away from her now! "No."

"Not at all?"

"Okay, I'm a little nervous. I haven't been in the spotlight for a while."

"You mean, you haven't had men undressing you with your eyes in a while."

Has that ever happened to me? I doubt it. "That, too."

"I'm glad it isn't me," Kim said.

"Why?"

"I like men, but I really don't *like* men, you know?"

Which is why she'll be perfect to play my "sister."

"I mean, they're nice to have around for a little while," Kim said, "but when it's time for them to go, they *got* to go."

Sonya frowned. "I'll be stuck with them for a long time."

"So kick them off sooner," Kim said. "I mean, what could they do if you, I don't know, cleaned house one episode, you know, dumped half of them?"

Yes. What could they do? "Wouldn't you want to help me with the dumping?"

"Well, yeah," Kim said. "That's why I'm here. But if you could, you know, speed things up a little . . ."

Sonya smiled. *I think Kim likes hanging with me.* "I could do that."

"I mean, all this is nice, but I'm liable to run out of things to do, especially since I don't have a car."

Ah. Transportation. "We'll get you one," Sonya said. "I'll get Michelle on it now that she's working for us." *Sort of.*

"Cool."

"And I won't call you every night," Sonya said. "Unless you want me to."

"Whenever." Kim shivered. "It's getting cold."

They returned to their room where Kim booted up her laptop and went to the *Hunk or Punk* Web site. "They're quick. Your picture is already on here."

I don't look like me at all, Sonya thought, *but I guess that's the point. I doubt anyone on earth*

142

would recognize me now. Are those really my lips? I didn't know I had any.

Kim pointed at a flashing word. "Live? You're going on live? I didn't know that."

Neither . . . did . . . I! Live? Are they crazy?

"I'll have to pop some popcorn," Kim said. "I wish I could tape it. This is going to be some classic stuff, I just know it."

Live? In that outfit? What if it rains, not that it would, I mean, this is Southern California and all, but . . . live? What if I freeze up? They said something about cue cards, but I wasn't paying attention.

"You know what would be funny?" Kim asked.

There's nothing funny about this!

"If I called you live on the air," Kim said. "Would you answer your phone?"

What? "You saw that dress. Where would I hide a phone?"

"Oh, yeah."

Live? There was nothing in the contract about live anything except for the eliminations.

"Are you nervous now, Sonya?"

Sonya nodded.

"Cool."

Not cool. I may be calling her the second I step out of the limo.

To come rescue me.

CHAPTER 9

John packed two suitcases before first service in exactly nine minutes.

He tried to pack his boots, but they wouldn't fit.

I have so little, but that's not a bad thing, John thought. *"Better is little with the fear of the Lord than great treasure and trouble therewith."*

The less I bring, the less trouble I'll have. Therewith.

The morning service ran smoothly, and despite an early January chill, fans still fluttered from "O Happy Day" to the benediction.

I'm going to miss New Hope. They've kept me going for fifteen years, and except for a case of bronchitis that knocked me out of a second service last February, I haven't missed a single service in twenty years. That has to be some sort of record, even for a faithful member of an AME.

After cleaning out and defrosting his refrigerator after service, also in nine minutes, John had a light lunch of leftover chicken soup, two heels of bread, and an apple. He spent his next two hours missing Sheila as he dusted, vacuumed, and swept the top floor.

Freshman year at Wheaton College. Foundations of Ministry 111. The first day there were maybe twelve of us in the class, all guys. Sheila smiled her way into the room and I smiled back. "Your smile told me I was in the right place," she told me. "I knew you were the man for me." I don't remember smiling at all. I was sitting near the window, so I might have only been squinting in the sun. I'm glad the sun was shining fiercely that morning. I might not have smiled.

Sheila was only one of ten black students at Wheaton that year, and despite my shyness and almost total lack of pigment, we hit it off after two slices of pizza and a soda at Jack Straw's. She cheered for me when I ran downfield on kickoffs and missed tackles — the coach often said I looked "like a moose on ice" — and she helped me survive senior seminar and the infamous honors thesis.

And when I proposed, I was as surprised as she was. I didn't have a ring. I didn't have a plan. I didn't say more than: "Please marry me." She fluttered her thick black eyelashes at me and said, "Really?" I nodded, she hugged me, we went and found rings at Stones Jewelry, broke the news to her family over the phone —

That *was interesting. Her mama must have said, "He's what?" a dozen times. "He going to be a pastor, Mama, and I'm going to be his wife." Her father asked, "Where?" "Down there, of course," Shelia told him. "You tell Uncle Charles he has a new youth pastor."*

And that was the extent of John's "interview" with New Hope AME.

I met her family at the rehearsal dinner. That was wild. Sixty people crammed into Zack's Restaurant over in Evergreen. My parents were quiet as mute mice while Sheila's family carried on and I ate too much, smiled too much, and said so little. But it was all right. Everything was all right. I was happy.

Yeah. I was a happy man once.

During the evening service in front of a scattering of people, most of whom worked Sunday mornings, Reverend Wilson spoke from 1 Corinthians 13, the Bible's "love chapter," and John tried to tune him out.

We were married right here. Her side was crowded. My parents were alone until some of the overflow crept up to within two pews of them. Most of Burnt Corn was here.

I wonder how my parents are doing. After Sheila died, I was supposed to run back to Chicago and be their only son again. Instead I stayed, and they've stayed more distant than ever. I doubt they'd ever watch a show like Hunk *or* Punk. *Maybe I should warn them.*

But what would be the point? They'd see me chasing yet another black woman, and for the whole world to see. If they had only gotten to know Sheila better, they'd understand why I couldn't leave even her memory behind.

"Though I speak with the tongues of men and of angels, and have not charity, I am become as sounding brass, or a tinkling cymbal . . ."

Reverend Wilson spoke from 1 Corinthians 13 on our wedding day, too. Not many weddings have full sermons anymore. All folks seem to want these days is a quick ceremony with a few songs, the vows, the reception, and the honeymoon. There was something so holy about our wedding. The ceremony was on God's time the entire time.

"And though I bestow all my goods to feed the poor, and though I give my body to be burned, and have not charity, it profiteth me nothing . . ."

I can't remember the last time Reverend Wilson spoke from this passage. Maybe he's trying to tell me something tonight.

"Charity — love — suffers long," Reverend Wilson said. "Some of us surely suffer a long time because of love."

Yeah, he's trying to tell me something. I've been suffering.

"Love bears all things, believes all things, hopes all things, and endures all things."

Amen, it is true, especially that enduring part. Love is an amazing gift, and it takes love to endure anything. Love even endures long after a loved one dies. Love never dies. There is always love.

"Faith, hope, and love. What's the greatest of these?"

Love. Sheila was my greatest love. I was at my greatest when I was with her. Lord, I want to feel great again.

"Do you have faith in love?"

John nodded. *Yes. I have no other choice.*

"Do you have hope in love?"

Tougher question. I hope to have hope in love.

"You have to have love in your heart to truly love someone." Reverend Wilson stepped away from the pulpit. "There is someone in here tonight who has so much love to give, many *years* of love building up inside, but that person has been holding back. God's been telling me to tell you to release that love now. You've been holding on to it for far too long. Let it go. Let it go."

Let it go.

I wonder if it's that easy.

On the two-hour ride to Montgomery early Monday morning, John and Reverend Wilson kept their own counsel until they got to Montgomery Regional Airport.

"We all still think about her, John," Reverend Wilson said. "I can still see her sitting next to you sometimes. But fifteen years is an awful long time to mourn."

"I know." *Though I could probably mourn for fifteen more.*

"You're doing the right thing here."

"I hope so." John shook Reverend Wilson's hand.

"We'll be praying."

So will I.

"You'll get her. Does she have a name?"

Here we go. "Jazz."

"Jazz, short for Jasmine?"

"No, just Jazz."

"How long you known her?"

And now for some ridiculousness. "Um, I'll meet her for the first time on Monday night."

"So you've been corresponding."

"Not . . . not exactly."

Reverend Wilson squinted. "So all this is a blind date?"

"You could say that." *A blind date for the entire country to see.*

Reverend Wilson blinked rapidly. "I, uh, I was gonna leave you with a special verse to see you through, but with what you've just told me, it wasn't a strong enough verse. A trip way out west to go on a blind date? You're gonna need Joshua one-nine then. 'Be strong and of a good courage; be not afraid, neither be thou dismayed: for the Lord thy

God is with thee whithersoever thou goest.' "

That's a good verse for those exploring unexplored territory. "Thank you, Reverend Wilson. For everything."

He shook his head. "We'll see each other again. Don't make this sound so final."

Yeah, you might be picking me up from the airport in a few weeks.

Once his plane to Dallas was airborne, John settled back and tried to rest. He wasn't exactly weightless, but at least he was moving.

I just wish I knew for sure that I was moving in the right direction.

After changing planes twice, snoozing for hours at two gates, and finally landing at LAX thirty minutes late, John walked through the tunnel to a swarm of people and a man holding a sign that read: BOND.

I hope that's for me, John thought.

Holding the sign was an elderly, tall, and tan Hispanic man who wore jeans, black boots, and a black leather jacket. "You Bond?" the man said with only a trace of an accent.

"I'm Bond. John Bond."

"Really."

John smiled. "John James Bond, actually."

"It is a good screen name."

"It's my real name."

The man crumpled up his sign and wedged

it into a trash can. "Do not change it."

"I don't plan to."

The man led John to baggage claim, where it seemed the entire world was waiting. "This is not good," the man said.

"Um, what's your name?"

"I am just your driver."

"Well, I'd like to know who I'm talking to."

"Manny."

John extended his hand.

Manny shook it, looking over John's head at the crowd. "This is not good."

Forty minutes later, John retrieved his suitcases, and he and Manny hustled to a green '66 GTO coupe with an AM radio, a real wood-grain steering wheel, and a grab bar over the glove box.

"What's the bar for?" John asked.

"You will need it," Manny said. "Strap in."

John belted himself, the straps forming an X across his chest. "This seat belt is different."

"You will need that seat belt, too. Hang on."

Manny drove John at speeds in excess of ninety miles per hour in and out of thick traffic, crossing four lanes at a time without signaling and generally leaving extended middle fingers and cursing in his wake.

Welcome to California, John thought. *Am I scared? Yes! This car has no airbags, no ABS, and no turn signals, apparently. We are two tons of steel — whoa! I could almost taste the bumper sticker on that van! Be strong and of a good courage. Yes, God, those are powerful words, but have You ever driven on a California freeway? You might be afraid, too!*

"They told me your hair would be auburn," Manny said.

I know it's turning white now. Slow down! "I'm just being myself."

"You are in LA," Manny said. "You can be anyone you want to be."

Right now I just want to be somewhere safe and not moving at — one hundred *miles an hour?*

"There is a packet for you in the glove box," Manny said.

John opened the glove box and took out a stack of papers. He scanned the cover sheet until he saw: "Arthur, thirty, film editor, Chicago." *It's so nice to be thirty again.* "Looks like I have to be someone named Arthur. Do I even look like an Arthur?"

Manny looked over. "You look more like a Fred."

Please watch the road! "Arthur the thirty-year-old film editor. King Arthur, leader of the knights of the round table, on my way to Camelot."

Manny didn't respond.

"Or a man dancing at Arthur Murray Dance Studios. They could have made me a dancer, which would be hilarious because I can't dance a lick."

Manny did not blink.

Manny is no fun, John thought.

John read through a list of do's and don'ts for the Crew, most of which he would never do. Don't do drugs. Don't curse too much. Don't get drunk on camera. *On camera. Oh. Get drunk on your own time.* Don't have your cell phone on during filming. *So we can have cell phones but we can't make calls out or communicate with anyone at any time. Huh? Oh. We can* get *text and voice messages, but we can't* send *them. Same with the Internet. Who would send me any messages anyway? My ancient phone doesn't even get texts or voice mail.*

Oh, and there's my "pay." One thousand two hundred fifty dollars a week. I'm guaranteed four weeks, so I'm guaranteed five thousand dollars. I'm getting paid to stay in a mansion and flirt with a beautiful woman. Only in America. And if I "win," I collect an extra fifty thousand dollars. If I stay the entire time and win . . . that's one hundred thousand dollars plus. There's something . . . wrong about that. Getting paid for winning a woman's heart.

Again, only in America.

A blur passed them. *Are you kidding me? We're doing one-ten, and someone passed us? Where are the cops? Maybe those* were *the cops.* "Um, Manny, is traffic always like this?"

"It is the day after New Year's Day, so people are still hung over and irritated. It is a Monday, and the people who had to work today are coming home from work hungover and irritated. And, it is Southern California. Today is the trifecta for *tremendo* traffic."

John gripped the bar over the glove box more tightly. "Are we in any particular hurry?"

"I must get you there before eight o'clock."

"Why?"

"You will see."

I just want to see the ground under my feet — both feet. If I had my boots, I'd feel safer.

After twenty harrowing minutes of bobbing and weaving through traffic, Manny pulled off the freeway and pointed at a hill. "You see all those lights up there?"

"Yes."

"That is the mansion."

All lit up like Christmas. "What a waste of electricity. You could probably see it from space."

"The lights are brighter because they are filming."

"Oh. Already?" *But I'm not there to be filmed.*

"They only use those lights when they are filming live."

Did he say . . . "What?"

"They did not tell you."

"No." *They like keeping the white man in the dark.* "But if those lights are on, that means

154

they are already filming, right?"

Manny checked his watch. "It is seven fifty-five. They are getting ready. They begin in five minutes."

"And how much longer until we get there?"

"Ten minutes."

"I'm going to be late. Is that good or bad?"

"Bad," Manny said, squealing tires up a winding, hilly street past massive mansions. "You are going to arrive after the princess's big entrance."

"Oh." *There are many degrees of bad, so . . .* "Um, will that be bad for me, bad for the show, bad for her, bad for you — what?"

"Bad for all concerned."

John looked at his clothes. "I look a mess."

"Yes."

"I need a shower, too." *I have travel funk.*

"Yes."

"This isn't good."

"No." He checked his watch again. "It is, as they say, showtime."

"How much longer?"

"Five minutes."

And now my stomach is crawling up my chest to my neck. Geez.

"When you get out," Manny said, "stay in the light."

"I'd rather hide in the dark."

"Yes." Manny pulled into a driveway a few car lengths from a long black limousine. "They have not begun introducing themselves to her yet. You may be okay."

"You don't think they're waiting for me, do you?"

"They are not waiting on you."

I feel so important. "I haven't even signed the contract yet."

Manny stared at the papers in John's hands.

"Oh." John signed all the places marked with an X.

"I will bring your suitcases inside. Just stay in the light."

John opened the door. "That's okay." *The ground feels good.* "I can carry them."

Manny got out and opened the trunk. John took out his suitcases. "Where exactly do I go?"

Manny shrugged. "Get in line. I recommend that you go to the end of the line."

"Yeah." *The last shall be first.* "Thanks for the ride." He extended his hand.

Manny shook it. "You are a funny man."

"I hope it's a good kind of funny."

Manny didn't respond.

"Um, what are the other guys like?"

"They are nothing like you."

I already knew that. "Is that a good thing?"

"It cannot hurt. Good luck."

John took a deep breath, hoisted his suitcases, and walked directly toward the lights.

Now I know how the Apostle Paul felt on the road to Damascus . . .

CHAPTER 10

As Graham McNabb, former child sitcom star and the gabby host of *Hunk or Punk,* had talked to hear himself talk, Sonya had sat in the limousine, hating life in general and her high heels in particular.

Why'd they choose Graham McNabb to host this show? He's a punk, not a hunk. He has to be the whitest black man on TV. Carlton Banks from The Fresh Prince of Bel-Air *was blacker. "Marky" Mark Wahlberg is blacker. The average white man has more soul than Graham does.*

But what am I? I'm a black Barbie in an electric blue party dress sitting in a limousine in Point Dume in the hills above Malibu. My hair keeps tickling my cheeks, and it's even getting in my mouth. I hate to have my own hair in my mouth. I don't know whose hair this was! I hate that I have to wear electric blue contacts. What was wrong with my hazel eyes? And these little torture chambers on my feet, these Pollini high heels, are like tourniquets for my toes. I just know I'm going to fall. I wonder if Cinderella felt this way on her way to the ball.

"Crew," Graham said, "it is time for you to meet your Nubian princess. Jazz, come out and meet the Crew."

There's my cue. Lord, You promise to uphold me with Your right hand. Please, I'm begging, use both of Your almighty hands to keep me vertical until I get to that little X on the ground.

Sonya had waited until the white-gloved chauffeur opened her door, had reached out her manicured hand, had grabbed onto the chauffeur's hand, had stepped out onto the driveway with one shaky foot, had followed that foot with another just like it, and her first thought when she had finally stood was: *Look at all that man meat.*

She had walked through the brightest lights on earth toward a vaguely host-shaped glow and had heard the glow say, "Crew, say hello to Jazz."

I can't see a thing with those lights in my face. Smile, girl. The whole blue world is watching.

Sonya had smiled.

And stumbled.

She had heard Graham whisper, "Jazz, say something to the Crew."

Oh, yeah. I have to speak. It's in my contract. "Hey, Crew," she had said. *That was stupid but not as stupid as what they wanted me to say: "Hello, my suitor princes."*

"Each member of the Crew will now —"

158

Sonya thought she had been prepared for just about anything, but when the white man arrived carrying his suitcases, his clothes wrinkled, his church shoes just plain wrong with those jeans, and he walked right up next to her, she thought, *Why is that man ruining my entrance?*

"Sorry I'm late, y'all," the man said. "Traffic was a mess."

What part of the deep *South is he from?* Sonya thought. *And why is he still standing next to me in all of his funk? What, did he ride his horse all the way from Texas?*

The man tipped an imaginary hat to her. "Ma'am."

Ma'am? I am not old enough to be a ma'am! Now . . . shoo!

The man carried his suitcases to the end of the line of man meat.

"Uh, okay," Graham said. "Now each member of the Crew will introduce himself to the Nubian princess."

Okay, Sonya thought, *let's see who is worthy of me.*

Let's also see if I can get some feeling into my toes. I see my feet.

I just don't feel them at all.

CHAPTER 11

Oh, God in heaven, what am I doing here?

John sized up the Crew and found himself lacking, and not just in pigment. Each of the Crew was taller, wider, and much better dressed. The man next to him had more teeth than two normal people. The man taking Jazz's hand had a linebacker's shoulders and a basketball player's legs. The tattooed man now hugging her should probably be playing for the Lakers. The next man in line had muscles on top of his muscles, his shirt crying for a much smaller man.

I am in the wrong place, I am in the wrong place, I am in the wrong place . . .

But she is so beautiful, she is so beautiful, she is so —

Not twenty-five.

John looked more closely at Jazz. *She looks older and wiser than an aspiring actress and surfer. Why'd they put such thick makeup on her? I bet she's fine under all that mess. Her voice was deeper and more textured than I expected it to be. I half-expected Minnie Mouse sucking on helium. She doesn't sound like an airhead, and she's very sexy. She has sense and sex appeal — what a combination. There can't be an ounce of fat on her. Curvaceous as the street I just came up. But her eyes are too blue — and they match her dress. What woman does that unless she's vain?*

She is definitely swaying in those high heels. Oh! Now she's switching feet!

John smiled.

That's what Sheila used to call it when her feet were killing her. She'd bend one knee to put all her weight on that foot to relieve the pressure on the other foot. Or she'd straighten a leg to let the other leg dangle in the air. I'll bet Jazz wants to kick those high heels off and leave them off.

Jazz has a lot of hair. Sheila used extensions a couple times but preferred her own hair, even though she wrestled and fussed with it every morning.

John frowned.

Why are they all pawing at her, touching her, hugging her, some even kissing her cheek? Y'all just met her! Show some restraint! That is a lady! She is not some —

Oh, Lord, it's my turn.

Be strong and of good courage.

And don't say or do something stupid.

161

CHAPTER 12

Are we done? I have so much cologne and body spray on me that I might asphyxiate! I think I even have bruises on my back from all those probing fingers. One left? Who is it? Oh. It's the show crasher. I believe that traffic was heavy, but I wouldn't be surprised if Bob and Larry didn't delay him on purpose for the effect his entrance would have on me.

Sonya watched the man approach, and unlike the rest of the Crew, he took his time, his eyes affixed to the ground, his smile hard to read. *Is he sneaky? Devious? Mischievous? At least he isn't staring at my chest like most of the others. But what is he looking at?* She looked down. *He's staring at my feet! And my toes have turned white! Geez, can you get gangrene from wearing high heels?*

"Hi, Jazz," he said. "I bet your feet are killing you."

Sonya looked into the man's brown eyes. "They are," she whispered.

He looked down. "Mine, too. Been traveling all day. Rode three planes to get here. They didn't want me to wear my boots. These church shoes look terrible with these jeans, but I didn't think I should wear running shoes on TV."

The man then slipped off his shoes.

Oh, no, he didn't. He just . . . took 'em off. Make yourself at home, pardner.

"Much better," the man said. "Oh, I showered this morning. Sorry about the funk now."

A man just took off his shoes on national TV in front of a Nubian princess. What kind of man takes his shoes off in front of any woman he just met? This has to be a setup. "Um, it's okay," Sonya said. *And he did call them church shoes. He was very clear about that. What man calls shoes "church shoes" unless he goes to church?*

The man had dropped almost an inch. "And now I'm shorter than you," he said. "I'm really sorry I ruined your entrance, Jazz. I should have just slipped in the back."

He seems sorry, but that could be part of a scam. "You didn't ruin anything."

The man looked down again. "I am worried that you're ruining your toes."

So am I. Sonya smiled. *I am about to make TV history, too. Oh no, the diva took off her heels! The folks at Pollini are going to be angry I took them off, but I don't care.* "My feet are killing me." She slipped off her heels, and

163

feeling returned to her toes. *Oh, thank You, Jesus! Thank You, Jesus! Thank You, Blessed Savior!* She looked at the man. "And now I'm shorter than you are."

"Your feet feel better?" the man asked.

"Much," Sonya said. "Um, what's your name?"

The man hesitated and looked up. "Um, my name is . . . Art. I think. No, it's . . . Artie. No. Arturo? No. It's Arthur. Yeah, that's right. Arthur, age thirty, film editor, Chicago."

Either he's extremely absentminded, or he has just told me that he's not really Arthur, thirty, a film editor, or from Chicago. He does have a cute squint. No, those are wrinkles. And he has worry lines around his eyes and on his forehead. Gray hairs, too? He's closer to my real age than to thirty. At least he has the good graces not to be touching on me. "It's nice to meet you, Art, Artie, Arturo, or Arthur."

He smiled. "May I ask you a question?"

Sonya looked at Darius Thompson, the director, who twirled a finger in the air. *I know, I know, Darius. Move it along. But I am having fun and relaxing for the first time. Calm down.* "Sure, Arthur. Ask me your question."

"Do you always match your dresses to your eyes?"

Sonya couldn't stop her mouth from dropping. "No." *The stupid producers do that for me!* "This is the first time."

"And now that you've met the Crew," Graham said loudly, "Nubian princess Jazz, welcome to your castle."

Arthur glanced at Graham. "Guess he thinks I'm taking up too much of your time, huh?"

"The show must go on," Sonya said.

"Yes," he said with a smile, his eyes narrowed and locked on hers. "The *show*. It *must* go on."

He is really into my eyes, Sonya thought. *I wish I could show him and the rest of the world my real ones.*

"Nice to meet you, Jazz." He picked up his shoes and returned to his place in line.

That was strange, Sonya thought. *Strange, but nice. He had soft brown eyes, and he really looked at my eyes and not my fake D cups. The others practically had their tongues down my —*

"Nubian princess Jazz?"

Oh, yeah. I'm on TV. How soon I forgot.

She wiggled her grateful toes and picked up her heels. The Crew parted, and Sonya walked a velvety black carpet into the house behind Graham. Instead of pausing in the two-story foyer, he rushed her through the kitchen and out to the pool.

This wasn't in the "script"! Aren't I supposed to admire the house and smile at the ridiculously overpriced inkblot paintings in the foyer prob-

ably done by three-year-olds? Larry told me we had to —

"We're behind schedule," Graham whispered. "Gotta catch up."

Whatever, Graham, Sonya thought. *It wasn't my idea to do this thing live.* She blinked at a glass table beside the pool that contained thirteen glasses full of bubbling champagne. *One of those bad boys is going to remain full.*

"Now it's time for each member of the Crew to toast the Nubian princess," Graham said. He held out a glass to Sonya.

"I don't drink, Graham," she said sweetly.

Graham looked past Sonya to Darius.

Darius glared and twirled his finger in the air.

I am really gumming up the works, aren't I, guys?

"Well, um, the Crew can toast you anyway," Graham said.

"Sure, Graham," Sonya said. *Sorry to confuse you with information you already should have known.* "You could get me a bottled water. I am a little thirsty."

Chapter 13

The UCLA-attendee doesn't drink, John thought. *She won't even hold a glass of champagne for show, and she seems to enjoy messing with the entire process. Man, if I weren't in this show, I would definitely be watching at home just to see what she'll do and say next.*

John also couldn't help thinking: *She's real.*

But now I have to toast her, and I have never given a toast to anyone in my life. I suppose I could give her a benediction. May the peace of God . . . No, that would be boring. And Larry said not to do the "religious" stuff.

While John tried to recall any toast-like verses from the Bible, the rest of the Crew poured on the charm:

"Here's to getting to know you better and better each day — and especially each and every night."

"Here's to my Nubian queen, the best-looking woman that I've ever seen."

"Here's to the hottest honey in the universe.

You have me buzzing like a bee."

"Here's to you and me . . ."

John backed away into the kitchen, opening a refrigerator that could have eaten two of his refrigerators, and took two Dasani bottled waters. By the time he returned to the pool, he was listening to Justin, by far the largest human John had ever met at six-eight and at least three hundred fifty pounds, rapping his toast to Jazz:

"Yo, Jazz, you are my princess, I must confess, I love that dress, and you don't take no mess. You came in nice wheels, you dropped them heels, you got nerves of steel, and before you I kneel." Justin eased down to a kneeling position, and he was still almost as tall as Jazz was.

Jazz clapped her hands. "That was great!"

And I have to follow that *performance?* John thought.

"Arthur?" Graham said.

Couldn't we go to a commercial or something?

Justin rose and stepped back. John edged through the rest of the Crew and stood in front of Jazz. He handed her a bottled water.

"Thank you," she said.

He held up his bottled water. "Here's to comfortable shoes, honesty, and quiet nights."

Why does everything get so quiet around here whenever I speak?

168

CHAPTER 14

He toasted me with Dasani water! Sonya thought. *Kim has to be busting a gut back at the hotel.*

"Thank you, Arthur," Sonya said. "That was sweet." *Especially the "honesty" part. But how'd he know I enjoyed quiet nights?*

"And now," Graham said, "it's time for Jazz to mingle with the Crew."

Darius shot his arm and five fingers into the air, folding his fingers one at a time into a fist. "Commercial!"

Three things happened simultaneously. Darius started cursing the world in general, half the Crew pulled out cell phones and checked for messages, and Graham picked up a glass of champagne, downing it in one gulp.

"That was horrific," Graham said.

"The champagne?" Sonya asked. *Or your inability to go with the flow and simply talk to people, Graham?*

"Not the champagne," Graham whispered.

"We'll be lucky to be on the air next week."

"Why?" Sonya asked.

Graham looked back at Arthur. "Him."

He's not the problem, Sonya thought. *This fantasy masquerading as reality is the problem.* "You're joking."

"He's been stealing the spotlight all night," Graham whispered. "He timed his arrival to get the most face time with you."

Arthur? He couldn't be that shrewd. I mean, the man took off his shoes on national TV. That was crazy, not shrewd. Hmm. But a lot of people are going to be talking about him and his shoes tomorrow. I'm sure people are online right now blogging their opinions about his socks.

"I've seen it before," Graham whispered after pouring and sucking down another glass of champagne. "It's always the ones you never expect."

"Turn off your cell phones!" Darius shouted. "I told you all to turn *off* your cell phones! I distinctly heard buzzing! Turn 'em off! We are on again in sixty seconds."

Sonya looked around. *Let's see who the drinkers are. Arthur doesn't drink . . . or at least he hasn't had anything to drink. He might still be trying to play me. Justin is drinking a Gatorade. Good. He could probably play lineman in the NFL as big as he is. He is definitely from Philly the way he talks. And that guy, what's his name? Gary. From Memphis. He could play linebacker. Tall, dark, and broad-shouldered. He's not drinking anything. Tony, slim, light-skinned, soft eyes. Where's he from? New Orleans. He has a bottled water. I have to learn these names quick. The rest are drinking like fish and getting seconds and thirds on the champagne. Hmm. But why aren't they fawning on me now?* She turned slowly in a circle. *Here I am, fellas. Aren't we supposed to be mingling?*

"Aren't your feet cold?"

Sonya turned to see Arthur staring at her feet. "A little." She looked down at his socks. "Are your feet cold?"

"No."

"Thirty seconds!" Darius shouted. "Get ready to mingle, and don't look at the cameras at any time!"

"Does he shout like that all the time?" Arthur asked.

"He seems to. I wish I had brought ear-plugs."

"I wish I had brought my boots." He smiled. "It gets kinda deep around here."

"Fifteen seconds!" Darius shouted. "Act happy!"

"I better step aside," Arthur said. "I don't want to be trampled by all your admirers."

"You don't have to go, Arthur." *I may need you to block for me.*

"I have, um, I've been getting too much face time with you."

Arthur has some excellent hearing.

"It is really good to meet you, Jazz." He backed away and headed for a poolside chair.

"Five! Four!" Darius silently mouthed the last three numbers.

And *then* the Crew descended on Jazz.

For the rest of the first episode.

So this is what claustrophobia feels like, Sonya thought. *I'm smiling so much my cheeks hurt. "Girl," "Ma," "Jazz." I miss my real name! So many conflicting colognes, so many perfectly white teeth. And the bling! It's blinding. I'm surrounded by tattoos, chests, muscles, and tattooed chest and arm muscles. And I'm not saying much. How can I whittle them down when I can't separate them out or even talk to them one-on-one? I may not know much about having a relationship, but this group thing going on around me is not the way to start one with* one *person.*

Sonya occasionally had glimpses of Gary, who had the nicest eyes, Justin, whose single leg would outweigh her, and Tony, who had the smoothest voice. They stayed just out of range of the huddle of faces, chains, and tight jeans around her. Once she spied Arthur looking out to sea. *Just like that stupid book cover on that personality test.*

"You look like you might have played some ball."

Sonya looked up. *Who is this tall person? Um. Aaron. The basketball player. From . . . Houston.* "I might have. Aaron, right?"

"Right," Aaron said. "Bet you got some smooth moves. Maybe we can play some one-on-one sometime."

Is he serious? "I am a team player."

"You can play on my team anytime, Ma."

I don't want to listen to this mess anymore. I have to leave. "I'm really tired, fellas, so . . ." *Where's Graham? Oh, there he is. The man is hammered. Good thing the table he's leaning on is sturdy.*

She tried to walk by Aaron, but Aaron stepped in front of her. "Excuse me," she said.

"I can walk you to your room," Aaron said.

And I can walk up some stairs all by my own little self. "That's sweet, but I'll be fine."

Aaron still wouldn't move. "Don't want you to get lost in your castle, Ma."

And I want you to get lost, boy. I'm old enough to be your ma. "I won't get lost."

"If you do, I'll find you," Aaron said, and he stepped aside.

And all that was just witnessed by a couple million people who probably think Aaron has game. He does — a little — but I just have to get some rest.

She said, "Good night, everybody," waved

for the cameras, and walked through the kitchen into the foyer, a cameraman following closely behind her. In the foyer she saw Arthur staring at one of the inkblot paintings.

And the camera is right on my sore heels. Geez. I can't escape!

Arthur turned from the painting. "Good night, Jazz. Sleep well. Dream happy dreams."

That was . . . odd. "I'll try."

She walked upstairs. *The camera is probably filming my electric blue butt now. I wish I could walk up the stairs backward.* She turned left at the top of the stairs, opened the door to her "wing," and closed the door.

That was the longest hour of my entire life. Triple-overtime games were shorter. Thank You, Lord Jesus, for getting me through it.

She drifted down a short hallway to her suite and locked the door behind her. Then she unpinned the wig and put it on a Styrofoam head on the dresser, shimmied out of the dress, removed her padded bra and contacts, threw on a T-shirt and sweats, and spent the next hour removing the makeup from her face and the cologne from her hands and upper body. Only then did she turn on her phone and find several text messages from Kim:

U look gud 4 an old lady LOL Thot u wld trip!

I thought I would, too, Sonya thought. *I will not wear Pollini ever again.*

Dat white man b old. funny tho. howd his feet smell? ROFL no dont. u wld b closer 2 his feet!

"Ha!" *I'm sure the rest of the world is wondering about him, too. He did save my toes, though. They are back to a healthy brown color.*

A few r gay. call me 4 who.

How does she know this? And if she's right about even one of them, what are they doing on this show? She opened the last message.

Aaron is hot. he da 1.

She is so young, Sonya thought, *but she's right. Aaron is chiseled, tall, smooth, a heart-throb. But he calls me "Ma." He's not the person I want calling me that.*
She heard a knock at the door. "Who is it?"
"Larry Prince."
Maybe he's here to tell me the show's been canceled already. How do I feel about that? Hmm. I feel relieved. She opened her door and stepped into the hall, closing the door behind her. "It's a mess in there."

"How are you?" Larry asked.

"Fine. What's up?" She leaned her back on the door.

"Um, well . . ."

Sonya nodded. "It didn't go too well, did it?"

"Oh, no, it was sensational . . . actually. Better than we had hoped."

Then why doesn't he sound so sure? "So . . . why the visit?"

"Bob thought I should, you know, remind you of a few important things."

"Oh. Did I leave the scene too early?"

"No," Larry said. "Your exit was done with style and grace."

And barefoot. "I shouldn't have taken off the heels. But they were killing my feet."

"How are they now?"

"Better." *Larry isn't mad at all. Hmm.* "Oh, I know I should have held the champagne glass, but y'all know I don't drink."

"It's fine."

"I'll try to be a better princess tomorrow."

Larry smiled. "And now that I have reminded you of those important things, I will go."

Huh? "You didn't remind me of anything important, Larry."

"And I don't ever plan to, Sonya," Larry said. "Keep doing exactly what you're doing. Keep on, how do they say it? Keep on keeping it real."

"Really?"

"You were marvelous." Larry smiled. "Keep it up."

Sonya smiled. "I'll try."

"I'll do my best to keep Bob happy," Larry said. "If that's possible." He chuckled under his breath. "You are amazing in front of a camera. You have such presence. Your reactions to everything Arthur did and said were priceless."

"That wasn't acting, Larry."

"I know," Larry said. "And that's what makes your reactions so priceless. I almost wish we could do the entire show live. We'll be taping and splicing all week for next Monday's show and for every show until the finale. The last fifteen minutes of every show will be live, though, and I'm sure those moments will be magical, but we're liable to lose some of the week's magic with all the splicing."

More live stuff? "The last fifteen minutes of every show will be live."

"That's when you send them packing," Larry said. "Bob says it's a bad idea, but I think it's the best idea. Viewers will see immediate reactions. No amount of editing can improve on that."

"What if they . . . go off?"

"We'll have it on a ten-second delay just in case."

Yikes.

"It will be fine, Sonya," Larry said.

"Um, do you think any of the . . . losers will get loud?"

"They might."

"I'll have to let them go gently, then, huh?"

"Let them go any way you want to." He winked. "Get some rest."

Sonya returned to her room and glided to the veranda overlooking the pool. She saw Aaron, Tony, and Gary sitting at a table and talking. *Yeah, those three are handsome, strong black men. The producers chose wisely.* She saw Justin and Arthur at the overlook talking. *And those two are my comic relief, two very sweet men. Arthur still isn't wearing shoes. The rest? Drunk, and the party is getting louder. I already miss the waves.*

I wonder . . . She quickly texted Kim.

Can i dump 7 guys @ 1 time?

A minute later, Kim replied:

Wch 7?

Sonya texted:

All but Arthur, Gary, Tony, Justin, & Aaron

Kim replied:

Gud choices exc 4 Arthur.

Why are we texting? And if I make one call, will they fire me? I don't think so. Sonya dialed Kim's number. "So what did you think?" *Of your old mother.*

"You were too blue," Kim said.

"I know." Sonya turned on her TV. "I was seeing blue, too."

"And you're supposed to talk a lot more, not just smile. You were cheesing the whole time. I kept saying, 'Speak, Sonya.' The people next door have to think I'm crazy."

"I know, I know. I was having enough trouble breathing, I was so nervous." She scrolled down the screen guide to the Travel Channel and *Man v. Food. Man, I've seen that one already. He eats an eleven-pound pizza. Disgusting, but entertaining.* "What do you think of my choices so far?"

"Arthur? Really?"

"He's different." *And older.*

"He's white."

"It's more than that, Kim. He's . . . funny. He's easy to talk to. The only time I relaxed was when he was around."

"Well, you can keep him," Kim said. "For now. Drop the other seven as soon as you can. All at once would be awesome. I've never seen more than one guy get dumped on a show like this. It will be unprecedented."

"They won't let me do that." *Larry might approve. He just said to let them go any way I*

179

wanted to. Bob, though. Bob will have a cow until his half-dollars squirt from his shoes and break windows.

"How could they stop you, *Jazz?* You are the star."

And if it's live . . . How indeed?

Kim yawned loudly. "I am so sleepy."

"I am, too," Sonya said. "It has to be the jet lag. Why don't you turn in early?"

"I'm already in the bed. There's nothing on TV tonight. No offense."

Sonya turned off her TV. "I know it. Call me tomorrow?"

"You might be taping."

"Call or text me anyway."

"Okay."

I wish she were here. "Make sure your door and windows are locked."

"I already did. Good night."

Sonya took one last look outside. Four members of the Crew filled the spa, water spilling over the edge, every one of them with a beer or a tumbler in his hand, two smoking cigarettes, one a cigar, all of them laughing and smiling. Four others, including Justin, had a card game going on one of the tables. *Looks like Spades. Fun.* She didn't see the other four members of her list, but that was just as well.

I guess I'm really here now, she thought. *I'm a princess in her castle.*

She frowned at her TV. *And when I'm not on TV, there's nothing on TV. What's up with that?*

CHAPTER 15

John unpacked, hanging up as much as he could in the only closet. Both Aaron and Justin, his suitemates, had a lot of clothes.

Enough for several months, John thought. *I'll have to do laundry in four days.*

He entered the bathroom and found no room on the counter for his shave kit.

They have turned our bathroom into a Walgreens.

He picked up and read labels. *Matifiant Shine Rescue? What does it do? Oh. It eliminates shiny skin and gives skin a "matte" finish. Who wants to look like a photograph? Fonteint Hydrating Enhancer? What does this do? It eliminates redness. I might sneak some of this stuff. I seem to have a natural knack for embarrassing myself. Cover Select Liquid Corrector, which reduces circles under the eyes.* He looked in the mirror at the circles under his own eyes. *Nothing will help those circles except sleep.*

He squinted at Alpha Hydrox, Kiehl's Line-

Reducing Concentrate, Paula's Choice, and MD Forte. He sniffed the top of Marvis Aquatic Mint Toothpaste. *Made in Italy? Imported toothpaste? And what's this? Supersmile Whitening Accelerator? Geez, just go to a dentist twice a year. Michel Germain séxûal pour homme deodorant? Liebling deodorant, which contains lemon balm, peppermint, lime extract, and propolis. What's propolis? And where are the American colognes?*

A Braun Oral-B Interclean Ultra System electric toothbrush and a Philishave 8000 Series Aquagenic Sensotec shaver were plugged into the only two outlets. *Whatever happened to simply using water and an Oral-B to brush your teeth? Whatever happened to using a razor and some shaving cream to shave your face?*

He looked at but didn't sniff the Roger & Gallet Extra-Vielle Cologne or the Creed Green Irish Tweed cologne. *The names barely fit on the bottles.*

Stacked in every other available space were vitamin supplements, none familiar to John. L-carnitine was touted for building lean muscle mass and increasing sperm count. "May cause nausea, vomiting, cramps, and diarrhea." *How can you please your lady if you're in the bathroom all night?* Casein protein powder was supposed to build muscle mass. "May cause rashes, cramps, bloating, and hives." *Hey, look at the muscular hives on that guy's arms.* Vitamin Q10, a disease-fighting antioxidant, "might cause dizziness, loss of appetite, sensitivity to light, irritability, headache, heartburn, fatigue, and insomnia." *The good news is that you don't have any diseases. The bad news is that you can't stand, eat, see, think, exercise, or sleep.* Selenium was reputedly good for healthy eyes and hair. *So if you have an eyelash stuck in your eye, rest assured that both are healthy.*

John shook his head while he snooped. *They even have real leather shave kits with a dozen compartments full of tweezers, clippers, combs, emery boards, and brushes. Vanity, vanity, all is vanity on this vanity.*

He looked into his own black vinyl shave kit. He sighed at the Old Spice deodorant, cologne, and shaving cream. He frowned at the Crest toothpaste, disposable razors, Oral-B toothbrush, and One A Day vitamins. *Y'all are out of place here.*

And so, apparently, am I.

He made a pyramid out of the supplements to give himself more space on the counter, then shaved, showered, and changed into a pair of threadbare sweats and a University of Alabama sweatshirt. He heard the thump and drone of hip-hop music below him, wished he had brought earplugs, and climbed into bed.

184

At four AM, he woke. *What is it, six or seven in Alabama?* He was wide awake and listening to Justin snoring like a freight train across the room. Aaron didn't seem to be conscious.

No use changing my routine.

He took his Bible, a pen, and a notepad downstairs through the kitchen to a huge room filled with comfortable couches and recliners. He turned on a lamp, settled into a comfortable overstuffed brown couch, and continued his study of Nehemiah.

Nehemiah was rebuilding the Temple, John thought, *and I am rebuilding my life.*

At four AM in a mansion in Malibu!

And then he prayed. *Lord, thank You for waking me up and giving me yet another interesting day . . .*

CHAPTER 16

Sonya couldn't sleep, her stomach gurgling. She had skipped dinner so her dress wouldn't strangle her, and now her body needed nourishment. She sneaked downstairs to the kitchen, taking an apple and a banana from a fruit bowl on a counter cluttered with empty and partially empty beer, wine, and liquor bottles.

What a mess. She sniffed a glass half filled with a greenish liquid. *Geez, what is that? Turpentine?* An empty Lucid Absinthe Supérieure bottle was in the sink. *One hundred and twenty-four proof? And it's called "Lucid"? Who are they trying to kid?*

She turned to leave the kitchen when she saw a light on in the great room. She peeked into the room and saw Arthur. *What's he reading? And why is he up at this hour?* She slipped into the room.

"Can't sleep?" she whispered.

Arthur turned his head. "Oh, hi, Jazz. Um, it's six or seven back home. I'm normally up at this hour."

An early riser. That's cool. Sonya sat across from him in a rocking recliner. "I haven't slept at all. All that noise. I hope they don't party like that every night."

Arthur only stared at her.

"What?"

"I like you better without makeup," he said.

"A woman doesn't wear makeup to bed, you know."

Arthur nodded. "I still like you better without makeup. That makeup was covering up your beauty."

Which is a compliment, Sonya. Take it. "Thank you, Arthur." *He's wearing sweats and reading the Bible. I do that sometimes, too.* "Um, what book are you reading?"

"Nehemiah."

He said that with no hesitation, no embarrassment, and no trace of fear. They let another Christian on this show? Bob must be tearing his hair out. "And you're taking notes."

"Yes. It helps me remember what I read." He looked at the ceiling. "Do you think they still have the cameras and microphones on?"

"I hope not," Sonya said.

"I hope not, too. I'll keep my voice down, just in case." He closed the Bible, leaving his hand on top of it. "Hi, Jazz, my name is John. I am not thirty, I am not a film editor, and I am no longer from Chicago." He smiled.

187

"Just thought you might want to know that."

An honest man. There's something comforting about that. "I figured as much."

"I am actually forty, I am my church's handyman, and I am a former pastor from Burnt Corn, Alabama."

Okay. That's a lot of information to digest in a short period of time. "You don't look forty."

"Thank you."

She raised her eyebrows. "How handy are you?"

"If it can break, I can duct tape it."

Funny. "Um, where in Alabama?"

"Burnt Corn. About halfway between Montgomery and Mobile. Small town."

It's too strange a name not to be real. "You also said 'former.' " *What'd he do wrong?*

"I am no longer married, and at New Hope AME, First Timothy chapter three is in full effect."

First Timothy chapter three. Something about requirements for ministers. But at New Hope AME? "And you're no longer married because . . ."

"My wife died."

That's so sad! "I'm sorry to hear that, Arthur, I mean, John."

"It was a long time ago."

I hate to ask, but I'm in interrogation mode. "How long ago?"

"Fifteen years."

188

Sonya didn't know what to say, so she only nodded. *Fifteen years alone! That would be horrible! Wait. I've got him beat. What's more than horrible? Atrocious?*

"I decided just last week to stop mourning her," John said, "and this, strangely enough, is how I'm going about it."

Sonya still didn't know what to say.

"You knew I wasn't thirty right from the start, didn't you?"

Sonya nodded. "You have these . . . worry lines." She rubbed her forehead with a finger.

John leaned forward. "So do you. Very faint, though. I'm guessing you're in your late twenties or early thirties."

Another compliment! "Guess again."

"I'll have to move closer," he said. "My eyesight is also forty."

"I'll move closer," Sonya said, and she moved from the recliner to the opposite end of the couch.

John stared at her for a full minute. "Thirty . . . one."

"I'm forty."

John blinked. "Wow. I never would have guessed it." He smiled. "And I like your hazel eyes, too. Why'd they make you wear contacts?"

Sonya smiled. "To match the dress, of course."

"Of course. For the *show*."

I like his sense of humor. I also like that he

doesn't take this show or himself seriously. "Yes, for the show."

John took a deep breath. "So, may I interrogate you now?"

He's definitely not slow. "To a point. I'm supposed to keep a few secrets."

"Understood. If it's to remain a secret, just shake your head. What's your real name?"

"Sonya."

"It's nice to meet you, Sonya. I hope I don't slip and call you Sonya when they're filming." He set his Bible on the arm of the couch. "And I take it you aren't an aspiring actress from UCLA who shops and surfs."

"No way."

John shook his head. "Reality TV, huh?"

"Not a whole lot of reality."

"Nope. Are there any real reality programs out there?"

"*Man v. Food* comes close."

John nodded. "Did you see him eat that eleven-pound pizza in Atlanta?"

He watches the Travel Channel. "Yes! That episode was on again tonight, but I didn't watch it. That was so gross."

"Not as gross as when he ate one hundred and eighty oysters in New Orleans."

And he watches it often. John is a couch potato, too! "Or the spicy tuna sushi in Charleston."

"I'll eat a fish," John said, "but you have to cook it for me first."

"Same here." She took a bite of her apple. *I'm glad my stomach woke me up. This man calms me.*

"Sonya, I'm really sorry I ruined your big moment."

"Don't worry about it."

"No, I have to explain. My plane from San Diego to LA was thirty minutes late, baggage claim at LAX took forever, and that traffic out there is brutal. I just want you to know it wasn't my choice to be late."

"I'm actually glad you arrived when you did. Just standing there looking like a princess is boring. And painful."

"How are your feet?"

"Better, but they still hate me. I don't normally wear high heels."

"I could tell."

This I have to hear. "And how could you tell?"

"I did have a wife once," John said, "and she kind of, well, tottered whenever she wore them. You were tottering."

Yeah, I was. "But I didn't fall."

"I'm glad you didn't."

And this is called comfortable silence. "Um, if you don't mind my asking, why'd you agree to do this show? I mean, you seem so . . . ordinary." *Like me.*

John sighed. "I am ordinary, and I don't mind you asking. I came to find a wife."

He didn't just say . . . "You what?"

191

"I came to find a wife."

And this is called uncomfortable silence.

"I know it sounds ridiculous," John said.

Sonya was once again speechless. *It is ridiculous. Who goes on TV to find a wife?*

"I just felt this . . . pull, this need to be here," John said. "I don't mean here on this couch, although I am liking this couch and the company with me on the couch very much."

He can't be serious! "Let me get this straight."

"Straighten away."

Sonya laughed. "You came to find a wife on a show called *Hunk or Punk.*"

"Yes."

"Um, I know we just met, and you seem like a really nice guy, but . . ." *I have to say this.* "That's crazy."

"Yep."

I have nothing to say to that.

"But who knows?" John said. "Maybe God just wanted me to come here to meet you."

Whoa. I can't tell him that's *crazy. I know God moves in mysterious ways and all, but c'mon! No one goes on TV to find a wife. A hookup maybe, even a date, but a wife?*

"Why are *you* doing this show?" John asked.

And now he'll think that I'm *crazy.* "My publicist, who is now my agent, signed me up without my permission. I could have said no, but I didn't."

"Why?"

I can't say it's because I want to bond with a daughter who won't call me "mama." I wish I could be more honest with him. She shook her head. "It's complicated."

John smiled. "You don't seem like a complicated person."

Is that a compliment? "I'm really not that complicated," Sonya said. "The situation is complicated."

"I won't pry," John said. "I like mysteries. I have probably watched every episode of *Unsolved Mysteries.* I will do my best to figure you out, though."

"What's to figure out?"

"No offense, Sonya, but I'm not really sure who you really are yet. So far I do know that you are not who the producers want you to be and that you don't like it very much that they don't like it. And I like it very much that you don't like it very much." He sighed. "Did that make sense?"

"Yes." *Perfect sense, actually.*

"And, um, I like this look, um, much better." He laughed. "This look I can deal with. It's natural, relaxed, and calm. I like natural, relaxed, and calm. The way you were before in that dress was . . . too much, um . . ." He wrinkled his lips. "I don't want to offend you."

"Just say it."

"Sonya, you were kind of busting out all over."

Sonya smiled. "I am *not* a D cup." *And why did I tell him this?*

"I can . . . see that." John's face reddened. "I mean . . ." He shook his head. "Sonya, I can see that you're not a D cup. You are beautiful the way you are now."

Wow. My little B-pluses are both happy and sad!

"You took out your extensions already?"

"It was just a wig." *Hold up. AME. White man. Extensions.* "What do you know about extensions?"

"My wife wore them from time to time. She claimed it helped her hair grow out. I don't think it did, but what do I know."

AME . . . extensions . . . he's on this *show, and he* chose *to be on this show.* "Was, um, your wife — was she black?"

"Yes."

"Oh." *Now what?* "So you thought you'd come on this show to woo a twenty-five-year-old Nubian princess with the ultimate goal for her to be your wife?"

"Yep," John said, "but it didn't make any sense at all to me . . . until this moment."

Oh. Now that I'm more his speed, it makes sense. "You better explain." *Because nothing about this makes much sense to me!*

"Now that I know that you aren't a twenty-five-year-old Nubian princess, I shall do my very best to woo you."

Sonya blinked. "So because I'm older, you'll do your best?"

John blinked. "I'm not making much sense, am I?" He sighed deeply. "Sonya, I guess what I'm saying is that I am *so* glad you're older and wiser. I was afraid I wouldn't have a single thing to say to you if you were a surfing actress airhead."

Well put! "Um, tell me about your wife."

"You want to know about Sheila."

Oh, geez, I've just asked him to tell me about his dead wife. "Only if you . . ."

"I don't mind. Sheila was light. She was sunlight. Everything about her glowed."

And his face is lighting up, too. No one has ever lit up like that talking about me.

"When I saw you glowing in all those lights," John said, "you reminded me of her, especially the heels. Sheila liked but she didn't like wearing heels, which is sort of the prerequisite of a pastor's wife. We had two services at church every Sunday, and New Hope likes to stand and get its praise on. Two hours minimum each service."

That's a lot of praising. "Ouch." *One praise service is enough for me, but I wear flats.*

"I would . . . rub her feet between first and second service and then after the second

195

service. It was kind of a routine. It helped her sleep, too." He seemed to wipe his hands on his sweats. "I could . . . No."

Was he about to ask if he could rub my feet? I would kill to have my feet rubbed now, but I just met the man! "You were about to ask if you could rub my feet, weren't you?"

"Yes. I'm especially worried about your left pinkie toe." He laughed. "But we just met. Who rubs the feet of someone they just met? I mean, that would be awkward."

"Oh, you're right." *But the foot rub would feel so good!*

"I mean, that would be about as brazen and shameless as hugging on or kissing a woman you just met in front of dozens of cameras on live TV while millions of people watched at home."

I wasn't expecting him to go there. But he's right. Those men were shameless and brazen.

"Sonya, I'm surprised you could breathe with all that cologne in the air. If anyone had lit a match around you after the introductions, you would have caught on fire."

True. "I had to wash that mess off the second I got upstairs." *And now I'm getting country with this country man.*

John sighed. "Sonya, I'm . . ." He turned fully to face her. "I have no idea what I'm doing. I mean, here I am practically begging you to rub your feet. What kind of man does that?"

A nice man with . . . large hands. I hadn't noticed those before.

"I haven't had a date, a real date, in fifteen years. I'm not sure how to behave."

"Trust me," Sonya said. "You're behaving very nicely." *Do I tell him that he's in good company and that I haven't had a date in seventeen years?* "You're being a gentleman."

"I'm trying to be, but . . ." John closed his eyes and opened them slowly. "You're sitting a few feet away from me looking so . . ."

"So . . ."

"Sweet."

Not beautiful? I should be hurt.

"And familiar, I mean . . . this scene is familiar. Just sitting on the couch talking." He looked at the wide-screen TV. "If the TV were on, we'd be commenting on what we were seeing, throwing popcorn at each other, changing channels, um, snuggling . . ."

My kind of date!

"I better change the subject," John said.

No. I like that subject! "Why?"

"I'm sometimes too honest for my own good, and I'm liable to say something you'll think is crazy."

You came on a reality TV show to find a wife. There isn't much crazier. "I don't believe it's possible to be *too* honest. What were you going to say?"

"I, um, I already like you, Sonya. You're easy to like."

He . . . likes me. Just like that.

"So, um, what do I have to do to keep your attention?" John asked.

Just keep talking to me, man. "Just keep . . . doing what you're doing." *And now I'm sounding like Larry.*

"Even if I don't know what I'm doing?" John asked.

You're doing just fine. "Just be yourself."

John nodded. "I can do that. I've had lots of practice."

Both of Sonya's feet began to throb, so she stretched her legs out in front of her to shake them out.

"I can fix them," John said.

I know he could fix anything with those . . . big ol' hands. "You don't have to."

"I want to."

Sonya swiveled to the arm of the couch, sliding her feet toward John. "Hook me up, then." *What am I doing? I'm handing my feet to a stranger! That didn't make sense. How can you hand your feet to anyone?*

"Are you sure?" John asked.

"Yes. They're killing me."

John took her right foot and began to massage it, gently but firmly. "Tell me if I'm too rough. I haven't done this in a while."

Lord Jesus, whoo! Yes, squeeze the pinkie toe, squeeze the pinkie toe!

"I'm not squeezing too hard, am I?" John asked.

Sonya shook her head. "No. Just right."

He took her left foot in his hands. "You have seriously strong feet."

Not exactly what every girl wants to hear.

"You do any running?" John asked.

Oh, yes, Lord! Grind that heel, grind that heel until it sings! "Some." *But right now my feet are floating!*

"This reminds me of something," John said.

I have nothing to compare this to at all. "What does this remind you of?"

"Something about a sandal in the book of Ruth."

He has my foot in his hands, and he's thinking about the book of Ruth? Oh yeah! "Ruth and Boaz."

John blinked. "Yes. Ruth and Boaz. Boaz took off his sandal . . . to, um, claim Ruth . . ."

As his wife!

"And you took off some high heels . . ." John said, his voice trailing off to a whisper.

Okay, Sonya thought, *this is getting awkward. But it feels so good! I better stop before I get too excited and make little yelping noises. I know I'm already panting.* She slid her left foot from his hand. "I'm getting sleepy, John."

"See? It works. Do your feet feel better?"

"Yes." *I don't want to walk on them ever again. Does this place have an elevator?* "Thank you, John."

"Anytime, Sonya."

Sonya stood, her feet still tingling. "Anytime? I may need your, um, services again."

"Anytime."

And for some reason, I know in my heart that he means that. "Good night. Thanks for . . . everything."

John looked out a window. "Sun's coming up, so it's good morning."

Something weird has happened here, but I like it. "Good morning, then."

John nodded. "God is good."

Sonya smiled. "All the time."

"Bob?"

"I know, I know, *Larry. That was pathetic! That was pitiful!"*

"Pitiful? This was one of the sweetest scenes I've ever seen. People will be talking about it for weeks."

"But we can't use any of this, can we?"

"Why not?"

"Nothing really happened. They talked. He rubbed her feet. Where's the romance in that? We can't use any of it."

Larry sighed. "I suppose not."

"These Christians! Do they have to be so chaste and honest with each other? They

practically know everything about each other!"

"She withheld a lot of information, Bob, and it does add a wrinkle to the proceedings, doesn't it?"

"But it's a wrinkle we can never put on the air. Except for the foot rub. That was kind of hot. Did you see her face? She was getting into it, but then she pulled away. Let's use the foot rub."

"Oh, no, Bob. We can't put that on the air unless we run the entire scene."

"Why not?"

"It wouldn't be right. It would be out of context."

"Of course it would be right. We have the right, right? And it would be great for ratings. Think of the promos we can run. 'Jazz gets a leg up on the next Hunk or Punk.' "

"But the phrase 'get a leg up' connotes —"

"I know what it means, Larry," Bob interrupted. "We're allowed to tease the audience, right?"

"They'll be disappointed when no, um, getting of the leg up happens."

"Hmm. Well . . . let's run the foot rub footage in front of the Crew at breakfast tomorrow."

"What? Would that be, um, would that be a good idea, Bob?"

"Controversy is good, right?"

"Yes, but Sonya and John, I mean, Jazz and Arthur have a certain degree of chemistry. They're already comfortable with each other.

We just watched an intimate scene, one they thought they were having alone. To share those intimate moments with the Crew, why, that's like casting pearls before swine."

"Chemistry is boring, Larry. No one tunes in to hear two people talking and being comfortable with each other, especially when those two people are on a couch at four o'clock in the morning and they aren't all over each other. Why didn't they, I don't know, start trading hands or something?"

"They're mature adults, that's why. They showed admirable restraint. This is how mature relationships begin. This is what helps mature relationships grow."

"By rubbing feet? We need more action than that! And this footage is guaranteed to start some action tomorrow at breakfast."

"Today. It's already tomorrow, Bob, and after the Crew's partying tonight, we'll have to show that footage at brunch."

"Whatever. Have the foot-rubbing scene ready to roll, but absolutely no dialogue. Just the rubbing."

"Bob, please reconsider."

"There's nothing to consider."

"Okay, Bob. I'll have it ready."

"Arthur won't see it coming. You think someone will open up a can of whup-ass on him?"

"A can of what?"

"The rest of the Crew isn't gonna like it that

the white boy has already moved in on their princess."

"Their *princess*? Bob, she's no one's princess until she makes her final choice."

"You know what I mean, Larry. The white boy arrived late, had all the best lines, and rubbed her feet while they were sleeping. He's winning."

"Yes. Yes, he is. And I'm happy for him."

"But no one will ever see him winning. You get me?"

"I don't agree with this."

"You don't have to agree. Now, what's our challenge tomorrow?"

"There isn't one. No challenge until the obstacle course Wednesday."

"Just as well. Arthur is going to have a very challenging day as it is."

CHAPTER 17

Just after sunrise, John took a jog through Point Dume beside mansions of the rich and famous.

My little apartment could fit inside one of their garages, John thought.

After taking Dume Drive to Cliffside Drive, he trotted past signs for Point Dume State Beach, where he panicked several rabbits and had to leap over a gopher snake. Looking out over the ocean, he saw several dolphins, heard more than saw sea lions, and even thought he saw a gray whale spouting in the distance.

This is not Alabama, John thought. *All this wildlife.* He looked behind him. *Better get back to the wildlife at the mansion. I'm sure the beasts will be stirring soon.*

He arrived tired and worn out, but he wasn't as tired as most of the Crew. He took a bottled water from the refrigerator and an apple from a fruit bowl and went into the great room.

"We've been waiting for you, Arthur," Graham said.

"Are the cameras on?" John asked.

"Always," Graham said.

Which means something dramatic is about to happen, John thought. *I am so glad I returned when I did.*

The rest of the Crew lounged on couches in front of a massive wide-screen TV, the gas fireplace behind it glowing.

John found an empty recliner near Justin and munched on his apple.

"Last night," Graham said, "something *very* interesting happened in this *very* room." He pointed to the brown couch where Aaron and Gary were sitting. "On *that* very couch." He clicked a button on the remote. "Watch."

Though the film was grainy and even a little gray, there was no doubt what John was seeing. *They* were *filming Sonya and me. Geez. There's nowhere to hide in this place.*

Most of the Crew sat up straighter.

"Our Nubian princess was *very* busy last night," Graham said. "And so was Arthur."

Instead of worrying what others were thinking, John analyzed his technique. *Not bad. I'm out of practice. I was concentrating so hard on her feet that I didn't notice her face. Is that peace? Ecstasy? A little of both. I still got it. I shouldn't have mentioned Boaz's sandal. Note to self: Never drop biblical references when you're rubbing a woman's feet. But where's the sound? Hmm. Maybe they couldn't hear us.*

When the clip ended, John looked around. He expected the Crew to be upset.

Most only shrugged.

"Gonna have to stay up later."

"She looked different."

"I knew she was wearing a wig."

"They got to fix the lighting in this room. I could barely see anything."

"Dag, man, I was *out*. I drank too much of that absinthe stuff."

"Yo," Justin said, "I ate too much. You all have any of those nachos? They were bangin'."

"Larry, why aren't they reacting? They should be reacting, throwing pillows, cursing, getting up in Arthur's face — something!"

"Well, I'll be."

"I'll be what?"

"They don't see Arthur as a threat. Here's yet another wrinkle."

"Quit saying 'wrinkle.' "

"Jazz and Arthur are *older than the others. They have wrinkles."*

"Larry, your wrinkles have wrinkles older than me. The Crew should be reacting! Arthur has gotten intimate with their princess. Get Graham in here."

"Why?"

"We need to stir up a hornets' nest in there.

This . . . this is one big nothing."

"Wait . . . Aaron's up to something. He just said, 'That ain't right.' "

"Finally."

CHAPTER 18

Aaron loomed over John. "What you up to, man?"

And so it begins, John thought. *"And they shall fight against thee; but they shall not prevail against thee; for I am with thee, saith the Lord, to deliver thee." How should I handle this? However I do this, I need to do it quietly. These guys look seriously hungover.*

"Up to?" John said. "Right now I'm eating. This apple is delicious."

A few of the Crew turned their heads in John's direction.

"I mean," Aaron said, his eyes two little brown dots, "what were you up to last night?"

I sense wrath, John thought. *Better give soft answers.* "I couldn't sleep. Y'all sure made a lot of noise. Justin, a locomotive has nothing on you, man. I thought a train was in the room."

"I have sinus problems," Justin said. "Didn't bring my Breathe Right strips."

"Yeah, man, I hear you," John said. "And I

still hear the echo." He paused to listen.

Justin laughed.

No one else laughed.

Aaron moved closer. "I am not going to ask you again. What are you up to?"

Just trying to win a wife. "I couldn't sleep, so I came downstairs to read my Bible. Jazz came in, we talked a bit, her feet hurt, and I rubbed them."

"Nothing else happened?" Aaron asked.

"Let's see . . . she said good night, I said it was morning, she said good morning, I said, 'God is good,' she said, 'All the time,' and I tried to return to studying the book of Nehemiah, but I really couldn't concentrate." *I better not bait him. He's not smiling.* "I eventually got up, took a jog down to the beach — fantastic view of the ocean down there. Y'all really ought to see it. And now I'm back watching myself rubbing Jazz's feet. She has very nice feet. Nice calves, too." *Okay, I couldn't resist rubbing it in.*

"What you *really* up to, man?" Aaron asked.

This man is a broken record. "I just told you."

Aaron scowled. "You know what I mean."

"Nope." *Although I think I do. I just want to hear him explain it.*

"Look, Artie." Aaron put his hands on the arms of the recliner. "You don't belong here."

I was just thinking the same thing last night,

but now I think I belong here. "I don't?"

"Nah, man," Aaron said. "Jazz isn't going to choose you."

"She's not?"

"No," Aaron said.

John shrugged. "Oh. I'm glad you told me that, Aaron. I guess I should just pack up and leave, then."

"You shouldn't have even come here in the first place," Aaron said. "You don't have a chance. None. You'll be the first to go. Home girl was just slummin'."

Nah, man, she wasn't. I think she was even doin' a little hummin' when she walked out of the room. "Jazz seemed perfectly content to be in the same room with me."

"Cuz you're harmless, man," Aaron said.

"Oh, I get it." *I think.* "So if you were in a similar situation, you know, sober, smelling like soap and shampoo instead of alcohol and cologne, reading a Bible, untattooed and un-pierced and restraining yourself from pawing at her and staring at her cleavage, you would have been harmless, too."

And once again the room is silent, John thought. *Why are they hanging on my every word? Maybe it just takes them a little longer to process what I say because of my accent.*

Justin chuckled. "Dag, Aaron. Whoo! Artie can talk."

Aaron let go of the recliner's arms and

210

stood. "Man, I am anything but harmless, and when Jazz and I get together, and it's gonna be soon, like Saturday night, I will be rubbing more than her feet, know what I'm saying?"

"Nope." *It got quiet again! All I said was "nope." That was surely a short enough word for them to process in a few seconds.*

"What do you mean, 'nope,' country boy?" Aaron said.

"I mean, nope, you won't be doing more than rubbing her feet," John said. "Jazz is a lady, and she's a Christian."

"What you trying to say?" Aaron asked.

I just said it. What is this, twenty questions? "I'm just saying that she obviously liked hanging out with me, and I am nothing like you, Aaron. She obviously prefers late-night conversation with me to whatever it was you were trying to do last night."

Aaron puffed up his chest. "And what do you think I was trying to do last night?"

I really shouldn't say this, but . . . "Before or after you groped her with your eyes?"

Aaron blinked. "What you talkin' about?"

"Aaron, the eyes are the window to the soul, and your soul had some unholy intentions last night," John said. "Jazz won't go for that."

Gary stood. "He's right, Aaron. Jazz is righteous."

Aaron wheeled around. "How do you know that?"

Gary shrugged. "She ain't like any woman I've ever met."

Aaron looked at the others, shaking his head. "Can you believe this guy?"

My turn to shrug. "All I know is that I have gotten more time with her being 'harmless,' as you say, than you have being unholy around her. I got some foot time, too. I mean, it's not every day that a woman gives up her feet to a guy she just met."

"This is some classic stuff, Bob. This is sensational! We have to show this to Jazz."

"What for?"

"So she can see what a jerk Aaron is and what a gentleman Arthur is."

"Isn't Aaron the former basketball player from Houston? Didn't she play college ball at the University of Houston? This is one of her people."

"That doesn't make him any less of a jerk. I like the way Arthur is handling this. I can only imagine how good his sermons are. Very quick-witted and under control."

"Larry, listen to yourself. You want to ask him out?"

"Of course not. I just think Jazz should know —"

"Jazz will not know anything about this conversation," Bob interrupted.

"She'll know we showed the foot-rubbing scene."

"How?"

"You mean . . . we won't tell her?"

"Hmm. Maybe we should. Yeah. We'll tell her we showed the scene, and then she'll get embarrassed about it. Maybe she'll even stay away from Arthur because of it."

"Why would she do that?"

"She betrayed her people, Larry."

"What?"

"We have eleven black men and one white man. She's betraying her race just by talking to Arthur."

"Bob, I told you from the beginning that I didn't want this show to have anything to do with race."

"I know, I know. It has to have romance and puppies and flowers and orchestra music. But where is the 'rainbow' cast you were trying to get for this show? Nowhere."

"And you're not worried that we'll lose our white viewers if Arthur leaves the show?"

"Of course I'm worried about that, Larry! But if what you're saying is true, she'll keep Arthur on the show a while, and that will raise ratings."

"I don't understand. You now want Arthur to stay on the show?"

"All the way to the end."

"But before you said —"

"I know what I said before," Bob interrupted. "But that was before." Bob sighed. "Okay, um, maybe not to the very end. Either he makes it to the end or he's the first to go."

"You promised him four weeks."

"And he breached his contract by telling Jazz the truth about himself. All bets are off." Bob looked at the monitor. "Hey, this is good. Look at Aaron trying to get the Crew to back him up. This *is classic stuff.* This *is sensational.*"

CHAPTER 19

Aaron stood in front of the TV. "Are we gonna let this white boy disrespect us like that?"

"Hey, now, Aaron," Tony said. "This doesn't have to get racial. That's a man sitting there. I don't feel disrespected. He was a man in the right place at the right time."

"Arthur got game, yo," Justin said. "Mad props, Artie."

I got game, John thought. *And mad props. Should I thank Tony and Justin? No. Better just to let all this run its course.*

"And anyway, Aaron," Tony said, "who's us?"

Aaron pointed around the room. "Us."

"Speak plainly, man," Tony said.

"Us *black* men," Aaron said. "We got a white man trying to steal our queen."

"She's a princess," Justin said.

"Whatever," Aaron said. "It's wrong, all right?"

"He has the same chance as any of us,"

215

Gary said. "What century are you living in anyway? Arthur didn't do anything wrong. Every last one of us probably wishes he was the one rubbing her feet last night." Gary smiled at John. "I underestimated you, man. I gotta try not to let it happen again." Gary walked out to the pool.

"I am definitely not drinking tonight," Justin said. He stood and stretched. "Gonna take me a nap so I can be awake later." He looked at his hands. "Gonna lotion up my hands, too. They are seriously ashy." Justin left the room for the foyer.

"Am I the only one who knows what's going on around here?" Aaron asked.

"The man is playing the game," Tony said, "and he's playing it well."

But, John thought, *it's not a game to me. Maybe that's why I'm "winning."*

"The rest of us have to step it up," Tony said. "This is a wake-up call." Tony went into the kitchen.

The rest of the Crew milled around in the great room for a few minutes before heading in all directions. Only John and Aaron remained in the room.

"Anything else?" John asked.

"What you mean, anything else?" Aaron asked.

"I am just dying to take a shower and then take a dip in that pool." He stood. "I think I will."

"Just watch your back, man," Aaron said.

"Why?"

"Cuz I'm gunnin' for you."

Is he serious? He sure looks serious. "Why waste your time gunning for me, Aaron? Shouldn't you be gunning for Jazz instead?"

Aaron's eyes popped.

"Just a thought," John said. "Have a good day."

"Now we're cooking."

"You see why we need Arthur on the show? He's the voice of reason."

"You're wrong, Larry. We need Arthur for the arguments and the conflicts, and I have a feeling they're going to get louder, and if we're lucky, there will be a fight. This is just the beginning. Aaron definitely has it in for Arthur."

"Arthur acquitted himself very well. He didn't even raise his voice."

"That will change, trust me."

"Why will it change, Bob?"

"Because you are going to prep Aaron to argue with Arthur every chance he gets. I want to see steam coming out some ears, Larry. I want to see men bucking on each other. I want to see fists flying. I want to see the rest of this sleepy Crew taking sides."

"I think a few lines have already been drawn, Bob. Gary, Justin, and Tony have shown respect for Arthur. I can't speak for the rest of the Crew.

217

Only Aaron seems to have a problem with Arthur."

"Well, I want this to build into a battle royale. Yes. I want to see fireworks, and Aaron obviously has to be the catalyst."

"I'll, um, try to help Aaron with his argumentative skills."

"He doesn't need any help. He was doing fine."

"He lost the argument."

"That was just one battle," Bob said. "This is going to be a war."

Chapter 20

Sonya woke, swiveled out of bed, and scrunched her toes into the carpet. *No pain, no throbbing, no aches. Even my pinkie toe feels joy. I've been healed. I have to hand it to John.*

I'd hand him my feet anytime.

After a quick shower, she left the bathroom and walked into two makeup artists and two hair stylists milling about in her room.

I cannot abide this lack of privacy, and I will not need them today. "I won't need your services today. Please leave."

And now they're frozen in place and blinking at me.

"Shoo," she said.

They trooped out.

They all must share the same mind. I've never seen four people moving in unison like that before.

A minute later, Larry was at the door. This time she let him inside her room despite the mess.

"You're not going to put on the dog today?" Larry asked.

"Not today," Sonya said. "Or any day."

"As you wish."

"No more wig either," she said.

"Fine."

I like the sound of that. "And I don't like anyone in my room without my permission. Everyone has to knock from now on."

"As you wish."

I am the princess, after all. He seems so agreeable today. Maybe it's Give Jazz What She Wants Day. Or he's just setting me up for something. "And I have decided that I want my, um, my sister here now."

Larry pursed his lips. "That's not supposed to happen until you get down to the final six."

Those stupid rules! "She doesn't have to be on camera until then. I just want her around. I want to spend some time with her, okay? I don't get to see her very often."

"I'll talk to Bob."

Who will say no. "There's nothing to talk about. I won't leave this room . . ." *Until she's here? It's such a nice day, and I don't want to waste it.* She looked out the window and saw John swimming. *Very muscular for a guy my age. I wish I could swim like that. He makes it look so easy.* She faced Larry. "I won't leave this room until you tell me she'll be here by dinner tonight."

"I don't have a problem with this, but Bob —"

"No sis," Sonya interrupted, "no this."

Larry bowed, said, "I will make your demands known," and left.

Sonya turned to the window. John was out on the diving board. *Nice lines. Great form on that dive.* Justin was next. *That poor diving board!* But when Justin executed a flawless swan dive, Sonya smiled. *Now Justin and John are talking. John seems to get along with everyone. It must be the pastor in him.*

No.

It's the Christian in him.

The rest of the Crew spilled out from the kitchen. *All I see are tattoos and ripped bodies. And Aaron has more tattoos than anyone. I wonder how close he was to making it to the NBA.*

Aaron stood on the diving board, took two giant steps, bounced, and flew into a front flip. *Not bad.* Other Crew members lined up at the diving board. *Oh, now it's a diving contest. Can they see me? Probably not. I'd have to be out on that little balcony.* She stood away from the window just in case.

A knock on the door. "Jazz, it's Larry."

Sonya opened the door, and Bob Freeberg — all five feet of him — walked in ahead of Larry.

"Sonya, I mean, Jazz," Larry said, "I'd like

221

you to meet the executive producer, Bob Freeberg."

He's just a kid! I have shoes older than his freckles! "Hi, Bob. Did Larry let you know my demands?" *They weren't kidding about the half-dollars. But no socks? Yuck. And the crease in his chinos could cut steel.*

"Yes," Bob said. "Your sister is on her way." *All right!*

"And it will save us about thirty thousand dollars," Bob said, sitting on the edge of Sonya's bed.

Get off my bed! "Do you mind?" Sonya stared at the bed.

"Oh." Bob stood. "Um, will you at least wear the wig? We got some nice play on the online blogs about your hair last night."

"No wig."

"Okay." Bob smiled. "No wig, then." He turned to Larry. "We'll have to adjust lighting and try not to do as many close-ups to, um, hide her age."

Jerk. "Fine."

"Is there anything else we can do for you?" Bob asked.

I don't like his fake tone one bit. I know Bob is setting me up for something. "What's the catch?"

"The catch?" Bob looked at Larry. "There's no catch."

There's always a catch. "What do I have to

do, then?"

"Just be you, Jazz," Bob said. "Just be you."

Oh really? "So I can be forty again?"

Bob looked away. "Except for that."

"And what else?" Sonya asked.

"The religion thing," Bob said.

I haven't even been religious on camera, have I? "I haven't been."

Bob bit his top lip. "We, um, filmed you and Arthur in the great room last night."

Where I was a bit religious . . . and had a foot rub. Hmm. Yep. They'd put that on the air to make me look like a hypocrite. Sonya sighed. "You're going to run that, um, footage."

Bob laughed.

I wasn't trying to be funny, Bob.

"No. That won't make the air." Bob's eyes narrowed. "So you'll be less religious from now on?"

Ah. If I agree to this, they won't show the foot rub. If I don't agree, they'll try to embarrass me. They've given me no other choice. "If I can't be, as you say, religious, then I can't be me, Bob."

"Can you just . . . imagine it's not Sunday?" Bob asked.

Which shows how much Bob knows about real Christians. "Every day is a gift from the Lord, Bob. I don't just act Christian on Sundays."

"What about this morning?" Bob asked.

223

"You and, um, *John* on the couch. How religious was that little interlude?"

"My feet hurt and he rubbed them," Sonya said. "Jesus washed folks' feet."

Bob blinked. "But the Crew has already seen the two of you in action. We showed them the, uh, *footage* this morning."

They've seen . . . Hmm. "And how did they react?"

"How do you think they reacted?" Bob asked.

"That's why I'm asking you, Bob," Sonya said. "I wasn't there, was I?"

Bob shrugged. "The Crew didn't like it one bit."

Sonya looked at Larry, who shook his head slightly. *Bob is lying.* "Okay, so they didn't like it. They'll get over it."

"They feel betrayed," Bob said.

Again Larry shook his head.

So this is how they "script" controversy. Well, I'm not going to be a part of it. She went to a drawer and took out her bathing suit. "I'm going swimming, Bob. Will there be anything else?"

Bob blinked. "Don't you . . . feel that you have betrayed them?"

"Bob, my feet hurt. John rubbed and made them feel better. The end."

"You sure looked cozy with John," Bob said.

"It *was* cozy," Sonya said. "And?"

Bob looked at Larry. "Um, well."

So that's the key to shutting up Bob. Just agree with him.

"Okay," Bob said. "Is there anything else we can do for you?"

Let's see . . . "One of the challenges has to be at a soup kitchen."

"What?" Bob said, his voice rising. "A challenge at a soup kitchen?"

"You put it in my fake bio that I volunteer at soup kitchens, and that was the only thing close to the truth in that bio," Sonya said. "I do volunteer my time at the Salvation Army and at local shelters. I've done four missions trips to Haiti. I was in New Orleans after Katrina. The soup kitchen *has* to be part of one of the challenges."

"It would be easy to set up," Larry said. "I know a few —"

"Just who do you think you are, Miss Richardson?" Bob interrupted. "You don't dictate how this show will go. Who does she think she is, Larry?"

Sonya towered over Bob. "I am a Nubian princess worthy of your *utmost* respect, and don't you ever forget it." She went into the bathroom and closed the door.

"I am paying you a *lot* of money!" Bob yelled.

Sonya opened the door. "I don't need your money, Bob. I have a Roth IRA, a healthy investment portfolio, my house and car are paid for, and I am already comfortably

225

retired." She closed the door.

"Bob, I did a documentary once down in Skid Row at the Hippie Kitchen," Larry said. "It won't be hard to set up at all."

"No, Larry! What an absolute cluster-f—"

Sonya opened the door. "And *don't* you be cursing up in my room, Mr. Freeberg. I won't have it." She closed the door and put on her swimsuit.

"Next time, Larry," Bob said, "get me an atheist."

Sonya laughed. "I'll pray for you, Bob!" she shouted.

She heard a door slam.

"Sonya?"

Larry didn't leave? "Yes?"

"Bravo."

She looked at herself in the mirror. *Thank you, thank you very much.*

CHAPTER 21

Sonya sat on the edge of the pool in the shallow end, her feet dangling in the water, a towel around her shoulders, while the Crew swam around in the deep end.

They're the sharks circling down there, Sonya thought, *and I'm the little guppy who can't swim way down here.*

John swam over and whispered, "I think we're safe. I haven't found any microphones around the pool. Sleep well?"

"Yes, and I think we better keep whispering, just in case." She leaned closer. "I didn't know they were filming us last night."

John smiled. "No harm, though." He grabbed her foot and squeezed. "All better?"

"Yes," she whispered. *And please squeeze it again!* "Is the Crew really angry with me?"

"Only Aaron." He looked at the diving board, where Aaron was doing half twists and flips. "He doesn't like me very much."

Because you're now a threat! "Um, Arthur," she whispered, "do you think you could teach me how to swim?"

"Sure. C'mon in."

In front of everybody? "Oh, not now. I, um, I'll need a private lesson." *And that sounded extremely naughty.* "I can't swim. At all. I never learned how."

John nodded. "Four AM again?"

"Why so early?"

"I'm on Alabama time, and you're on . . ."

He's fishing in a pool for my hometown. "North Carolina time," Sonya whispered.

"I thought I heard a little Southern belle in you. It's mixed with something . . . northern. I like the mixture."

Sonya smiled.

"Don't be late," John said. "The water won't be this warm at four AM."

"I won't be late." *I'm going to learn how to swim! Who said you can't teach an old lady new tricks?*

John backstroked away.

"How you doin', Ma?"

Sonya felt Aaron's shadow before she saw him. *Be nice.* She looked behind her to see him toweling off. "Good afternoon, Aaron." *Hungover? Sweating out that turpentine?*

"Why don't you get in the pool?" Aaron said. "The water's great."

"I'm fine."

Aaron sat beside her, his towel on his shoulders, his leg nudging hers. "You lookin' good, Ma."

This "Ma" noise has to stop now. "I prefer that you call me by my name."

"All right," Aaron said. "You lookin' good, Jazz."

Do I take this compliment? I guess I should. "Thank you. So, did you ever get the chance to play in the NBA?"

"You heard about me?"

The tattoo on his bicep is a naked black mermaid with triple E's. How quaint. Why do men put this pornography on themselves? And why do some women consider these pornographic tattoos attractive? "I read your bio, Aaron."

"Oh. Yeah."

"So, did you ever make it to the show?"

"I went to a few tryout camps after college," Aaron said. "Led LaSalle in scoring for three years. Fourth all-time leading scorer. Honorable mention All-American my senior year."

"Impressive."

"I had tryouts with the Clippers, Hornets, and Bucks," Aaron said.

"Yeah?" *That's more impressive, even if those teams aren't annual contenders.*

"But I had an old knee injury from high school." He pointed to a sizable but faded scar on his knee. "Tore the MCL and the ACL. They didn't want to take the chance

229

on me even though I proved I could play four years in college. The City Six in Philly was no joke, and neither was the Atlantic Ten."

Yeah, Philly has some great teams, and A-10 teams always gave us fits in the NCAA tournament.

"I played in the NBA Developmental League for a few seasons until the team folded," Aaron said. "Led that team in scoring every year, too."

I guess it isn't really bragging if it's true. "Was it always your dream to play in the NBA?"

"Yeah. Ever since I was a little kid growing up on the mean streets of Philly."

Philly? He isn't from Philly. He has no Philly accent. I played ball with a girl from Philly, and instead of saying she was reading some poems by Walt Whitman, she said, "I'm reading Wall Women." Aaron's from somewhere much farther west. Wait. His bio says he's from Houston. Geez. Why would he lie about something I could check?

"You, um, you still have that dream?" Sonya asked.

Aaron smiled. "You're the only dream I see now."

That was actually sweet. But you ain't from Philly. And what's that black thing on his towel? Is that a bug? No. It's not moving. "You have something on your towel."

Aaron glanced at it. "It's just the microphone."

"The what?"

He pointed at something on her towel. "You have one, too. All the towels have them. State of the art, huh? They're even waterproof."

Which means . . . Bob and Larry know about my little rendezvous tonight with John. Terrific. Unless the water noises drowned us out.

"They say," Aaron said, rubbing his shoulder on hers, "these little mikes can pick up ants farting."

Nice image, Aaron. And, yep. Bob and Larry heard. Should I still go? Yeah. This is my show, right? "Um, Aaron, you just said that I was a dream."

"You are."

She looked around. "Where are the cameras?"

"Everywhere, I guess." He pointed to a spot in a palm tree. "Think that one's a fisheye. Takes in the whole pool area. Every room has them here and there. There's one right over the kitchen table so the world can see us pigging out."

"What about the cameras they follow us around with?"

"They only use the hand-held ones for live stuff," Aaron said.

I am such a fool! I read it in the contract! I am being filmed twenty-four-seven wherever I go.

"Well, take it off."

"Take it off? Ooh, Mama."

"No, Aaron." She plucked the little microphones from his towel and her towel and threw them into the water.

"Why'd you do that?" Aaron asked.

"So we can *really* talk, Aaron," Sonya said. "Now what were you saying about me being a dream?"

"Huh?"

"You called me a dream."

Aaron looked around. "Yeah. So?"

Just as I suspected. "So you only said I was a dream because you knew you were being recorded."

"Well, isn't that the point of the show?" Aaron asked, breaking into a broad smile.

"You really want to get to know me?"

Aaron hesitated. "Of course I do, Jazz."

Yeah, right. You just want to win the game. "Then don't come around me only to *act* interested." *And that gives me a great idea.* She stood. "Everybody. Throw your towels into the pool."

"She can't do that! Is she out of her mind? Larry, why is she changing everything?"

"She wants a real experience."

"What?"

"She doesn't want to be treated like a princess."

"Every woman wants to be treated like a

princess, Larry. It's in a woman's genes."

"I don't think Jazz does. She wants to be treated like a normal person. She wants to be treated with respect. She wants to have real conversations with the Crew."

"You can't have real conversations on a reality show, Larry. You know that."

"Bob, you know the camera does strange things to people, and Aaron is the worst. He only talks to Jazz and uses those obviously rehearsed lines when he's on camera. Arthur mostly talks to her when he thinks he's not on camera. You see the difference?"

"But those mikes are the best! They cost a fortune!"

"We've already miked every palm tree, light fixture, chair, table, couch, and ceiling in the house. I don't know why we needed so many. And didn't we just save thirty thousand dollars?"

"Yeah, I better call Casa Malibu."

"You mean you haven't called Jazz's sister yet?"

"I was just bluffing, Larry. Who's running the show here, her or me?"

"Well, you had better call her now."

"It's just down the highway, Larry. Relax. Everything's under control."

"I'll call her for you."

"I'll do it."

"You know, Bob, by ditching all the towel mikes, the Crew might begin to act natural around the pool."

"I don't want natural, Larry. Natural is boring. Natural has no glamour. Natural is for real life. This is TV. I want come-ons. I want to hear those lines, rehearsed or not. I want those men to show some real game."

"Bob, this could be the first reality TV show to be really real. Think of the possibilities."

"Look at the scene, Larry. Nothing is happening."

"They're swimming in the pool. They're talking. They're flirting. So what if it isn't in your face. I think it's charming."

"Larry, you've been making too many documentaries."

"Now look. They're throwing all the towels into the pool. That's not boring at all."

Bob sighed. "I just hope they don't find the other mikes."

"What others?"

"The ones sewn into their clothing."

"When did this happen?"

"Larry, why do you think we took the Crew to the beach all day Sunday?"

"But, John, I mean, Arthur —"

"We took care of that when he went running this morning. It only took five minutes. The man has very few clothes."

CHAPTER 22

As a result of the microphone dunking, it was *much* quieter around the pool for the rest of the day. While most of the Crew frolicked around the pool and played drinking games involving quarters and Ping-Pong balls, Sonya corralled Gary and Tony to help her make a huge salad to go with the steaks Justin and John were cooking and seasoning to perfection on the grill.

"Steak and *salad,* Jazz?" Justin said.

"Low-calorie dressing, too," Sonya said.

"No ranch dressing?" Justin asked.

"Nope." *These men put ranch on everything, even their pizza.*

"No potatoes?" Justin asked.

"Nope."

Justin sighed. "I hope we at least have some dessert."

"You get fruit," Sonya said.

"Man," Justin said.

"You need good food to give you energy for the challenge tomorrow," Sonya said. "You need protein. Ranch dressing, potatoes, and dessert will only weigh you down. That obstacle course is going to be no joke."

"C'mon, Jazz," Justin said, "at least throw some croutons up in there."

"Not gonna happen."

After dinner, while Sonya and John cleaned up the kitchen and while Aaron, Justin, Tony, and Gary played Spades at the kitchen table, the rest of the Crew started partying again outside.

And not one of them complimented any of the chefs, Sonya thought.

"Is it louder tonight?" John asked while drying dishes.

"Seems like it," Sonya said. "Why do they do that? Why do they drink away their limited brain cells?"

"Boredom, I think," John said.

"A bunch of frat boys," Justin said. "They don't know any different."

Gary shook his head. "You and Aaron were putting 'em away the other night, man."

"But I was a frat boy," Justin said. "For about a minute. Once that rushing mess started, I quit."

"I only drink light beers," Aaron said.

It's still beer, Sonya thought. "Well, I don't get any of it," Sonya said. "They could be bowling or watching TV or, gee, getting to know me better." She looked at Tony's hand. "What'd you bid, Tony?"

"Five," Tony said.

She looked at Tony's partner, Aaron. "Get ready to help this boy. He only has three and a possible."

"Watch me get it," Tony said.

Tony didn't get his bid, Aaron got mad and left, and the game ended.

Tony shrugged. "It was worth a shot."

"You didn't even have any off aces, man," Sonya said.

Tony smiled. "So I take risks."

Gary and Justin stood.

"I'm goin' bowling," Justin said. "You with me?"

"Yeah," Gary said. "Gotta work off all that healthy salad. You comin', Tony, Artie?"

Tony stood and stretched. "I'm beat. I'm goin' up."

"I'll catch up with y'all," John said. "Almost done with these dishes."

After they left, John whispered, "You should be resting for your lesson."

"I'm not that old," Sonya whispered.

"It will be quite a workout," John whispered.

I am already tired of cleaning up after a dozen men. "I'll just get off my feet for a while, then. You don't mind finishing up?"

"I am a horrible bowler," John said. "If I bowl half my weight, I'm happy."

That's pretty bad. "What's your high score?"

He looked up. "Think I broke a hundred once."

Geez. I hardly ever bowl, but I always get at least a hundred. "After you finish, you need to go practice," Sonya said. "I'm sure they'll want to make bowling one of the challenges."

John shrugged. "If they put up those gutter guards, I have a shot."

"Good night, um, Arthur," Sonya said.

"Good night, um, Jazz," John said.

She went upstairs and had barely hit the bed and grabbed for the remote control when she heard a knock on the door.

Kim!

She went to the door, opened it, and saw Larry and all his wrinkles.

"Where's Kim?"

Larry looked past Sonya into her room. "She's not here? Bob was *supposed* to call her."

Which means Bob didn't call her. She picked up her phone and pressed number two.

Larry smiled. "You're not *supposed* to be making calls."

"And people are *supposed* to keep their word."

"What you want?" Kim asked.

Sonya heard loud voices and traffic noises. "Where are you?"

"At Grauman's Chinese Theatre to see all the handprints and footprints," Kim said. "Ooh, there's Denzel's! What's up?"

238

"They're letting you move in tonight," Sonya said.

"Why so early? I haven't seen all I want to see. I haven't done half of what I want to do, Sonya."

I did promise she could see the sights. "How much time will you need?"

"Gimme a week at least. I haven't been to Disneyland, San Diego, or Tijuana yet."

"Tijuana? What for? And do you have a passport?"

"I have a passport, Sonya, and, I don't know, I just want to go there to say I've been there. I may get another tattoo."

"In Tijuana?"

"Why not?"

"Why not?" is this generation's excuse for doing anything stupid. "Well, can't you knock all that out in three days?"

"Sonya, I'm on vacation. I want to take my time and enjoy myself."

Shoot! I can almost control a TV show, but I can't control my daughter. "Just be safe, okay?"

"You know I will."

I don't know that for sure. "I'll see you in a week, then. Keep your phone with you at all times, okay?"

"Okay. Ooh, there's Will Smith's. Why didn't he put his ears in the cement? Gotta go." *Click.*

Hmm. Why didn't *Will Smith put his ears in*

239

the cement?

Sonya tossed her phone onto the bed. "So Bob didn't even try to call."

"He only *said* he would call," Larry said.

Jerk! "Bob says a lot of things he doesn't really mean, huh?" Larry nodded.

"But I didn't *say* anything."

At least I can trust Larry. "Kim will be here in a week."

"And we'll be ready for her." Larry walked to the window. "They sure have a lot of energy, don't they?"

"Misguided energy," Sonya said. "They need to do something constructive that doesn't involve drinking."

"Good luck," Larry said, and he left.

And here I am about to veg and watch something on this little TV when I could be watching something on the huge TV downstairs. Whose castle is this anyway?

When Sonya went downstairs to the great room, she found John, Justin, Gary, and Tony sitting on a couch watching *Man v. Food.*

"I thought y'all were bowling," she said, settling into a recliner behind them.

"No balls," Justin said. "Oh, sorry."

What? "There's a bowling alley but no balls?"

Gary shook his head. "Triflin', ain't it? It wouldn't even turn on."

Sonya stared at the screen. *Oh, this is a*

gross episode where Adam eats seventeen hot dogs in an hour at a place in Chapel Hill.

"Remind you of home?" John asked.

"A little. Chapel Hill and Charlotte are worlds apart. He's never come to Charlotte."

John smiled. "So you're from Charlotte."

Sonya nodded.

"He's never come to Alabama either." John stood. "Why don't you join us?"

Such a gentleman. She left the recliner and sat in the middle of the couch flanked by Gary and Tony, Justin anchoring the rest of the couch. She took the remote from Tony. "House rules."

"Yes, ma'am," Tony said.

Grr. There's that word again. "Um . . ." *What's his other name?* "Arthur, if Adam did come to Alabama, what would y'all feed him?"

John sat in a recliner. "Home cookin' till he busted a gut."

"I miss that," Sonya said.

"So do I," Justin said. "At least at home they put potatoes on the table."

"Hush," Sonya said.

"And at least a few croutons," Justin said.

"Hush, I said," Sonya said.

After watching Adam suck down a half-dozen hot dogs, Justin tapped the couch arm with his hand. "We should do this." He nodded. "Yeah, we should have a hot dog–eating contest."

241

Is he kidding? "We just ate. And I doubt the Crew out there will want to participate." *Alcohol is* their *food.*

"I bet I could eat twenty dogs in an hour," Justin said. "No problem."

"With the bun?" Gary asked.

"With the bun," Justin said.

Sonya looked at Justin. "Oh, please don't. I don't doubt you can do it, but we just had dinner."

"That was just an appetizer," Justin said. "I have plenty of room."

John jumped out of the recliner. "I'll fire up the grill. Shouldn't take long." He started for the pool.

"No!" Sonya shouted.

John stopped.

I have power! "I mean, do we even have any hot dogs?"

Gary went into the kitchen and came back with three eight-packs of hot dogs. "We have dogs. Beef ones, too. Not the rooter-to-the-tooter kind."

Shoot. "We have buns, too?"

Gary nodded. "We have plenty. Justin, you want 'em plain or kitted out?"

Justin smiled. "Can't eat a hot dog without mustard, ketchup, onions, and coleslaw. Oh, and chili, if you got it."

Sonya blinked. "Y'all can't be serious."

"As serious as the heart attack he's going to have," Tony said.

Gary shrugged. "Why not?"

"Why not?" Sonya said. "Justin, you have an obstacle course challenge tomorrow."

"So I'll need some extra protein," Justin said. "And it ain't likely I'm gonna win, right?" He turned to Gary and John. "Y'all gonna hook me up?"

"I'll cook 'em," John said.

"I'll prepare the buns," Gary said.

"I'll prepare the bucket," Tony said.

Gross! "I guess I can make the chili."

While browning the ground beef, Sonya borrowed one of the show's many laptops to surf the Internet. *The average hot dog with a bun is two hundred fifty calories. Add my chili and the fixings, and the dogs Justin is eating will be around three hundred calories. That man is about to eat six thousand calories in one hour! I might eat that many calories over three days! And at, say, four ounces per hot dog, he's about to eat five pounds of food after dinner!*

I'm glad I'm not rooming with him.

Sonya marveled at the precision of her hot dog–making crew. After John filled each bun with a charbroiled hot dog, Gary and Tony "kitted them out" and placed them on several plates. Sonya added a layer of chili, and in less than thirty minutes, Justin was at the kitchen table, a huge linen napkin tucked into the top of his shirt.

"Who's keeping time?" Gary asked.

Tony checked his watch. "I got it."

"Justin," John said, "you have to eat one hot dog every three minutes."

"Piece of cake," Justin said. "Let's do this."

Justin inhaled *half* the hot dogs in only twenty minutes.

Oh, nasty! Sonya thought. *And I'm sure Bob will use this mess as a promo for next week's show. I feel so sorry for our viewers!* She looked at the light over the table. *Is that the camera lens?* "I am so sorry you're seeing this, America," she said. "I tried to stop them."

By the time Justin finished his fifteenth hot dog, the rest of the Crew, all reeking of alcohol and smoke, had drifted in to cheer Justin on.

Nobody light a match! Sonya thought.

With five minutes to go, Justin was down to his last hot dog. "Mmm-mmm," he said. "I think I'll try to taste this one."

"Amazing," John whispered in Sonya's ear.

"Disgusting," Sonya whispered back.

With the Crew counting down the seconds, Justin finished his last hot dog, took a swig of water, gargled, and swallowed. He opened his mouth just as Tony yelled, "Time!"

The noise was deafening, high-fives all around —

And then it was over.

The rest of the Crew returned to their

drinking, and Gary pulled out a deck of cards.

"I need a snack," Justin said.

And I need a nap! Sonya thought. *Watching someone overeat in front of me is more tiring than watching Adam scarf down food on TV. But now there's another mess in the kitchen.* She went to the sink to run some water.

"I'll clean up," John said from behind her.

"It's okay," Sonya said. "I let this thing happen."

John tugged her elbows until she faced him. "Rest."

Sonya rolled her eyes. "We're not swimming a marathon tonight, are we?" she whispered.

"No," John whispered. "You just look tired."

I am a little tired. "Okay."

"We'll try to keep it down," John said louder.

Sonya looked at the card players. "I'm not worried about y'all. It's *them* I'm worried about."

And "them" kept Sonya awake for most of the night. That and her nervousness. *What if I can't swim? What if I sink? What if I make a total fool of myself?* A verse came to mind. "I sleep," she whispered, "but my heart waketh."

When the alarm clock went off at 3:45, all was quiet in the mansion. Sonya put on her swimsuit and a rubber swim cap, wrapped herself tightly in a robe, slipped on some sandals, and went down to the pool, where

John was already doing laps.

She shivered in the wind. "Is it cold?"

"The water is warmer than the air," John said. "It was cold at first."

Sonya looked around. "Is everyone else asleep?"

John nodded. "Justin tried to stay up but crashed an hour ago. Guess his little snack did him in."

She took off her robe, kicking her sandals behind her. "I just want you to know that I *am* athletic. I just never took any swimming lessons." She dipped a toe into the pool. "It *is* warm."

"I would never lie to you, Sonya."

And I believe him. Crazy. Whenever John speaks, I believe him. "Okay. I'm ready. I think." She went to a ladder and eased into the water. *Brr. Not terrible, but not exactly like a nice warm bed.* "Okay, Coach John, let's do this."

"Your first lesson will be how to float."

But I came here to learn how to swim! "Not swim?"

"It's for balance."

"Okay." Sonya moved to the middle of the pool. "You're the coach."

"Um, take a deep breath, lie back, and let your legs float to the surface," John said. "If necessary, wave your hands under the surface to keep yourself stable and horizontal."

Sonya leaned back and lay on the water,

her legs shooting to the surface. No matter how hard she tried to stay in one place with her hands furiously paddling the water under her, her butt kept dropping. She stood. "Why can't I stay up?"

"That was great."

Was he even watching me? "But I sank."

"You just proved to yourself that you're not afraid of the water."

I did? I did. Cool. "But how do I stay up?"

"You may need to wave your hands, um, lower, under your center of gravity."

"My what?" *I didn't know that swimming was this technical.*

"Your . . . um." John pointed at his butt.

Oh. My butt is my center of gravity. Why didn't he just say "butt"? "You can say butt."

"It's not the nicest word."

"It is what it is." Sonya lay back again and worked her hands lower. After a few shaky moments, she was stable and horizontal. "I'm floating."

John moved closer. "To stay up longer . . ." He slid his hand under the water and pushed up slightly on her lower back. "Keep your, um . . ."

"My chest?" *It's about time he touched me somewhere other than my feet.*

"Yeah. Keep that up as best you can." John removed his hand.

Sonya peeked at her "girls." *Not exactly bob-*

bing like buoys, are you? "I'm not that en-
dowed."

"I didn't mean that." John floated away.
"Once you can float for a few minutes, we'll
go to the next step."

*I'm actually not sinking. This is so peaceful,
and I'm hardly expending any energy.* "You've
taught others to swim before."

"Yes. Well, only one person. Sheila."

I don't know why this matters to me, but . . .
"Did she float like this the first time?"

John smiled. "Oh, no. She sank like a stone
because she had, um . . . She had bigger . . ."

He is so cute! "Sheila had a bigger butt and
bigger girls than me."

John turned away. "Yes."

So he likes thick sisters. "Did you teach her
to swim anyway?"

"Yes. Eventually she could out-swim me."

We sisters are powerful like that. "You think
about her a lot."

John moved closer, the waves rocking her
slightly. "All the time. Too much of the time."

"Did you date anyone after . . ." *Why do I
keep bringing this up?*

"I tried. But I kept seeing Sheila's face."

*That's either sad, or wow, here's a man who
really loved his wife.* "Do you still see her
face?"

John smiled. "Right now, I only see you."

That's so sweet. "Because you don't want
me to drown."

248

"No. I only see you, Sonya."

Sonya turned away. *The man only sees me. How do I feel about that? I guess I feel good. I have his complete attention, which is a million times better than most of that stupid Crew.* "And what do you see?"

"Beauty."

Wow . . . "Anything else?"

"Very nice legs."

He got that right. I built these legs up from scratch.

"Time's up," John said.

Sonya stood.

"Tired?" John asked.

"Not really." *He saw beauty and my legs. I'm more fully awake now.* "What's next?"

"Kind of lie on your stomach, but keep your head up and looking at me."

"Just . . . do a Superman?" *I should have said "Super Woman."*

"I'll hold you up." He stood beside Sonya and placed his left hand on her stomach. "Wow. Do you do sit-ups?"

He likes my stomach. I'm kind of proud of it, too. "Not as many as I used to do."

"Your stomach is a muscle. It's a one-pack."

And despite the cool water, his hand is so warm! "Thank you."

"Um, go ahead and lay out," John said, "and I'll, um, keep you horizontal."

Sonya stretched her arms out and rested

249

her head on the surface as her legs floated to the top, John's hand keeping nearly her entire body above the water. *He's holding me up with one hand! I love water. It's so buoyant. And why is Song of Solomon suddenly coming to mind? "His left hand should be under my head, and his right hand should embrace me."*

"You okay?" John asked.

I'm weightless, and a man has his hand on my one-pack. He sees beauty when he sees me. He admires my legs. Why wouldn't I be fine? "Yes."

"I'm going to give you a little support while you learn the crawl."

I have to tell him. "You're holding me up with one hand."

"It's the buoyancy. And, you're pretty light."

Okay, I was fishing for a compliment in a pool. "Thank you."

"Okay, without kicking your legs, just let them stay limp, cup your right hand and reach out ahead of you, pulling the water under you."

Sonya cupped her right hand, reached ahead, and pulled the water back to her.

"Now the left," John said.

She repeated the motion with her left hand. *That's all there is to it?*

"Now alternate, right, left, right, left."

This is easy!

"You can stop."

Sonya stopped.

"Now we'll add just your legs. Straighten your legs, point your toes, and kick but try not to splash."

Whoa. I just leaped forward! Is that another hand I feel holding me just above my hip? Do I mind that he has both hands on me? My hip surely doesn't mind. If I were in a bikini, his hand would be right on the little tie. Whoo. Sorry, Lord, but . . . whoo.

"Now we'll put it all together."

"Don't let go." *Of my hip. That feels real nice. Sorry, Lord, but a hot hand on my hip is nice.*

"I'll try not to let go, Sonya. You, um, you've got some powerful legs."

"Just keep a hold of me, and don't be afraid to squeeze." *I can't believe I just said that. Whoa! And now he's squeezing. Very nice. He even has a finger or two on my booty. I may have to invest in a bikini.*

"Ready to rock?" John asked.

And roll, man. Keep squeezing. "Yes."

As John did all he could to restrain Sonya, even pinching and holding the fabric of her swimsuit, Sonya surged forward as she reached and kicked. *I am really doing this!*

"All stop," John said.

Sonya stopped. "Should I just . . ." *Let you hold me like this? Yes. I should let you hold me like this until I turn into a prune.*

"Um, yes, just rest," John said. "You can stand."

But I don't want to! Sonya stood, feeling a twinge in her right shoulder. "Wow, that really works the shoulders."

"Yeah. Um, I may have gotten ahead of myself. I didn't explain breathing."

Sonya smiled. "I know how to breathe, John."

"I know you do, but breathing while swimming is different. Some swimmers do two strokes before breathing, some do four strokes before breathing, and some even do eight strokes before turning their bodies and heads to the side and taking a quick breath."

"What do you suggest?"

"You're an athlete, Sonya, so you could probably go eight strokes before breathing."

"I'll just stick to four strokes for now."

"The key is exhaling while your face is in the water." He dunked his head in the water and blew bubbles. He popped up his head. "So it goes stroke, stroke, blow, stroke, stroke, turn your head and breathe. In a pool this size, though, you could probably get to the other side in one breath. Let's practice, um, blowing bubbles."

Sonya dunked her head and blew. *This is silly, but I suppose it's necessary.* She raised her head out of the water. "I think I'm ready to swim. Are you going to hold me in the beginning?" *Please say yes!*

"Sure. I hope I haven't been squeezing you too hard."

Just right. And if your hand should slip farther down my booty, I won't hold anything but me against you. Yes, Lord, I know that was a carnal thought, but c'mon! My booty has been untouched for so long. "I won't break."

"Um, once we begin, I'll gradually let you go," John said. "Just keep swimming until you get to the other side. We're only in four feet of water, so if you get tired or scared, just stand up."

"I'm not tired." *Or scared. What was I thinking all these years?*

"And when I let go, don't stop crawling, kicking, exhaling, and breathing until you get to the other side. Ready?"

"Ready."

John winced. "Um, I'm not. You see, I can't get a good hold of you from the side. I need to go under."

Sonya blinked.

"I'll be holding your, um, your hips. Oh, if it's all right."

It's quite all right. In fact, it's an absolute necessity. "So . . . you're going to hold your breath."

He nodded, took a deep breath, and went under.

There is a man — whoo! I'm horizontal, and his hot hands are squeezing my hips so nicely.

253

What do I do? Oh, yeah. Start swimming!

Sonya began stroking and kicking, and after ten seconds or so, she felt John's hands sliding from her hips to her thighs to her shins, and then . . . *I'm on my own! Where's the other side? Breathe!* She reached her hands out and felt the opposite wall. *Ain't nothin' to this thang!* She turned and didn't see John.

"John?"

He surfaced next to her. "You have excellent form. I was watching you under the water."

And that somehow makes me feel . . . shy?

"You already knew how to swim, didn't you?" he asked.

"I didn't. Really. You're an excellent teacher."

John wiped some water from his nose. "And you're an amazing athlete."

And I'm still shy. "For someone my age, you mean."

"I'll bet you could still play whatever sport you played." He smiled. "And I'll bet you were very good at it."

Well, I was *pretty good. I just don't wear the rings.* "What makes you think I was an athlete?"

"You definitely have an athletic body."

Well, I don't know about that. I try to stay in shape . . .

"And you look so familiar. I know I've seen

you before." He circled around her. "On TV. At the Olympics." He nodded. "You played basketball for Team USA."

How can he tell this just from a swimming lesson? What did he see under the water?

"And you played in the WNBA." He snapped his fingers. "You're Sonya . . . Richardson. Houston Comets. Number twelve. Always wore a ponytail."

Wow. I shouldn't tell him he's right, but wow! He recognized me. And if he could recognize me, so could the rest of America.

"You look almost the same now as you did then," John said.

Say what? "Almost?"

"You have a few gray hairs, but other than that . . ."

"Other than that, what?"

He bobbed closer. "You could be rookie of the year all over again."

This is amazing. Why do I keep thinking that word? "How did you recognize me? I'm not exactly a household name."

He drifted backward. "I live alone. I watch ESPN long into the night. I like watching the WNBA. Y'all play with a whole lot more passion than the NBA players do."

"We tried." *And now I've admitted who I truly am. Oh well. Bob and Larry will just have to deal with it.*

"You were the best point guard in the

league. Great crossover, and those bullet passes you made? *Zing!* Clutch three's in the championships. You have a few rings, too. Three?"

Wow. He really *paid attention.* "Four. I didn't get one for the thumb."

"And you're in the Hall of Fame. You're basketball royalty."

Well, I am . . . "What sports did you play?"

"Football. Kickoff and return teams mostly. Made a few tackles here and there, two or three good blocks in four years. Missed more tackles and blocks than I made."

And he's so humble about it. "Ever play any basketball?"

"Only after I became a pastor. Sometimes on youth nights we'd go to Monroe County High School to play ball. About the only thing I was good at were free throws, fouls, and turnovers. Sometimes I got picked last when I got picked at all."

"You shoot free throws in pickup games?"

"Oh, no," John said. "I just shot them while I was waiting to get into the game. I got a lot of practice shooting free throws."

Nobody's that terrible. "You're really that bad?"

"I tripped over the lines. I dribbled better with my knees. The backboard was scared of me. The rim and nets yawned at me. On a scale of one to ten, I was about a two. Which is the most points I usually scored in a game, by the way. I usually got double-doubles in turnovers and fouls."

His eyes just . . . light up when he talks . . . about how bad *a basketball player he is.* "So you're a hacker."

"No, I was just slow-footed and reached a lot." John looked at the water. "Maybe you can give me some lessons."

Why am I drifting over to him? There's no current in this pool, is there? Oh. My little feet are moving closer to him all by themselves. And now my little feet are standing on top of his big feet. "I could do that."

"I wish there was a court around here," John said. "This place has everything else."

"Yeah, who doesn't put up at least a half court somewhere?"

"The theater is kind of nice," John said. "All that sound."

"Yeah. Sure beats my setup."

"I have a console TV," John said. "Looks more like furniture than a TV. It's also a great table for all my junk. I had to use rabbit ears and everything when we first got it."

He said "we." He still has the first TV he and his wife used.

"Final exam time," he said. "I want you to swim lengthwise once without any help."

But I like the help and your hot hands, man! "Could I start at the deep end?"

"Sure."

As they drifted to the deep end, Sonya grabbed for and held John's shoulder as he swam. "Just hitching a ride."

John turned and smiled. "No charge."

She gripped the cement lip jutting over the water under the diving board. "Stay close to me."

"I will."

Sonya took a deep breath, kicked off the wall, and swam the length of the pool.

Without taking a single breath.

She gasped for air as she wiped water from her eyes at the other end. "I forgot to breathe."

"It happens." John leaned on the wall beside her. "You're very fast."

"I was swimming for my life, man," she said.

"Don't we all," John said.

"Yep." *How long have we been out here? An hour? Not even. I don't want this date, I mean, this lesson to end.* "What can we do tomorrow morning?"

John peeked over the lip. "Tomorrow? Why not today? We can go jogging as the sun rises all the way down to the beach. It's about two miles. The view down there is amazing."

And now he's *using that word.*

"Unless you're too tired," John said.

I'm too alive to be tired. "I'm okay. Um, thanks for the lesson."

"Thanks for . . ." John shook his head. "Just . . . thanks."

"For what?"

"For giving me a chance . . . to get to know you better. I doubt I'll win any of the challenges."

"Oh, I have a feeling you will." *And it's a good feeling because I am inches from a good man in a warm swimming pool at five in the morning, and I feel . . . peace. My heart is floating in my chest.* "I'll just throw on some sweats and meet you . . ."

"At the end of the driveway."

Where all this madness began. "See you in a few." She climbed out of the pool.

"Good morning, Sonya."

She looked at John, who was backstroking away from her. "Good morning, John." Sonya removed her bathing cap and dried out her ears. *He's watching my every move when he thinks I don't notice him watching. He's watching me. He's sponging me up. He sees me. He sees beauty in me.*

I like to be watched.

"That was sweet."

"Is this man romantically retarded, or what?"

"Bob, you have to know his history. He's been through so much tragedy that —"

"She was ripe for the taking!" Bob interrupted. "They were inches apart! She was standing on his feet! Her breasts were rubbing on his chest! And when he went under the water to hold her,

259

he barely kept his eyes open! What good are underwater cameras if they don't capture a man staring at a woman's naughty bits?"

"Naughty bits?"

"So I'm a fan of Monty Python."

"The chlorine in that pool is very strong, Bob."

"Not that strong. What kind of man nearly closes his eyes when he can get up close and personal with a woman's —"

"C'mon, Bob," Larry interrupted. "He's being careful, and so is she. This is how relationships begin in the real world. One step at a time. Or in this case, one lesson at a time."

"You saw how she was looking at him, Larry. She wanted more, much more."

"Maybe, maybe not."

"If they had kissed or even hugged we'd have more fireworks to shoot off at brunch. A swimming lesson just won't do it. Unless . . ."

"Unless what?"

"Unless we manipulate what they said to our advantage."

"You mean, take what they said to each other out of context."

"Precisely. Have the writers and editors have at it."

"I don't like this, Bob."

"I don't care if you like it, Larry. It'll be great for ratings. Yes, we're going to turn the swimming lesson into something much more interesting."

CHAPTER 23

I'm jogging with a premier athlete goddess while the sun rises behind us, and she's hardly breaking a sweat, John thought. *While I am having cramps in my calves, she is still smiling. Her ponytail swishing through the air has more energy than I have. I am so out of shape in so many ways.*

"How you doin', John?" she asked.

"Sweatin', Sonya."

She laughed. "And this is only the downhill part."

"I know."

When they reached the beach, they slowed to a leisurely stroll, neither one speaking.

I've forgotten how to talk to a woman, John thought. *What do I say? What did I say to Sheila when she was quiet? It's been so long. Maybe this:* "You seem lost in thought."

Sonya pointed down the beach. "Just missing my sister. She's down that way at a hotel. She's supposed to help me weed y'all out in a few weeks."

"I shouldn't ask, but . . . she isn't your opposite, is she?"

Sonya laughed. "Just about. She's . . . she's something."

"Oh." *That doesn't sound good.* "Um, how *something* is she?"

"About as *something* as anyone I've ever known." She stopped walking and looked out over the ocean. "She's quite the little heathen."

"I'll be praying for her," John said. *And I'll be praying for me when she does arrive.*

"Thank you." She turned and smiled. "I've been praying for her for twenty-six years. Fervently."

"It will one day avail much, Sister Sonya."

"Ooh, listen to the preacher man talk." She sighed. "We should probably be getting back to the castle, old man. That hill isn't getting any lower."

John rubbed his knee. *Maybe if she sees me rubbing my knee . . .*

"I see what you're trying to do," Sonya said.

What am I trying to do? Oh, yeah. I'm catching what little breath I have left in my body. "You've figured me out."

"To the castle," she said.

"Yeah. To the castle."

As John struggled to keep up, he tried not to stare at Sonya's . . . *Butt, man. You can think it. It's an excellent piece of God's crafts-*

manship. She has honed and toned and chis-eled that part of her anatomy for most of her life, and she deserves to have it looked at. You are a man. You are allowed to take in the beauty of God's handiwork. You are allowed to stare hard at a woman who is not looking back —

"You okay back there?" Sonya asked.

John smiled. "Yes."

"Why are you running so far behind me?"

"I like the chase." *Don't say it, don't say it . . .* "And the view." *You said it! And now you're blushing.*

Sonya slowed until she was beside him. "You staring at my booty?"

"Yes. I know it's not very godly, Sonya, but God made it, and I'm just praising it."

Sonya's mouth dropped open. "How . . . You just turned . . . Ooh, you *are* a preacher man. But I didn't hear a hallelujah."

John dropped back. "Hallelujah!"

"Stop!"

"Lord God in heaven, You are so good!" John shouted.

Sonya slowed until he caught up. "Please stop."

"Forgive me, Sonya. I've been alone a long time. You are much more than a pair of legs and a tempting, uh, butt running up a hill. You're a smile brighter than the sunrise. I hope to chase after you some more."

Sonya looked up at the sky. "The things you say."

"I mean every word."

"I know you do, but tomorrow I'm letting you go ahead of me."

"Why?"

"I want to say hallelujah, too."

Despite the aches and the pains in his legs, John sprinted ahead.

"Amen!" Sonya yelled.

John looked back. "No hallelujah?"

Sonya caught up to and passed John with ease. "I'm playing hard to get, John."

After showering and changing into a clean pair of sweats, John walked into yet another meeting of the Crew in the great room.

"What's up?" John asked Justin.

"Who knows, man," Justin said.

"How's your stomach?" John asked.

"Empty," Justin said. "They're not feeding us until after this is over. Probably another video."

Of a swimming lesson, no doubt, John thought. *Hmm. This could get dicey.*

Graham swept in from the foyer and stood in front of the TV. "Crew, there were more clandestine activities last night involving Jazz . . . and Arthur." Graham clicked the remote. "Just wait until you see this."

The video was grainier than the previous one, and the fisheye lens skewed and rounded the rectangular pool, but there was no doubt who was in the video.

I was that close to her? I guess I was. Oh, yeah. She stood on my feet. That was a nice sensation. But why are they filming us from behind? And where's the sound? We were talking the entire time.

And then John heard:

"It is warm. I'm ready."

"Um, take a deep breath. You may need to wave your hands, um, lower. Yeah. Keep that up as best you can."

"Like this?"

"Yes."

"Eight strokes. Stroke, stroke, blow, stroke, stroke, breathe. Let's practice that. If you get tired or scared . . ."

"I'm not tired. You're a good teacher."

"I'm good."

"Yes."

"On a scale of one to ten, I was about a two."

"Yeah. Um, thanks for the lesson."

John took a deep breath and exhaled. *Oh, Lord, mind my tongue.* He stood and went to the center of the room, looking up at a ceiling fan. *I hope there's a camera in there.* "I want to see one or both of the producers right now."

The rest of the room was speechless.

"None of that happened like that," John told the Crew. "They cut and spliced the entire thing to make it look like something it wasn't. I simply taught Jazz how to swim and that's all."

Aaron pounded a pillow with his fist. "You and Jazz got busy in the pool?"

"That's what the producers want you to think," John said, his voice steady but his anger rising. "I gave Jazz a swimming lesson, only they" — he pointed at the ceiling — "didn't include the lesson. The producers edited all that out and only used parts of our conversation to make y'all angry. Didn't you see the tape loop? We weren't standing next to each other for more than ten seconds the entire time. That tape loops at least two times."

"I saw it," Tony said.

"So did I," Gary said.

"Oh, man, that's shameful," Justin said. "Oh, not giving Jazz a swim lesson. That wasn't shameful, Artie. That mess they made on the screen was shameful."

John continued to look at the ceiling. "I said I wanted to see a producer. Larry? You better get down here." He scanned the room. "If they could do it to me, if they could manipulate what I did and said in a perfectly harmless activity, they could do it to you, too. That isn't what happened. That would never happen."

"Don't sweat it, Arthur," Tony said.

"Yeah, man," Gary said. "That's some trifling mess."

"Ain't it," Justin said.

Aaron jumped up and stood beside Graham. "How can we be sure that what we just saw *didn't* happen?"

"The video repeated itself, man," Gary said. "Only the dialogue changed, and it was so fuzzy we couldn't even see their mouths moving."

"I didn't see that," Aaron said. "Did the rest of you see that?"

"Well, then, we'll show it again," Gary said, "and we'll show you where the tape repeats."

John shook his head. "Gary, I'd rather you didn't. That was an abomination."

Aaron snatched the remote from Graham. "I want to see."

While the video ran again, Gary stood at the TV. "There, you see that? The entire scene repeats after this. You see that now, don't you, Aaron?"

Aaron clicked off the video and the TV. "All right, all right." He squared his shoulders. "But you all are missing the point. Artie here got with our princess *again.* In the pool late at night. He seems to like to sneak around and stab us all in the back like that. And what if it doesn't repeat or loop as you say? Artie was out there trying to ruin Jazz."

"Oh, man, like hell he was, Aaron," Gary

said. "Show it again in slow motion this time."

"Don't worry about it, Gary," Tony said. "Aaron only sees what he wants to see. We could show it to him a hundred times and he still won't see it."

"Because it's not there," Aaron said, slapping the back of his hand into his other palm. "Artie was getting busy with Jazz."

John sighed. "Larry, you're about to have a mutiny here." *Lord, what do I do? Jazz would be devastated to see this. Hmm.* He went to the DVD player and hit the eject button. "I'm sure Jazz has a DVD player in her room." He took out the DVD and held it up. "I'm sure she'll just love seeing how you twisted our words and made her look like a harlot."

"A what?" Aaron asked.

"A ho, Aaron," Justin said. "Dang. Ain't you never been to church?"

"Jazz isn't a ho!" Aaron shouted.

"I *know* that, man," Justin said. "But the producers are tryin' to make her look like one. For ratings. Understand?"

Larry appeared, his hands behind him, and he walked slowly toward John. "What seems to be the trouble?"

John showed him the DVD. "This is a complete lie."

Larry nodded. "Yes, yes, it is a lie. And this wasn't my idea at all, though I must confess that I had our editors rig it up." He turned to the Crew. "Arthur gave Jazz a swim lesson this morning. That's all that happened. We altered the truth to get a reaction out of you." He looked up at the ceiling.

"Why?" Aaron asked.

"To piss us off," Gary said. "And especially to piss *you* off, Aaron. Don't you see that you're getting played?" Gary stood. "I don't know about the rest of you, but I'm about to walk. This is one shaky, shady show, and I can make just as much working back in Memphis."

Justin stood. "This is some serious BS, Larry. But I ain't pissed off. I ain't mad at Arthur. The man got game. I should be taking some lessons from him. Two nights in a row. I even tried to stay up. Arthur, don't you ever sleep?"

"I'm still on Alabama time, I guess," John said. He looked around the room. "Look, fellas, I noticed yesterday that Jazz was the only one not swimming. I've seen that look before. It was as if she were afraid of the water. You saw her sitting at the shallow end, right?"

"Yeah, I saw her, and I sat with her," Aaron said. "So what?"

"So I asked Jazz to meet me at the pool, and she agreed. I didn't think she'd want a lot of people watching, and four AM seems to be the only time it's finally quiet around here. I mean, it's kind of embarrassing for an adult not to know how to swim, and you don't want an audience for your first swim lesson." *Whoa. And her bio says she's a surfer. I hope no one in here remembers that!*

"Where were you two later in the morning?" Aaron asked.

"We went for a jog down to the beach and back," John said. "We were just swimming and jogging today, nothing more." *Okay, I felt her one-pack and stared at her butt and nice, muscular legs. I even said hallelujah a couple times.*

Aaron nodded to himself so much John thought his head would fall off. "You see? You see? He's getting *dates* with her before he earns the *right* to get a date, and that ain't right."

"Those weren't dates," Justin said. "That was only a foot rub, a swimming lesson, and some jogging."

"And there's no rule against it," Tony said. "It's supposed to be every man for himself, right, Mr. Prince?"

"You are correct, Tony," Larry said. "And the challenges begin today, gentlemen. We'll be taking you out to the obstacle course right after lunch."

"Nah, nah," Aaron said. "That isn't good enough. I think there needs to be a *rule* about seeing Jazz alone at any time that isn't a date. If it isn't a date, you can't be with her alone. We all agree?"

"Man, just let it go," Gary said.

"What do the rest of you think?" Aaron asked. "Let's take a vote. Majority rules."

"Man," Justin said, "that's just some more BS. This ain't no democracy. This is supposed to be romance, yo. Romance is war, not congress. And he's taking a vote. Who does he think he is?"

I have to calm Aaron down. So much rage! "It's okay, Justin," John said. "Take your vote, Aaron."

Aaron's eyes narrowed for a second. "All right, all in favor of a rule forbidding contact with Jazz alone unless it's a date that you have *earned,* raise your hand."

Three hands went up.

"C'mon," Aaron said, "this is our queen."

"Princess," Justin said.

"Whatever," Aaron said. "Are we gonna let him win this thing?"

More hands rose until eight hands were in the air. Aaron nodded and smiled. "All right. That's what I'm talking about. Eight in favor. It's now a rule." He pointed at John. "No alone time with Jazz unless you *earn* it."

"A rule's a rule," John said. *And there goes my future basketball lesson and jogging with her tomorrow. I was even going to suggest an early-morning Bible study together.* John shrugged. "So how is this going to work?"

"What you mean, work?" Aaron said.

"We're in the same house with her, Aaron," John said. "There may be times she's in a room alone. Do we have to travel in pairs or what?"

"Yeah, dog," Gary said, "do we need chaperones or what? I'm a grown-ass man. I don't need no chaperone."

"These are valid points, Aaron," Larry said.

"You all know what I'm saying," Aaron said. "As long as we all stay together, no one of us is going to get extra face time with her, all right?"

"So we need to travel in packs," Tony said. "Like wolves, and no lone wolves."

"Right," Aaron said. "Right. That's right. We travel in packs."

Justin winked at John. "Until the challenges, right?"

"Well, yeah," Aaron said. "Every wolf for himself, then." He smiled. "And since I wasn't up all night swimming and out running this morning, this wolf is gonna win him a date with a princess today, and there's gonna be some real fireworks Saturday night."

He probably will win, John thought, *though Tony might make it close. But if I know Sonya, Aaron is one wolf who will be howling at the moon Saturday night.*

Alone.

CHAPTER 24

"I've faced many obstacles in my life," Sonya said as the wind whipped her ponytail back and forth at Topanga State Beach, "and I've survived them all with God's help." Sonya smiled. *I wasn't supposed to say the last three words. I'm sure they'll edit them out, but at least God and the Crew heard me.* "Today, I want to see how you rise to a new challenge as you complete this obstacle course." She looked at a dozen men dressed in the finest running gear Nike could provide. *This looks more like a Nike ad than a challenge.*

But what's up with John? He's going barefoot. Why doesn't this surprise me? He probably has blisters from trying to keep up with me and my booty this morning.

"I will be waiting at the finish line for the winner," she said. "Good luck."

Graham, also in a Nike outfit, addressed the Crew. "The winner of this challenge will earn the first date with Jazz, so get after it, yo. And don't be the last man to finish, or you are officially a punk."

"Just do your best," Sonya said. She held up a little silver whistle. "Wait till I blow the whistle."

As she jogged to the finish line, Sonya worried most about Justin. *I hope he doesn't spew twenty hot dogs all over this beach. Or even half of them. I'll bet little Bob Freeberg would just love for that to happen. They'd probably show it over and over in the promos in excruciatingly slow motion.*

At the finish line, she turned and looked out over the obstacle course. *I'm glad I'm not running that thing. I could handle the logs and the tunnel, but that cargo net is no joke.* "Ready?" she yelled. *I'm sure they didn't hear me.*

She blew the whistle.

Twelve men zipped under the first log. *Hey, they're all even. Cool.* Ten men were able to roll over the second log without too much trouble. Eight ran across the sixty-foot log without falling off. Six came out of the forty-foot tunnel without bumping their heads. Five hurdled the three-foot wall, three vaulted the five-foot wall, and after the tires, only two hit the cargo net at the same time.

Tony and Aaron. I hope Tony wins.

Tony reached the top of the net first but had trouble kicking over, his foot snagged on a rung. Aaron hulked himself over the top

274

and dropped twelve feet to the sand, sprinting to the finish before Tony could extricate his leg from the net.

"And the winner is . . . Aaron!" Graham said.

Am I supposed to be smiling? Ooh, and now Aaron's coming over to hug me? Dude, you are seriously sweaty.

"I won," Aaron said, smiling and panting.

"Congratulations, Aaron."

Now, where is Justin?

More importantly, where is John?

CHAPTER 25

John had no trouble with the logs, the tunnel, the walls, or the tires, but when he saw Aaron breaking the tape ahead of him, he caught his breath in front of the cargo netting and looked back for Justin.

Justin was resting inside the tunnel.

John trotted back to the tunnel. "C'mon, Justin. Let's finish this thing together."

Sweat streamed down Justin's face. "I don't know if I can make it, Artie."

"Don't sweat it, Justin. We'll finish together no matter what, okay?"

Justin nodded. "Who won?"

"Aaron."

"Figures."

"Yeah."

"Evil rises to the top, huh?"

John smiled. "Not always. Come on."

With a little encouragement, Justin made it to the cargo nets in just under five minutes.

"I ain't gonna make it," Justin said. "You go on."

"Nah," John said. "We'll go up together and come down together."

Justin looked up. "Go on, man. The rest are done. I'm done."

John shrugged. "We're in no hurry, then. This is just another beautiful day at the beach."

Justin doubled over. "I am so out of shape. I'm the punk."

John crouched beside him. "If we tie, no one loses, right?"

"Huh?" Justin said.

"I mean, if we cross at the same exact time, we *tie* for last, so technically, *neither one* of us came in last."

Justin straightened up. "And neither one of us will be a punk today."

Technically. Not sure the producers will see it that way. "Right." He patted Justin on the back. "Let us run with patience the race that is set before us."

Justin shook his head. "You got a Bible verse for everything, don't you?"

"Yep."

Justin smiled. "Preach on, man." He looked at the top of the cargo net. "And when I get up there, do some prayin', too. I ain't too fond of heights."

The going was slow and shaky, the net stretching under Justin's considerable weight. John had to climb almost sideways to keep his balance and footing. Once Justin and John were at the top, Gary and Tony left the finish line and stood on the other side.

"Yo, Justin!" Gary yelled. "Get a leg up!"

"You ain't funny, man," Justin said.

John felt the wooden rigging leaning dangerously to Justin's side. "Justin, I may have to jump off the other side. I won't leave you, all right? I'll be waiting for you. Take your time."

John put his right leg over, swung up his left, put his feet into a rung, and jumped off, the semisoft sand cushioning his fall. He turned in time to see Justin contemplating a jump.

"Back it up," Tony said. "I think he's gonna jump."

Justin shook his head slowly. "You crazy? I'm climbing down. Don't want to set off no earthquakes."

Sonya strolled up. "How's the view, Justin?"

Justin smiled. "I can see Hawaii from here."

As Justin started down, John felt Sonya's eyes on him. He turned and saw her eyes cutting to the finish line. *Oh. Right. Don't be a punk. I'll never be a punk, and right now, I just want to be a friend.*

Once Justin was safely on the sand, he and John walked in step past Sonya to the finish line. "How we gonna do this?" Justin whispered.

"The ol' one-two-three step," John whispered.

"I hope this works," Justin whispered. "I ain't ready to go home yet."

Neither am I, John thought.

They stood in front of the finish line. "On the count of three," John said. "One . . . two . . . three."

They put their right feet on the line at precisely the same time.

"It's a . . . tie?" Graham said. He looked at Darius.

Darius shrugged and twirled his finger.

"Um, okay, it's a tie," Graham said. "Um, Aaron, you are the hunk today, and that means that you have immunity at this week's elimination and a date with Jazz Saturday night." Graham clapped once, and no one joined in.

Sonya skipped up to Justin. "Way to go, man! I didn't doubt for a second that you would make it."

"*I* did," Justin heaved. "Whoo. I need to eat more salads and fewer hot dogs."

Sonya hugged him. "I'm really glad you didn't spew."

Justin nodded. "So am I."

Sonya smiled at John. "Never leave a man behind, huh?"

"Right," John said.

She looked at his feet. "You couldn't wear shoes again?"

"They weren't my color." He smiled. "Or my size."

279

Aaron stepped between John and Sonya. "I can't wait for our date."

And I can't wait to soak my feet! John thought. *I have bark and rope burns!*

Chapter 26

Sonya called Kim the second she was safely locked in her room.

"Where are you?"

"San Diego."

Sonya heard a whirring sound. "What's that noise?"

"I'm getting a tattoo."

Don't ask, don't ask . . . "Of what?" *And where?*

"I'll show it to you when I get there. What's up?"

"We had our first challenge today," Sonya said. "An obstacle course. Guess who won?"

"Aaron."

The child is no fun at all. "How'd you know?"

"I told you he's the one, Sonya," Kim said. "How'd Tony do?"

"He came in second."

"Who came in last?" Kim asked.

No one, really. "Justin and Arthur tied for last."

"Arthur? He seemed like he was in good

shape. What'd he do, fall or something?"

"He helped Justin finish."

"What for?"

Because he's a good man. "He was helping out a friend."

"He must not want a date with you."

As in shape as John is, there was no way he was outrunning Aaron, Tony, and some of the other Crew. "I know he does." *And we can have some mini-dates of our own every morning anyway.*

"Where are you and Aaron going on your date?" Kim asked.

"Catalina Island."

"Ooh, watch out, now."

"Watch out for what?"

"Aaron is hot, Sonya. You're going to an island. He has big hands."

Which probably means something else entirely. "The cameras will be following us everywhere."

"Maybe he'll drag you into a dark alley."

"On an island?" *Wait. Is this how Kim gets her jollies?*

"I'm kidding, Sonya. You may be the one doing the dragging."

"Me? Why would I even consider getting frisky with Aaron?"

"Frisky, ha! That's a good one."

Why would I get frisky with Aaron at all? He is definitely a hunk, and he probably already has an online fan club and a fan page on Facebook. Tall, lean, muscular, tattooed, athletic, a fierce competitor — he's the kind of man I would have liked when I was really twenty-five. But now I want a man I can talk to. And flirt with. And learn new things with . . .

"You be careful, Sonya," Kim said, "and keep your cell phone with you at all times."

Grr. "Funny. Where are you going next?"

"I'm staying overnight here and doing a day trip to Tijuana tomorrow."

What else was she planning? Oh, Disneyland. "And Mickey and the Magic Kingdom after that?"

"I don't know. I may be a little old for all that."

Which could mean . . . "So you might show up here earlier?" *Please!*

"I might. Gotta go. Battery's low. See ya." *Click.*

Sonya lay back on the bed. *My body's battery is kind of low, too.* She snuggled under the covers. *I better rest up for the first date I've had in seventeen years.*

Lord, let me have a nice time, please? And please help Aaron refrain from pawing at me.

If that's possible.

After an hour's limo ride from the mansion to Huntington Beach Harbor on Saturday morning, Sonya's knee hurt because Aaron's knee couldn't help getting frisky.

"Do you mind?" Sonya asked.

"I can't help it," Aaron said to the onboard camera. "My knee has a mind of its own."

At least he has a mind somewhere *in his body,* Sonya thought.

Sonya and Aaron finally boarded the *Gecko Gecko,* a power catamaran from Gecko Yacht Charters, followed by an army of camera-men.

It was a crowded ride.

Once Captain Randy motored out of the harbor, he let Aaron and Sonya take turns steering the catamaran in the direction of Catalina Island while dolphins followed and leaped in their wake. Aaron took off his shirt to provide some eye-candy moments for the cameras, boasting: "I was always good at driving the lane."

Sonya softly coughed.

Larry, wearing his usual boat shoes and shorts, looked right at home. "Bob wanted you to put on a skimpy bikini for the ride, but I talked him out of it."

"Thank you," Sonya said, rubbing her shoulders. "I am getting sunburned already."

Larry found and brought her a Wind-breaker. "It's all I could find."

"Thank you," Sonya said. "How much longer to the island?"

"We first have to let you two do some

snorkeling," Larry said.

"Snorkeling?" *So the world can see my booty bobbing in the ocean.* "Larry, I just learned how to swim a few days ago."

"You'll be wearing life vests," Larry said.

"That's not the point, Larry," Sonya said. "I just want to get out of the sun."

"You won't be out there long," Larry said.

Sonya became a salty prune in fifteen minutes. Her shoulders turned red. Her feet cramped because of the tight swim fins on her feet. Sonya also learned that Aaron was an octopus, his hands never missing a chance to touch her, rub her, and squeeze her.

"Gimme a break, Aaron," she whispered, a cameraman in an inflatable kayak a few feet away. "Let's just swim, all right? You know, you use your hands to move *you* around."

"I can't help myself, Jazz," he said to the camera. "You're so touchable."

Where are the sharks? Come get you some ham.

Sonya tried to be civil and asked Aaron what kind of fish they were seeing.

"Oh, look at that yellow one," he would say. "That one reminds me of Tony. And that dark black one. That's the Gary fish, isn't it? Oh, look at that eel. That is definitely Arthur. Oh, that orange one likes me. I don't see any fat Justin fish."

Sonya was sorry she had asked.

After an hour of listening to Aaron name

285

the fish and fending off Aaron's tentacles, she climbed aboard the catamaran. She went directly to Captain Randy.

"Get us to the island," she said. *"Now."*

Though Captain Randy broke speed records getting to Avalon, a town made up of houses walking up the hills, Sonya arrived at Catalina Island sunburned, ashy, worn out, and bruised.

An oversize Jeep without a top met them at the docks.

"And now, you're to go on a forty-mile tour of the island," Larry said.

"Larry, there's no top on that Jeep," Sonya said. "I'm going to fry."

Larry handed her some sunscreen. "It's the best I could do."

SPF 15. Is he kidding? I need at least SPF 50. She rubbed some sunscreen on her cheeks and shoulders anyway and put on the Windbreaker. "I'm not having a good time."

"I know," Larry said. "And I'm sorry."

For the next three hours, Sonya's stomach grumbled while they looked at "romantic" seascapes, walked across "secluded" beaches crawling with cameramen, explored "mysterious" coves littered with plastic bottles, and posed for "candid" pictures at every overlook.

As they bumped along, Aaron pointed at the sky. "Look, Jazz! That's a bald eagle."

"That's a seagull, Aaron," Sonya said.

"No, I'm sure it's a bald eagle."

No, fool, it's a seagull. Bald eagles don't hover over a Jeep looking for food, or in my case, fried flesh.

Upon returning to Avalon, the Jeep deposited them at Luau Larry's, a "Food, Spirits, Oyster Bar." Sonya went immediately to the bathroom to inspect the damage. *My hair! It looks as if I've been playing ball for five hours! The red spots on my cheeks make me look like a clown. Even my eyes feel sunburned.* She patted the Windbreaker, and dust plumed into the air. *I am not happy. Aren't dates supposed to at least smell good? I am so funky right now.*

To top it off, Aaron put a huge straw hat on her head when she came to their table.

Sonya took it off.

"It'll be fun," Aaron said, straightening his matching hat.

No, it won't.

Then she watched Aaron slurp down a dozen oysters, drink a Tazmanian Zombie, and inhale a plate of fried calamari while he watched an NFL wildcard playoff game on a TV hanging over the bar. Sonya tried several times to engage him in conversation, but Aaron was content to hoot and yell for "his" team.

Sonya picked at her Luau Salad and tried not to make eye contact with all the fake parrots inside Luau Larry's. *This is a bar that oc-*

casionally serves food. When Aaron ordered his second Tazmanian Zombie, Sonya stared at Larry.

Larry shrugged.

Sonya stood. "I'll be waiting on the boat, Aaron."

Aaron smiled. "Be out as soon as the game ends and I finish this drink."

I hope you'll be out, *all the way home,* Sonya thought. *Drink another. Get one to go. Drink like a fish. Why not? We're on an island, and we're about to get on a boat. And as we roll over the waves, make sure you puke into the Pacific. It will be the perfect ending to our date.*

Captain Randy seemed to sense Sonya's fury, and he made record time back to Huntington Beach. While Aaron drank beer and told stories to the cameras about how great a basketball player he was in college, Sonya went to the stern to watch the sunset.

It's a nice sunset, God, she thought, *but Aaron is definitely not the man I want to share it with. Ever.*

Unfortunately, Aaron didn't vomit over the side of the *Gecko Gecko.*

Fortunately, Aaron dozed on *his* side of the limo on the way back.

Unfortunately, he woke once the limo stopped in the mansion's driveway.

"How 'bout we hit that hot tub, Ma," he said lazily.

Sonya got a contact buzz from Aaron's breath. "No. I'm going to sleep now."

Aaron reached for her, but she stepped out of the limo and was up the driveway before he could stumble out after her. She opened the front door and had almost closed it when Aaron's head popped in.

I've seen this scene before in The Shining. *I will have nightmares.*

"How 'bout a good night kiss, Ma?" Aaron lurched forward and swooped in for a kiss, his eyes closed and his lips pursed.

Sonya leaned back, and Aaron almost kissed the fronds of a potted plant.

"Good night, Aaron."

Aaron opened his eyes. "I'll walk you up," he said to the potted plant.

A cameraman struggled through the doorway and froze just behind Aaron.

And now to finish this night in style. "I don't need you to walk me up, Aaron." She snapped her fingers several times.

Aaron wheeled from the plant to face her. "Huh?"

"In fact, Aaron, I don't need you to do anything for me, because the entire day wasn't about me at all, was it?"

Aaron blinked several times. "What you mean? Didn't you have a good time? I had a good time."

Sonya sighed. "Exactly. *You* had a good time." She pointed to the great room where the rest of the Crew was watching another football game. "Go catch the rest of that game, because, man, you don't have any game."

The cameraman gave her a thumbs-up.

Sonya smiled.

Aaron staggered into the great room.

Someone called to Aaron, "Yo, what up, dog?"

That man isn't a dog, Sonya thought. *That man is a dogfish.*

As soon as she was safely in her room, Sonya called Kim.

No answer. No one wants to talk to me tonight.

"Kim, when you get this message, give me a call. I don't care how late it is. I want to tell you about my date from the lowest depths of hell. Be safe. Bye."

But maybe John will be awake early. Yeah. John will be awake, and I can tell him all about my evil date.

She took a cool shower, didn't scrub her shoulders or cheeks too hard with the washcloth, put on her sweats, set her alarm for 4 AM, hit her pillow, and winced. *Ow.*

After lightly rubbing her shoulders and cheeks with lotion, she tried again to sleep.

Foot cramp . . . ow, ow, ow, ow.

She grabbed her big toe until the cramp

subsided.

She tried calling Kim again and got no answer.

Where is she?

After tossing and turning for most of the night, she woke at four and slipped down the stairs and into a dark great room.

No John to talk to. Maybe he's getting used to the time change.

At 6 AM, she dressed in her sweats and running shoes and walked gingerly out to the driveway.

Still no John. Guess he's not running today.

She frowned at the clouds muddying up the sunrise.

Man, I can't get a break today.

CHAPTER 27

John woke early, took a shower, and was shaving when Justin came in yawning.

"Yo, Artie, you gotta learn to sleep in," Justin said.

"Going to church," John said. "There's an AME over in Oxnard. Interested?"

"Yeah." Justin leaned out and looked at Aaron. "Aaron is out cold, man. Think he'll go with us?"

Let him sleep or annoy him? John thought. *Everyone needs Jesus.* "I'll try to wake him. Go see if anyone else wants to go."

"All right," Justin said, and he left the room humming, "God's Got a Blessing."

I knew Justin was AME, John thought. *Just something about the way he looks at life.*

John gently shook the foot of Aaron's bed. "Aaron."

Aaron turned his head from his pillow. "What?"

"You up for going to church? A couple of us are going."

Aaron squinted. "Jazz goin'?"

I hope so. "Don't know."

"Nah, I'm good."

Um, no . . . I don't think you are. And you talk in your sleep, man.

John put on his best gray suit, really the last suit he owned that didn't have tears or pulls in the fabric, and while Justin got ready, he went into the kitchen, popped some bread in a toaster, and started a pot of coffee. He read several Psalms and munched on some toast and jam until Gary, Tony, and Justin came in.

Whoa, John thought. *These guys should do commercials for suits and Stacy Adams. What's my problem? Oh, yeah. New Hope frowns on any suit color that isn't black, white, or gray.* "Y'all preachin' today?" he asked.

Justin laughed. "Gotta look good for the ladies in the choir." He wore a mustard yellow suit, mustard yellow shirt, and matching mustard yellow tie. "Think I'm overdoin' it?"

"Nah," Tony said. He smoothed his gray tie and buttoned his black jacket. "Mustard yellow doesn't stand out at all." He looked at Gary. "Now Gary, here." He smiled. "Man, I don't know if you're a Vegas lounge singer or a traveling tent preacher."

Gary spun around, his crushed blue velvet suit sparkling. "I'm a little of both. C'mon. Don't want to be late."

When they walked down the driveway to the limo, the driver folded his newspaper and opened the back door. "Where to, gentlemen?"

"Bethel AME in Oxnard," John said as Gary, Justin, and Tony got inside.

"Wait up!" Sonya called from the door, waving her Bible. She wore a long-sleeved white blouse, medium-length black skirt, and black flats.

And she is even more beautiful when she's not trying to be, John thought.

Sonya caught up. "You look good," she said.

Not really. "So do you."

She smiled. "Where are we going?"

"Bethel AME over in Oxnard," John said.

"And you were going to leave me?" she asked.

Oops. "I thought you might be sleeping in after your late date."

She walked past John to the limo. "I never miss church." She turned her head and squinted. "Oh no."

John saw Bob steaming out the front door. *He can't have a problem with this, can he?*

"Where are you going?" Bob asked.

Sonya stepped in front of John. "There's no filming today, so we're going to church."

"Bethel AME in Oxnard," John said. *I wonder if I've set some sort of record for saying that.*

"Church is fine," Bob said, "and I've alerted First AME of LA that you're on your way. Cameras will follow your every —"

"No," Sonya interrupted.

Bob's mouth shut. "No? Stevie Wonder and Obama have been to First AME. It's a famous church. The, uh, ..." He looked at John.

"Bethel AME in Oxnard." *That* has *to be a record.*

"No one famous goes there," Bob said.

Sonya shook her head. "We don't go to church to be seen by anyone but God, Mr. Freeberg."

"But a woman going to church with four men is exciting," Bob said. "And we can be better prepared at First AME than at —"

"No, Bob." Sonya frowned. "And don't have a camera crew following us either. This is supposed to be a free day. Let it be free, okay?" She stepped into the limo and sat facing Tony, Justin, and Gary.

John smiled at Bob. "We'll, um, we'll be at the —"

"I know, I know," Bob interrupted. He stepped closer. "This was your idea, wasn't it?"

"Church?" John said. "Well, actually, *the* church began a long time ago. I believe *the* church began when Jesus called the first disciples, but others believe it began at Pentecost."

Bob blinked.

"Just saying that church wasn't my idea," John said. "Have a blessed day, Bob."

John got into the limo next to Sonya. "I don't think Bob is a churchgoer."

The limo circled the drive and was flying up Pacific Coast Highway in minutes.

"Y'all look nice," Sonya said.

Her face is so red! "You get sunburned?" he asked.

"Yes," Sonya said. "My shoulders hurt the most."

I could fix them, John thought. *There are aloe plants growing all around the property.*

"Have a good time, Jazz?" Justin asked.

Sonya sighed. "I survived."

Justin turned to Tony. "*Told* you she didn't have a good time."

"You heard different?" Sonya asked.

"Aaron said you two had a nice time," Tony said, "but I didn't believe a word he said."

Sonya sat up straighter. "What'd he say? Wait. They got cameras in here?"

Justin nodded. "That's how they got all our arrival pictures."

Sonya tapped on the glass, and the driver opened the divider. "Yes?"

"You aren't filming us, are you?" Sonya asked.

"No filming today," he said.

Sonya closed the slider and looked directly at John. "What did Aaron say?"

She knows I would tell her the truth. "He

296

made a few claims that none of us believed." *And all of them were sexual. Not exactly what we should be talking about on our way to church.*

"Do I want to know what he said?" Sonya asked.

"The man was drunk off his ass, I mean, his butt," Gary said.

"He was talking out his butt, too," Justin said.

Sonya nodded and leaned forward. "Here's the truth, though I doubt you'll see it in any video they'll show you. I had a *lousy* time. The *worst* part was watching Aaron flex his mermaid tattoo on the boat ride to Catalina. It was all *downhill* from there."

All four men sighed and smiled, as if on cue.

"And that makes y'all happy, huh?" Sonya asked.

All four men nodded, also on cue.

"Do you think he's any competition to you *fine* men dressed so *sharp* for church?" Sonya asked.

All four men shook their heads, John only shaking his head slightly. *I don't look fine or feel all that sharp this morning compared to Gary, Tony, and Justin.*

Sonya sighed and rolled her eyes. "Let's go get our praise on and forget yesterday."

"Amen!" Justin shouted.

Yes, amen, John thought.

The service at Bethel AME was crowded, fun, loud, and hot. John had the misfortune of sitting between Gary and Justin in a pew built for much smaller men, and when the music swelled to a crescendo, he had to stand sideways during the singing to get some fresh air.

Justin knows all the songs, John thought. *But why am I surprised? He's a man of many layers.*

They sang "Back to Eden" and "I Call You Holy." They listened to a heartfelt, soul-lifting prayer. They listened to the choir sing "Bread of Life" and "He Saw the Best in Me." They opened their Bibles to Philippians 4.

Reverend Robert Cox read: "Rejoice in the Lord always: and again I say, rejoice."

Thank You, Lord, for another day, John thought. *Thank You also that Sonya had a lousy time. I know that's selfish, but thank You anyway. Please help her sunburn heal.*

"Let your moderation be known unto all men," Reverend Cox said.

Lord, thank You for keeping me from alcohol. And mermaid tattoos. And the sin of pride. When will moderation become a virtue on this earth again? Just asking.

"Be careful for nothing," Reverend Cox said, "but in every thing by prayer and supplication with thanksgiving let your requests be made known unto God." *Thank You that Sonya . . . is now sitting right next to me. How'd that happen? I need to pay better attention.*

He smiled at Sonya.

"Justin had to use the restroom," she whispered. "I hope you don't mind."

"No." *Thank You that Sonya is sitting right next to me with . . . her leg pinned to mine. They need to expand this church! Wait. No. Lord, thank You that this pew is too small. My leg is very happy now.*

"In everything," Reverend Cox said, "let your requests be known to God."

Lord, here's my request for today. You know my overall request. You remember. The get-a-wife thing. And now it doesn't seem so ridiculous. Today I ask that I get a chance to talk alone with Sonya without breaking that stupid rule.

"And the peace of God, which passeth all understanding," Reverend Cox said, "shall keep your hearts and minds through Christ Jesus."

Our knees are touching, they're practically moving in together and looking at carpet swatches, and she doesn't seem to mind. I think she's even doing most of the pressing. Don't look at her calves, don't look . . . Wow, those are nice cuts. Look away, look away . . . She sure does like to get her praise on. I sure do like watching that skirt of hers moving back and forth when she feels the Spirit. And those legs? God, You are so good! And that booty. Hallelujah!

"Finally, brethren," Reverend Cox said, "whatsoever things are true, whatsoever things are honest, whatsoever things are just, whatsoever things are pure, whatsoever things are lovely, whatsoever things are of good report; if there be any virtue, and if there be any praise, think on these things."

Sorry, Lord. Sonya is more than a spirit-filled woman swaying in the pew. But You have to admit, God, that she makes even a simple skirt look good. Hallelujah!

After the service, an ancient woman cornered Sonya on their way out. "Aren't you Jazz?"

Sonya smiled. "Yes. How are you?"

The old woman smiled at Justin, Gary, and Tony. "Such handsome men. How will you ever choose?"

Why isn't she looking at me? John thought. *Oh, yeah. I'm white and wearing a wrinkled gray suit.*

Sonya laughed. "God will help me choose."

"You be sure to pray about it," the woman said. "And you gentlemen be sure to come back."

"Yes, ma'am," Justin said, giving the woman a gentle hug. "I can't wait to come back."

"It has definitely been one of the few

highlights of my week," Sonya said. She smiled at John.

Lord God Almighty, make me a highlight of all her days.

I mean, at least make me another highlight today.

And, Lord, let me be on the receiving end of every one of Sonya's smiles.

And do something about this suit.

Amen.

CHAPTER 28

While John introduced himself to Reverend Cox, Justin talked to a tall, buxom choir member, and Gary and Tony were surrounded by women, Sonya stood alone on the sidewalk outside.

Hello? Sonya thought. *Um, I know it's a free day, but c'mon, y'all, free yourselves and let's get going.*

John broke away first.

Now maybe I can talk to him alone for a few minutes.

John took several steps toward Sonya and froze, returned to Justin, and touched his elbow, nodding at Sonya.

No, John. I just want you. Don't bring him.

Justin gave a hug to the choir member — *the hussy!* — and called out to Tony and Gary. The four of them walked up to her.

"Sorry to keep you waiting," John said.

Now why did John do that? Sonya thought. *He had me all to himself and called in the posse.*

On the ride home, Justin couldn't stop

gushing about the soloist. "That girl *sanged* that song. Whoo. She *kilt* it. Gave me goose bumps."

"Me too," Sonya said.

"I thought the speakers were gonna explode," Justin said. "What a voice!"

Uh-huh, Sonya thought. *What a body, right, Justin? I think Justin has a crush.* She glanced at Gary, who was looking out the window. *Gary broods a lot. Or maybe he's just thinking.* She looked at John, who was also looking out the window. *I know John's thinking. I just want to know what!*

"Arthur," Sonya said, "what did the reverend have to say?"

John turned to her. "Oh, I did most of the talking."

That's hard to believe, Sonya thought.

"I introduced myself and gave him my regards from Reverend Wilson back home," John said.

By the book, Sonya thought. *John is always going by the book. The world needs more people like him.*

"Gary, what did you think of the service?" Sonya asked.

Gary wrinkled up his nose. "A little low-key for me."

"Low-key?" Sonya said. *The man is tripping.* "We were jamming in there."

Gary shook his head. "At Mississippi Boulevard in Memphis, they get down, get funky, and get loose. That choir was small. We got at least three times as many in our choir. And service sometimes doesn't end till two. It's only one o'clock."

Gary the brooder likes church. Interesting. "Tony, where do you attend?"

"Second Free Mission Baptist in New Orleans," Tony said. "Bethel kind of reminds me of Second Free."

She stared at Justin.

"Oh," Justin said. "I go to Zion AME."

"And you have to sing there," John said.

"Yeah, they're probably missing me," Justin said. "I'm in the chancel choir, the male choir, and the Zion ensemble."

Very interesting, Sonya thought. *Everyone in this limo attends and participates in church.* "We will go every week no matter what. Okay?"

Justin smiled. "Deal."

When they returned to the mansion, two of the Crew whistled at them, but Tony set them straight. "Y'all are just jealous that we got to spend four hours alone with Jazz while y'all were still sleeping."

Sonya approached one of them, and though she tried to remember his name, she couldn't. *Booker? Timbo?* "Um, where is everybody?"

"Out shopping mostly," he said. "What you have in mind, baby?"

I am not your baby. "And when did you get up?"

"Dude, I just woke up."

And I am not your dude, dude. "Is Aaron around?"

"Man, I don't think you'll see him until tomorrow, yo," he said. "That boy is still unconscious."

You snooze, you lose.

After John and Gary made hot ham and cheese sandwiches for everyone, Sonya tried to corner John at the sink.

"I didn't see you this morning," she said.

John drifted to the entrance of the great room. "I slept in a little." He waved at Tony.

Tony nodded.

What's going on? "And you don't jog on Sunday?"

"No," John said. "My body needs to rest."

Why does he keep looking at the TV instead of me? "Can we . . . go somewhere . . . to talk?"

John looked at the floor. "There's a new house rule, Jazz. We can't be alone with you at any time unless we win a date."

What a stupid rule! "Whose idea was that? Bob's?"

"Aaron's, actually," John said. "I didn't vote for it, and neither did Tony, Gary, or Justin, but majority ruled."

Sonya sighed. "How can I get to know anyone if I can't talk to them alone?"

"You'll have to be gregarious and let us suck up to you, I guess." John winked. "As if you'd ever let that happen." He looked at the game again.

"You know I don't operate that way," Sonya said. "And I'm over here, man."

John turned to face her. "Sorry. I'm trying to keep the rule. And I'm also trying to keep the Sabbath."

"By watching a football game?"

"By not looking too long into your eyes," John whispered. "Makes me crazy." He looked at the TV again.

"Oh." *And that was a compliment.* "Um, what are you going to do all day?"

"I plan to rest, relax, maybe even watch a game, I don't know," he said. "I'm glad we all got our praise on today. I needed it."

"So did I." *I wish he'd look at me! This is making me crazy! When John looks at me, I feel sane.* "I've never heard so many hallelujahs." She stepped closer and whispered, "I like to hear you say it to me. Just to me, though, remember?"

John nodded. "I miss the reason I say it." He blinked. "And now I'm not respecting the Sabbath again."

"You aren't?"

"I'm seeing you running ahead of me and thinking about your, um . . ." He stared into her eyes briefly. "I better finish the dishes.

Enjoy your day." He moved past her to the kitchen.

And he thinks he can just get away that easily? She moved next to him as he worked on a frying pan. "Is that all you see, John?"

John shook his head. "Justin!" he called. "Gimme a hand with these dishes!" He glanced at Sonya. "I also see your smile, your ponytail, your legs, your calves, and your eyes," he whispered quickly. "I see all of you, Sonya, whenever I close my eyes."

"Then why'd you call Justin just now?"

"He walks the slowest," he said with a wink. "I miss our alone time, too, more than you'll ever know."

"Zoom in," Bob said.

A video operator pressed a button.

"Man, she looks . . . What is that look, Larry?"

"I think she really likes him, Bob."

"How can you tell?"

"She seems to be pining for him."

"Pining?"

"That's a face that is yearning for her man, Bob. That's a face of longing and desire. She craves Arthur's attention. She seems to need his attention, too."

"I didn't expect this. Of all the young, ripped flesh in the house, she falls for the oldest and hardest to focus on."

"And she may try to change that silly rule so

she can be alone with Arthur more often."

"We won't let her. It won't matter after tomorrow anyway. She has to dump either Arthur or Justin."

"Does she? She could send any of the Crew packing. That's explicitly in the rules. The challenges are just there to —"

"I know, I know, Larry. But she should dump one of them for losing. That's what the audience expects."

"And Jazz has certainly done the expected since she's gotten here."

"Yeah. Hmm. Well, she needs to keep Aaron. We need him."

"Do we? I think Jazz would send Aaron packing today if she could."

"They had a great time."

"She wasn't having any fun with Aaron at all, Bob. She just wanted to get back here to see Arthur. You saw her wandering around looking for him this morning."

"Maybe she just couldn't sleep."

"She was searching for Arthur."

"Or she just couldn't sleep because of her date with Aaron. We'll cut yesterday to make it look like she had the time of her life."

"I'm sure we will."

"I just don't understand! Out of all the beef in the house, she has to latch on to Arthur."

"They're kindred spirits."

"There are no such things as kindred

spirits, Larry."

"Then they're soul mates, and it took them forty years to find each other."

"You're making me sick, Larry."

"I know, Bob. I know."

CHAPTER 29

Kim arrived at the mansion Monday afternoon.

The Crew playing in the pool noticed.

While Sonya watched Kim dragging her suitcase up the driveway, several of the Crew stood at the gated entrance to the pool area and gawked.

It's shameful the way they lust after her, Sonya thought. *Of course, she is only wearing a black sports bra and tight jean shorts with her cheeks hanging out. Throw in her new hair and — what's that? A dragon tattoo? Geez! Throw in all that and my daughter's a certified —* Sonya didn't want to think it, but she did. *She's a certified hoochie, and this Crew sure loves a hoochie. Put your tongues back in your heads, fellas. Eww. That man is actually drooling. Nasty!*

Sonya raced out of her room and down the stairs, meeting Kim in the foyer.

"It's about time," Kim said.

Sonya put a finger to her lips. "Shh. We'll

310

talk upstairs." She picked up Kim's suitcase. "Geez, it's heavy," she whispered.

"I did some shopping," Kim said. "Why are you whispering?"

"Cameras are everywhere," Sonya whispered, pointing at the ceiling and walls.

"So?"

Sonya rolled her eyes and carried the suitcase up the stairs, Kim following.

Once inside Sonya's room, Kim threw herself onto Sonya's bed. "Is that all the Crew does all day?"

"Basically," Sonya said, rolling Kim's suitcase to the dresser. "They drink all night and play all day. You want to unpack?"

"Eventually." Kim pulled a pillow under her. "Sonya, where's your hair?"

Sonya closed the curtain to the balcony and sat on the edge of the bed. "I ditched it. I'm not going diva anymore. No makeup, no hair, no fancy clothes. I'm just doing me from now on."

"Scary," Kim said.

"Hush." *No scarier than that dragon you're letting the world see.* "I called you a couple times."

Kim rolled over, the pillow still covering her chest. "I was busy."

"You could have spared a minute or two to return my call."

Kim looked around the room. "Um, there's only one bed."

311

And she ignores me. She seems to do it most when I try to act motherly. "I'll get Larry to put in another bed."

"Not a rollaway, okay? Those things are murder on my back. That bar in the middle is a pain."

I'm not gonna ask about that. "So . . . what'd you see? What's Tijuana like?"

Kim rolled to her side, sliding the pillow under her head. "I didn't go to Tijuana. I liked San Diego." She smiled. "Like my tattoo?" She traced the tail of the dragon that started at her shoulder and disappeared between her cheeks. "The dragon's head took the most time."

A snake in front, and a dragon down below, Sonya thought. *Yep. That fits my daughter perfectly.*

Kim sighed. "Then there was this sailor . . ."

Terrific. While I was worrying about her, she was having a hookup. "Did he have a name?"

"No," Kim said dreamily. "No names. That's what he said."

Lord, when will she wise up?

"We met at the tattoo parlor."

And I'm sure it was love at first injection.

"We compared tattoos all night." She rolled off the bed. "I got the coolest bikini, too." She went to her suitcase, opened it, and took out a lime green bikini. "Isn't it nice?"

Where's the fabric? It's practically see-

through! The Crew will easily see where the dragon ends! "You can't wear that down at the pool."

Kim modeled the bikini top in front of the mirror. "Why not? Someone around here has to show a little skin. It'll be good for the ratings."

And her ego. "And they'll have to fuzz out your . . . your stuff."

"Maybe they won't."

My daughter, the exhibitionist. "They'll have to, Kim."

"Shani, Jazz," Kim said. "I am Shani, and I'm beautiful, aren't I?"

"Yes, you're gorgeous, but there's something called good taste."

Kim giggled. "There is?"

Is this child still a little drunk? "You been drinking?"

Kim nodded. "I'm almost sober. I could use some sleep. Mind if I use your bed?"

"No."

Kim slipped under the covers.

"You sleep with the wig on?"

Kim nodded.

"Isn't it uncomfortable?"

Kim shook her head. "I like the way it feels on my skin."

She's almost asleep already! "Do you want to hear about my date with Aaron before you doze off?"

"I can tell already that it sucked." Kim

turned away from Sonya. "If it was great, you would have told me about it already."

"It was as if I weren't even there, Kim." *Hmm. Like now with Kim.* "Aaron flexed in front of the camera. He smiled for the camera. He talked to the camera. He kissed up to the camera. If he could have, he would have made out with the camera."

"That wouldn't have been in good taste."

"Right."

"Yeah, a camera probably tastes all metallic." Kim giggled.

I'm talking to myself. "Aaron only interacted with me if they were doing a close-up on him. I wish I could dump him tonight."

Kim turned and blinked at Sonya. "Oh, yeah. You have to get rid of someone tonight. That could be fun."

"Dumping someone is not a fun thing to do."

Kim rolled over onto her back. "It can be. I mean, once you get used to doing it, it's not so bad. Kind of liberating, actually. Frees you for the hunt."

She loves 'em and she leaves 'em. "I'm supposed to dump either Justin or John."

"Who's John?" Kim asked.

Oh, yeah. Oops. "That's Arthur's real name."

"How do you know his real name?"

"He told me his real name."

"Why'd he tell you his real name, Sonya?"

Is there an echo in here? "John is an honest man."

"He just . . . busted out and told you his real name."

"Yep."

Kim seemed to ponder that for a few moments. "You're the most honest person I know, so . . ." Her mouth dropped open. "What'd you tell *him?*"

Is she sobering up? I can't tell. "Not much. He already figured out who I really am."

"What?"

She's getting louder. Yep, she's sobering up.

"You didn't tell him *everything,* did you?" Kim asked.

"He knows I'm older and that I played ball. He remembered seeing me in the Olympics."

Kim sat up straight against the headboard. "You *have* to get rid of him, then."

"Why?"

"He'll blab it to the others, and they'll want to get off the show."

John wouldn't do that. "How do you know they'll want to leave?"

"When they find out that you're old enough to be their mama, they're gone, Sonya."

"Thanks for reminding me that I'm old."

"You are." Kim sighed. "And Arthur or John — if that's even his *real* name. He might be scamming you, Sonya. He's bound to tell your business sooner or later."

"He's not that kind of man."

315

"Oh, you've known so many men that you can trust the first white man who comes along."

Hmm. My snake- and dragon-tattooed daughter is spitting venom and fire today. "You have a problem with his color?"

Kim looked away. "I've gone out with white guys, Sonya. Geez. I don't have a problem with his color. But they all seemed to have ulterior motives. I mean, he's the *only* white guy on the show. I'm sure he has some weird reason to be here."

Yeah, he came to find a wife; an honorable motive, but I can't tell her that yet. "Well, if he wanted to bust me out he would have done it already, right?"

"Come on, Sonya. Use your head. He might be saving the information for another time. I'll bet he's just waiting for the right moment to bust out with your business. You need to dump him tonight."

Not a chance. "I am not dumping him tonight."

"You'll regret it."

"I like him, so he's staying."

Kim scowled. "You like any man who talks to you."

True. "I also like any man who *listens* to me."

Kim shook her head. "Whatever." She slid down the headboard and pounded a pillow. "Like you ever have anything to say anyway."

316

She buried her head in the pillow.

And now I'm losing her. "You never told me who you thought was gay."

Kim rolled her eyes. "Timbo and Boogie are gay."

Who are they? Those can't be their real names. "How do you know?"

Kim rolled over to stare at Sonya. "It's a look they have, okay? It's a way they move, the way they look at the other guys, a way they look at each other, a way they *didn't* look at me a few minutes ago."

Oh, that had to hurt your self-esteem, Miss Hoochie. "They might be, what's the term? Metrosexual."

"They're gay, Sonya. They're only on this show to brag later about how they crashed a hetero show. They'll get gigs on Logo for sure."

"You might be wrong."

"As if you'd know."

Well . . . she is right about that. "I hardly know some of these guys because they don't talk to me at all. That leaves me to base my decision on the ones I can talk to."

"Talking."

"Yes, talking. Conversing, back-and-forth communication. Talking. With our clothes on."

Kim rolled her eyes. "Whoopee."

"So far I know I can talk to John, and Tony, Gary, and Justin."

"Figures," Kim grumbled. "You can talk to Wider Wesley, the Tiger, and Jumbo."

"Huh?"

"I nicknamed all of them to help me remember who they are," Kim said. "Gary is a wider version of Wesley Snipes so he's Wider Wesley."

Gary kind of, um, is, only without the little gap in his teeth. "Who's the Tiger?"

"Tony. He's Creole or a Cajun from Louisiana. You know, the LSU Tigers?" Kim smiled. "He seems like a tiger, too, like he's constantly on the prowl."

Tony on the prowl? He has manners! "And Justin is Jumbo, huh? I don't need an explanation there. Do you have a nickname for John?"

"No, he's just the white guy. I could call him OWG. Old white guy. How old is he really?"

Should I tell her? Can't hurt. "He's my age."

Kim laughed. "Yeah, he's scamming you. He can't be more than twenty-eight. I'll bet he puts gray in his hair every morning."

Now that is ridiculous. Sonya sighed. "It's real gray hair. You can't fake gray hair."

"You'd be surprised what some men will do to get with you." Kim rolled onto her stomach. "So, who are you going to dump tonight?"

Sonya sighed. "I'm supposed to dump either John or Justin because they came in

318

last in the challenge, but they're both very sweet men, and I don't want either one of them to go."

"Boot them both, then," Kim said.

"But I can talk to them, Kim. They're good people."

"So?"

"The world needs more good people. I need good people around me."

"And you asked *me* to come here sooner?"

Funny. "You're good people, too, Kim. You just need to let more of that goodness out."

"My name is Shani," Kim said. "Please use it."

"Yes, *Kim.*" *She hasn't earned that magical name yet.*

Kim turned on her side. "Well, what are the rules of this game anyway?"

"I'm supposed to send a punk packing every week."

"Your text told me you might dump seven."

"I can't do that." *Can I?* "The producers won't let me, and that would shorten the show by almost two months."

"Won't the elimination be live?" Kim asked.

"Yes."

"So who'll be able to stop you from doing that on a live broadcast?"

No one. Hmm. "But I'm supposed to weed from the bottom up. That's what's expected on these shows."

"So do the unexpected," Kim said. "Simplify your life. Isn't that what you preach at me sometimes?"

Not enough, evidently. "Have you simplified your life?"

"I did a few days ago. I skipped Tijuana to stay in San Diego another day."

"Because of a navy man."

Kim shrugged. "So I like a tattooed man in uniform. I like him better out of uniform. And just about everything he had to offer me was tattooed, even his —"

"Spare me the details, Kim," Sonya interrupted. "What should I do about this elimination? If you were me, what would you do?"

"If I were you," Kim said, "I'd put that wig back on."

"Hush."

"Okay, I'd get down to the ones I can actually stand and go from there. Five is manageable, I guess." Kim rubbed her eyes. "And I'll come out there to help you do the weeding."

"No, that's not a good idea." *Not tonight when you're going to be hung over and cranky.*

"But I'm already here, Sonya, and I want to help."

She wants to help, but do I want the world to see my daughter just yet? Not really. "I have to do the first elimination on my own, Kim."

"Suit yourself." She slid out of bed and opened the curtain slightly. "Will I be able to see the elimination from here?"

"Yes. We'll be out in the driveway."

320

"A driveway. Wow. How glamorous and romantic. I know, I'll stand here in the window and give you a thumbs-up or a thumbs-down."

"You don't even know these guys."

"I know the type, right?" Kim said. "They're my age. But make it easy on your-self. I say dump seven."

"That can't happen."

"You were always setting records in college and in the WNBA. You had sixteen assists in a game a couple times and eleven steals in another."

She knows about my records? And they still stand?

"Set another record tonight," Kim said. "Give people something to talk about tomor-row morning."

I didn't think she cared about my career. "You know I don't make snap decisions like that."

"C'mon." Kim returned to the bed and dis-appeared under the covers. "It'll be fun."

Right. Fun.

And the idea is very tempting.

And it does sound like fun.

Chapter 30

While John packed up in nine minutes and Justin worked on loading his third suitcase with his toiletries, Aaron sauntered into their suite.

"Y'all see that nice, fine piece of hot ass out there?" Aaron asked. "That tattoo was hot! And her hair! Daa-em. Who *was* that?"

John had seen Sonya's sister briefly and thought she was Sonya's twin. "Jazz's sister."

"How do you know?" Aaron asked.

"They look alike," John said. "Same eyes, same facial features, same height." *Same legs. The tattoos, though. Yowzers.* "They could be twins."

"Yeah, they could be," Aaron said. "The sister has more tats than me. How old you think she is?"

Twins fifteen years apart? I have no clue on ages. "Mid-twenties, I guess."

Aaron smiled. "If Jazz won't have me, I'll take the sister, know what I'm sayin'?"

John set his suitcase by the door. "No,

Aaron, I don't know what you're sayin'."

Justin hoisted a suitcase onto his bed. "She isn't supposed to be here now, is she?"

"All I know is that Jazz has been missing her," John said, "and today she's here."

"And Jazz gets what Jazz wants," Justin said.

"Well, fellas, been nice knowin' one of you," Aaron said. "Gonna go down to the pool, see what I can see. Hope she goes swimming so I can see where that dragon's tail ends, though I think I already know."

After Aaron left, Justin shook his head. "He's off to be seen."

"Pride goeth before a fall," John said.

"Yeah," Justin said. "Maybe he'll fall into the pool and dissolve."

"I hope not. I like that pool."

"Good for giving lessons, huh?"

"Yes." *And the memory of that lesson isn't fading. I keep replaying it in my mind. Why is that? Water, the sun rising, Sonya standing on my feet . . .*

Justin came over and shook John's hand. "Nice knowing you, Arthur."

"What makes you think you're leaving? Or do you mean me? I may be gone instead of you."

"Dog, you rubbed her feet, taught her to swim, jogged with her, cooked with her, helped her clean up the kitchen, and sat next to her in church." Justin smiled. "I saw y'all's

323

knees rubbin' together. You're the mack daddy around here, not me."

The daddy what? "I seriously doubt that. Justin, you make Jazz laugh. You make her smile. No woman would get rid of a man who makes her day brighter. Don't sell yourself short."

"But I'm tall."

John laughed. "Yes, you are."

"Nah, man," Justin said. "Honeys like Jazz don't go out with big and tall fat guys. Nah, man. I'm out."

"Oh ye of little faith."

"And that's another thing, Arthur," Justin said. "You're righteous."

"So are you. You didn't have a second thought about going to church yesterday, did you?"

"No. I always go. Been goin' since I was small."

"You were small once?"

"I wasn't born big." Justin laughed. "Actually, I was. Ten pounds, nine ounces."

Whoa. And ouch. "And you know every song."

"I am built for gospel, all right? If I hear a song once, I can sing it. I'll be singing back in Philly soon."

"C'mon. Jazz also talks to you. She doesn't even speak to the others unless she has to. She likes conversation, and you're easy to talk to."

"Yeah. I've always been good at that," Justin said. "But she talked all day Saturday to Aaron —"

"Who is a narcissistic fool," John interrupted. "She *had* to speak to Aaron. She had to be polite."

"Ten hours with that guy." Justin shook his head. "I can't stand him for more than a few minutes at a time."

"I have a good feeling that you and I are safe," John said. "You don't want to go back to Philly yet, do you?"

"Nah, man. I'd much rather stay here. It's twenty-five degrees and snowing in Philly."

The Crew sat in the great room watching the taped portions from the past week while the lighting and sound crews prepared the driveway for the live elimination. John's "face time" was shortened to "I'm Arthur?" The foot rubbing and swim lesson footage — both the actual scenes and what was shown to the Crew — were nonexistent. Aaron's conversation with Sonya at the pool ran in its entirety except for the microphone destruction. Justin's hot dog–eating stunt lasted five excruciating minutes, a blinking counter marking his progress from one to twenty. Aaron's win at the obstacle course ran in slow motion.

Justin's problems at the obstacle course ran in slower motion.

Sonya's date with Aaron took up fifteen minutes, and while John watched, he felt helpless. *He has his hands all over her! And without asking! I asked! I got permission! The way they've edited this, I can't tell if Sonya's having a good time or not. He's definitely pawing at her, and the camera only shows her smiling. Aaron is a handsome man, an athlete, young, virile, and doesn't have nearly as much baggage as I have. What is this I'm feeling? Am I feeling anger? Frustration? Fear? Jazz is smiling at the sunset, but Aaron's not beside her. That's a good sign. I should be beside her.*

The scene faded to black with Aaron standing in the doorway bleary-eyed, Sonya smiling on the stairs.

No way she smiled, John thought. *No way.*

When the commercials began, Boogie clapped. "What happened after that, dog?"

Aaron stood. "Y'all know what happened after that. I went up those stairs and got me some."

Timbo stood and gave him some dap. "What was she like?"

"Oh, man," Aaron said, "she couldn't get enough of me."

"That's a lie," Tony said.

"Yeah, man," Gary said. "You came in here and passed out while we were watching the game."

"Yeah, man," Justin said. "Don't front."

326

They should be filming this *conversation live,* John thought.

"How y'all know what happened *later*?" Aaron asked. "You weren't there. We had us a *good* time."

Justin shook his head. "Man, you didn't move from your bed all night. Why you lyin'?"

"How you know I didn't get some while you were asleep?" Aaron asked.

Tony stood and stretched. "Man, this show is so twisted that the producers *would* have shown exactly what happened if anything happened at all. They didn't show what happened because nothing happened."

"You calling me a liar?" Aaron asked.

Tony nodded. "Yeah, man. You're a liar."

"I ain't lying, yo," Aaron said.

"On our way to church yesterday," Gary said, "Jazz told us she had a lousy time with you, dog, and I believe her."

Aaron shrugged. "She's just protecting her reputation, yo. She doesn't want any of y'all to feel bad that I got in there first. And it was *good,* yo. Tasty and tight."

And that's where I come in. "Aaron, that's enough. There are no cameras to lie to in here."

Aaron wheeled to face John. "And I told you —"

"Lies," John interrupted. "I'm your roommate, too, and I don't sleep, remember? Your stench kept me up all night. Nothing moved except the alcohol evaporating from your body."

"Why don't you just shut up when you don't know what you're talking about?" Aaron said.

"Jazz had a lousy time on your date," John said, "and the only reason you don't know that is because you were drunk off your butt for most of the time you were *supposed* to be paying attention to her. You can't remember what happened, can you, Aaron?"

"All I know," Aaron said, "is that I woke up smelling like her."

"You nasty," Justin said. "You woke up smelling like alcohol and your own funk."

"Get to your marks, gentlemen," Darius said. "We go live in two minutes."

Aaron stared at John. "This ain't over."

"Nothing is over that has never begun," John said.

"Why am I even listening to you?" Aaron said. "You're about to be goin' back to Butt Crack, Alabama, white boy." Aaron cocked his head toward Justin. "Either you or that clown."

"I got your clown, yo," Justin said, rising to his full six-eight. "Anytime you want to do some clownin', see me."

"Justin," John said quietly, shaking his head. "Let it go."

"Yeah," Aaron said, walking to the foyer. "Time to let one of you go."

Lord, John prayed, *I don't ask You for much, but could You make a way? And while You're doing it, could You maybe, I don't know, have Aaron fall flat on his arrogant face in front of ten million viewers?*

Just askin'.

Amen.

CHAPTER 31

Sonya wore a reasonably sexy lavender dress, lavender flats, a little makeup to cover up the sunburn, and only gold hoop earrings instead of all the previous bling, and when she took her position in front of the Crew, she saw eleven men with suitcases.

Geez, she thought, *some of them brought more stuff than I did. And why is Justin looking so sad? Don't worry, big guy. I got you.*

"And now it's time for the first elimination," Graham said. "Tonight we'll find out who our first punk is. Aaron, because you won the obstacle-course challenge, you're safe from elimination. Stand by Jazz."

Oh, Aaron is so smug. And here he is trying to take my hand. The nerve. My eyes put those groping hands behind his back where they belong. If you want to grab some butt, Aaron, grab your own. I'm sure you've had lots of practice.

"Jazz, it's time for you to choose who else is safe from elimination," Graham said. "If

Jazz calls your name, you are still a hunk and have earned the right to stand beside Jazz."

What? Sonya thought. *This is not the way I thought it would go. I just want to dump!* Sonya looked up at Kim standing on the balcony. *Maybe I should have had you down here with me.*

"Jazz, I know it's a tough decision," Graham said. "Tell us who else is safe."

Singling out until the final two are standing up there is so cruel. It does build suspense, though. Make a choice, Sonya. "Gary."

"Gary, you are a hunk," Graham said. "Come join your princess."

Sonya looked up and saw Kim wiggling her hand. *So what if Wider Wesley isn't your type, little girl.*

Gary walked to Sonya and only squeezed her hands. "Thanks."

"Jazz," Graham said. "Who else is safe?"

"Tony." *Oh, I get two thumbs-up from Kim for that selection. Tony the Tiger, huh?*

"Tony, you are a hunk," Graham said. "Come join your princess."

Tony came and gave Jazz a little hug. "Thanks."

"Jazz," Graham said, "who else is safe?"

And now it's time to make America say "huh?" It's show time! Sonya smiled. "Justin."

A light stand fell, several lights shattering on impact with the driveway. Darius dropped his clipboard. Several of the Crew coughed. Kim shook her head. Aaron seemed to growl.

"Um, Jazz," Graham said, his eyes blinking rapidly, "are you sure?"

"Positive," Sonya said. *But why isn't Justin coming to me? He's probably as shocked as everyone else.* "Justin, come on down here and gimme a hug."

"Um, Jazz, he, um," Graham stuttered, "he tied for *last* with Arthur in the obstacle course."

"I've made my choice, Graham," Sonya said. "Justin is a hunk."

Justin was in front of her in three huge steps. "Thank you, Jazz." He picked her up and hugged her. He set her down. "Sorry about that."

"It's okay, Justin," Sonya said.

Graham practically put his big nose in Sonya's ear. "But, Jazz —"

"Hush, Graham," Sonya interrupted. "Completing an obstacle course in the fastest time is not a true indicator of any man's heart. Justin had the *most* heart out there, and I guarantee you that he burned the most calories out on that course."

Justin nodded. "I did. I lost at least three pounds. This jacket fits better now." He took his place beside Tony.

"There's more to being a hunk than having athletic ability," Sonya said. "Justin never gave up, and I have to respect that. A good man never gives up." She smiled at Graham. "It's your turn, Graham."

Graham looked at Darius.

Darius shrugged.

"Um, okay, Jazz," Graham said, "who else is safe?"

Another easy decision. But why did I make him wait so long? Oh, yeah. He's trying not to speak to me because of a stupid rule Aaron made. Don't say the wrong name now. "Arthur."

A cameraman fell forward, his camera clattering to the ground. Darius slapped his clipboard on his thigh. Several Crew members said or mouthed, "What?" Kim frowned and put one thumb up. Aaron *really* growled.

"But, Jazz," Graham whispered tersely, "Arthur came in last, too."

"Arthur, come to your princess," Sonya said.

Arthur smiled and drifted down to her.

"Arthur could have easily finished in the middle of the pack, but he proved himself to be a true friend," Sonya said. "He didn't leave Justin behind. He didn't leave a man behind. He took a risk, did the right thing, and he should be rewarded for his loyalty. He's a team player. I like team players."

John stood in front of her, his hands behind his back. "My princess."

No hug? He's too much of a gentleman some-

times. Sonya stepped forward and hugged John. *I knew he was put together well. He has a one-pack, too. And he smells nice. I like his scent.*

"Um, Jazz?" Graham asked.

I don't want to let John go. Shh.

"Jazz?" Graham said. "Who else is safe?"

Sonya stepped back.

John winked.

Sonya blushed.

"Who else is safe, Jazz?" Graham asked.

Sonya looked up to the balcony, mouthing, "Who else?" Kim only shrugged. *A princess has gotta do what a princess has gotta do.* "That's . . . all."

"What do you mean, that's all?" Graham asked.

Sonya watched Darius's clipboard fly off into the night. *I can't believe I'm doing this!* "That's it. The rest of them can go."

"Jazz," Graham said, his voice rising in pitch, "you're only supposed to eliminate one member of the Crew."

Sonya sighed and walked to where the rest of the Crew stood. *The Seven Drunk Dwarves. Hmm.* "No offense, fellas, but we didn't really connect, you know? I barely know any of your names." *It's time to take a stand.* "And I can't abide any man who drinks, smokes, or parties." She glanced back at Aaron. "I also can't stand a man who drinks instead of thinks."

She turned to face the Crew. "You all have such magnificent bodies and hopefully bright futures. Why try to mess any of that up? Take care."

Graham left his mark and stood beside Jazz. "But, Jazz, you can't dismiss seven guys in one show."

Sonya smiled at the nearest camera. "I just did, Graham."

"Commercial!" Darius bellowed.

And then, chaos reigned on the set of *Hunk or Punk.* Darius fussed at the camera crew, Graham, and even the limo driver. The seven "gone" Crew members had their hands in the air and cursed whomever was closest. Aaron made a beeline for Larry, who was smiling and chuckling. Tony, Gary, and Justin exchanged a little dap. Only John didn't move a single muscle.

Bob pushed through the chaos, his face so red it could stop traffic. "You can't do this!"

"I just did, Bob, and there's nothing in my contract that says I can't," Sonya said. "It says I will eliminate *players* each week. There's an *s* on that word. 'Players,' not 'player.' And all of them are players." *Even Aaron. Hmm. He's got to go. If he didn't win the date, he'd be out of here, too.*

Bob puffed up his little chest. "That's *not* the way this *game* is supposed to be played!"

"That's the way I play this game, Bob, and

335

please stop shouting at me," Sonya said. She looked at the men she had just dismissed. "Why are they still here?"

Bob ran both of his hands through his hair. "This show is supposed to last a *minimum* of —"

"I know, I know, Bob," Sonya interrupted. "And it still might. But you can't script any of this. It takes some people many months or even years to fall in love. You can't limit me in the way I feel. What, I'm supposed to love all but one of them every week and call the loser a punk? None of these men are punks. Maybe some weeks I don't kick anyone off because I can't decide."

"And you might clean house again," Bob said.

True. "I might. But it *will* make people tune in every week to see what I'll do next, right?"

Bob started to say something and stopped. "Hmm. I'll make you a deal."

"No deals, Bob," Sonya said. "I have my own mind, and I intend to use it."

Bob looked around. "Where's Larry?"

Darius pointed to the mansion.

"Figures he'd run out when all hell is breaking loose," Bob said. "Could you *try* to keep these five for a while?"

"I may keep them for six months, and I may tell all but one of them to take a hike next week," Sonya said.

"Jazz, be reasonable," Bob said.

"Come on, Bob," Sonya said. "Loosen up. In real life, women make crazy, impetuous decisions all the time. It's how we roll. These five standing here are like a basketball team, and I'm the coach. Right now, impetuous me needs them all. Justin's my center, John's my point guard, Tony and Gary are my forwards, and Aaron's . . ." *Well, at least for now.* "And Aaron's my shooting guard." *Who dribbles when he drinks.*

Bob stared at the stars. "But you have no one on the *bench!*"

"I don't want a *bench* player, Bob," Sonya said. She waved at Kim. "Hey, can my sister come down now? It'd make a wonderful end to this episode."

Bob's head snapped down. "No!"

"Work with me here, Bob." She waved Kim down, and Kim zipped inside their room. *I hope she changes into something nice.* "It will be fine. I know just what to say, too."

"Miss Richardson," Bob whispered, "you can't just —"

"Be myself?" Sonya interrupted. "Isn't that what you told me to be?"

Larry arrived out of breath but smiling. "Bob, the phone lines are lit up like Christmas. The online blogs are cooking like never before. So far it's two-to-one in favor of Jazz's decision. Let me read a few comments." He looked at a printout. " 'OMG Jazz is the bomb! She no princess, she a queen, yo!' 'She chose the same five I would have, even the old white guy.' 'Dag, this show is the junk!' 'It's about time somebody put reality in reality TV.' "

"See?" Sonya said. *Old white guy? John's not that old!* "We've just put reality in reality TV, Bob. Congratulations."

Bob scratched at his neck. "What do you think, Larry?"

Larry shrugged. "What's done is done, Bob. I say we run with it."

"Thirty seconds!" Darius shouted.

"You still have to say these guys are punks before they go," Bob said.

"That's not in the contract either, Bob," Sonya said.

"It's in the script!" Bob shouted.

"And what have I said about *scripting* any of this? I will not call these men punks. I'm sure they're pretty nice guys when they're sober. I don't know them well enough to call them punks because they rarely even spoke to me. And anyway, I'm not the kind of person ever to call anyone a punk." She looked at the losing Crew. "They're still here? Man, if they're still here when we come back from commercial, what will people think?"

Larry turned to the Crew. "Do as your princess says, gentlemen. You have to go, and quickly."

As Darius counted down the seconds, the

338

losing Crew filed out and Kim slipped through them wearing a form-fitting, bright red dress and heels, that dragon tattoo peeking out.

No panty lines, Sonya thought. *My daughter's debut on TV and she's looking like a dragon lady.*

Darius pointed at Graham, and Graham put on his fake smile. "Crew, um, remaining Crew, Jazz has someone she wants you to meet."

"Team, not Crew, Graham," Sonya said. "Team, I'd like you to meet my sister, Shani. Shani, meet the Team."

Kim only nodded.

"Shani is going to help me choose which one of you I end up with. She's going to be my conscience, my confidant, and my relationship advisor." *And one day, she might even become my daughter.* "Trust me: Shani doesn't play. We are *very* close. If you hurt her, you hurt me. And if you hurt me . . ."

"You're nothin' but a punk," Kim said, her eyes fierce. She walked up and down the row. "Things are going to be different around here from now on. You got that?" Kim poked Gary in the chest. "Y'all got to shape up." She poked Tony in the chest. "Ain't gonna be no carryin' on." She stopped in front of John and stared him down. "There's another sister in town, and she . . . means . . . business."

CHAPTER 32

The fallout from Sonya's decision began later that night.

David Letterman was first to take a few potshots. "Before the show, Paul Shaffer and I were watching this new show on another nameless network called *Hunk or Punk.* The princess on that show, what was her name, Paul?"

"Jazz, David," Paul said. "It was Jazz. Great name, David. Really jazzy."

"We watched Jazz dump *seven* men in one night," Letterman said. "*Seven* men in one night."

"Like hot potatoes, David," Paul said.

"Liz Taylor, Zsa Zsa Gabor, and Joan Collins are home right now saying, 'Why didn't *I* think of that?' "

"I'm rooting for the white guy," Conan O'Brien said. "Someone has to, right? Let's hear it for the white guy!"

Conan was the only one clapping.

"Yeah, you're right," Conan said. "What

340

am I thinking? He's toast. Plain, white toast."

Early the next morning, LA's number-one morning radio show, *The Bubble Bill and Juicy Show,* cranked up the hate.

"Juicy, you see that *Hunk or Punk* show last night?" Bubble Bill asked.

"Oh, yes," Juicy said. "Wasn't that amazing?"

"Amazing? She broke all the rules of shows like that. Isn't it supposed to be one man at a time?"

"I don't think she broke any rules, Bubble Bill," Juicy said. "I bet there are millions of women who would love to dump seven men in a heartbeat like that."

"But why'd she keep the white guy?" Bubble Bill asked.

"She likes him. You saw how long she hugged him."

"Well, I thought he was jumpin' her. The only thing a white man can jump is a car, and I should know. I haven't left the ground since I was born."

"I would have kept Arthur, too," Juicy said. "He's polite, charming, and has charisma."

"What's charisma?"

"It's something you don't have, Bubble Bill," Juicy said. "I bet you can't even spell it."

"It sounds like a disease," Bubble Bill said. "I got a bad case of the charisma."

"You'll never be infected," Juicy said.

"C'mon, Juicy," Bubble Bill said, "can you see Arthur dancing at a club? I can't. He'd be pouting for sure, cuz I know he can't dance."

"Not all women want a man who can dance at a club, Bubble Bill."

"The man's obviously a redneck. I bet he sold the dirt from his front yard for the plane ticket out here."

Juicy laughed. "Is that how you got to LA?"

"Nah, I sold my truck and my best cow."

Canned laughter filled the air.

"Did you know that the dump scene went viral on the Internet?" Juicy asked.

"It went viral? Well, it was pretty sick."

"That scene got twenty-five *million* hits," Juicy said. "I've watched it twenty times. You see the looks on those punks' faces? Priceless."

"I'd hate to be their agents," Bubble Bill said.

"Dumping seven guys at once has to be a record," Juicy said.

"Oh, and I knew her hair was a wig. She ought to give it back to the horse she stole it from."

"That wasn't nice, Bubble Bill," Juicy said. "And I think she looks better natural anyway . . ."

The Internet headlines were surprisingly positive:

Jazz Dazzles!

***Hunk or Punk* Is a Slam Dunk!**

No Junk on *Hunk or Punk*

Seven Drunk Punks Sunk

Kim, lying on a queen mattress in front of Jazz's bed, surfed the Web all morning Tuesday and found a glowing review at ET Online. " 'Jazz knows what she wants, and what Jazz wants, Jazz gets.' "

Sonya looked up from her Bible study. "I like the sound of that."

"Don't interrupt," Kim said. " 'Never before in the history of reality TV has a bachelorette had so much power — and the willingness to wield it to her advantage. Instead of the tried-and-true *formula* of dumping one guy every week, Jazz chose to clean mansion using one simple: "That's . . . all." She later explained to the stunned punks: *No offense, fellas, but we didn't really connect, you know? I barely know any of your names. And I can't abide any man who drinks, smokes, or parties. I also can't stand a man who drinks instead of thinks. You all have such magnificent bodies and hopefully bright futures. Why try to mess any of that up? Take care.' "*

I said all that? Sonya thought. *Cool. I thought I was babbling.*

" 'According to producer Larry Prince, the show is still slated to tape through June, though that may change as Jazz changes her mind. *It is indeed a woman's prerogative to change her mind,* executive producer Bob Freeberg said. *I can't wait to see what Jazz does, and with the addition of Jazz's sister, Shani, who knows what will happen next . . .' "

Sonya mangled a pillow with both hands. "What a hypocrite! Bob hated the idea last night. But now that the reviews are good, he's in love with the idea."

"It's all about the money, Sonya," Kim said. "You just made him some serious money. I'll bet new sponsors are fighting each other to get a hookup."

"I don't see why," Sonya said. "I shortened the show."

"Like you said, you could keep 'em all for a few months."

"I probably will." She smoothed out the pillow. "Did you see the look on Aaron's face?"

"Was he growling?" Kim asked.

"I think so."

"He's a jerk, Sonya," Kim said. "He's not the one." She stood and rubbed her neck. "We have to get a desk in here." She climbed into Sonya's bed. "You know, all this means that this week's action has to be more spectacular than last week's action."

No, it doesn't. "It doesn't have to be spec-tacular. Maybe it will actually be meaningful. The next challenge is supposed to be a mini-triathlon. Swimming, bicycling, and run-ning." *Blood, sweat, Justin needing an ambu-lance or John helping Justin finish, Aaron winning again, Aaron drunk again, Aaron ignor-ing me again, Aaron's hands on me again, Aaron kissing the plant again . . . No.*

"You know Aaron will probably win the tri-athlon," Kim said.

Maybe I can put a mask on that plant, Sonya thought. *That might be funny.*

"So why don't you make the next challenge more cerebral?" Kim suggested. "Have them take a test or make them list their likes and dislikes or have them write you a poem. Something different."

Definitely not a triathlon. "What kind of test?"

"The parts of a woman's body," Kim said. "So many of 'em don't know we have more than one part. I have yet to meet a man who can arouse my entire body."

Is that even possible? And if it is, where is this man? And if he's in this house, why isn't he here with me now? "No tests. A poem might work." *A poem written to me? No one has ever written a poem to me before.*

"All right, a poem," Kim said. "You'll be able to find out who has soul and who doesn't have soul in a matter of seconds."

I'd rather have a man who has a *soul than soul.* "I like that idea. Oh, but what if they're horrible poems?"

"It will be great comedy."

True, but . . . "I don't want to laugh at them."

"Then laugh *with* me," Kim said. "But we have to jazz it up more, Jazz. Why is there only one challenge every week? I mean, what do you do here when the cameras aren't on?"

Not much. "We watch TV, we play cards, we cook, we eat, we swim. I swim now." She smiled. "John gave me a lesson."

"He did?"

Sonya nodded.

"Then why didn't they show it on TV?" Kim asked.

"Well, it was at four o'clock in the morning."

"What?"

Yeah, it does sound kind of risqué. "Neither one of us could sleep. He's a very good teacher."

"Sonya, you just . . . got into a pool at four AM with some strange man you just met?"

"And you just slept with a sailor you just met?"

Kim was silent.

"We kind of had a Bible study first." *Sort of.*

"And he taught you how to swim in, what,

an hour? That's not possible."

"I am still a good athlete," Sonya said. "He was a great coach."

"Whatever." Kim sighed. "Y'all don't have much fun around here at all. It all sounds boring to me. We need to liven up this place."

Sonya's stomach grumbled. "You know, they should also cook a meal for us."

"I was thinking more like having them do pole dances in G-strings while singing 'Beat It,' " Kim said.

Where did that idea come from? "No."

"Tony would look so fine in a black G-string," Kim said.

"No, Kim."

"Justin wouldn't," Kim said. "He'd need a Z-string. But the ratings would skyrocket."

I don't want that image in my head. "Hush."

"Yeah. I doubt there would be a pole strong enough to hold either him or Gary. They'd have to use telephone poles."

Sonya laughed. "Stop!"

"Sonya, they are big."

"So?"

"You're not," Kim said. "Why you like big men?"

"They're *good* men," Sonya said. "That's the kind of man I like. The package isn't as important as a man's goodness."

"Sonya, the package is *everything.* Trust me."

Oh, this nasty child.

"But having them all cook for us instead of doing pole dances?" Kim said. "That's so . . . domestic."

"It's real." *And I'm hungry.*

"That kitchen isn't big enough for all of them."

"So we'll expand the kitchen somehow." *And if I want my men to cook for me, they are going to cook for me.*

"I'm going to starve," Kim said.

"You won't starve, and it might actually be fun."

"I doubt it."

And I like being around John in the kitchen for some reason.

These thoughts, these thoughts.

But she's right — that's a lot of beefcake to fit into one kitchen.

In the great room Tuesday morning, Sonya and Kim stood in front of the fireplace with Graham while Justin, Tony, Gary, John, and Aaron lounged on couches in front of them.

Graham cleared his throat. "All right, Crew —"

"Team, Graham," Sonya interrupted.

"Okay, *Team,*" Graham said, "Jazz and Shani have an announcement for you."

"Team, there will be not one but *two* challenges this week," Sonya said. "First, you will cook for me."

All but Aaron smiled. *That's right, Aaron.*

348

We ain't running this week. But why are the rest of them smiling?

"Wait a minute," Sonya said. "Y'all can cook, can't you?"

Justin patted his stomach. "Look at me. Don't I look like I know how to cook?"

"A single man who likes to eat has to know how to cook," Gary said.

Aaron raised his hand. "Um, I thought the next challenge was a triathlon."

"We wanted to do something different, Aaron," Kim said. "Something without too much sweat. Being a man isn't all about sweating, you know."

And she said that? I might be rubbing off on her. Or she's just being ironic. "Y'all might be sweatin' in the kitchen, though," Sonya said.

"No sweat," Justin said.

Kim frowned at Justin. "Then we'll have to make it more difficult, won't we, Jazz?"

Justin's smile faded.

"Um, yeah, and to make it more difficult, what you cook . . ." *I don't want them fixing me something like ostrich.* "What you cook has to represent where you're from. I want you to give me a taste of your hometowns."

"Yes!" Gary said.

"No problem," Tony said.

"Piece of cake," Justin said.

"*And,*" Kim said, "you have to impress *both* of us with your cooking." She stared Justin

349

down again. "I am a picky eater. If I don't like it, you're gonna hear about it. I send steaks back all the time at restaurants. Whatever you fix has to be perfect. I want whatever you cook to melt in my mouth and not give me any trouble in the bathroom the next day." She smiled at Sonya. "Tell them the second challenge."

I'll say one thing for my daughter — she knows how to handle men. "In the second challenge, you will have to amaze me with an original poem."

All but Aaron smiled again.

Oh, come on! This is too easy, too? What's a challenge if it isn't a challenge? "Y'all can write poetry, can't you?"

Justin stood. "My skills are not fictitious, in fact they're quite ambitious, my cooking is so delicious that you'll want to eat the dishes."

Aaron raised his hand again. "Are we *ever* going to do a triathlon?"

Maybe I should have stuck to the triathlon, and we could have had it at sunrise when Aaron was hungover. "I don't think we will, Aaron." Sonya shook her head. "I thought these would be hard challenges." She shrugged. "Just make them romantic poems, okay?"

"*Ma chère, mon chou, je vais lui écrire en Français,*" Tony said softly.

Kim blinked. "What'd you say?"

"I'll tell your sister on our first date,"

350

Tony said.

Kim crossed her arms. "Your poetry must be deep and have meaning, Tony. And if you write it in another language, you have to give us the translation as well. And you must move both Jazz and me *emotionally*. Make us cry. Make us laugh. Make us say, 'True dat.' Make us *feel* something. Think you can handle that?"

"Word," Justin said.

Aaron didn't raise his hand this time. "Does it have to rhyme?" he asked.

"No," Kim said.

"*Should* it rhyme?" Aaron asked.

"It's your poem, man," Kim said. "Do what you want with it."

"What kinds of poems do *you* like, Shani?" Aaron asked.

Aaron is so shameless! Sonya thought. *Hitting on my daughter right in front of me.*

Kim frowned. "Poems that make me think and poems that prove to me that *you* can think. Deep poems. Poems from the heart. You got heart, Aaron?"

"Yo, Ma, I got mad heart," Aaron said.

Kim gave him the same kind of withering stare she gives me whenever I annoy her, Sonya thought, *which is most of the time.*

"Just don't write a Hallmark card," Kim said, "or I will slam you. Hard."

"You won't have to slam *me*, Shani," Aaron said. "I got mad writing skills that thrill and

351

kill, um, Bill, and instill the hills with, um, thrills."

Kim laughed. "Oh, that was *swill,* Aaron."

Aaron smiled. "Thank you."

That man has an ego the size of Texas and an intellect as small as a thimble. "So, you'll first be cooking with food," Sonya said, "and then you'll be cooking with words."

Darius handed a card to Graham. "Tomorrow," he read, "you will shop at Ralph's." Graham smiled. "Ralph's? I shop at Ralph's. Thursday you will prepare your meal here in the mansion. Friday you will try to amaze Jazz and Shani with poetry. And the winner will be going on a date with Jazz Saturday night."

"How's that for a busy week, Team?" Sonya asked.

"*Don't* disappoint us," Kim said.

And there's John not saying a single word, Sonya thought. *I wonder what he's thinking.*

Chapter 33

Shani, John thought, *is like the quarrelsome wife from Proverbs 27. She's the dripping of a leaky roof, and controlling her is as easy as controlling the wind or grabbing oil.*

Shani is slippery.

She may be the spittin' image of her sister, but all she spits is venom. She is so unlike her sister. Maybe that's the way of the universe. For every good, wholesome, kind person, there is a not-so-good, worrisome, mean person as a counterbalance. Either that or Shani just didn't get enough warm fuzzies in her life. Maybe that's it. Sonya got all the attention for her amazing athletic abilities, and Shani felt left out.

John was the last to leave the couch, and Shani and the others were already in the kitchen eating snacks or going out to the pool. Sonya cut her eyes toward the foyer, and John hesitated, then followed her to one of the inkblot paintings.

"You were awfully quiet," Sonya said.

"Aaron's rule is still in effect," John whispered. "I should be anywhere you aren't."

"But you're not," Sonya said.

John nodded. "You're a bad influence on me." He went to the foot of the stairs. *Put one foot higher than the other on the stairs so if anyone comes in, it will look as if I'm just going up the stairs.* "I have a lot of writing to do."

"Gonna write me an epic poem, John?" Sonya asked.

"I'll try not to. It's only an hour show."

"Right," Sonya said. "If you're up, say, at four and want some company . . ."

John took two steps higher on the stairs, then leaned on the banister. "I always want your company, Sonya. Always. But rules are rules."

"Even if seven of the people who voted for that stupid rule are gone?"

"That's a very good point," John said. "However, Aaron is still here, and I don't want to butt heads with him today." He winked. "I don't want it to affect my creativity. You don't want an angry poem, do you?"

"No." She stepped closer to the stairs. "But I miss you, and this makes me angry."

John rolled his eyes. "We practically live together, Sonya."

Sonya smiled. "True."

"And I don't think your sister likes me very much either. True?"

Sonya nodded. "Not yet. I'll try to bring

her around."

"You do that," John said. He looked to the top of the stairs. "I'll be upstairs if you need me."

"You inviting me to your room, John?"

I'd like nothing better, Sonya. "Just holler if you need me."

"Arthur!" she hollered.

I'm sure people in Oregon heard that. "Thank you," John said. "It's nice to be needed." He continued up the stairs.

"Where are you going?" Sonya asked.

"To write you a poem."

"Now? I just hollered for you."

John smiled. "And that will inspire me. I intend to win this one."

Sonya sighed. "Well, go on, then."

She's pouting. Shoot. John trotted down the stairs, pulled Sonya to him, gave her a firm hug, squeezed her hands, elicited a smile, and then tore up the stairs two at a time to his room.

"Arthur!" Sonya hollered again.

This could become habit-forming, John thought.

He sped down the stairs, hugged her again, elicited a laughing smile, and went up to his room.

The poem flowed out of John's pen, and so did the tears.

God, I have two women in my head. Two.

Why can't I separate them? They're blending together on this page, and I can't help it. It's as if I'm writing the ending of one thing and the beginning of another, and the ending of the one thing is making me cry. Sheila . . . Why can't I say good-bye to Sheila? Is it because I didn't get the chance to?

He reread the poem silently. *I guess this is my good-bye to her.*

Justin popped his head into the room. "You okay?"

John wiped his eyes with his palms. "Yeah."

"You must be feeling it." Justin sat on his bed.

"I'm just thinking about my wife."

Justin shook his head slightly. "You're married?"

"Was." He put his notepad down. "She died. Her name was Sheila." He took out his wallet and pulled out a small wedding picture, handing it to Justin.

"She's . . . daa-em, Artie. She fine. Oh, sorry." Justin handed back the picture.

"She *was* fine," John said. "Sheila was so amazing that I was always amazed she was with me." He looked at the picture. *I have never looked better in a suit in my life.*

"How long were you married?" Justin asked.

"Five years."

"Don't take this the wrong way, Artie, but I

didn't know why you were even on this show," Justin said. "Now I can see why. Sheila, right?"

John nodded, tucking the picture back into his wallet.

"Sheila was beautiful, man."

"Is. She's still beautiful. In my head." *And she visits me in my dreams, too,* John thought, *but I can't tell Justin that. I can't tell him I always wake up crying.*

"Yeah. Man, Artie, I'm real sorry to hear that."

And here come more tears. I have to let them fall. "Yeah. It's been hard. Real hard." He went to the bathroom and took two tissues, blowing his nose. "Sorry, man."

"It's okay."

John sat on his bed. "Writing this poem has helped some."

"Gonna be deep, huh?"

"Maybe too deep. I doubt Shani will be impressed."

"You ain't writing for her, right?" Justin asked.

"Right."

"I ain't that deep," Justin said. "I'll just try to make them both laugh. It's what I'm good at."

"A feast is made for laughter," John said.

"True dat," Justin said, "and there's gonna be lots of laughter after our feast."

■ ■ ■ ■

"Please tell me we'll run some or all of this, Bob."

Bob seemed deep in thought.

"Bob?"

"You didn't tell me he had a dead black wife."

"I tried to tell you, Bob. I told you that Arthur had been through some tragedy. This is that tragedy."

"How long has she been dead?"

"Fifteen years."

"And he's still crying over her?"

"True love is like that, Bob. I still think about my wife, and she's been gone for thirty years."

"You dream about her?"

"She drops in occasionally. 'For a visit,' she tells me. And when I wake up, I look at her picture and say, 'Soon, dear, soon.' "

"You're not going to drop dead on me anytime soon, are you, Larry?"

"I'll try to stay among the living until the show ends, Bob. Now are we going to run any of this conversation?"

"No. It's too heavy. A man crying? We run this and she keeps him another week or longer and we lose all credibility."

"How so?"

"A man who cries is a punk, Larry. You know that. And if she keeps a punk, what's the point of having any hunks?"

CHAPTER 34

On the ride to Ralph's Wednesday morning, Justin broke the silence. "What y'all gonna make? I'm makin' her an authentic Philly steak 'n' cheese."

"She's getting gumbo and a po' boy from me," Tony said. "Something spicy, something sweet."

"I'm from Memphis," Gary said, "so you know I gotta make her the world's best barbecue."

"We Texans make the world's best chili," Aaron said. "And I use secret ingredients."

Justin blinked. "You're going to cook two beautiful women . . . chili."

"Yeah," Aaron said. "It will melt in their mouths."

Gary laughed. "Never heard about no chili melting in anyone's mouth."

"Trust me, fellas," Aaron said. "They'll ask for seconds."

Justin looked at John. "What about you, Artie?"

John sighed. "I'm having a little trouble deciding. I'm originally from Chicago. That means pizza, sausages, and cheesecake — not the best combination."

"Nope," Justin said. "For them. Sounds fine to me."

John smiled. "I've been living in Alabama for over twenty years, so I'm going home-cooked. Fried chicken, real mashed potatoes, cornbread, and greens."

"This is California, Artie," Tony said. "I don't know if all these beautiful people even eat greens. You might not be able to find any fatback either."

"You gonna cook them greens at the mansion?" Gary asked.

"I'll have to," John said.

"You're gonna stink up the whole house, man," Gary said.

"Yep." *And that's the point. Sonya will smell them percolating, and it will remind her of home.*

"Well," Justin said, "at least we're all giving them something different."

Gary shook his head. "And Shani ain't gonna like any of it."

"True dat," Justin said.

"I guarantee she'll love my chili," Aaron said.

Gary shook the limo with his laughter. "I ain't never heard no one ever say, 'Yo, I just *love* chili.' "

"Just you wait, man," Aaron said.

Out in front of Ralph's, a small crowd of shoppers surrounded the limo, many taking pictures with their cell phones as the Team left the limo to stand on five X's taped to the sidewalk. Graham and several camera crews waited near the doors.

"Gentlemen," Graham said, "welcome to Ralph's. You each have one hour to shop and only fifty dollars to spend on your meal for Jazz and Shani. A camera crew will follow each of you as you shop. Go!"

John headed first to the meat section. *Whole chickens at sixty-nine cents a pound. Do I want to cook a whole chicken? It'd save money. I'd have to cut it up, though. My meal won't cost that much anyway. Maybe a pack of drumsticks? No. That's childish. Unless I give them some variety. There's more meat in a breast. Hey, Foster Farms chicken parts are fifty percent off. Cool.*

He put packs bursting with breasts, drumsticks, and wings into his cart. The camera crew recorded the event.

This can't be a fun job for them, John thought. *Maybe I should say something to liven it up?* "On to the potatoes!" he said with a smile.

The sound man gave a thumbs-up.

Standing in front of the potatoes, John decided to think out loud. "Hmm. Yukon gold are the best for making mashed potatoes, but

361

these russets are a buck ninety-nine for five pounds. A mix? Yes." He smiled directly into the camera lens. "I take my smashed spuds seriously, y'all."

He put a bag of Yukon gold and a bag of russets into his cart. "On to the greens!" he yelled, one finger high in the air.

I'll bet that's a first for TV.

Ralph's had greens in abundance. John decided on collards. He displayed the bunch of collards for the camera. "These are good for you, America." He put them in the cart.

He backtracked to the meat section. "Ham hocks or fatback? Decisions, decisions." He chose two ham hocks, holding them up to the camera. "These are not as good for you, America, but they sure do make the greens taste better." He smiled broadly for the camera. "And now, I am going to race through Ralph's to make the rest of my purchases. Ready? Let's roll!"

He flew back to produce and collected two sweet onions, nearly colliding with Aaron. He tipped an imaginary hat to Aaron and raced down every aisle in the store, collecting a bottle of apple cider vinegar, two boxes of Jiffy cornbread mix, a half gallon of milk, a box of butter, and half a dozen eggs. He spent a long time in the spices aisle selecting sea salt, white pepper, basil, parsley, ground ginger, and a bottle of Lawry's.

"And now, I will pay for my purchases,"

John said to the camera. "Isn't this exciting?"

In the checkout line, John picked up two Snickers bars and put them into his cart. "Shh, America, don't tell. I like chocolate." He raised an eyebrow. "Don't snicker at me, now."

John finished first with his purchases, Aaron coming outside last.

"Yo," Aaron said to the Team, "y'all got any money left over? I need another ten bucks."

The Team pooled its change and gave it to Aaron, who rushed back inside.

Not even a thank you, John thought.

"Why we helping him?" Justin asked.

"Curiosity, I think," John said. "We all want to know what sixty-dollar chili tastes like."

Gary grimaced. "Do we really?"

"Nah," Justin said.

"No," Tony said.

"Nope," John said.

With the bathroom door closed, John perfected his poem and worked on reciting it in front of the mirror.

Justin knocked on the door. "Yo, Artie, what rhymes with 'booty'?"

John opened the door. "You're not going to use that word in the poem, are you?"

Justin nodded. "Got to. Goin' for laughs."

John closed his eyes. *And now I'm seeing Sonya's booty. Better open my eyes.* John opened his eyes. "Um, beauty, cutie?"

"I used them already," Justin said.

John ran the alphabet in his head. "Um . . . duty?"

"Nah, man. Too serious."

"How about . . . fruity."

"*You* serious?" Justin asked.

"Might be funny."

Justin wrote something down. "Maybe. What else?"

John looked at the ceiling. "Um, Doug Flutie, snooty, sweet patootie."

"Huh?"

Either he's too young, or I'm getting too old. "Doug Flutie was an NFL quarterback. Think he even played up in Canada. 'Snooty' is, well, kind of how Shani is, and 'sweet patootie' is an old-fashioned term of endearment."

"Yeah?"

John nodded.

Justin wrote it down. "Sweet patootie. That could work. Thanks, Artie."

And for some reason, John thought, *I think I just helped Justin win this challenge.* He looked at his own poem. *Would "sweet patootie" work somewhere in here? Nope.*

I'm not changing a thing in this poem because . . .

Because I can't change my heart.

CHAPTER 35

Sonya woke Thursday morning to the smell of greens.

Someone had to be up at sunrise to start them greens, she thought. *Who could it be? It could be anyone, but I'll bet it was John. Shoot. I could have gotten up early to get him alone for a few hours.*

She got out of bed and bounced on Kim's mattress. "Wake up!"

Kim opened one eye. "What's that smell?"

"Greens," Sonya said. "And Lawry's, and Old Bay, and ginger, I think."

Kim sat up and sniffed the air. "I smell chocolate, too. Who's baking us cookies?"

Sonya shrugged. "That has to be an incredibly crowded kitchen. Want to go with me to find where they get all the live feeds?"

"You want to watch them cook?" Kim asked.

"Don't you?" Sonya asked.

Kim smiled. "Yeah. It could be good comedy, and I already know where they sit and watch us."

"You do?"

"The windows to the garage are painted, Sonya. A mansion with painted glass windows? Bob and Larry have to be in the garage."

They dressed and sneaked down the stairs and out to the front door to the garage. Sonya tapped on a side door, and Larry opened it.

"Can we watch?" Sonya asked.

Larry ushered them in to the "eyes" of the house, where six technicians wearing headsets sat in front of long banks of monitors, each labeled with a section or room in the mansion. Most of the monitors were blank. Larry led them to four wide-screen monitors showing different views of the kitchen.

What a madhouse that kitchen is! "You brought in more ovens?"

"No," Larry said. "Those are countertop stoves."

They're elbowing each other every time they turn around! "So they're sharing the oven?"

"Only John will be baking anything," Larry said.

Cookies? Yum!

"I feel like such a voyeur," Kim said. "But where's Gary?"

"Gary is watching TV while his food cooks," Larry said. "Most of them have been going back and forth between the TV and the kitchen. You have missed most of the preparation. This is as busy as it's been for the last two hours."

"They have covers on most of their pots. I can't see what they're cooking." Sonya smiled at Larry. "You know what they're cooking, don't you?"

"It is supposed to be a surprise," Larry said. "For the integrity of the blind taste test. You're not supposed to know who cooked what."

"C'mon, Larry," Kim said, looking at the monitors. "We'll figure it out. We know where they're from."

John has all four burners going, Sonya thought. *Oh, he's opening . . . Yep. Them are greens. John only checks them. Grandmama used to say, "Don't worry the greens, just let 'em be." John's giving me a home-cooked meal. He's over at the sink now . . . peeling potatoes. Two different kinds. Greens, mashed potatoes, going to bake something maybe later, big old cast-iron frying pan on two eyes . . . It has to be chicken. I'm getting so hungry!*

"This is boring," Kim said. "I'm going back up."

"I'm staying," Sonya said. *This is better than the Food Network.*

"See ya," Kim said, and she left the garage.

Mmm, Sonya thought. *He cuts those potatoes so fast. Don't lose a finger! Straight into the pot, the water already boiling. I hope he leaves his mashed potatoes lumpy!* She pointed at a box on the counter. "Can you zoom in on that?"

"Sure." The technician pushed a little toggle switch forward, and the picture grew until the box filled the screen.

Jiffy. Cornbread, too. Man, John is trying to take me home. I hope it tastes okay. "Can I, um, can I . . ." She pointed at the toggle switch.

"Sure," he said. "You can go right and left, too." He stood. "I need a break anyway."

"Yes," Larry said. "Why don't you all take a break?"

The technicians filed out.

"You're leaving me alone in here?" Sonya asked.

"We're only leaving so you and John can be alone," Larry said.

Sort of. "Um, thanks."

"I'll be waiting outside," Larry said. "Take your time."

For the next hour, Sonya zoomed in and out, focusing on John as he worked. She watched his big ol' hands. She zoomed in on his face. She zoomed in on his chest. She zoomed in on his booty. *Now I feel like a voyeur. I wonder if I should tell him that he has a tiny hole near the back right pocket of those jeans.* She zoomed closer, the tiny hole filling the screen. *White drawers.*

The door to the garage opened, a technician entered, and Sonya quickly pulled the little toggle switch back.

"Larry told me to tell you to get ready for dinner," the technician said.

Sonya looked back at the screen at John starting to fry chicken. *Hot and fresh, too.* She looked at another screen and saw Gary putting long strips of ribs on the grill outside. *I am going to eat well tonight.* She stood. "Thanks for letting me play around."

"You get any good shots?" the technician asked.

"Shots?"

"We're always filming," he said. "Twenty-four-seven."

Which means they'll have my close-ups of John's booty. "Um, not really. I'm sure you'll get better ones. You're the professional, not me. You can just . . . trash what I've done."

Oops.

Graham stood at one end of the long dining room table, Sonya and Kim to his right and left, five covered platters spaced down the length of the table. The Team sat at the far end of the table.

"For our first challenge this week," Graham said, "the Team had to cook a meal representative of their hometowns. Jazz and Shani have no idea who cooked what."

"That's not true, Graham," Sonya said.

369

"It's what the card says for me to say," Graham said.

"Well, it's not true," Sonya said. "Shani and I watched y'all cooking. And since we know where everyone's from, we would have figured it out eventually, right? Watching y'all in the kitchen was better than watching the Food Network."

"I'm hungry," Kim said. "Let's eat."

Graham carried the first platter to them, removing the large silver cover.

"Gumbo!" Kim cried. "This yours, Tony?"

Tony nodded.

"And a po' boy," Sonya said. She looked up. "Um, I feel kind of strange eating in front of y'all. You, um, mind maybe waiting in the great room for us?" She looked at Darius. "Is that all right, Darius? Maybe you can send the feed to the big TV in there or something."

Darius sighed. "C'mon, fellas."

The Team trooped out.

"That was rude," Kim said, taking a bite of the po' boy.

"I think it's rude to eat in front of other people who aren't eating," Sonya said. "And this way, we can make comments as we eat without hurting their feelings."

"They'll see us eating on the TV," Kim said. "And they're still gonna hear what we have to say." She dipped her spoon into the gumbo and blew on it.

Sonya smiled at Darius. "Could you, um,

mute the room?"

Darius sighed and shook his head. "Sure, Jazz. Anything for you."

Darius hates me. "Thank you, Darius."

Darius said something into his headset.

"You can go, too, Darius," Sonya said.

"Thank you," Darius said, and he left.

"What's with him?" Kim asked.

"We're messing with his program, I guess," Sonya said. "He probably took hours setting up all the shots." She slipped a spoonful of gumbo into her mouth. "This gumbo is so spicy." She took a sip of ice water. "My tongue is burned."

"You kidding?" Kim said. "I could eat this gumbo all day. The po' boy is kind of bland, though."

"It's to counteract the spiciness of the gumbo," Sonya said. "Only it's not doing it very well for me." She opened up the hoagie roll. "He has red pepper in here. All of this is too spicy for me."

"And it's just right for me," Kim said.

Sonya sighed. "So we tie on Tony."

"Whatever."

They split on Gary's barbecue ribs, too.

"I like wet ribs," Kim said. "These are dry."

"I love dry ribs," Sonya said. "Less mess."

"Another tie," Kim said. "I hope we agree on something."

They also split on Justin's Philly cheesesteak.

"Why'd he put mushrooms in it?" Kim asked. "Mushrooms are nasty."

Sonya swallowed her third bite. "It's delicious! The mushrooms counteract the onions."

"And the cheese isn't American," Kim said.

"It's provolone, Shani. This is authentic."

Kim pushed her Philly away. "Gee, another tie."

They even split on Aaron's chili.

"Whoa, I'm tasting peanut butter," Kim said. "And chocolate. Very sweet. Different."

"The meat is a little too rare for me," Sonya said. "I don't think he cooked it all the way through." *He spent more time in front of the TV than in the kitchen.*

"The corn and rice are a nice touch," Kim said.

"The beans should be much softer than this," Sonya said. "He should have been up early this morning cooking them."

"Another tie?" Kim asked.

"Yes," Sonya said. *Now bring on the John.*

When Kim took off the cover, Sonya closed her eyes. *Thank You, Lord, for the food I am about to love.* She snatched a drumstick and bit into it. "Ooh, this chicken is crispy, cooked to the bone, and seasoned right." *I wonder if this is Sheila's recipe or his own? Either way, it is the bomb.*

372

"Needs more salt," Kim said, nibbling on a wing.

"You can always add more salt." Sonya took a spoonful of mashed potatoes and audibly sucked it into her mouth. "Perfect. Just the right amount of butter, salt, and pepper."

"It's lumpy," Kim said.

"Lumpy means it's real," Sonya said. She bit off half a square of cornbread. "You have to appreciate this cornbread."

"It tastes like Jiffy," Kim said. "Jiffy is easy to make."

"Ain't nothin' wrong with Jiffy." She took a forkful of greens and sucked it in. "Man, that's nice. Mixing the onions and vinegar with the greens. Strong hint of ham. Very nice."

"You act like you're tasting wine," Kim said. "These greens are nasty."

"Everything on this platter is good," Sonya said. *How can I change her mind?* "Try the chicken again."

"None of this works for me," Kim said. "TV dinners are better."

"I think this is wonderful."

Kim shook her head. "Oh, boy. Another tie. We disagreed on everything. Go figure."

Sonya smiled. "Can we at least agree that we're disagreeable?"

Kim rolled her eyes. "No."

Sonya waved her hands in the air above her head.

"What are you doing?" Kim asked.

"Getting them to come back in. Watch."

In moments, the Team reentered with Graham and Darius.

"Jazz and Shani," Graham said, "it's now time to let the Team know what you thought of their cooking."

"Tony," Sonya said, "I loved the po' boy except for the red pepper, but that gumbo singed my tongue. It was extremely hot."

"I loved 'em both, Tony," Kim said, "especially the gumbo. I love hot things that make my tongue happy."

Nasty flirt. "Gary, I love dry ribs. I want the recipe for your rub."

"But I love wet ribs, Gary, the wetter the better," Kim said. "When I eat a mess of ribs, I want to make a mess. What's the point of eating ribs if you can't lick your fingers afterward?"

"Justin, that Philly was hittin' the spot," Sonya said. "That meat was so tender!"

Kim sighed. "But did you have to put mushrooms in it? Fungus and steak should never mix."

And now for Aaron's candy chili. "Aaron, your chili was a little too sweet for me."

"I loved it, Aaron," Kim said. "I even had seconds. It was like eating a hot and spicy Reese's cup."

No, it wasn't. It was like eating a Reese's cup with pinto beans in it. "Arthur, I wish I had more room for your meal. I may sneak down later to eat some of the leftovers." *Hint.* "The whole meal reminded me of my grand-mama's kitchen. Those greens were so tender, and the chicken was banging. You have to give me that recipe, too."

Kim swiveled to face John. "Greens are nasty, Arthur, and you stunk up the whole house for the last twelve hours. That wasn't very considerate, was it? Your mashed pota-toes were way too lumpy. You didn't mash 'em up enough, you know? Your cornbread was from a box that any child could make, and the chicken was just okay. I could do bet-ter at a Popeyes or a Bojangles'."

That was harsher than it had to be. "This means that y'all tied," Sonya said. "And it also means that your poems will break the tie."

Kim stood. "Some of you had better get to work tonight, because if your poems are anything like your cooking, you're in trouble."

Friday night, while Sonya and Kim settled into a couch facing a low stage set up in front of a crackling fire in the fireplace, soft jazz music played. Lights dimmed, and a spotlight illuminated a single stool and a floor micro-phone on the stage.

Now this is romantic, Sonya thought. *And I'm nervous. Why am I nervous? I'm not read-ing a poem. I guess I'm just nervous for John.*

Lord, help his words touch Shani's heart. Or at least help them thaw it out a little.

If that's possible.

"Our first poet tonight is Gary," Graham said. "His poem is called 'You and Me.' Gary?"

Gary walked in from the kitchen and sat on the stool. "It's kind of short." He cleared his throat and read:

"I'll always stand beside you,
your strong hand in mine.

Whatever you want to do, baby,
I will always make the time.

Whatever *you* want to do, baby,
I will *always* make the time.

And if you're ever scared,
I'll hold you all night long.
Cuz, baby, when you're with me,
Ain't nothin' gonna go wrong.

Cuz, baby, when you're with *me,*
Ain't nothin' gonna *ever* go wrong."

"Thank you, Gary," Graham said. "You may return to the kitchen now."

After Gary left, Kim turned to Sonya. "Not very flowery. 'Mine' and 'time' don't rhyme."

"It was close," Sonya said. "You said it

didn't have to rhyme."

"Well, if a poem tries to rhyme," Kim said, "it should rhyme correctly. It didn't move me at all."

"It was from the heart. Kinda jazzy, bluesy. Direct. I liked it."

"It lasted fifteen seconds," Kim said. "He had days to write something that lasted fifteen seconds? A definite no from me."

And we're split again.

"Our second poet tonight is Tony," Graham said. "His poem is called *'Mon Coeur'* or 'My Heart.' Tony?"

Tony sauntered in, took the mike from the stand, and stood in front of the stool. *"Mon Coeur."* He dropped to one knee and read:

"Amour de ma vie,
je t'aime de tout mon coeur.
A toi, pour toujours
parce que il a pour réchauffer le coeur.

Love of my life,
I love you with all my heart.
I am yours forever
because love warms the heart."

"Thank you, Tony," Graham said. "You may return to the kitchen now."

After Tony left, Sonya turned to Kim. "Kind of simple, huh?" She smiled. "Though his voice could melt butter, right?"

Kim nodded.

"And he used the same word to make his rhyme." *I think.*

"The man speaks French," Kim said. "It doesn't matter what he said or how he said it. That was *so* hot. A definite yes. It made me sweat."

"But it only lasted fifteen seconds, too," Sonya said.

"I don't care," Kim said. "That poem's gonna echo in my head all night."

We're split again.

"Our third poet tonight is Justin," Graham said. "His poem is called 'Oooooh.' I hope I said that right. Justin?"

Justin ran in and wrestled the microphone from the stand. "How ya doin'?" He clapped a few times until Sonya and Kim joined in.

"Girl, you are a beauty
A real classy cutie
It ain't all about the booty
I ain't throwin' passes like Doug Flutie

Ooty oooooh . . .
Ooty oooooh . . .

Girl, it is my duty
I ain't proud or snooty
No one can call me fruity
Cuz you're my sweet patootie

378

Ooty oooooh . . .
Ooty oooooh . . ."

Justin bowed and ran back to the kitchen.

"That was . . ." Sonya doubled over in laughter. "That was hilarious!"

Even Kim was giggling. "That man is a trip. Thumbs up."

"I agree. Ooty oooooh . . ."

"Our fourth poet tonight is Aaron," Graham said. "His poem is called 'My Love.' Aaron?"

Aaron strolled in, grabbed the microphone, and knelt on the floor a foot away from Sonya and Kim.

"My love,
you're the only one I think of.
My dove,
with you I can rise above.

My dove, my dove, my *dove,*
with *you* and only *you* I can rise above.

My only love,
when push comes to shove,
I'm like a rose in a fisted glove,
and with you I can rise above.

I'm a rose, I'm a rose, I'm a *rose,*
and with *you* and only *you* I can rise
    above."

Then Aaron took and kissed each of their hands before leaving.

Sonya wiped the back of her hand on the couch.

"Um, he did graduate college, didn't he?" Kim asked.

"He played basketball for four years, but that's no guarantee of a diploma," Sonya said. "Um, wow. He had two days to do that?"

"Yeah, um . . . I didn't feel it at all." Kim looked at the back of her hand. "And the kiss was sloppy and wet."

"Do 'of' and 'love' even rhyme?" Sonya asked.

"Only on greeting cards. You're a dove? You ain't white, Jazz."

"He's a rose? He *is* thorny."

"And horny," Kim said.

No argument there. "He wasn't into this kind of challenge, was he?"

"And his chili gave me the shits this morning," Kim whispered.

"You had diarrhea?"

"No, I had the shits," Kim said. "I've been dropping the kids off the bus all day. And it came out looking like the way it went in. Sweet coming down, sour coming out."

"Ew. That's nasty."

Graham smiled at them. "Are you ready for the last poet?"

Sonya nodded. *Okay, John, turn it on.*

"Our last poet tonight is Arthur," Graham

said. "His poem is called 'Another Chance.' Arthur?"

John walked directly to the stool and sat. He adjusted the microphone slightly before reading.

"You once told me sunrises were frowns
that became fiery mouths of praise.
I miss our sunrises.

You once told me sunsets were shouts
that faded to colorful whispers echoing into
    the night.
I miss our sunsets.

The days . . . the days . . .
they go by so slowly,
the nights . . . the nights . . .
they never seem to end.

I miss our days.
I miss our nights.
I miss our sunrises.
I miss our sunsets.

You were the soul of me,
the heart of me,
the good of me,
God's gift for me.

God never let go of you, did He?

He always held your hand.

But now my hand is empty,
my days are empty,
my nights are empty,
my joy . . . empty . . .
until I stood on the beach . . . with you
and we watched a sunrise frown turn to
    praise . . .
and endless hallelujahs."

Sonya felt tears forming behind her eyes. *He wrote that with Sheila in mind, and there I was with him at the beach in the end. That was totally from the heart. Wow. Sunrise frowns and endless hallelujahs.*

After John nodded once and left, Kim grabbed Sonya's wrist. "What the hell was that about?"

More than I can ever explain to you, Kim. "Wow. That's all I can say."

Kim released Sonya's wrist. "Wow? You get it?"

Sonya wiped a tear. "Yes, and you have to try to understand the feeling. I liked it. A lot."

"You're crying?"

"It moved me, Shani." Sonya rubbed her chest. "It got me. Right here."

"It didn't do a thing for me," Kim said. "Not a thing."

"It had the most heart," Sonya said. "Believe me."

"Heart? I didn't understand a single line, much less a stanza."

Because you've never really known loss like John and I have. Sonya sighed. "So I guess that means we agree on Justin's poem."

"I guess so." Kim laughed. "You and Jumbo. What a combination. Hey, they can send you two to Sea World, and he'll be part of the whale show."

"Hush."

The Team trooped in and stood on the stage with Graham. "Ladies," Graham said, "it's now time for you to give our poets some feedback."

"Gary," Sonya said, "I liked the rhythm and the soul in your poem."

"I didn't," Kim said. "I didn't hear the rhythm, and it did nothing for my soul. It was way too short and full of lame rhymes. Saying something louder doesn't make a poem more effective."

Geez. Just say you don't like it and leave it at that. "Tony, yours sounded nice, but only the French part."

"I liked the whole thing, *mon chere,*" Kim said. "Every bit."

"Arthur, you got me in the heart." Sonya smiled at Kim. "Your poem will echo in my head long into the night."

Kim scowled. "I still don't know what all that was about, Arthur. You were way too vague. And it wasn't very poetic. No rhyme or rhythm, you know? Sunrise frowns? What medication are you on? A definite thumbs-down."

Yet Arthur is still smiling. He knew Kim wouldn't like or "get" it, but he read it anyway. "Um, Aaron, it was . . . okay. Not very, um, creative."

"I told you not to write a Hallmark card for me, Aaron, and you wrote one anyway. What's up with that? Your rhymes were lamer than lame, and that kiss? What were you thinking?"

Hmm. I was hoping she'd say more. And now for my next date. "Justin, you are a trip. Ooty oooooh!"

"It was funny, Justin," Kim said. "Ooty oooooh!"

Graham stepped to the microphone. "And the winner is . . ."

"The only one we *both* liked," Sonya said. *I hope John understands.* "Justin."

"All right!" Justin shouted. "Oh, I have to tell you that Artie helped me with some of the rhymes."

Kim sat up straighter. "Artie helped you rhyme?"

"Yeah," Justin said. "He has a huge vocabulary."

"And that means that Justin and Jazz will go out on a date tomorrow night," Graham said.

Darius counted down, the lights came up, the fire died down, and the stage disappeared within minutes.

"I don't know about you," Sonya said, "but I'm going back to the dining room."

The rest of the Team followed her.

There were no leftovers.

Except for Aaron's chili.

While the others were out by the pool, Sonya stayed behind to watch John nibbling on a drumstick.

"I really liked your poem," Sonya said. "Thanks for putting me in it."

"To be honest," John said, "I didn't start out with you in mind."

"I know. And it doesn't bother me. Really."

"But then . . . there you were on the beach with me." He smiled and put down his chicken bone. "I was saving the best for last."

"Yeah. I felt that."

He dabbed at his lips with a napkin. "I hope the hallelujah line didn't embarrass you."

"It didn't. It's good to know that you think about me."

"I was only thinking of parts of you, though."

"And those hallelujahs won't be endless," Sonya said, pushing away from the table. "There are these things called age and gravity."

"I can always use my imagination." He

closed his eyes. "Mmm. Nice."

"Stop."

He opened his eyes. "I didn't impress your sister enough to win the date, though."

"You don't have to win *her* heart."

"I wasn't trying to." He stood. "Sometimes when you lose, Sonya, you win."

Sonya watched him collect a few plates, including hers, and go into the kitchen.

Yeah, he's winning by losing. My heart just beats faster around him, gets hotter, my hands get warmer . . . and I'm going out again without him by my side.

God, I don't like irony. It's too . . . ironic. This is so twisted. The man I want to be with the most is considered a loser on TV. You know that I could lose myself with him. I know that I could. I could get lost in those brown eyes of his. I'd just like to get lost with him somewhere, Lord, on a beach watching a sunset and listening to all those endless hallelujahs.

Sometimes when you lose, you win.

He's winning, Lord.

She stood.

Oh, yeah. I was praying.

Amen.

CHAPTER 36

Justin held the door for Sonya.

"Such a gentleman," Sonya said, and Sonya got into the limo.

They had to do this four times.

For the cameras.

The lighting was wrong, the angle was wrong, the glare off the windshield was wrong, they could see the camera in the window, they couldn't hear her, the third take they had a case of the giggles . . .

The fourth time, Sonya stayed put. "Let's just go." She tapped the driver's glass, and he slid it open. "They didn't tell us where we're going."

"To Milan Vineyards over in Topanga," the driver said.

She shook her head. "I don't drink."

"Neither do I," Justin said. "*Much.* But I don't do wine at all."

"Where can we go?" Sonya asked. "I want to have some fun."

The driver turned his head. "There's always

Sea World."

Kim would love it if we did that.

"Or the San Diego Zoo," the driver said.

"I've never been to a zoo," Sonya said.

"Might be crowded," Justin said.

"Yeah," Sonya said. "They'd send those stupid cameras to follow us around. I don't want to draw attention to us."

"Yeah." Justin looked at his hands.

"Justin, I didn't mean . . ." Sonya sighed. "It's not a real date if there are cameras everywhere. My first date with Aaron taught me that. I want to be able to talk to you without someone else in my grill, you know?"

"I get you."

"Why not go to the Safari Park instead?" the driver suggested. "You can get private tours there."

"Justin? What do you think?"

"I never been on a safari," Justin said.

"Let's go on a safari, then."

Larry tapped on the window, and Sonya rolled it down. "What's the holdup?" he asked.

"We're not going to the vineyard, Larry," Sonya said. "We're going to the Safari Park."

Larry smiled. "I like that idea much better. I'll, um, reroute the camera crews to your location."

"Don't go to any trouble," Sonya said.

"I see," Larry said. "Hmm. I'll, um, I'll just

send them to the Los Angeles Zoo by mistake, then."

Sonya squeezed his hand. "Thank you, Larry."

Larry looked at the sky. "You have the right sunblock this time?"

Sonya nodded. "Right here in my fanny pack."

"Have fun," Larry said. "The, um, crew *might* catch up to you eventually, it might not."

Sonya shrugged. "At least we'll get away from them for a little while. Thanks again." She closed the window. "Let's get our safari on."

"This is gonna be great," Justin said.

And it was.

After learning how to ride an off-road Segway X2 two-wheeled personal transporter, and also learning that an off-road Segway X2 two-wheeled personal transporter could indeed support a man one hundred pounds over their supposed weight limit, Sonya and Justin took a slow, leisurely tour with their guide. They saw giraffes, rhinos, cape buffalo, ostriches, zebras, wild swine, antelope, cheetahs, lion cubs, elephants, and gazelles. A baby rhino calf took a liking to Justin just as the film crew finally arrived.

"They sent us to the wrong place twice," Darius said. "What did we miss?"

Everything! Sonya thought.

After posing with the baby rhino and a panda, Justin whispered, "Jazz, I'm real hungry."

They decided on eating at a nearby Brigantine Seafood Restaurant where they ate the light lunch combo: half a swordfish sandwich, a cup of clam chowder, and a side spinach salad. Only one camera followed them in, two little microphones clipped to the table.

"Is that going to be enough for you?" Sonya asked as she looked at Justin's empty plate and her half-full plate.

"Yeah," Justin said. "I gotta cut down. Um, thank you for the date. My first in a long time. To be honest, I've never really had a date before."

That's so . . . sweet. What will he think later when he finds out his first real date was with a forty-year-old woman? "I find that hard to believe. Never?"

"Do church dates count?" Justin asked.

"Sure. They're the best kind of date."

"I've had plenty of them," Justin said. "Just sitting with a girl in the pew isn't exactly a date in my mind, though. I mean, a date is when you're alone with someone, you know?"

"As if we're alone now." She nodded at the cameraman.

"Yeah." Justin made a face for the camera. "Jazz, I'm the guy people hang with, have fun with. I'm not the guy girls want to be alone with."

This boy is plucking at my heart. "You're fun to be with, Justin. I had real fun today. And technically this was only my second date ever."

Justin blinked. "Only your . . . second date . . . ever?"

I can't tell him about Archie. "I don't get out much."

"But you were with Aaron last week," Justin said.

"That wasn't a date. That was a photo-op for him. This was fun." She squeezed his hand. "And we have a group date at church in the morning, right?"

"Yeah." Justin looked away. "Thank you, Jazz."

"For what?"

"For making me feel special."

"You *are* special, Justin."

Justin turned back. "I mean, you didn't treat me differently because I'm the size of a rhino."

"You're a big man in many ways, Justin. A woman would be glad to have someone who has your big heart, big laugh, and big smile."

"Any woman?" Justin asked.

Danger, danger! Do not lead this wonderful man on! "Not just any woman. A woman after your heart. The right woman. The woman God made especially for you."

"How do I know which woman is for me?" Justin asked. "I mean, what if it's you?"

My heart is definitely not going this way, and I don't want to hurt him. There's something so innocent and pure in this man. I have to tell him the truth. "Justin, I like you very much."

Justin looked down. "Like."

"Hey, man, we just met," Sonya said. "And I don't like many people very much. You can ask my sister."

Justin smiled. "You're easy to like."

"Thank you."

He drank more of his ice water. "That rhino wasn't really checking me out, was it?"

"It only had eyes for you."

Justin laughed. "I need to lose more weight, huh?"

"No," Sonya said. "I can't see you skinny, for some reason."

Justin nodded. "Neither can I. Um, Jazz?"

"Yes?"

"Can I . . . hug you at the door?" Justin asked.

So sweet! "Of course," Sonya said.

And at the door, Sonya hugged Justin, the cameras mere feet away. "I had a blast, Justin."

"So did I."

She pulled his face down and kissed him on the cheek. "You earned that, man."

Justin's smile lit up the night. "Thank you." He opened the door. "See you in the morning."

"You know it."

Justin walked past the great room entrance and took the stairs three at a time.

Lord, I think I just made that man's day. Thank You for taking care of us, especially when that rhino started eyeing Justin.

CHAPTER 37

Justin floated into the room and flopped on his bed. "Wow," he said.

John looked up from his notepad, his Bible open to Nehemiah. "How'd it go?"

"Jazz is . . . Jazz is amazing."

"Yep." *I expected no less.*

"She makes you feel like you're the only person on earth, you know?" Justin said. "I've never known anyone like that. My hands were sweaty the whole time. Every time she smiled, I started acting like a kid and saying the stupidest stuff."

I know the feeling. "You were nervous."

"Yeah."

"Were you as nervous talking to the woman at church?" John asked.

Justin smiled. "You noticed, huh?"

"Hard not to."

"Yeah, at first I was nervous," Justin said. "But then we got to talking . . . and I didn't feel nervous as much. Her name is Brandy. She can sang." He rolled over and looked at the ceiling. "I know I don't have a chance with Jazz."

"We all have an equal chance," John said.

"I don't know," Justin said. "She's . . . she's a lady, and I'm just a guy, you know? She had me eating healthy at a seafood restaurant. Normally, I see food and I eat it. Today I ate right."

"She's good for the body and the soul, isn't she?"

"Yeah. And my weight. She makes me feel weightless."

"I know what you mean, man," John said.

I know exactly what you mean.

CHAPTER 38

When the alarm went off in Sonya's room at seven, Kim stirred.

"Why are you getting up so early?"

"It's Sunday," Sonya said. "And I've already been up for an hour." She took a scarf from her head. "And we are going to church."

Kim slumped back into her pillow. "*We* aren't going anywhere."

Sonya dried her ears with a towel. "There are <u>other</u> we's in the house. Justin, Gary, Tony, and John are going."

"Not Aaron?" Kim asked.

Hmm. I can't leave Kim alone in a mansion with a pool knowing there's a man with octopus hands out there. She'll put on that see-through bikini, and Aaron will be grittin' on her snake and her dragon. "I'll invite him." She put on some deodorant. "What about you?"

Kim sat and stretched. "I *guess* I'll go. What do I wear?"

Sonya pointed to the closet, her hand shaking. *God, keep me calm. She's about to go to church!* "Just pick out any of the churchy outfits in there."

Kim stood and opened the closet. "These aren't outfits, Sonya. They're uniforms."

"But they'll fit," Sonya said. *And cover up all your tattoos.*

Kim held out a black skirt. "Can you see me in this?"

"Yes." *And I'll take your picture and put it on the wall in my hallway for everyone to see.* "Now get in the shower before the men take all the hot water."

As soon as the bathroom door closed, Sonya hit her knees in front of her bed. *Thank You, Lord! Thank You, Thank You, Thank You.*

Kim stepped out of the bathroom completely naked. "Forgot a towel." She snatched a towel from the dresser. "What you doin'?"

Praying. "Saying my morning prayers."

"Oh." Kim returned to the bathroom.

And, Lord, if somehow You could perform a miracle in that bathroom this morning and have her wash off all those tattoos, I'd be eternally grateful.

Sonya dressed quickly and went to the pool, where she found Aaron reading a newspaper. "Aaron, do you want to go with us to church?"

Aaron rolled his eyes. "First Artie last Sunday, and now you."

John and I think alike, especially when we

see lost people. "Will you go?"

"Y'all are such Holy Rollers." He folded his newspaper. "Church ain't for me, Jazz. Church has never been for me."

"Why?"

"Why what?" Aaron asked.

"Why isn't church for you, Aaron?"

He dropped the newspaper to the ground. "It's a waste of time. It's a waste of a perfectly good day off."

"How often have you been to church?" Sonya asked.

Aaron tapped the arm of the chair. "Never been and don't intend to go."

"If you've never been," Sonya said, "how do you know it's a waste of time?"

Aaron blinked. "I just know, all right?"

That made no sense. "Do you believe in God?"

Aaron sighed. "No. God doesn't exist."

Yep. He's lost, all right. "How do you know that God doesn't exist?"

"Cuz of all the mess in the world," Aaron said. "War, death, poverty. All that."

"All that mess is man-made, Aaron," Sonya said. "God created a perfect world, and we messed it up, not God."

"Well, if God is truly God, He'd fix all that mess," Aaron said.

"He did fix it," Sonya said. "He sent His son, Jesus. He deserves our praise for that. And that's why I go to church. To praise Him for what He's done for me."

"Oh, right." Aaron scowled. "I'm supposed to give glory to God for what I accomplish. Where's the logic in that?"

"Where's the logic in your statement?" Sonya asked. "Didn't God give you your abilities, Aaron?"

"God didn't give me anything," Aaron said with a scowl. "I earned everything I got. Where was God when I messed up my knee, huh? Was God out there keeping me safe or healing me afterward? No."

Such bitterness. "You made it further than ninety-nine percent of the basketball players on this planet did. And God *did* heal your knee."

"Physical therapy healed my knee, not God," Aaron said. "And anyway, God could have kept me from hurting it in the first place, and then I wouldn't be here talking to you. I'd be playing in the NBA."

"But then you might not have learned perseverance, dedication, and hard work," Sonya said. "You needed to learn all that. That's why God gives us trials and tribulations."

"Well, if there is a God," Aaron said, "He doesn't like me."

That's the first true statement he's made. "You're right."

Aaron turned sharply to Sonya. "I am?"

"God doesn't like you, Aaron," Sonya said.

"He *loves* you. God may not like what you do or what you say, but God will always love you."

"Whatever." He reached down and picked up the newspaper. "Is your sermon over?"

"That wasn't a sermon, Aaron," Sonya said. "That's how I roll."

"Rolling holy all the time, huh?" Aaron said.

"It's the best way to roll."

Aaron shook his head. "Y'all have a good time."

"Go with us, Aaron."

"No."

Do I take no for his final answer? No. "At least go so you can logically say it isn't worth your time."

Aaron opened the newspaper. "You gonna ask me every week?"

"Yes."

"Don't bother, Jazz." He turned a page.

"I will ask you every Sunday." *Every Sunday that you're here, that is.* "It will make me very happy if you go with us today."

"No, thanks."

I tried, Lord. Maybe today I was just supposed to bug him about it. I'm the bug in Aaron's ear. "I'll be praying for you."

"Don't bother, Jazz," Aaron said. "There's no one to hear you."

Sonya smiled. "Then I'll just have to pray louder, huh?"

She went back to her room to check on

Kim's progress. What she saw took her breath away. *Don't overreact, Sonya. Try to act casual. This is your daughter as you've always wanted her to be. Just stand behind her at the mirror and act as if you're primping.*

"How's everything fitting?" Sonya asked. *Wow. That black skirt, that sky blue blouse, those black flats, and hose, too? Put a Bible in her hand, and she can go door to door witnessing.*

"The skirt's itchy," Kim said.

"You wearin' a slip?" Sonya said. "There's one in the drawer."

Kim opened a drawer, found the slip, and instead of removing her skirt, she wormed her way into it. "That's much better."

Sonya saw a sliver of slip showing. "Your slip is showing."

Kim wrestled it higher. "Better?"

Sonya nodded.

"How do I look?" Kim asked.

Such a loaded question. "Honestly?"

Kim's eyes dropped. "Yes."

Sonya hugged her. "You look like an angel."

Kim stepped out of the embrace and started brushing her long black hair. "You're just saying that."

"Nope." Sonya collected her Bible and purse. "See you downstairs."

" 'Kay."

Sonya had to hold on to the banister all the

way down the stairs. *I just hugged my daughter, and she didn't tense up. She let me hug her. Yeah, she turned around quick, but . . . for a moment, she wanted to be hugged. By me.*

This is going to be a very good day.

During the service at Bethel, Kim sat next to Tony and paid more attention to Tony than to the service, but that was okay. She was in the building, she was in a pew, and she was even clapping and singing. When the sermon began, Sonya sent her Bible down the row to Tony so she could share a Bible with John.

And touch him, Lord, Sonya thought. *Just to see if he's still there.*

Her hand brushed John's leg, and John shifted his weight toward her. She slid her hand under the Bible. *Is that his thumb? Yeah. My pinkie and his thumb are talking now. Oh, and now they're hugging. I hope this sermon doesn't end.*

During the benediction, Sonya slipped her hand into John's.

This is right, this is good, this is mine, she thought. *I hope this is mine. What You have for me is for me, isn't it, God?*

When the benediction ended, she slipped her hand to her side.

"Make sure you hug someone on your way out," Reverend Cox said.

She turned to John, but John was already hugging a little biddy in the row in front of them.

"You're my favorite," she said to John.

"Thank you," John said. He turned to Sonya. "I'm her favorite."

Sonya hugged John. "Mine, too," she whispered in his ear.

The little biddy touched Sonya's arm. "Who will you call a punk tomorrow night, honey?"

Sonya turned from the embrace but kept her hands on John. "I won't call any man a punk."

The little biddy smiled. "But if the shoe fits . . ."

Sonya turned to check on Kim and saw her embracing Tony for quite a long time. Gary had already gone to the back, Justin had gone to the front to talk to that singer, and only John was left in the pew.

"I, um, could use another hug, Sister Jazz," John said.

Me too. And since no one is watching us . . . She reached around him, locking her hands. "I might not let you go this time."

John pulled her closer. "Might not? This time?"

She pressed her head into his chest. "Just hold me, man." She felt his arms pulling her dangerously close. She looked up. "Any closer and I'll be behind you."

"And then you can say hallelujah," John whispered. He relaxed his grip on her. "We better get going."

She slowly slid her hands around his waist. "And you better win the next challenge. I don't want to only go on church dates, man."

"I'll try."

She fixed his tie. "Try harder."

Sonya and Kim made a huge bowl of popcorn and had a mini–slumber party in their room while the men did promos around LA.

"Since Justin is immune, who are you going to dump?" Kim asked.

Sonya threw a piece of popcorn at her. "I don't like the way you phrased that."

"You caught that, huh?" Kim said.

"Yep. Justin is a nice man. Big, but nice. Gary, too."

Kim took a sip of a Coke. "Gary is a brute."

"Gary has soul," Sonya said. "He just doesn't express himself as smoothly as you'd like him to. I'd also keep Tony."

"Yeah. He's something."

I think my baby might be sweet on Tony.

"That leaves Artie and His Heirness," Kim said. "Try to let Artie down gently."

She's just trying to bait me. "John is staying. Aaron is going."

"What? Because he wouldn't go to church with you today?"

"That's only part of it," Sonya said. "But add it up. Aaron was a jerk on our date. Aaron drinks too much. Aaron told lies about what happened on our date. Aaron made the nasty chili. Aaron wrote the fakest poem."

"But he's eye candy, Sonya," Kim said. "He's why women are watching the show."

"I'm not interested in eye candy," Sonya said. "And the arrogant way he refused my invitation to church sealed the deal. I can't abide arrogance."

"I've refused to go to church with you, too," Kim said.

"True, but you weren't so . . . angry about it." *Hmm. She was once. Even threw a shoe.* "Aaron showed me a hateful side today that was so ugly. He may be a very handsome man, but handsome is only skin deep."

"And ugly is to the bone," Kim said.

"Yep." Sonya smiled. "I'm so glad you went to church today. You don't know how happy that made me feel. What'd you think of the service?"

"It was loud."

True. "I saw you dancing."

"Hey, so I like to dance," Kim said. "That music was bangin'."

Sonya took a sip of her Sprite. "I saw you hugging on Tony, too."

"The preacher told us to," Kim said.

"In Christian love, Kim," Sonya said.

"So I was feeling especially Christian today." Kim stuck out her tongue. "You were practically grinding on Johnny Boy."

Yeah, I was. I almost popped a button on my

405

blouse. "I really like him. I hope you can accept that."

"He doesn't do anything for me," Kim said.

"He's not supposed to," Sonya said. "He makes me feel warm, you know? And Aaron only makes me feel cold. That's why he has to go."

Kim rolled her eyes. "But dumping Aaron is stupid. Aaron is the basketball player. You two can play out in your driveway or something."

"Tony is just as handsome, and Tony also has some sense," Sonya said. "You're assuming that everyone who watches the show is only interested in what they can see. Tony has substance. Tony has personality."

Kim threw a few pieces of popcorn in the air and caught them in her mouth. "Well, he is kind of . . . hot."

"And he can dance," Sonya said. "You like to dance, right?"

Kim nodded. "I'll bet Johnny Boy can't dance."

"I'm no dancer, Kim," Sonya said. "And I'm sure he can slow dance, and at my age, that's all I'd need for him to do."

Kim sighed. "I can't believe you're going to keep a punk and dump a hunk."

"John is not a punk."

Kim squinted. "When's the last time you went to an eye doctor?"

"John is a very handsome man," Sonya said.

406

And he has an amazing body for someone his age. Not an ounce of fat on him.

Kim rolled over. "You should do that Lasik surgery."

She'll never see what I see or feel what I feel. "Hush."

"So Aaron's really leaving us, huh?" Kim asked.

"Yes."

Kim threw her pillow at Sonya. "This show is going to the dogs."

Sonya fired the pillow back. "Aaron is a dog."

Kim swung her pillow at Sonya. "A cute dog."

Sonya smacked Kim hard. "Cute or not, he's still a dog."

"Ow," Kim said. "What you got in your pillow, rocks?"

"It's the same pillow as yours," Sonya said. "I just have more muscles."

Kim smiled. "No. Your pillow must be filled with your marbles, because you've definitely lost your marbles, old lady."

Sonya laughed. "At least I have some marbles to lose." She let Kim's pillow bounce off her face. *Lord, thank You for getting this child to at least act like my sister.* "I'm about to go wet a towel."

Kim jumped to her feet. "You can't hit what you can't catch, old lady." She ran out of the room.

Sonya drifted to the window, peering out in the off chance that she'd see the limo returning with "her men." Instead she saw Kim diving fully clothed into the pool. She stepped out on the balcony. "How's the water?" she yelled.

"Cold!" Kim yelled. "Come on in!"

"Be down in a minute!"

She thought briefly about putting on her swimsuit. *Nah. This is a slumber party. I'll just go in with my SpongeBob pajamas.* She froze. *And if the guys come back while we're in the pool, they're going to see a whole lot of us.*

She took her robe, just in case.

CHAPTER 39

After breakfast the next morning, while the men were again doing promos, this time at Venice Beach, Bob Freeberg came to visit. While Kim swam in her transparent green bikini, Bob and Sonya sat at a poolside table.

"So, Jazz," Bob said, "are you giving anyone the boot?"

Geez, I can see the entire dragon from here. I need to get Kim a black wool one-piece that comes down to her ankles. "You'll find out tonight, Bob."

"May I make a suggestion?" Bob asked.

"No."

"Then I'll just talk," Bob said. "Assume I'm your executive producer and that you're under contract and are supposed to listen to me."

Oh, yeah. I signed a contract. Rules are rules. "I'm listening."

"Fair enough," Bob said. "Justin has immunity, but he should stick around. Justin is very funny. Older women find him as adorable as a teddy bear. Gary is a little rough, intimidating, um, scary, but you've proven that he's also a soulful teddy bear."

A soulful teddy bear? Bob is seriously tripping.

"Aaron is closest to who you are and what you've been," Bob said. "Two athletes. In a poll we ran at the *Hunk or Punk* Web site, eighty percent think you'll pick Aaron in the end. You two seem destined to be together. He's from Houston, you played in Houston. You played in the WNBA, he almost played in the NBA. Get where I'm coming from?"

No. "Eighty percent out of how many?"

"One hundred and sixty thousand people participated in the survey," Bob said.

Geez. That's a lot of people. "Why should I care what anyone else thinks?"

"I'm just talking, okay?"

And I'm barely listening. "What about Tony?"

"Tony is a future film star," Bob said. "Smashing good looks, and forgive me, he has skin light enough that he appeals to all races."

How nice. Racism isn't dead, especially if you can cash in on it. "Really?"

"This is a business, Miss Richardson. We have to take these things into account. More white people watch TV than any other race." Bob tapped the table. "As for Arthur? I can't say much about Arthur. One percent — just *one* percent — in that survey had you two

410

together in the end."

Good thing I took that survey last night.

"He tied for last in the obstacle course challenge," Bob said. "He cooked you ordinary
food that anyone could have made. He made
you cry with his poem."

"He massaged my aching feet," Sonya said.
"He taught me how to swim. Why wasn't any
of that in the show?"

"What I'm *saying* is —"

"Going in one ear and out the other, Bob,"
Sonya interrupted. "Thanks for stopping by."

Bob stood. "Do me one favor."

"Maybe."

"Please don't dump anyone tonight," Bob
said.

"Why?"

"That will be another first for a show like
this," Bob said.

"And?"

"And the ratings, my dear," Bob said. "The
ratings."

*Oh, yes. The ratings. We must behave ac-
cording to the ratings.*

He pushed in his chair with a loud screech.
"A full fifty-two percent think you're going to
dump all but Justin and Aaron tonight."

Those people are high! "I'm not going to do
that."

"Good."

After Bob left, Larry came from the kitchen
to the pool.

"Y'all tag-teaming me, Larry?" Sonya asked.

"I am not here to kibbutz or kvetch," Larry said.

"What?"

"I'm not here to meddle or complain," Larry said. "That's what Bob does. I only want to suggest that you build up the suspense tonight. With fewer, um, players, fifteen minutes is a bit harder to fill. I'm just suggesting that you talk more."

A good suggestion. "I'll try to build up the suspense. I plan to talk the last two to death."

"Good," Larry said. "Um, which two?"

"You'll find out tonight."

Larry nodded. "I feel the suspense already."

"Quick question, Larry. Is Bob married?"

Larry nodded. "Why?"

"Does he have kids?" Sonya asked.

"Yes," Larry said. "A cute little baby girl. Clare is her name, I believe. Why do you ask?"

"I was just wondering how a man with a wife and a daughter could be so cold and calculating about romance."

Larry sighed. "It's his business to be cold and calculating."

"And what's yours?"

"Keeping things *less* cold and less calculating." He smiled. "And I have you to thank for making my job so much easier. Have a good show tonight."

"Thanks."

When Larry left, Kim slinked up out of the pool. "What'd they want?"

Geez, and she shaves down there, too. "Please put on a robe, a towel, something."

Kim looked down. "Oh." She wrapped herself in a towel. "So what'd they want?"

"They wanted a preview of tonight."

Kim smiled. "And you didn't give them one."

"Nope."

"Good." Kim opened up the towel and looked down. "Man, I need to shave again."

The first forty-five minutes of the show were hilarious. Watching men shop at Ralph's was fairly dry until John started racing around the store.

"You are a trip, Arthur," Sonya said. *And I'd love to go race-shopping with you anytime.*

When footage of Sonya zooming in on John's butt appeared, Kim shouted, "Oh my God, Jazz! What were you doing?"

Oops. Sonya winced at John, and John mouthed, "Hallelujah?"

Sonya nodded several times.

After the first batch of commercials, Kim's acidic cooking comments took center stage. Only Justin's poem ran in its entirety, and all of Kim's poetic criticisms ran.

They're turning my daughter into a shrew, Sonya thought. *How can we change that?*

Sonya's date with Justin took up only ten

minutes, but they were a fun ten minutes with several close-ups of Justin "playing" with the baby rhino. The room quieted during the conversation at the restaurant.

Wow. They ran it all. That was nice of them. That scene will endear Justin completely to America.

"Two minutes, people!" Darius yelled. "Get to your marks."

Here we go.

Sonya went to her mark, turned, and saw only Tony, John, and Gary with suitcases. *Aaron has no suitcases? Why is that? He must think he's safe. He didn't even dress up, his chest and chains hanging out of an old wife beater, Nike sweats, and Nike slides on his feet. Wow. Pride goeth before a fall, Aaron, and it's gonna be a hard fall for you tonight.*

When the lights came up and Darius finished his countdown, Sonya took a deep breath.

"Since Justin won the date this week," Graham said, "he has immunity. Justin, come join your princess."

Justin came down and gave Sonya a peck on the cheek, standing to the right of Kim.

"Jazz," Graham said, "who else is safe?"

Let's rock this. "First of all, I want all of you to know that I enjoyed my time with you this week."

"For the most part," Kim said.

"Yes, for the most part," Sonya said. "You fed me, and you read poetry to me. You filled my stomach, and you touched my heart. And I didn't get heartsick or sick sick."

"I did," Kim said. "That chili was illy."

That child has a future in TV for sure now! "I had a wonderful date with Justin at the Safari Park, and I didn't get sunburned. I'm even thinking of adopting a baby rhino." *Deep breath.* "I have thought long and hard about my decision. I've even prayed about my decision."

Bob and Darius are shaking their heads. Good.

"My director and producer don't want me to be 'religious.' I'm not religious. I'm a Christian, and I pray whenever I'm faced with a decision. After I prayed, the decision became easy."

"Um, Jazz, Justin has immunity," Graham said. "Who else is safe?"

"Don't rush me, Graham," Sonya said. "I wasn't finished."

"Oh, sorry," Graham said. "But we're kind of pressed for time, Jazz."

Sonya rolled her eyes. "No, we're not, Graham. Relax. As I was saying, I have peace that passes all understanding about this decision because I prayed about it. Okay, Graham. *Now* say your line." *For the third time.*

"Justin has immunity," Graham said. "Who else is safe?"

"Tony."

Kim smiled.

Tony came down and gave both Sonya and Kim quick hugs.

"Tony, you are a hunk," Graham said. "Jazz, who else is safe?"

"Gary."

Kim rolled her eyes.

Gary came down and hugged only Sonya. "Thank you," he whispered.

"Gary, you are a hunk," Graham said. "And that leaves only Aaron and Arthur."

Sonya left her little X and walked up to John and Aaron. *Time to build a little suspense and ruin more of Darius's carefully planned-out angles and shots.* She took John's hands. "Arthur, you really know how to win a girl's heart. You made me a home-cooked meal that truly reminded me of home. Your poem made me cry but in a good way. You wrote it from your heart to mine. I will never forget it. I am looking forward to getting to know you better." She pulled him to her and hugged him. She stepped back and squeezed his hands again. "You're safe."

John nodded, smiled, and walked around Sonya to stand beside Tony.

Sonya stepped in front of Aaron and sighed. *Should I do what Ephesians says and speak the truth in love? Or do I let him have it?* "Aaron . . ."

Aaron smiled. "Yes, Jazz?"

And now I'm blinded for real. He used all fifty of his teeth. Hmm. Doesn't Proverbs 27:5 say that "Open rebuke is better than secret love"? I guess that this man is going to get a rebuke.

"Aaron, Aaron, Aaron," Sonya said dreamily. "Where do I begin? Let's start with that chili. Your chili might have been good had you put any actual chili in it. The beans you did put in it were crunchy, not soft. I thought I was chewing on my own teeth."

Aaron's eyes widened.

"And save the peanut butter and chocolate for Reese's cups," Sonya continued. "And that 'poem' you wrote? Your poem could have been taken from the inside of any greeting card at the Dollar Store. It meant *nothing* to me, and I have a feeling that it meant nothing to you, too. As for our date last week . . ."

Aaron looked away.

"I had an absolutely *horrendous* time, but they cut and spliced it to make it look as if I had a 'magical' time," Sonya said. "There was nothing magical about our date, Aaron. I wish I knew some magic so I could have disappeared from our date. And I practically *did* disappear, didn't I? I could have vanished on our date and you never would have flinched because you had your shirt off and your drink on. The best part of the date was when it ended. And how did it end? The producers didn't want the world to know what a boozer

417

you were. They just faded it out. We know what really happened, don't we? When you tried to kiss me, I stepped far away from your whiskey-sour breath, and you missed my lips by a mile. Then you nearly kissed a ficus plant because you were so drunk."

Aaron set his jaw. "I wasn't drunk, Jazz."

"Yes, you were," Sonya said. "You could barely walk."

"I wasn't drunk," Aaron said.

"So you're normally sloppy and slurring your words?" Sonya asked.

Aaron didn't respond.

"That's what I saw," Sonya said. "But most of all, when I invited you to church yesterday morning, you didn't just turn me down — you turned God down. In Psalms it says, 'The wicked, through the pride of his countenance, will not seek after God: God is not in all his thoughts.' " *And now for the big finish.* "Aaron, you are arrogant, close-minded, and too full of yourself to have any time for me or for God. Good-bye, Aaron. I hope one day that you find what you're looking for. It will *never* be me." Sonya turned her back on him.

Aaron smiled. "You're joking, right?"

Unbelievable. "You're still here?"

"Jazz, you aren't playing the game according to the rules," Aaron said. "There are rules to this game, and you're breaking them all."

Oh, yeah? Sonya turned to face him. "There are no real rules when it comes to real relationships, Aaron. You broke quite a few rules of *decency* on our date, and I have the bruises on my body to show for it. What gave you the right to put your hands on me, especially after I asked you to stop?"

Aaron's eyes narrowed. "You wanted to be touched, Jazz."

"Not by you," Sonya said. "*Never* by you."

Aaron took a quick breath. "You're just saying that."

"Yes, I *am* just saying that," Sonya said. "And millions of people just heard me say that. And now I'm telling you to go."

Aaron slapped the back of his hand into his palm. "That's not how this game is played!"

Sonya took a step closer. "I am true to *the* game. You're only true to yourself. Now . . . shoo."

Aaron froze, looking over Sonya's head.

Darius, Bob, and Larry can't help you, boy. "Oh, that's right. You thought you were safe tonight. You didn't even pack your suitcases, did you? And that just proves what I was saying about how arrogant you are. Go inside and pack, Aaron. We'll wait for you out here."

"This ain't right," Aaron said.

"It sucks to be wrong, doesn't it?" Kim said. "Do what Jazz said to do. Shoo."

"You gonna regret this," Aaron said.

Sonya stepped to within an inch of Aaron's chest. "My only regret, Aaron, is that I couldn't get rid of you sooner." She returned to her mark.

Aaron looked at Darius, and Darius shrugged, pointing back to the house. Aaron shook his head several times and went up the sidewalk, slamming the door behind him.

"Commercial!" Darius yelled.

Kim gave Sonya some dap. "Nice job, Sis."

Bob burst from the garage and made a beeline toward Sonya.

Sonya met him halfway. "I don't want to hear it, Bob."

"I *told* you —"

"And I *told* you," Sonya interrupted. "I told you that I am what you see and hear. I will not put on another face, attitude, or appearance that isn't me. I have made my choice."

"You made the wrong choice," Bob hissed.

"For you. But this show isn't about you, is it?" *Now . . . shoo, Bob.*

Bob sighed, cursed, and strode over to Darius.

A bottled water materialized in front of Sonya's face. "You look thirsty," John whispered.

Sonya took the water, opened it, and drank half of it. "Thank you. I've never talked so much in my life."

"Yes, you have," John whispered. "On the couch. In the pool. See you in the kitchen."

"Why the kitchen?" Sonya asked.

John winked. "We're celebrating." He walked away.

Sonya started for the mansion, but Larry and Bob cut her off. "Not now, guys."

Larry held out his BlackBerry. "I have the results of the online poll. Eighty percent in favor, Jazz."

Bob took the BlackBerry. "What? How many took the poll?"

"Two *million*, Bob."

Bob blinked. "That fast?"

"As soon as Jazz started in on Aaron," Larry said, "the numbers rose exponentially. They must have known what was coming."

Bob stared at the BlackBerry. "Two . . . *million?*"

That means one point six million think I was right, Sonya thought. *It also means there are four hundred thousand misguided souls out there. Hmm. Probably Aaron's relatives or the state of Texas taking the poll again and again.* "Anything else, Bob?"

Bob handed the BlackBerry to Larry. "No. Um, nothing else." Bob wandered away.

"What's his deal?" Kim asked.

"Jazz, Shani," Larry said, "if two *million* people were online and watching TV simultaneously, how many more millions were *only* watching the show?"

"I don't know," Sonya said. "More than two million?"

Larry nodded. "Many, *many* more. Sonya, we may have the number-one show on TV

421

this week. We may be bigger than the NFL playoffs. That doesn't happen. *Ever.*"

Cool. "See what happens when you do the right thing?" *And this is cause for celebration, too.* "I'm, um, I'm going to the kitchen."

"What for?" Kim asked.

"To celebrate," Sonya whispered.

Their celebration consisted of popcorn, tortilla chips, seven-layer dip, bottled water, fruit smoothies, and a Spades tournament.

Sonya tried to teach Kim to play, but it was a lost cause. They lost badly to Justin and John and even worse to Tony and Gary. After the men split two games, they played the rubber match while Sonya circled the table and Kim flirted with Tony.

"Tony," Justin said, "you keep dealing me *feet* instead of hands. I got maybe one here, Artie."

"Want to concede the victory?" Tony asked.

"No," John said. "We're all right, Justin. I have seven and a possible here."

Justin looked at the score sheet. "They only need forty points, yo. All they have to do is go board."

"Let 'em," John said. "If we take the rest, we win by ten. We bid nine. Y'all goin' board?"

Tony looked again at his cards. "What you got, Gary?"

"Two and a possible," Gary said.

"So do I," Tony said. "Should we just go board?"

"Your call," Gary said.

"If I bid five and we don't make it, they win," Tony said. "If I bid board and they make it, they win. If I bid five and we get five, we win. If I go board and we get five, we win."

Gary shrugged. "Go board, then."

Tony tapped his cards on the table. "We're going board."

Sonya circled the table, analyzing hands. *Justin has a* stank *foot of a hand. Only one little spade and a queen of clubs that* might *get him one. Tony and Gary are right about their bids, and it's possible those possibles of theirs will cancel themselves out if diamonds goes through without trump three times. John won't let me see his cards, but if the other hands are any indication, he might have eight books in there — but only as long as he keeps the lead.*

"My lead," John said, and he threw out a ten of clubs.

What's he doing? Why didn't he lead an ace? I sometimes throw low on my weakest suit, but not when I've bid eight. Gary throws a king, Justin a nine, Tony the ace.

"Sorry, Gary," Tony said.

And that means Tony is out of clubs. Now Justin's queen is useless. They are so set!

Tony led the ace of hearts, and John

trumped it.

"Damn," Tony said.

Ah, John has no hearts. Maybe he does have a chance.

John collected the book. "I mean no disrespect, but I might have the rest."

Tony stared at his hand. "No way, man. Play your cards."

John sighed. "All right." John played the big joker, the little joker, the ace of spades, and the king of spades.

Uh-oh. Spades are done. What's John doing?

"That's five," John said, straightening the books.

Justin smiled. "Four more, big daddy!"

John threw out an eight of clubs.

Justin's queen won the book.

How did John know?

"That's six," Justin said. He studied his hand. "No hearts, no trumps . . ." He looked up at the ceiling. "This has to be the card." He threw out the five of clubs. "Tell me I'm right."

John smiled. "You're right." He took the book with the jack of clubs. "Does anybody have clubs?"

Three heads shaking.

John nodded. "So these three clubs are good." He laid them on the table. "That makes, um, eleven, I think." He flipped up his last card, an eight of diamonds. "Y'all can have that one."

424

Justin jumped up, high-fiving John. "We are the champions!"

Tony threw his remaining cards on the table. "How'd he do that? He bid nine and led off with a measly little ten of clubs."

John smiled at Sonya. "I knew I couldn't pull out the big guns at the beginning because I didn't have any off aces, just some high spades and a slew of clubs. I had to draw out the spades so my clubs would go through. I'm glad Justin didn't play a red card or we'd have been sunk. I had to disarm you all first, you know?"

Sneaky devil. Smart, too. John is always full of surprises. He's quite a disarming man.

Quite a charming, disarming man.

He still should have been set.

CHAPTER 40

Bubble Bill and Juicy went at it early the next morning on the radio.

"She dumped the ballplayer?" Bubble Bill said. "Is she crazy? She lost all her credibility right there."

"I'm surprised you know that word," Juicy said.

"Just don't ask me to spell it," Bubble Bill said. "Maybe Jazz was a late bloomer who got burned by some players before, and last night she got her revenge on all of them. Now look who's left. The white boy, a thug, a gay guy, and a fat guy."

"Who's the gay guy?" Juicy asked.

"Tony's gay," Bubble Bill said.

"Tony's not gay," Juicy said.

"You hear his voice when he read that poem? He's gay."

"That's what French sounds like," Juicy said.

"Well, French sounds gay to me. The only reason she's keeping the white guy is so white people will tune in to watch and they won't lose their sponsors."

"Maybe Jazz actually likes him," Juicy said. "Ever think of that?"

"Puh-lease," Bubble Bill wheezed. "They're probably paying her extra *not* to dump him."

"You don't believe in love, do you, Bubble Bill?"

"Hell no, Juicy. No one finds true love on these shows. But you watch. As soon as she dumps Arthur, the ratings will tank."

"My money's on him," Juicy said.

"You gonna be broke, Juicy."

"There's just something about his eyes," Juicy said. "I can't explain it."

"You sound like you're in love with him, Juicy."

"He's deep," Juicy said. "I like deep."

"Deep, huh?" Bubble Bill said. "Dense is more like it. And why'd they pick such a Holy Roller for a princess? Dag, she makes the Church Lady look hot."

"The Church Lady was Dana Carvey in drag," Juicy said.

"That's what I'm sayin'!"

"You're just mad that Jazz told Aaron the truth about himself," Juicy said. "I'm glad she told him off."

"But she had a good date," Bubble Bill said. "She was smiling out on that boat. She was always looking at him and smiling."

"Bubble Bill, she was squinting. And what

about that date? They couldn't have shown the entire date. She looked so bored in what they did show."

"She was pensive," Bubble Bill said.

"You know that word, too?" Juicy asked.

"Yes, though I don't know what it means," Bubble Bill said.

"Aaron only talked about himself the entire time and showed no interest in Jazz," Juicy said. "He always seemed to make sure his good side was framed in the camera at all times. She had much more fun with Justin."

"I couldn't tell him apart from the rhinoceros."

"You're bigger than he is, Bubble Bill."

"Ha, ha." Bubble Bill rang a bell. "But, Juicy, you're still missing the point. Aaron was the ballplayer. He was the stud. He was the only hunk left."

"They're all handsome men," Juicy said.

"You only say that because you're as hard up as Jazz is," Bubble Bill said. "She probably couldn't handle Aaron anyway. Aaron was a man."

"Lame date. Lame chili. Lame poem. Aaron was lame."

"And Arthur isn't lame?"

"No."

Bubble Bill laughed. "How can you still be rootin' for the white guy, Juicy. He's at least fifty."

"Well, if he's older than thirty, he wears it

well," Juicy said. "I'd go out with him."

"You went out with me once, and that ain't sayin' much."

Juicy groaned. "We never went out, Bubble Bill."

"Must have been another Juicy, then," Bubble Bill said. "Speaking of juicy, the white boy's chicken wasn't juicy at all."

"It was crisp and cooked, Bubble Bill," Juicy said.

"I'll bet they added sound effects to make it sound crispy," Bubble Bill said. "You know us white folks don't make anything crisp but twenty-dollar bills."

"The chicken looked fine," Juicy said. "I love a man who can cook in places other than the bedroom."

"Juicy, you'd love a man who didn't throw up on you on a date —"

Sonya snapped off the radio. "All because I told Aaron the truth about himself. At least Juicy understands." She leaned back on two pillows propped against her headboard.

"And Juicy is a sister," Kim said from her perch on the dresser. "What's she doing on that redneck's show anyway?"

"What does her race have to do with anything?" Sonya asked.

"Bubble Bill is sloppy and white," Kim said, "and he disagreed with your decision."

"And your point is?"

"I'm just saying . . . that even white people

don't understand you keeping John."

One sloppy white man. "Bubble Bill does not speak for all white people. He can barely speak for himself. You think I did the wrong thing?"

"No," Kim said. "I'm just saying that you could have let Aaron down more gently."

"This, coming from you. You don't pull any punches."

Kim slid off the dresser and picked up her hair. "But that's *me,* Sonya. I've never heard *you* be so mean. You're turning into a diva." She threw on her hair.

Look who's the diva now. "No, I'm not. I'm being my ordinary, *honest* self."

"Couldn't you have let Aaron go with a smile on his face?" Kim asked.

No. His teeth blinded me enough as it was.

Kim began to brush her hair. "You could have massaged his ego a little, told him he was hot but that you didn't have any chemistry, you know, lied to his face like normal bachelorettes do on these shows."

And that wouldn't have been honest. "Aaron's ego is far too big for anyone to massage. A hundred women couldn't massage his ego with *both* hands. And anyway, there's probably some hoochie out there right now consoling him. 'Oh, you poor, poor baby. Let me help you get over the *truth* that woman said about you. Hey, that's a really cool mermaid you have there. What's her name?' "

"Sonya, you're tripping." Kim dropped her brush and walked over to the window.

Sonya shook her head. "Aaron is going to milk my rejection of him into a whole lot of draws. Bob Freeberg is probably negotiating with him right now for another show all about him in the future."

"I'd go on that show," Kim said.

"Would you? Tony might not like it."

Kim opened the curtains wider. "Why would I care what Tony thought?"

"You like him, that's why."

Kim turned. "Tony's okay. That's all. He's just . . . okay."

"Uh-huh."

"Tony only likes the hair and what he can see."

"Like someone else I know in this very room." *And there isn't much else left for Tony to see.*

"You think I only go for eye candy, don't you?" Kim asked.

"Yes." *And the sour variety, too.* "John is white. Aaron is a hunk. Gary's too dark. Justin's too fat. You let your eyes make your decisions for you."

Kim turned back to the window. "So?"

"So in order to attract 'okay' Tony, let your hair down, don't even wear it, see with your heart instead of your eyes, and be you," Sonya said. "And if he's still attracted to you after this monumental change . . ."

Kim turned back sharply. "What?"

She's actually listening? Cool. "If he's still attracted to you, we'll get him checked out psychologically."

"Hey! That wasn't nice!"

Sonya grabbed her pillow. "Then do something about it."

Kim picked up a pillow.

Half an hour later, down feathers filled their room.

CHAPTER 41

Once they had run out of pillows to break open, Sonya rested on her bed in a pile of feathers. "For the next challenge, I want them to fix something."

"Like what?" Kim said. "These pillows? That would be fun to watch."

"Like, oh, a clogged toilet or a sink or even fix a flat tire," Sonya said. "You know, the stuff real men fix every day."

Kim blew a feather off her nose. "I can't see any of them doing that."

I can. John is a handyman. "Then we'll do it. It will be good comedy."

"I meant the producers, Sonya. Where's the romance in fixing a clogged toilet? Can they even show shit on TV?"

Yeah. That's nasty. "A flat tire, then."

"Isn't that what Triple-A is for?" Kim asked.

She has an argument for every one of my arguments. "I'm just saying that a real man should know how to fix stuff."

Kim shook out her bedspread, feathers

floating into the air. "Shoot, if a man can fix me some microwave popcorn, I'm straight."

"You need to raise your expectations, Kim."

"Okay, have them do some ironing," Kim said. "I have never met a man who could iron very well."

Wrinkled John ironing? He's full of surprises. An iron is really just another tool, if you think about it. "All right then, our next challenge will be for them to do some ironing." *I hope he can iron.*

John couldn't iron.

A lick.

John came in dead last, the outfit he ironed looking worse *after* he ironed it, the white bed sheet sporting several scorch marks.

Since the challenge ended in a tie between Tony (Kim's choice) and Justin (Sonya's choice), Bob appeared.

"You have to break the tie, Jazz," Bob said.

"Why?" Sonya asked. "They both won."

"Just . . . make a decision," Bob said. "You've already gone out with Justin. Say Tony wins this one."

"I won't," Sonya said. "Justin kicked butt on the outfit, and Tony kicked butt on the bed sheet. Either both Tony and Justin go on our date or no one goes on *any* date."

"You want to go out on a date with two men?" Bob asked. "Aren't you worried about your reputation? A single woman out with *two* men?"

"I go to church every Sunday with *four* men, Bob," Sonya said. "What's your point?"

Bob closed his eyes. "Jazz, you *have* to pick one. You already went out with Justin, so it's Tony's turn."

"It's no one's turn," Sonya said. "They tied for first. They both must go."

"No."

Oh well. "Then we don't go. Have fun filling up forty-five minutes before the elimination."

"Okay, okay." Bob sighed. "The three of you can go to the winery you skipped out on last week."

"No way," Sonya said. "No winery."

"I'm letting you go on your double date," Bob said. "Work with me here. Compromise."

"No," Sonya said. "I guess we'll just lounge around the pool for a few days, maybe play some cards, eat leftovers."

"Miss Richardson," Bob whispered, "please be reasonable."

"I'm actually being very reasonable," Sonya said. "Has anyone on a show like this ever done three on a date?"

Bob took a breath and held it. "No." Bob smiled. "Not yet."

"So we'll be the first. We're always breaking new ground, aren't we, Bob?"

Bob shook his head. "Whether I want us to

or not, right? Well, what do *you* want to do on your date?"

"I want to go . . ." *What haven't I done in a long time?* "I want to go fishing."

Bob's eyes popped. "Fishing? I'd think the last thing you'd want to do is get on another boat."

"I'll be better prepared this time," Sonya said. "Sunscreen, a hat, long sleeves. And I know I'll have two men who will pay attention to me."

"Fishing, huh?" Bob said.

I am wearing this man out. "Yes, Bob, fishing. Just like I'm fishing for a man."

Bob smiled. "A metaphor."

"Yes," Sonya said. "A metaphor, Bob. TV shows still use metaphors occasionally, don't they?"

Bob nodded. "Yes. We do." He shook his head. "You're a piece of work."

Sonya winked. "And I work for peace, too. Now if you will excuse me." *I have to go rag on John.* She caught up to John in the kitchen, where he was making Sloppy Joes.

"Don't say it," John said.

"Say what?" Sonya asked.

"Something like, 'Who taught you how to iron?' "

He read my mind. "Sheila did all your ironing."

John nodded. "She tried to teach me how

436

to once, and, well, the results back then were actually better than the results were today."

Sonya moved close enough to smell John's neck. *I need to know what his cologne is. It's so fresh.* "I tried to do an, um, handyman-type challenge this time," she whispered, "but a clogged toilet wouldn't make for good TV."

John turned from the stove. "Don't go to any trouble on my behalf."

"But I miss talking to you." *And having you touch me.*

John smiled. "We're talking now, right?"

"Not like before."

"I'm a patient man," John said. "What does the Bible say? 'Tribulation worketh patience, and patience, experience, and experience, hope.' I hope to win a challenge soon."

"I hope so, too."

"I hear you're going fishing," John said. "Have fun. If you catch it, I'll cook it for you."

"Deal."

Sonya, Justin, and Tony went to Newport Beach and Davey's Locker to take the sixty-foot *Hercules* out on the high seas to San Clemente Island. They bragged about how many fish they had caught in their lives, how adept they were at fishing, how great it would be to pose in front of a marlin.

They caught one fish. It weighed slightly under two pounds.

The captain promised an abundance of swordfish, shark, bonito, tuna, snook, and yellowtail. After nine hours of feeding pounds of anchovies to the fish and losing several big ones, Sonya caught a little two-pound sea bass that reminded her of Aaron. Though she wanted John to cook it up for her, she let it return to the deep.

Including the production costs of the film crew, boat and fishing rig rental, and all those anchovies for bait, the little bass cost Warner Bros. about sixty thousand dollars a pound.

Back on shore, they ate at Hokkaido Seafood Buffet, an irony not lost on anyone. While Justin and Tony pigged out on crab, New York steak, and yellowtail sushi, Sonya stuck to salads and an order of honey-glazed shrimp.

At the door to the mansion, they did a group hug for the camera.

Eww, Sonya thought. *We smell like anchovies.* "Fellas, I need a bath."

"We could go sit in the hot tub," Justin said.

"No way," Sonya said. "We'd turn that hot tub into anchovy soup."

Chapter 42

As Justin and Tony showered off nine hours of fishing funk, Gary and John had a quiet talk in John's room.

"If both Tony and Justin have immunity, that leaves you and me," Gary said. "I haven't exactly impressed anyone, especially Shani."

"Ah," John said, "but I burned the sheets."

"I don't know how you didn't see the flames, man," Gary said. "The smoke detectors were going off."

John smiled. "Maybe I didn't want to win that one."

Gary widened his eyes. "You tanked it?"

John shrugged. "I didn't use enough starch, I guess. But when I saw y'all putting razor-thin creases in those pants, I knew I was sunk. So I had a little fun."

"Why'd you do that, man?" Gary asked. "Don't you want a date with Jazz?"

"Sure."

"You're going about it a strange way," Gary said. "She really digs you, man."

"I know." *And I dig her.* "Maybe I'm just making Jazz sweat a little, you know, putting her on the spot."

"But she has to eliminate someone," Gary said. "And if she digs you, it has to be me."

"Not necessarily," John said. "She might not eliminate anyone."

"You think?"

John shrugged. "Today's date was a first. If she keeps everyone, that would be a first, too. I think Jazz likes breaking new ground."

"I hope you're right," Gary said.

I hope so, too.

It was much quieter at Bethel Sunday morning, and Sonya seemed to notice. Instead of whispering during the service, she wrote a note to John on the back of the church bulletin.

What's wrong?

John wrote back:

Thinking @ 2morrow nite

And then they had a conversation.

U R safe

I shouldn't B

U R

Y

I like u. I like having u @

I burn things

Cuz U R hot

So R U

How hot?

Scalding

LOL

What @ Gary

He's safe 2

Which means . . .

We R family now

We R

Yes! Can't break up family

Right

U OK now

Yes wish I could hold yr hand

John took Sonya's hand and pulled it under his Bible as an old Sisters Sledge song rolled through his mind . . . *We are family . . .*

Only John and Gary had packed bags in the driveway Monday night, Tony and Justin flanking Sonya and Shani.

"Both Tony and Justin have immunity this week," Graham said. "Jazz, who's safe?"

All of us, John thought. *We are family.*

Sonya smiled at John. "Gary."

Oh, that wasn't nice, John thought. *The old smile at one man and make the other man's day. And she thinks* I'm *the one making her wait.*

"Gary, you are a hunk," Graham said, smiling. "And *that* means that *Arthur* is —"

"Safe as well," Sonya interrupted.

Always keep 'em guessing, huh, Sonya? Thank You, Lord. I owe You another one. Hmm. I better get down there.

"They're *all* safe, Jazz?" Graham asked as John strolled down. "But Arthur torched the sheets! He ruined a pair of Theory pants and a Ralph Lauren shirt! He came in dead *last* in the challenge!"

Sonya smiled. "I'm not done with him yet,

442

Graham."

John went to Sonya and hugged her, brushing his lips against her ear as he whispered, "You kept me waiting a long time."

"Look who's talking," Sonya whispered.

John took his place next to Gary.

"Jazz, you can't *not* eliminate someone," Graham said.

"Can't not?" Sonya said. "You can't expect me to truly know a man in only a few weeks."

"But it's part of the game," Graham said, sweat beads forming on his forehead.

"I'm keeping all my options open," Sonya said. "Anyone who plays a game keeps all the options open. And a woman can never have enough options, Graham. Women shouldn't be forced to make snap decisions, especially if a man is doing the forcing."

"Then what's the point of doing challenges?" Graham asked.

Yeah, John thought. *Why can't I just go out with you without the challenge?*

"The point of the challenges is education, Graham," Sonya said. "I am *learning* about each of these men. They have all tried their hardest. Yes, Arthur burned the sheets. But what woman on earth would be angry if a man set her sheets on fire?"

Did she mean to say that? John thought. *I don't think she did.*

"I mean," Sonya continued, "a woman

443

could always use another set of new sheets, right? And if she gets new sheets . . ." Sonya turned to Shani.

"Then she'd have to get a new comforter," Shani said. "And new pillows . . ."

"New drapes, new carpet . . ." Sonya smiled.

Then Shani actually smiled. "New blankets, new furniture, a whole new bed."

Sonya looked directly at John. "Arthur is just a bedroom makeover waiting to happen."

Nice save, Sonya, John thought. *What does a bedroom makeover cost? It must be expensive.*

After the lights dimmed and winked out, Bob and Larry approached Sonya, Bob with his usual anger and Larry with the all-important online information on his Black-Berry.

"You are bound and determined to change all the rules, aren't you?" Bob asked. "You were supposed to dump either Gary or Arthur, but, no, you can't make up your mind! You're destroying the integrity of the show!"

"You *told* me to keep them for a few weeks, Bob," Sonya said. "So I've kept them all for another week. And I did make up my mind, Bob. I *decided* to keep them both."

"I never said . . ." Bob blinked. "Oh, I did, didn't I?"

"I'm glad you did, Bob," Larry said. "Online, a full ninety percent think you did the right thing, Jazz." He looked at his Black-Berry. "Listen to these comments. 'Like, Jazz is my hero,' and 'You can't rush love' and 'I hope she keeps 'em all till summer' and 'She made the only reasonable choice she could make' and 'I couldn't decide either.' " Larry shrugged. "You're a hit because you didn't make a choice."

"But I *did* make a choice," Sonya said. "I *chose* to keep them all." She smiled down at Bob. "Anything else, Bob?"

Bob shook his head and disappeared into the garage. "How are the numbers, Larry?" Kim asked.

"We're really no match for the NFL playoffs this week," Larry said, "but I'm almost positive we'll be a close second." Larry laughed. " 'What woman on earth would be angry if a man set her sheets on fire?' Classic stuff! Keep it up." Larry, too, went into the garage.

"Classic stuff," John whispered, "from a classic lady."

Sonya drew him to the pool area. "You think maybe I said something I shouldn't have said?"

"I'd like to set fire to your sheets," John said. *Whoa. And now I've said something I shouldn't have said.* "I mean, um, I'd like the opportunity to . . ." *Wrong direction.*

Sonya put her hand on his face. "I'll bet you could do it, too."

"I'm a bit out of practice . . ." *And now I'm*

saying more *things I shouldn't say. What is this woman doing to me? No. What am I allowing this woman to do to me?*

"You any good with babies?" Sonya asked.

John looked around for anyone within earshot. "From burning sheets to babies, Sonya? It is a logical progression, you know, burning up the sheets and making a baby, but . . ."

"I hope you're good with babies, John," Sonya said, "because the next challenge involves babies."

"Whose idea was this?" *Ah, the evil sister strikes.* "Shani's?"

"Mine." She bit her lower lip. "I want to know that, um, my man can do his part should I one day have a child."

"And you're, um, actually planning to have a child?" John asked.

"Two, actually," Sonya said. "A boy and a girl."

My elbows are sweating. Why are my elbows sweating? "And who's the lucky father?"

"Win the challenge," Sonya said, "and I'll let you know."

I have to win this next challenge.

CHAPTER 43

The producers asked Graham to take a few days off, and Graham was only too glad to oblige them. Darius assembled the Team in the great room Tuesday morning.

"I have created a unique challenge, guys," Sonya said, "and it's going to be fun."

"Y'all are going to be shopping at Costco today to properly equip a baby bag for an infant," Shani said.

Equipping a baby bag, John thought. *That doesn't sound too hard to do.*

"Your bag must be adequately filled to last for an eight-hour outing," Sonya said.

"You're not allowed to ask for help at Costco or go online to look at lists," Shani said. "You're completely on your own."

An eight-hour outing, huh? Babies sleep half the time, don't they? Good babies do. I will have a good baby. So I really only have to prepare for four hours of awake time. Three, no, four diapers ought to do it. Let's see . . . I'll need wipes, a burp cloth or whatever they call it, a

baby bottle, a rattle, and a pacifier. Done.
Piece of cake.

Later, each member of the Team unpacked his bag in front of Shani and Sonya.

Justin unpacked first. "I put in a full package of diapers and two packs of wipes, cuz my baby gonna like to eat." He pulled out a huge blanket. "My baby also gonna be big." He waved a stuffed rhinoceros in the air. "For entertainment." He took out a bottle, pacifier, several candy bars, and two cans of Red Bull.

"What are the candy bars for?" Shani asked.

"Me," Justin said. "For when the baby's asleep."

"And the Red Bull?" Sonya asked.

"Babies take the energy out of you, right?" Justin said. "I'm just putting some energy back."

Tony displayed a full package of diapers, one package of wipes, a change of clothes but no socks, and a bottle.

"You have a lot missing there, man," Shani said. "Good idea on the clothes, but no socks? Baby's feet gonna get cold."

"It'll be a hot day," Tony said.

"And no pacifier?" Sonya asked.

"I heard they can mess up a baby's teeth," Tony said.

"This is an infant, Tony," Shani said. "They have no teeth."

"I know that," Tony said, "so when the baby

does have teeth, they won't be messed up."

John's diaper bag contained four diapers, a package of wipes, a burp cloth, a baby bottle, a rattle, and a pacifier.

"Four diapers?" Shani said with a laugh. "Are you kidding?"

John smiled. "My baby likes to sleep. A lot."

"One pacifier?" Sonya said. "What if he drops it?"

Oops. "Um, *she* won't drop it because she's going to be a future athlete, and if she does drop it, I'll wash it off."

"No change of clothes?" Shani said. "No blanket?"

Yeah, I screwed up there. "Um, we live in the desert, and we have a swimming pool."

Shani shook her head. "Then where's your sunblock?"

Shoot! "We'll, um, we'll sit in the shade of our, um, our cactuses." *Cacti?*

Sonya sighed.

I have just lost another challenge.

"Let's see what Gary has," Shani said.

Gary counted out ten diapers. "One for each hour and two extra just in case."

I didn't know there was any math involved.

"I got wipes, diaper-rash cream," Gary said.

Oh, yeah. And I was standing right in front of that gooey stuff.

Gary pulled out two cloths. "These are for the mess." He held up a nice outfit with some tiny socks, and then he pulled out what had to be a XXXL T-shirt. "This shirt is for me in case the baby spits up on me." He pulled out and displayed sunblock, a baby bottle, and two toys. "One toy for each hand. My baby gonna be two-fisted and ambidextrous." He removed a small blanket and a stuffed teddy bear.

"So cute," Sonya said.

Oh, rub it in, why don't you!

John thought Gary was done.

Gary wasn't done.

Two pacifiers, a changing pad, a bib, and two large freezer bags followed. "For the mess, you know, the diapers and wipes and such."

John compared his little pile to Gary's huge pile. *My baby would hate me.*

Sonya stood. "Fellas, there's no doubt who the hands-down winner is on this one. Gary. You've done this before."

"Yeah, I have," Gary said.

"The rest of you . . ." Shani said. "Wow. Your babies are gonna be cryin' for most of those eight hours."

John tried to catch Sonya's eye, but Sonya wouldn't even look at him. *C'mon, Sonya,* John thought. *You would have packed the bag for me, right?*

When Sonya finally did speak to him after dinner, she only said two words — "Four diapers?" — and continued up the stairs to her room.

I should have followed Gary around, John thought. *I should have crammed one of everything from that baby section into my bag. I should have paid more attention to the mothers at New Hope. I should have —*

John sighed. *I should have researched babies the second Sonya warned me about the challenge, but that wouldn't have been fair to the other guys.*

Lord, please help her make the next challenge something physical. It is obvious that my mind is not up to these challenges.

CHAPTER 44

Instead of going on an all-day visit to David W. Streets Beverly Hills Fine Art, Galerie Michael, Spencer Jon Helfen Fine Arts, and the Sundaram Tagore Gallery in Beverly Hills, Sonya and Gary instructed their driver to take them to the Knott's Berry Farm amusement park.

And big, tough Gary was afraid to ride any of the rides.

With an enormous amount of coaxing, Sonya eventually got Gary to ride the bumper cars and the Calico Mine Ride.

Gary was unsteady on his feet after the mine ride.

He was even a little nervous going up in the Sky Cabin.

The last ride they attempted, the Dragon Swing, made Gary sick.

Gary was later, however, still able to eat a XXXL Fatburger containing twenty-four ounces of beef and a large Fat Fries at Fatburger, where a single cameraman recorded him inhaling his meal in less than five minutes.

Sonya only had the Small Fatburger and Skinny Fries.

"Sorry about the rides," Gary said, munching on some fries. "I had a time on that plane ride out here, too."

"It's okay," Sonya said. "I'm not too good with heights either. You know, it's still kind of early. We could go to a movie."

I have to make this date last longer, Sonya thought. *I have to punish John as much as I can. Four diapers? What was he thinking? I mean, I told him about the challenge. He should have been prepared. Maybe I just have to be more specific with him.*

"It's okay," Gary said. "I'm kind of tired."

But this is my *date, man!* "I did have fun."

"You probably think I'm a punk," Gary said.

"I don't think you're a punk." *I know you're a punk, but only when it comes to amusement parks. Who gets sick on the Dragon Swing? He was even looking weak in the knees in the Sky Cabin.*

"But you wanted to ride the big rides," Gary said.

I did. "The little rides are just as fun if you're with the right person."

Gary nodded. "Yeah. It's all about being with the right person. Or people. My kids are

453

going to think I'm a punk."

"I knew you had kids," Sonya said. "Your diaper bag was perfect. How many?"

"Two. Two daughters." He showed Sonya their pictures. "This one's A'isha. She's three. And this is Bria. She's twenty months."

Oh, they are so cute!

"I really miss them," Gary said. "Don't tell the producers," he whispered, "but I've been talking to them just about every night."

"As you should," Sonya said. "And don't whisper. You don't have to hide your love for your children."

"You're right." Gary smiled. "I really do love them. And, um, I'm not really that tired. I just promised I'd call them before they went to bed. With the time difference, I have to call them by six. I left my cell in my room."

Sonya looked at the cameraman in the next booth. "You can use mine." She gave Gary her phone. "Call them now."

Gary looked at the cameraman.

"Why don't you take a break, get some food," Sonya said. "You know, give the man some privacy."

"Nah, it's okay," Gary said, pressing the numbers. "Y'all can listen in." He smiled. "I mean, this way I can get my girls on TV. Hey . . . Yeah, I know it's a little early. I just went to Knott's Berry Farm . . . I won a date, can you believe that? For properly filling a diaper bag . . . You taught me well."

That has to be his baby mama, Sonya thought, *and is that some . . .* like *in his voice? I think it is. There's some definite respect there. But what's he doing on this show if he still likes her? Maybe they parted as friends. Hmm. Who does that anymore?*

"Put A'isha and Bria on the phone," Gary said. "Hey, sweeties, it's Daddy."

This is too . . . This is something I could have done . . . Sonya stood. "I'll give you some privacy, Gary. I'll be out in the limo."

Gary nodded. "You think I look bigger on TV? You like that doll I got you? What name did you give her? Oh, sure, we'll play when I get home . . ."

Sonya stepped over to the cameraman. "C'mon."

The cameraman tilted down the camera. "I'll get something to eat."

Sonya sat in the limo thinking about Kim. *All those little moments I missed with Kim. I missed seeing her waking up, missed her running downstairs at Christmas, missed her birthdays, missed . . . too much. And here's Gary keeping his kids in his mind all the time. He wasn't brooding before. He was just missing his kids. Maybe that's what I was doing during my playing days, too. Brooding. Missing my little sweetie.*

Gary came to the limo, got in, and returned Sonya's phone. "Thanks."

The limo pulled away.

"Why'd you come on this show?" Sonya asked.

"Like the rest of the guys did, I guess," Gary said. "Exposure. Maybe I could make some more money for my kids, you know? I did some modeling for Casual Male XL to make a few extra bucks, and a friend of mine convinced me I had a shot to do TV because of my looks and my voice. The producers of this show came to Memphis, and I talked to the old guy."

"Larry."

"Yeah," Gary said. "He loves them shorts, doesn't he?"

"Unfortunately."

"I didn't expect to be picked," Gary said. "I'm kind of intimidating."

"In looks only." *Should I tell him? Why not?* "Shani calls you 'Wider Wesley.' She thinks you look like a bigger Wesley Snipes."

"I've heard that before," Gary said. "Not true, though."

So humble. "How are your kids?"

"Good," Gary said. "Real good. They miss me."

"There's a lot to miss."

Gary smiled. "She makes jokes."

"I didn't mean your size, Gary," Sonya said. "I bet you're a great father."

"I try." He looked down. "You won't tell the fellas about, um, me not riding the rides,

456

will you?"

"I'm sure it will be on the recap Monday night." *It might even* be *the recap.*

"Oh, yeah," Gary said. "Think they'll make me look like a punk?"

Sonya shrugged. "They might."

"I can take it."

And take it, he did.

After twenty minutes of the baby bag reveals and shots of the Team's promos at Venice Beach, a full twenty-five minutes were devoted to Gary's hesitance, fear, and vomiting, the last scene near the Dragon Swing running several times in slower and slower motion. What made the date one of the most memorable moments in television history, however, was Gary's phone call to his daughters. The big, hulking man afraid to ride a rollercoaster was desperately in love with his kids, and the camera captured it all.

The elimination was nearly a repeat of the previous week.

"Gary has immunity this week," Graham said. "Jazz, who else is safe?"

Sonya skipped the suspense. "They're all safe, Graham."

Darius threw his clipboard into the pool. It floated for a moment before sinking.

Tony, John, and Justin gave Sonya hugs. Only Tony smiled at Shani.

"Um, Jazz, we have ten more minutes to fill," Graham said.

"I'll fill them, Graham." *I have a lot to say tonight.* She walked toward the lights. "They're all amazing men, and I still need them all. Even the one who only put four diapers in his bag. What was he thinking?" She looked at John and closed her eyes, shaking her head.

"But we lived in the desert," John said.

Sonya opened her eyes. "Uh-huh. Even babies in the desert need more than four diapers over an eight-hour period." She looked into the camera. "None of these men will ever be punks, even if three of them can't fill a baby bag properly. Red Bull, Justin? Really? No socks, Tony? Really? And Gary isn't a punk for not riding the big rides. I know some of you are out there thinking he is. He's not. He and I could have gone to a movie after our fun at Knott's Berry Farm, but he was more interested in talking to his daughters. I'm not angry or upset about that at all. In fact, I am *overjoyed* that there are men in this world who are *that* interested in their children. He has been calling them every night, even though it's against the rules of this show. He knew that if he were caught, he'd have to leave. He called anyway. That's love." *And I'm about to cry. Geez.* "Before you judge any one of these men, judge the whole man." She smiled. "And I'm just not through judging them yet."

CHAPTER 45

How can I get John to win a challenge? Sonya thought. *He said he could shoot free throws, and that's what we'll do.*

They went to an outdoor court at Knapp Ranch Park in nearby West Hills on a chilly, blustery day. Kim was poorly dressed for the weather, wearing only a tight white T-shirt and some tighter jean shorts. The rest were kitted out nicely in Nike sweat suits, and this time John wore the basketball shoes Nike provided.

John almost looks athletic, Sonya thought. *Lord, help him make his shots today.*

While Gary and Justin threw up some seriously loud bricks and made only half of their twenty shots, Tony made eighteen and John made seventeen, most of them swishes.

John can *shoot free throws, and he has excellent form. More importantly, John is in second place! For the first time!*

In the second round, both John and Tony made nine out of ten.

John is . . . still in second place. Geez, Tony, screw up, why don't you. It's John's turn, not yours. My daughter wants you, not me, anyway.

"I'm freezing, Jazz," Kim said. "Let's end this thing. Tony wins. He made twenty-seven out of thirty."

"They *tied* in round two," Sonya said. "Okay, um, for round three we'll shoot one shot at a time. The first person to miss loses."

For the next *fifteen* minutes, neither Tony nor John missed a shot. *Incredible! What was that, thirty in a row? C'mon, wind, knock Tony's ball out!*

The wind wouldn't cooperate.

Those are some of the most forgiving rims I've ever seen! Just about any shot that hits the rim goes in.

"Jazz, come on," Kim said, her teeth chattering. "Let's end this thing."

"I wasn't the one who dressed for a day at the beach," Sonya said. "I told you to wear sweats."

"The sun was out," Kim said.

"And I'm not ending this thing and declaring a winner because they're both on a roll."

"Well, take 'em both out or something," Kim said.

No way. I want John all to myself. "Um, okay, since y'all don't want to miss, we'll do the next ones . . . with your eyes closed."

John smiled. "That's what I've been doing."

No, he hasn't. He squints.

"And no peeking," Kim said. "I'm going to stand in front of each of you to check."

Tony smiled at Shani, closed his eyes, dribbled once, and shot.

Oh, geez. A swish. That ain't even right. "Did he peek, Shani?"

"Nope."

Shoot. C'mon, John. Make one for me.

John closed his eyes. "I am going by faith and not by sight, Jazz," he said, shot, and loudly banked it in.

All right! Yes! "Right off the square." *That poor backboard.* "Um, Arthur, you go first this time."

John squinted over Shani, closed his eyes, and shot the ball.

Over the backboard.

And into a tree just outside a tennis court.

Sixty feet away.

Kim clapped. "Not even close!"

What's the deal, man? No one has that much adrenaline, and the wind was in your face, man!

"C'mon, Tony!" Kim yelled.

C'mon, Tony? She knows how much I want to go out with John, but I can't say a word. I'm not supposed to show any favoritism.

Tony calmly stepped up to the line, closed his eyes . . . and made another swish.

How is that possible? This is so unfair!

"Tony wins!" Kim yelled, and she gave

Tony a hug.

Let go of my date, Kim.

Kim let go and bounced over to Sonya. "Now can we go home? My ass is frozen."

"Yes." Sonya dribbled a ball up to John, who squatted on the baseline shaking his head, a camera recording his pain. "Not bad, Arthur."

"Not good enough." He looked up.

"You made thirty in a row, man," Sonya said. "That was some nice shooting. Except for that last one."

"Sorry. I was counting on the wind to blow that one back."

"You would have needed a hurricane to blow that one back," Sonya said. *That was harsh.*

"I was, um, hyped," John said. "I don't think I've ever made that many in a row before."

"You easily made ninety, ninety-five percent of your shots," Sonya said. "You have nothing to be sorry about. Tony just got lucky."

"I didn't make the shot that mattered, though," John said.

Sonya held out her hand. "C'mon. Shani is freezing to death."

John took her hand and stood. "That wasn't very nice having us close our eyes."

"You must not have had enough faith, Brother Arthur," Sonya said.

"Oh, I had plenty of faith," John said. "I

didn't have enough wind."

She walked fast to the limo, John picking up his pace beside her. "Did you tank that shot or what, dude?" she whispered. "It's only fifteen feet to the rim. You launched it a hundred feet."

"Yes," John whispered, "I tanked it."

Sonya stopped, faced him, and grabbed him by the elbows. "Why?" she whispered.

"I wouldn't have been last," John said. "And I want to be first. If I go on a date with you before Tony does, I won't be last."

What? "What are you saying?"

" 'So the last shall be first, and the first last.' Matthew chapter twenty."

He's quoting scripture? He can't be serious! "You think that if you come in last in everything that you'll eventually win?"

"Yes."

"That makes no sense."

"Sure it does," John said. "I have to be the last to date you so that you can compare the others to me the entire time we're out so you can find them seriously lacking and find me irresistible. If I was the first to win, you'd be comparing me to *them* instead of *them* to me, which is so much more important. Of course, if I had won first, and I was really trying to with the meal and the poem, then I might have been in your head during the other dates. Hmm. That would have been —"

"I get the point," Sonya interrupted. "You

463

really believe that by losing you'll win."

"Yes," John said. "I even ruined a pair of nice pants, a shirt I could never afford, and some sheets to make sure."

Sonya narrowed her eyes. "You *can* iron?"

"Yes," John said. "Sheila taught me well. She wouldn't let me out of the house unless I looked sharp."

"And you really knew how to fill a baby bag?" Sonya asked.

"Nope," John said. "Not a clue. That was a legitimate loss. I know how I'll fill one in the future, I mean, if you're still planning on having twins."

Sonya tried not to smile, but she couldn't help it. "I didn't say twins."

John smiled. "Twins would be nice, though, huh?"

Sonya sighed. "I don't get you, man. I thought I did."

John shrugged. "Maybe I'm playing hard to get now."

Instead of spending the day at the La Brea Tar Pits and the Los Angeles County Museum of Art, Sonya and Tony attended a Lakers basketball game.

"And I don't want to be miked," she told Bob. "I want to enjoy the game."

She and Tony were fairly anonymous until their faces and names appeared on the Live 4HD scoreboard hanging over center court.

That's when the autograph seekers descended on them in waves, especially during time-outs.

This is so weird, Sonya thought. *I played ball against the LA Sparks in this very building, and no one has recognized me yet. Oops. I think I signed that one "Sonya" instead of "Jazz." Oh well.*

Tony signed more autographs than Sonya did.

Sonya had to shoo a few teenage girls away, one of whom wanted Tony to sign her thigh.

"What do you really think about my sister?" Sonya asked as the Lakers girls performed at halftime.

"She's all right," Tony said.

No, she isn't. "Tony, tell me the truth."

Tony set his Coke on the ground. "She's mean."

Yep. "As a snake?"

"As a swamp rat."

I may have to agree with that, too. "She's not mean to you, though. She liked your gumbo and your poem."

"Yeah, that's what I don't get," Tony said. "How can she be so mean and nice at the same time?"

Kim is an inconsistent person. "You mean she's mean to the others and nice to you."

"No, it's like she has a huge chip on her shoulder or something," Tony said. "She hardly ever smiles, and she's usually only smiling when she's being mean."

And I have to take some of the blame there. I helped that child to be born with that chip on her shoulder.

"Jazz, you don't seem to have an evil bone in your body," Tony said. "Um, how'd she turn out so different from you?"

"Different daddies," Sonya said. *It's partially true.*

"Oh," Tony said. "That explains it."

And different mamas, but I don't want to burden him with that. "What about her appearance?"

Tony looked away. "What about it?"

"A bit too . . . revealing, isn't she?"

Tony sighed. "I don't think I can answer this question and not make someone mad so I will plead the fifth."

"Just answer it."

Tony sighed again. "Your sister is certifiably hot. Bangin'. Drop-dead gorgeous. Sexy. A feast for the eyes. *Tres érotique.*"

"All that, huh?" *And I feel a tinge of pride now. I made a beautiful daughter.* "She's smart, too. Magna cum laude from Rutgers."

"I knew she was smart," Tony said. "She's quite a . . ."

"Handful."

Tony nodded. "You said it. I just wish she wouldn't flirt so much with me, and right in front of you."

"Excuse me?" *As if I didn't already know this.*

"Just being truthful," Tony said. "You have to appreciate that. She flirts with me all the time, and right under your nose."

"I've noticed, Tony, but who's doing most of the flirting, huh? She wouldn't flirt unless her target was interested."

Tony blushed. "I'm not supposed to be interested, right?"

"But you are."

"Yeah, but I try not to be." He picked up his Coke and took a sip.

"Tony, you can't change your nature because you're on a TV show," Sonya said. "If you're interested, you're interested, right?"

"I suppose."

She rubbed his shoulder. "You like . . . what's the word? Edgy. You like an edgy girl."

"Yeah."

"Shani has an edge all right." *And it's cutting and sharp.* "I'm pretty much her opposite, huh?"

"No," Tony said. "I think the best parts of her are in you."

What a nice thing to say. I wish it were true. "Thank you for saying that."

"So, did y'all fight a lot when you were growing up?" Tony asked.

"No. We've only begun to fight recently."

Tony laughed. "I fought all the time with my brothers and sisters. I have five brothers

467

and six sisters, and all of them are older than me."

That's a big family! "You're the baby of the family."

Tony nodded. "My oldest brother is forty-two. He's old."

And I'll be there in two years. I'll be old, too. "Tony, why are you really on this show?"

"To win."

No, he isn't. "C'mon. You said you were trying to be honest. Stay honest."

Tony turned to her. "I studied to be an actor, and although I like the theater, the pay is so much better on TV and in the movies."

"You wanted exposure."

"Yeah." Tony nodded. "Exposure. I need it, and this show provides it for me." His body jolted in the seat. "Oh, Jazz, I didn't mean that I didn't care about you."

"Don't worry yourself," Sonya said. "You didn't know me when you made the decision to be part of this show. It's okay."

"I hope I didn't offend you."

Tony has a soul. My daughter needs a soul. She needs to hang out with Tony every chance she can get. "You didn't offend me."

Tony laughed softly. "I won't get *the* hug tonight."

"*The* hug?"

"Justin and Gary call it *the* hug," Tony said. "You must do it right or something."

How else is there to do it? "You'll get your

hug, boy."

"I don't deserve it," Tony said. "I've practically told you that I think your sister is hotter than you."

"You didn't practically do nothin', man," Sonya said. "She *is* hotter than I am and will probably always be."

"In an edgy sort of way."

After the game, which the Lakers won over the Clippers in a landslide, they went to Tito's Tacos in Culver City, ate too many tacos and enchiladas, and snoozed on the ride back to the mansion. At the door, Sonya gave him her usual hug.

"Did I do it right?" Sonya asked.

Tony stepped back. "You really care about us, don't you?"

"Yes. I care about all of you," Sonya said. "So . . . did I give you *the* hug?"

"Yeah." Tony smiled.

"What did it feel like?" Sonya asked.

Tony opened the door and looked back. "It felt like . . . love."

Do I mind that a camera practically in my back pocket recorded all that? No. I do hug people with love.

Sonya stepped inside and looked up the stairs. *Kim sitting on the top step. Hmm. Waiting up for your mama and her date? I should dip Tony to the floor and kiss him passionately to mess with her.*

469

"Um, good night," Tony said.

My daughter is giving me the Evil Eye. Hmm. Sonya kissed Tony on the cheek. "Thank you for a wonderful date."

Tony nodded, waved at Kim, and went into the great room.

Sonya took her time going up the stairs and down the hall to her room, Kim trailing behind.

As soon as Kim shut the door behind them, she asked, "Well?"

How should I play this? Coy? Mysterious? Nah. I'll just play dumb. "Well what?"

"How was your date?" Kim asked.

Sonya sighed and kicked off her shoes. "I'm not even sure what the score of the game was." She smiled into the mirror. "I was so busy talking to Tony that I didn't even notice the game had ended."

"What'd you talk about?" Kim asked.

"Oh, this and that," Sonya said. She took off her jeans and put on some sweats. "Nothing you'd be interested in. I mean, we were only having a conversation. You're not one for talking, right?" She went to the bed, picked up the remote, and turned on the TV.

Kim went to the TV and hit the power button. "What'd you talk about, Sonya?"

She is really interested. "Oh, his family for one thing. He's the youngest of twelve."

"What else?"

"Let's see." *I don't want to overdo this.*

"Hmm. Oh, his career. He would rather do TV and movies than do theater. He says the pay is better."

Kim sat on the edge of Sonya's bed. "And what else?"

Should I? I think I should. "We also talked about you."

"Me?"

Sonya nodded.

"Did he bring me up or did you?" Kim asked.

This really matters to her. The order of things is important to her. "I did."

"Oh."

She seems hurt. Oh well. It's the truth.

"Why'd you bring me up?" Kim asked.

Sonya propped a pillow against the headboard. "I was curious what he thought of you."

"What does he think of me?" Kim asked quickly.

Wow! He really matters to her. "He says you are *tres érotique.*"

Kim's mouth opened and shut several times. "He said that?"

Sonya pulled the covers back and got into bed. "Yep. He also said you were mean as a swamp rat."

"I am not!" Kim yelled.

"Yeah. He got that wrong. You're mean as a junkyard dog."

"I am not," Kim said softly.

And now she's pouting. Good. "You're mean to everyone *but* Tony. You were cheering for him to win at the park."

"So?"

"So . . . he's noticed. Oh, he said you were a feast for the eyes. He must like to eat snakes and dragons, huh?" *That didn't come out right.*

"How much did y'all talk about me?" Kim asked.

"Most of the time," Sonya said. "I think he has a serious crush on you."

"Oh." Kim slid up beside Sonya, her eyes wide. "Oh no. You're not going to dump him because of that, are you?"

"I ought to," Sonya said.

"You wouldn't!" Kim cried.

"But I can't this week," Sonya said. "He has immunity."

Kim pulled the covers up to her waist. "What about next week?"

Sonya smiled. "A lot can happen in a week. Who can say?"

"So you're thinking about dumping him?" Kim asked.

Was that a tremor in her voice? I think it was. "I don't plan to. Why?"

"Well, after what he said about *me, you* should be upset," Kim said.

"But I'm not upset. He's excellent company." *And now it's time to test the waters of jealousy.* "Except when the Lakers girls came up to get his autograph. I had to excuse myself so they could all surround him. A few of them even gave him phone numbers. One of those hussies even wanted him to sign his name just above her breast, and on camera, no less."

"No, they didn't," Kim said quickly. "I watched the entire game."

So she was spying on us! "It's amazing how fast those girls can climb stairs during commercials."

Kim seemed to hold her breath. "Did they really give him their numbers?"

Sonya squeezed Kim's leg. "No, Kim. He paid attention to me and only me the entire time."

"Well . . . good."

My daughter likes a boy, and I'm here to see it. "It's a pity you don't like him. I think you two would hit it off just fine."

Kim slid out of bed and went to the window.

"Is he out there?" Sonya asked.

"Yes."

And she said that in her soft voice. I didn't know she had a soft voice. And she didn't ask which "he" I was referring to. "What's Tony doing?"

Kim turned. "He's just sitting at a table, and I think he's looking up here."

He's out there waiting on her. Sonya yawned. "I'm kind of thirsty, Kim. Could you get me a bottled water?"

"Sure," Kim said, and she ran to the door. She turned the knob, leaned over to look at herself in the mirror, fixed her hair, and zipped out.

Sonya kicked off the covers and went to the window, peeking through the curtains. In less than a minute, Kim appeared at Tony's table carrying a bottled water and an apple. She handed Tony the apple.

She's not exactly Eve, and he's not exactly Adam, but . . . Wow. She's actually shy around him. Look at the way they're smiling and not making eye contact. Yep, this is turning into a matchmaking show all right, just not the one America expects to see or will probably ever see. She turned away from the window. *I wish I could match myself with the one I want to be with, but, no, he has to win a challenge first.*

She returned to her bed, wormed under the covers, and flipped through the channels. *What might John be better at doing than the others?*

I mean, other than getting a serious grip on my heart.

CHAPTER 46

Sonya tried Putt-Putt next.

John came in last.

He actually putted better while wearing a blindfold on one of the holes.

Justin won in a landslide. "Tiger ain't got nothing on me."

She and Justin flew by helicopter to play golf at Pebble Beach, hitting balls everywhere but the short green grass in the fairway.

"If I can score under my weight for the entire round, I'll be good," Justin said.

If I can score under my age on each hole, I'll be happy, Sonya thought.

She scored under her age only three times in nine holes.

They both gave up after nine holes.

Sonya next tried the soup kitchen idea. Though they all worked extremely hard and served breakfast and lunch at the Hippie Kitchen, the staff chose Gary, mainly for his ability to lift heavy boxes and the barbecue sauce he made. Their date, originally scheduled for Cicada at a one-hundred-dollar-per-meal minimum, ended up back at the Hippie Kitchen.

"Those folks have so little," Gary said. "I can't see myself spending a hundred bucks on one meal when that kind of money can feed fifty."

"Let's have a working date, then," Sonya suggested.

After serving dinner and helping to clean up, they ate slices of apple pie in the dining area.

"How much do you miss your kids, Gary?" Sonya asked.

"A lot," Gary said. "The calls help, but not being with them is hard."

I know all about that. "Can I be honest?"

"You're always honest, Jazz," Gary said. "I really like that about you."

"I don't think I could ever tell you to leave the show, Gary. You're a good man." *A good man is so hard to find, and there should be more good men on TV every week.*

"I'm . . . Thank you."

"You're good people, Gary."

Gary smiled. "So are you, Jazz. So are you."

But late at night, Sonya only thought of John. *He's the best people. He served everyone at the Hippie Kitchen with a smile and a "God bless you" and carried trays and opened cans and did dishes and mopped. Lord, I need a challenge where he can win. Please provide that challenge to me now!*

Sorry, Lord. Also give me some patience.

Now, if You can spare it.

Sonya decided to let Kim plan the next challenge.

"I want to see if they know anything about fashion," Kim said.

And John will come in last again! "What did you have in mind?"

"I want them to dress me."

How should I take that one? "You want them to turn you into Barbie?"

"Something like that."

"Well, it sure beats having them undress you with their eyes," Sonya said. "Do they have to match the colors of your dragon and your snake? I'm sure they'll be peeking out of whatever you wear."

"I'll even wear something tasteful, okay?" Kim said.

This Sonya had to see.

CHAPTER 47

John took his place on the couch, the same couch where many weeks ago he had rubbed a woman's feet. Though Sonya had "kept" him week after week, he was starting to feel hopeless.

Maybe I'm just challenge challenged, he thought. *I hope the challenge this week involves something outdoors. Maybe we can have a weed-eating contest. I know I'd do well on that.*

"Team," Graham said, "Shani will explain this week's challenge. I don't know why we even have challenges. The losers never get booted off."

Sonya smiled. "There are no losers here, Graham. Yes, fellas, Shani has an interesting challenge for you this week. Shani?"

Shani came out wearing a white collared shirt dress that hit her just above the knee. None of her tattoos were visible, and she stood in front of them barefoot and without the wig.

Wow, John thought. *She* is *Sonya's twin. Very cute and even feminine.*

"Gentlemen," Shani said.

John sat up straighter. *She's never called us that before. We're in trouble.*

"This week you will accessorize this dress, which I found at the Gap," Shani said.

John shuddered. *Accessorize. What an evil-sounding word.*

"This dress is white," Shani said. "It shouldn't be too hard for you to accessorize."

"What's their budget?" Sonya asked.

"Thirty dollars each," Shani said. "I expect you to accessorize me from head to toe."

"Yes, Team," Graham said, "you will be shopping at The Grove in LA. Good luck, and good hunting."

I have already lost this challenge, John thought. *What's the point of even trying? I should just get her a gift card for thirty bucks to some accessory store.*

Once the Team was dropped off at The Grove, John swore he saw tumbleweeds and heard the distant sound of coyotes.

They walked four abreast through the mall, followed closely by a camera crew.

"Fellas," John said, "I've never accessorized a thing in my life."

"We know, Artie," Justin said. "I'll help you."

"Thanks," John said. "I don't even know

where to begin."

They walked each level of the mall, they looked in every window of every store, they drew a sizable following — and then they found Forever 21, the ultimate accessory store.

They commenced to rummage.

"Was it a bright white or an off white, Artie?" Justin asked.

There are different shades of white? I'm sunk.

"It was kind of cream, I think."

"The lighting in that great room turns everything amber," Justin said. "Maybe it was antique white."

"So white isn't always white?" John asked.

"Right," Justin said.

"That's just . . . wrong," John said.

Gary came to them empty-handed. "Man," he said, "there's just too many choices in here."

"Look, y'all, we're not here to impress Shani, right?" Justin asked.

"Right," John said.

"So why are we in here in the middle of all this mess?" Justin asked.

"I never knew white had so many shades," John said. He picked up a black-and-white-checkerboard beanie. He read the tag. "This is cool. It's a black-and-white earflap beanie doohickey hat. It has some shade of white in it, doesn't it?"

Tony arrived carrying a pair of brown

boots. "This is hard, man. These cost thirty-five, but they'd be perfect. What's with the hat, Artie?"

John pointed at a spot. "It has white in it."

Justin held up a scarf and read: " 'Aztec diamond shimmer shawl.' There's some white in this, but I doubt it will match the white of that dress."

"I don't know why we just don't find a Gap and borrow another dress from them," Gary said. "Then we'd be sure of the color."

Tony held up the boots. "These folded-cuff knee-high boots are tight, but I'll need five more bucks."

"I found her a pocketbook back there," Gary said. "It's huge, though. Black leather-ette satchel. It's big enough to hold a bowl-ing ball, and it'll take all my money."

Justin laughed. "We suck at this." He turned to the camera. "We *really* suck at this."

And this gives me an idea. "We could all . . . suck at this together."

Tony shook his head. "Artie, don't you want to win?"

"Like Justin said, we're not here to win Shani's heart," John said. "We're here to win Jazz. Maybe if we make Jazz laugh hard enough, she'll take all of us out."

"A group date," Justin said.

"Right," John said. "At least it's a date, right?"

"Works for me," Justin said.

John smiled at the camera. "America, is any of this accessorizing really necessary? I thought the dress looked fine like it was." He turned to the Team. "Fellas, we just have to make her accessories, um, as hideous as possible."

Justin smiled. "And that means more sequins."

"Rhinestones, too," Gary said.

"And nothing can match," Justin said.

Tony sighed. "But these boots are great."

John patted Tony on the back. "And they'll go so badly with everything we're going to choose."

"We were each supposed to accessorize her, right?" Tony asked.

"So we'll act like we didn't hear her right," Justin said. "I get tired of hearing her anyway."

"Could you at least try to match the boots?" Tony asked. "I mean, we could match this brown . . ."

Justin towered over Tony. "Dude, we know you like Shani, but come on. We're a team, remember? We got to stick together on this, and teams stick together no matter how hot the girl is."

"Yeah, but . . ." Tony looked at the camera. "America, I just don't want Shani mad at me, you know?"

"Bro," Gary said, "no matter what we do, that girl gonna be mad at us. We might as well have some fun with it."

Tony hugged the boots to his chest. "I'm keeping the boots."

"Fine," John said. He held up a sparkly clutch. "Pink okay?"

Justin handed him a floral print clutch. "Looks like my grandma's couch. Use this one instead."

John smiled. "Perfect."

Tony sighed. "Y'all are wrong."

Justin put his face in the camera lens. "Yep. We're stinkers."

Gary laughed. "I'll go get her some purple leggings."

"Oh, man," Tony said, "that dragon of hers is gonna spit fire."

"Dude," Justin said, "I would pay good money to see that."

"And now," Graham said, "it's time for the Team to accessorize Shani. Shani, will you come out?"

Sonya led Shani, wearing a blindfold, to a mirror where the wide-screen TV used to be in the great room. Once Shani was in place, the Team took out their accessories and showed them to Sonya.

Sonya had to run down to a couch to cover her face with a couch pillow so she didn't laugh too loudly.

Graham, however, was not as quiet. "Good God in heaven! What are you doing?"

Sonya put her finger to her lips.

Graham didn't get the hint. "Oh my goodness!"

"Graham, shut up," Sonya said. "Um, okay, Team." She mouthed, "Y'all are wrong," to John. "Let's accessorize Shani."

"Who's going first?" Shani asked.

"Shani," Sonya said, "I think it will be fairer if you don't know."

And now, John thought, *we're going to decorate Shani as if she were a maypole or a Christmas tree.* He, too, put his finger to his lips. He nodded at Justin.

Justin draped several garish, hot pink scarves around Shani's neck.

"Feels like silk," Shani said.

I doubt silk costs four ninety-nine. John set the black-and-white checked beanie on her head.

"A hat?" Shani said. "Nice touch."

Gary wrapped a wide, rhinestone-studded lavender belt around Shani's waist, clipping the "grandma's couch" clutch to it.

"All right," Shani said. "Whoever's doing this is doing it right."

Sonya briefly left the room to laugh in the kitchen.

Tony helped Shani into some electric blue leggings and the brown boots.

"Oh, so warm," Shani said. "And they fit just right."

Sonya returned in time to see John putting

cheap, gaudy silver and gold necklaces and bracelets on Shani, finishing with a half dozen macramé earrings in every color of the rainbow.

John mouthed, "We're done," to Sonya, and Sonya dropped her pillow and went over to Shani. "Oh, they've done so well, Shani."

"They?" Shani said.

"I mean," Sonya said, "*he* has done so well." She turned Shani to the mirror. "You can take off your blindfold now."

Shani removed her blindfold.

I didn't know a person's mouth could actually bounce *off the floor. I hope they show that in super-slow motion on Monday night.*

"Oh, hell no!" Shani screamed. She tore off the hat and earrings. "Y'all didn't even try!"

Sonya's smile broke into laughter, and the Team joined in. "But *everything* matches a white dress, Shani!"

Shani ripped off her belt and scarves. "No dates this week. None."

Sonya seemed to have recovered, though she was still dabbing at her eyes. "Can we do that?"

Graham's face turned to stone. "Y'all can do whatever y'all want. You know y'all are dead wrong."

Shani had removed all but the leggings and the boots. "Y'all need to be punished." She looked down. "Though these boots are all right."

"I told you," Tony whispered to John.

"And as punishment," Shani said, "we're all going to go see an art film."

Sonya put on the black-and-white checked beanie. "That doesn't sound like punishment."

"The movie is in Portuguese," Shani said.

"Portuguese is a beautiful language," Tony said.

"Suck-up," Justin whispered.

"And the movie takes place in the world's largest garbage dump," Shani said, "where all these accessories should be."

"Except for the boots?" Tony asked.

Shani smiled. "You get these?"

Tony nodded.

"And yet you let them do this to me?" Shani asked.

Tony winced. "I tried to get them to do it right."

Shani stalked over to Tony. "Just for that, you have to sit next to me for the entire movie, and you better not fall asleep."

At the Art Theatre in Long Beach, Sonya, Shani — wearing the white dress and the boots — and the Team watched *Waste Land,* a documentary about an artist from Brooklyn who went to his native Brazil to the world's largest garbage dump outside Rio de Janeiro. The artist photographed the *catadores,* the scavengers in the garbage, who later re-created photographic images of themselves out of the garbage. The artist sold the photographs, and the *catadores* received the money.

Amazing, John thought. *Art from waste. It's the wrong title, though. It should have been called* Saved Land. *It may have been a wasteland, but nothing was ever wasted.*

They decided to eat greasy pizza at La Rizza's afterward.

There is something extremely ironic about this, John thought.

Shani, who sat at the head of the table, stood. "I need to test y'all to see if you were paying attention."

"Why?" Sonya asked.

"This is still part of *my* challenge, Sonya," Shani said. "Hush. They embarrassed me. I'm gonna embarrass them. I want to see if they can think. Intelligence is a plus in a man, isn't it?"

"Of course," Sonya said.

"Justin," Shani said, "what did you think of the movie?"

Justin chewed and swallowed. "They were eating what people threw away. Man, that's horrible."

"Anything else?" Shani asked.

"I just can't get those images out of my mind," Justin said. "Especially because I'm eating now."

"No exposition of theme?" Shani asked.

Justin looked at John. "Huh?"

Don't look at me, man, John thought. *You're on your own with this one.*

Shani sighed. "Never mind. Tony? Your thoughts?"

Tony smiled at Sonya. "I stopped reading and just enjoyed it. Art from garbage. What a concept."

"It was amazing, wasn't it?" Shani said.

"Such beauty from the ashes, you know?" Tony said. "Like a phoenix."

Shani nodded. "And what about the phoenix, Tony?"

Tony looked at John. "Um, well, there was this bird in one of the Harry Potter movies, see, and —"

"I meant," Shani interrupted, "the real, mythological phoenix. Any thoughts on that?"

"Um, I don't . . . I think . . ." Tony shook his head. "No more thoughts."

Shani smiled at Tony anyway. "Nice try. Gary, what did you think?"

Gary shrugged. "I don't know, um . . . They were honest people. The movie was honest. It showed the good and the bad but mostly the good and bad about people in a good way."

Shani blinked. "You mind explaining what you just said?"

Gary nodded. "Yeah. I do."

"No dichotomies to explore?" Shani said. "No metaphors?"

Gary blinked at John. "None . . . I could see."

"Didn't think so." Shani turned her attention to John. "Arthur, what about you?"

I guess I'll just lay it on thick. "I saw the juxtaposition of dignity in the face of despair. Thematically, the film proves that reality can be beautiful, that even filth can be useful on a literal, visceral level in modern society. We *can* recycle ourselves. We can rise from the garbage, the ashes, the dirt, and the slime and achieve rebirth from what's been cast away. We are all phoenixes in our primal souls. They say art mirrors life, and sometimes life mirrors art. In this movie, life *is* art."

Shani had no further comments and sat, pushing a crust of pizza around her plate.

John smiled at Sonya. *That has to mean something. Shani . . . is silent. And so are the rest of the people at this table.* "Who wants the last slice?"

"Yo, Artie," Justin said. "You deep, man."

John took the last slice. "I try."

Sonya rolled her eyes.

And from now on, I have to try harder than my hardest.

Chapter 48

While Sonya tried to digest her pizza later that evening, Kim surfed the Internet.

"Geez, these people have too much time on their hands," Kim said.

"What people?" Sonya asked.

"The online people," Kim said.

"I'm an online people."

"Not like this," Kim said. "You surf. These people *submerge.*"

Sonya lay on Kim's mattress. "What are they up to?"

"They've been analyzing the order you've 'saved' them during the last four eliminations," Kim said. "Gary and Justin are either first or second one hundred percent of the time. Tony is usually third, and Johnny Boy is always last."

Always? "Maybe I'm saving the best for last."

Kim coughed. "Yeah, right. Listen to what they're saying. 'She should do it alphabetically so Arthur doesn't have to stand there fidgeting so long.' "

He's not fidgeting. His old knees are just getting tired.

" 'I feel sorry for Arthur cuz she's just stringing him along.' " Kim looked at Sonya. "Are you just stringing him along?"

"There's nothing further from the truth," Sonya said.

Kim returned to the screen. " 'I hold my breath every show, and when she keeps everybody, I breathe a sigh of relief.' That's what I'm talking about, Sonya. There are people out there who are practically *living* this show."

"But isn't that a positive thing to say?"

Kim clicked over to another Web site. "But the critics are starting to turn against you. 'People only watch to see if she keeps people, not dumps people.' "

"So? At least they're watching."

" 'While it's somewhat interesting that no one wins or loses and that Jazz refuses to break ties,' " Kim read, " 'it's been two months of the status quo — something has to give.' "

Has it been two months? It has. But I like the status quo. It's . . . comfortable.

"Listen to this one," Kim said. " 'Jazz has turned into TV's ultimate tease, and the whole show has become a tease.' "

"I am not a tease." *Am I?*

"Yeah, you are," Kim said. "Here's another:

'Yes, they've all become friends, and that's a beautiful thing, but the point of the show is for her to make decisions and she's only choosing not to decide.' "

Am I doing that? I'm making decisions. I choose for them to remain, right?

"Oh, this one is harsh," Kim said. " 'They should rename the show *Hunk* because she refuses to see the punks on the show.' "

That was harsh and totally inaccurate. None of my men are punks. "Any more?"

" '*Hunk or Punk* is quickly becoming a real-life *Friends* episode that never ends.' "

"That's not so bad," Sonya said.

"Oh, here are some more favorable ones," Kim said. " 'It's like chilling with some friends every Monday night and it shows black men can be friends with women and not be all about the drawers.' "

"Amen," Sonya said.

" 'There's something magical about the whole thing, something genuine, something real,' " Kim read. " 'Even the laughter is real.' "

Now they're talking. "Keep reading."

" 'The Team respects her so much, and she respects them even more.' "

And they deserve my respect.

"Oh," Kim said. "Here's one about me. 'Shani is a trip! She should get her own TV show.' " She giggled. "I have some fans."

And I'm your biggest fan.

Kim clicked on a few keys. "Why *do* you always choose John last?"

I honestly didn't know I did that. Hmm. "Maybe because I know he can handle the pressure, the wait, the anxiety of waiting."

"Or maybe he's an afterthought, like, oh, yeah, the white guy. Come on down."

Does it look that way? "That's not it."

"Oh, the Nielsen ratings are in," Kim said.

Whee. "What did the preselected American TV families watch last week?"

"We came in second." Kim bit her lip. "Second, Sonya."

"Okay." *That's still crazy good according to Larry.*

"Except for football games, which don't count in my mind, we've been first for nine straight weeks," Kim said. "We're slipping."

I am not going to get caught up in this hoopla. "What beat us?"

Kim nodded. "It's not so bad. We came in second to *This Is It.* Every time Michael Jackson comes on, the world still stops."

"Being second to the King of Pop isn't all that bad, is it?" Sonya asked.

"No, I suppose not, but it wasn't the first time it was on network TV," Kim said.

"The numbers were still good, right?"

Kim nodded. "They actually went up a few hundred thousand, but *NCIS* is creeping up on us."

"We're fine," Sonya said. "And when *NCIS*

becomes a series of reruns, we'll be back on top."

"Yeah, but . . ." Kim sighed. "The show is getting stale, Sonya. You really should let go of somebody soon."

"What do you mean, let go?" Sonya asked.

"You're holding on to all of them," Kim said. "Drop somebody. It's getting boring."

"No, it isn't." *Not for me!* "More people are tuning in to watch every week. Larry told me our numbers haven't begun to plateau yet."

"But the reviews are starting to turn against you," Kim said.

I didn't hear that many negative reviews. "Those reviewers are reviewing reality, and they're not used to reviewing reality. They're used to reviewing fantasy, and what we're giving them makes them think too much. Reviewers don't want to think. Critics don't want to think. They just want to make snide remarks and criticize and sound important and use big words. I'm not going to give them fantasy so they can gush, 'It was so magical how they manipulated that scene to be romantic.' "

Kim closed the laptop. "But the reality is that you have to get down to one guy. Please dump someone this week."

No. "I don't want to."

"You're being selfish."

Am I? Well . . . yeah. I have four handsome men in my life who care about me. Why wouldn't

494

I want to hold on to them? "So I'm selfish."

"So . . . folks are only tuning in to the last fifteen minutes now to see if you dump anyone."

I doubt that. "How do you know that?"

"It stands to reason," Kim said. "Common sense. It's what I'd do if I were watching at home."

Because you're in the text-him-a-breakup-message generation that has no patience with anyone or anything. "You wouldn't watch the challenges or see recaps of the dates?"

"No."

Because you're not featured in them, Miss Exhibitionist. "They're tuning in, right? At least they're watching."

"Yes, but, Sonya, this can't go on forever."

And this is true. To every thing there is a season, and a time to every purpose under the heaven. "You're not getting bored, are you?"

"No," Kim said. "This is the best paid vacation I've ever had. It's just . . . I think something should happen. You are narrowing them down in your mind, right?"

I have only one man in my mind. He just hasn't won a date with me yet. "Yes."

"Then . . . start narrowing."

"Okay, if I *absolutely* had to get rid of someone," Sonya said. "who would *you* suggest?"

"John," Kim said. "It's obvious."

Ouch. Baby girl, you just punched the man who's residing inside my head and my heart. "Why? Because he's white?"

"No," Kim said. "Because he hasn't won a single challenge. He's a loser. You're a winner. You're incompatible."

What kind of logic is that? "John never gives up, and he loses with grace, a joke, and a smile. That's cool to me."

"And he dresses badly."

Well . . . "John's not about the clothes." *He doesn't have many clothes to be about.* "He looks fine to me in whatever he wears. You've seen him in his swimsuit."

"And he's old, Sonya," Kim said. "Yes, he has a young body, but he's not that handsome. Did you see the little sprouts of hair in his ears?"

"It comes with age," Sonya said. "And anyway, I see with my heart, not my eyes."

"Your heart needs glasses."

No, it doesn't! "John is sweet, helpful, kind, a strong Christian, hard-working. But most of all, he listens to me. I can talk to him about anything and know he's listening. He focuses on me."

"Cuz he's hard up for a date he couldn't get anywhere else but on this show," Kim said.

Wow. Lord, give this child a heart. "Everything is genuine with him. His motives are pure. He impressed you after the movie, didn't he?"

"So he's somewhat deep and knows some big words," Kim said. "Maybe he reads the dictionary in his spare time down in Butt Crack, Alabama. He's still wrong for you, Sonya. I mean, if you two hooked up, that would make him my daddy."

"What?"

"How could I tell anyone that the biggest loser on TV is my dad?" Kim asked.

"That . . . that makes no sense."

"Your liking him makes no sense either," Kim said.

"To you."

"Whatever." Kim yawned. "What's our next challenge that won't really be a challenge and will only end up in a tie or the loser will still be safe from elimination no matter how badly he botches the challenge? Setting fire to something? John could win that easily. Oh, I know, we could see who snores the loudest. Wait. No. We'll have them watch TV with you, and the one who tunes into your favorite show fastest, wins."

"Hush." *But when she puts it that way, the show is sounding stale. What else can I do to help John win? What else can he do?*

He can sing.

Why didn't I think of this before? At Bethel he sometimes gives me goose bumps when he harmonizes. Hmm. He only harmonizes. Can

*he sing the melody, too? God, I hope so. I'm
running out of ideas here.*

"What about a singing contest, Kim?"
Sonya asked.

Kim didn't respond.

Still mad at me. "Kim, what about a singing
contest?"

Kim didn't even look Sonya's way.

I'm not having this. She reached back and
shook Kim's foot. "Kim."

"What?" Kim said.

"I just asked you a question."

"You did?" Kim turned. "Sorry. I guess I'm
getting used to hearing Shani. What's your
question?"

And that's . . . kind of cool. "For our next
challenge, we will be having a singing contest."

"That could work," Kim said. "And it
might actually be fun. Justin can really *sang.*
And if we add dancing . . ."

Oh no, not that! "Why would we add dancing?"

"Song and dance," Kim said. "Those two
words just go together."

*John can sing, but can he dance? He sways
nicely in the pew and claps on beat most of the
time.* "That might work." *God, I hope it does.*
"Okay. Song and dance it is."

Kim laughed. "John is never going to win a
challenge, is he?"

"Miracles can happen."
Miracles better *happen.*

CHAPTER 49

Oh, gee, it's another challenge, John thought. *I can't wait to find out another area in my life that's deficient.*

"I used to like watching *American Idol* and *America's Got Talent* until they became more about the hosts and their bickering than the contestants," Sonya said.

Ouch, John thought. *Take that, Fox and NBC.*

"Your challenge is to sing me a song as if you were on one of those shows," Sonya said. "I want you to croon for me. I want you to move me only with the sound of your melodious voice."

This, I can do. All right. I'm feeling good about this. Oh, yeah. Justin is the singer. Shoot. Maybe he'll have an off night. Oh no. Shani is smiling.

"And you have to *dance* for her, too," Shani said.

I hate it when Shani smiles.

"And I don't mean do a dance and then

500

sing or sing and then do a dance," Shani said. "You must dance and sing at the *same* time."

I am in some serious trouble, John thought. *Walking and talking gives me fits sometimes.*

"Here are the ground rules," Sonya said. "Soundtracks are okay. They'll have some headset microphones for you to use. Costuming is optional, and there's a three-minute minimum."

Shani smiled directly at John. "Some of you have a *lot* of work to do."

And "some of you" would be me. John shook his head. *I can't win. I thought I had a chance when I was only going to sing, but now I have no chance.*

Okay, I have one chance in four. Calm down. There is a time to mourn and a time to dance, and since I'm no longer mourning, it's time for me to dance. The race is not to the swift, nor the battle to the strong. I am not the swiftest or the strongest, but time and chance happen to us all. It's my turn, my time, it has to be. Run so you may obtain the prize.

Lord, help me dance so I may obtain the prize.

Um, Lord, just help me look *as if I can dance.*

"You okay?" Sonya asked.

John looked up into Sonya's eyes. "Just praying."

"So am I." She sat next to him. "I originally only wanted a song. Shani added the dance."

"And I will dance for you," John said. "To

the best of my ability."

And I'll be forever enshrined on YouTube as the worst dancer in world history.

"Artie, what song are you gonna sing?" Justin asked.

John looked above the bed at the camera he just knew was recording his every hiccup, twitch, sneeze, and fart as he slept. "I'd like to tell you, but I don't want to tell them."

"What you lookin' at?" Justin asked.

John pointed at a black dot in the ceiling. "The camera." He waved. "Hi, Larry, Bob. I hope you are enjoying my discomfort."

"Think there are any in the bathroom?" Justin asked.

John shrugged. "Don't know. I wouldn't put it past them."

"C'mon," Justin said, and the two left the room, collected Gary and Tony from the kitchen, and went to the bowling alley. "I think we're safe here." He sat on the ball return. "What are you going to sing, Arthur?"

Maybe if I whisper it, it won't sound so foolish. "It's an Earth, Wind and Fire song called 'Reasons.' "

Justin's eyes popped. "Nah, dog."

"Yep," John said.

"You sure about that, man?" Gary asked.

"Yep," John said.

"I mean, can you hit all the notes?" Tony asked. "There are some really high notes in

502

that song."

"Yes, I can hit those notes." John winced. "Most of them." He sighed. "I might only *hit* them, though. I doubt I can *hold* them. I'll just have to sing faster, I guess."

"Artie, please pick an easier song, like some Elvis," Justin said. "You can shake your hips, can't you?"

"Yes," John said. "But they might not return to their normal state if I do." He smiled. "I am going to sing 'Reasons,' fellas. It's my destiny."

"Artie, you'd have to be crazy to sing that song," Tony said. "Even if you hit every note but one, Shani will ruin you. Why are you tempting fate like that?"

It's my destiny. "I have a feeling that Jazz likes this song, and I must sing it."

"We can't talk you out of it?" Gary said.

"My mind is made up," John said.

"Oh, man," Justin said. He rubbed his head with a huge paw of a hand. "It'd be easier to sing Stevie Wonder's 'Overjoyed,' man. Even the national anthem is easier to sing."

"I can do it." *I hope.*

"What do y'all think?" Justin asked.

"Maybe just the effort will be enough," Tony said.

"Artie," Justin said, "you gonna need help. We gotta back you up."

"Nah, that's okay," John said. "I'd rather fail alone."

"Artie, you've had my back the whole time I've been here," Justin said. "I wouldn't be here at all if you hadn't tied for last with me in that obstacle course or helped me with those rhymes."

"You didn't need my help, Justin," John said. "I mean, all I really gave you was Doug Flutie."

"I never would have thought of him or 'sweet patootie,' " Justin said.

Because, John thought, *you're not old enough to have seen Doug Flutie play.*

Justin turned to Tony and Gary. "Let's back Artie up, y'all. We'll be the Three Tops or The Jackson Three."

Gary laughed. "The Jackson Three? Isn't that what they're down to anyway? And fellas, if we're gonna be Earth, Wind and Fire, we're gonna need some serious costuming."

"And dance lessons," John said. *There's that quiet I've missed. Was that a cricket? What's a cricket doing in a broken-down bowling alley inside a mansion?*

"You . . . can't dance," Tony said.

"Yep. I don't have a dancing bone in my body." *There's that cricket again. I wonder if it's as lonely as I'm going to be after this challenge.*

"I'll get a laptop," Tony said, and he left the bowling alley.

"What do we need a laptop for?" John

asked. "I need to learn how to dance in less than twenty-four hours."

"It's called YouTube, Artie," Justin said. "We're about to watch a whole lot of video."

They watched dance videos long into the night. They analyzed Earth, Wind and Fire album covers for costuming ideas. They made a list of what they'd need: African robes, fake Afros, and platform shoes. They taught John simple dances.

"For God's sake, Artie, use your arms!" they yelled.

"You dancin' to the words or the music, man?" they asked.

"Dude, please loosen up and feel the flow," they said.

It was a very long night.

John's feet hurt after thirty seconds of something called the Jerk. His arms ached as he tried to Dougie. He became immediately lost and ran into Tony during his first attempt at the Electric Slide.

"I'm hopeless," John said.

No one disagreed.

The next morning, while Sonya and Shani were out shopping, they helped Artie dance along to "Reasons" as he practiced on a stage set up outside near the pool.

"Keep the music low," John said. He looked into a tree. "The producers are watching."

"Let 'em," Gary said. "They probably can't

dance either."

Ouch.

"Oh, sorry, Artie," Gary said. "I didn't mean any disrespect."

John stood in front of a silver microphone stand. "You ain't lyin', though."

Tony cued up the music.

"Oh. I'm, um, going to save my voice, okay?" John said. "I'll just mouth the words as I do a little, um, dance. Y'all just . . . do something fantastic behind me so she'll watch y'all and not me."

As he mouthed the words, he swayed, he stepped, he moved his arms, and did everything *but* dance. "I can't dance a lick, fellas."

"You're doing fine, Artie," Justin said, spinning flawlessly along with Gary and Tony.

"Maybe it's the shoes," Gary said.

"It's the DNA, Gary," John said.

Tony stepped away from the line dance behind John. "For such a slow song you don't need to do much dancing. Just imagine Jazz is the mike stand and slow drag with her."

"This mike stand is far too skinny to be Jazz," John said. "She has, um, more curves."

And then *the* idea struck John like a lightning bolt through the top of his skull. He stopped dancing. "I'll figure something out. Y'all please sing the background loudly. I'm sure my voice is going to crack."

"Just don't fall in them platform shoes, man," Gary said.

"I won't," John said.

Because eventually, I am going to have someone to hold on to.

CHAPTER 50

Sonya could barely contain her excitement, running her feet in place as she and Kim drank fruit smoothies at a table in front of the stage.

"This is gonna be good," Kim said.

My hands are really sweating! "I'm so nervous," Sonya said.

"Why are you nervous? You're not singing, Jazz."

No, but I'll be praying my guts out.

The lights grew in intensity, and Graham, wearing a tuxedo, walked from the kitchen to the stage.

"Jazz, you are in for a real musical treat tonight," Graham said. "The Team has been hard at work all day. Did you enjoy your shopping trip?"

Oh, get on with it, Graham! "Yes. It was nice."

"I'm sure it was," Graham said. "First up for the song-and-dance competition is Tony, singing 'Whip Appeal.' "

Sonya didn't recognize Tony, who wore a

sharp white suit, shirt, and tie, but she did notice Kim's feet running under the table. From the first word out of Tony's mouth to the last, Kim didn't seem to be breathing.

The boy is definitely workin' it, Sonya thought. *Way too much for my taste, and only, it seems, for Kim. Did Babyface gyrate like that? I don't think so. Tony hasn't even made eye contact with me yet. The nerve! I'm not that mad about it, cuz the boy can sing and I've never seen that look on Kim's face. She almost seems scared, anxious, and hyped at the same time. Is that what love is? Being scared, anxious, and hyped that you won't get picked by the one you love? I'm so scared John will bomb this challenge and give up completely, but I'm also hyped that, miracle of miracles, he's gonna nail it.*

And all this is making me anxious!

After Tony bowed and blew a kiss in the general direction of their table, Sonya grabbed Kim's arm. "You can put your tongue back in your mouth now, Shani."

Kim closed her mouth.

"Next on our show tonight," Graham said, "is Gary, singing Luther Vandross's 'A House Is Not a Home.' "

Strange choice, and yet . . . it's not. And dag, he looks absolutely huge in that velvet purple suit. And, yes, he's sangin' *it, and a whole lot deeper than Luther did. But he's not singing it*

509

to me or to Kim. He's only looking into the cameras. He's singing to his baby mama back home. He's singing to his children. That is so sweet. Maybe this is what love is. Ignoring the world and focusing only on the people we love.

Gary did a simple bow and left the stage.

"Third on our song-and-dance program," Graham said, "is Justin, singing Biz Markie's 'Just a Friend.' "

No . . . way! As good a voice as that man has, he's singing that song? He's nailing it, though, and Kim and I are trippin' fierce! So funny! And he's so nimble on his feet, spinning, sliding, clapping, doing a one-man cha-cha slide with a little mashed potato thrown in. But of course. The man loves him some potatoes.

Justin moonwalked off the stage.

"That man is a trip," Kim said.

Sonya nodded. *Maybe he's no longer "Jumbo" to her anymore. There is always something more to a person than meets the eye.*

Graham returned to the stage holding a card. "Um, I've just been handed this card."

"Duh," Kim said before Sonya could think it.

"It reads: 'One moment while we change into costume for the grand finale.' " Graham slipped the card into his pocket. "I guess they're, um, changing, for the, um, grand finale."

"What grand finale?" Kim asked. "Arthur hasn't gone yet."

"Maybe Arthur *is* the grand finale." *And there go my feet again. Geez, I'm gonna need another foot rub soon!*

Justin, Tony, and Gary entered the stage wearing African robes, bell bottoms, and big Afros. *They look exactly like Earth, Wind and Fire! Which song? And where's John?*

John stepped onto the stage wearing a golden African robe, a smaller Afro, and shiny white platform shoes.

Oh . . . my . . . goodness. Am I breathing? Is that really John?

The intro to "Reasons" filled the air.

Oh . . . wow. "Reasons"! O . . . M . . . G . . . This is . . . wow. He hit the first note! He's really crooning, and he's hitting all the notes. This is . . . wow. And he craves my body, oh, yes, Lord! I am definitely in the wrong place for any of this to be real, but this is real, this song is real, what he's singing to me is real — but only for one night? I know it's just a song, but that's all I've wanted, one date, one night, and this show is a game of love, all right. And he even sang "hypmotized" instead of "hypnotized"! Oh, squeeze me real tight all night! Who cares if your Afro's slipping over your eyes—

What's this?

He's beckoning to me?

Sonya stood, mesmerized by the man with

511

the falling Afro and the three men behind him dancing absolutely in synch. She ran up to that stage and stuck out her hand.

John pulled her up onstage with him.

And now he's singing to me and we're dancing and his hand is dangerously *low on my back and his voice is so pure, so right, and his eyes never leave mine and, God, please keep me from laughing at the line dance back there because now they're doing some old Jackson Five moves and I'm smiling so much my face may explode all over this stage and the cameras and, hey, his thigh is getting right frisky with mine, and he's pulling me in for a . . . hug . . . and he's doing it right, he's doing it right and it feels like love and . . . Oh, a whispered "thank you" in my ear . . . And why does the music have to end? Why couldn't this be an extended version?*

As the music faded to nothing, Kim broke the silence with loud laughter. "Oh . . . my . . . God!" she shouted over and over.

John led Sonya down the stairs and back to her chair. He bowed before her.

Sonya started clapping.

"You can't be serious!" Kim shouted.

"That . . . that was amazing," Sonya said.

"Yeah, it was," Kim said. "It will be a viral hit on the Internet in seconds under 'White Guy Can't Sing or Dance.' That was too funny!"

He won, he won, he won, he won . . . my heart.

The Team arranged themselves onstage while Sonya tried to remember how to breathe.

"And now it's time for Jazz and Shani to give the Team feedback," Graham said. "First up is Tony."

Where am I? Am I back on earth yet? "Um, Tony, you were workin' it. You kind of worked it more for Shani than for me, though, huh?"

"I'll say," Kim said. She fanned the air in front of her face. "You got that whip appeal, boy. You can work it on me anytime."

"Next up is Gary," Graham said.

"Gary, you really sanged it," Sonya said. "I love me some old Luther."

Kim shook her head. "Not very romantic, though. You could have chosen something more appropriate. And you didn't move from your spot the entire time."

"Luther didn't dance that much either, Shani," Sonya said.

"He was supposed to sing *and* dance," Kim said. "He didn't dance."

Sonya smiled at Gary. "Gary, I felt it." *Ignore her. She's very young.*

"You need your hearing checked, too, Jazz," Kim said. "He was flat. And Luther didn't sing it that low either."

"It moved me, Gary," Sonya said. "Thank you."

"Next is Justin," Graham said.

"Justin, funny as usual," Sonya said. "I think Biz Markie would be jealous. I mean, you actually sang the song instead of whatever Biz Markie did to it."

"You seriously need to be on *Def Comedy Jam,*" Kim said. "Or on *Dancing with the Stars.* You got some serious moves, man."

"I couldn't help singing along," Sonya said.

"And last up is Arthur," Graham said.

John took off the Afro.

There's my man. Sweaty but sweet. "Arthur, man, it's about time. You *kilt* that song."

Kim laughed. "I'll say."

Sonya stared Kim down. "I meant that in a good way, Shani. That is one of my all-time favorite songs. You amazed me. I can't sing those notes, even in the shower. And you guys *kilt* the backgrounds. Y'all should go on tour."

"Ahem," Kim said. "Artie, darling, you hit a *majority* of the notes. Some of those notes, though. Ouch. Pitchy. They sounded like fingernails on a chalkboard. And if that was dancing, I'd rather not go to the prom, know what I'm saying?"

Now that's enough, Kim. "He danced with me just fine."

"He was supposed to dance alone, Jazz."

"You only said he had to dance," Sonya said. "You didn't say he couldn't dance *with* me."

Kim shook her head rapidly. "But that wasn't dancing, Jazz. That was some in-the-basement-with-the-lights-out-hoping-no-one-sees-you, old-school slow-dragging."

"Yes, it was. I like in-the-basement-with-the-lights-out-hoping-no-one-sees-you, old-school slow-dragging. By the way, Arthur, I love your shoes."

John looked down at his shiny white platform shoes. "I don't." He kicked them off into the pool. "Much better."

"Jazz!" Kim shouted. "That's *twice* this man has taken off his shoes in front of you." Kim fanned the air in front of her nose.

Sonya stood and kicked her own shoes off, one flopping into the pool. "What's your point, Shani?"

"Artie, darling, you are no singer," Kim said, "and I can't call what you did dancing. It looked more like you were boxing with Jazz than dancing with her. I give you a C-minus for effort and a D-minus for execution."

When will she stop? "Shani, you didn't give grades to the others."

"Because they were all B or better," Kim said.

"Don't listen to her, Arthur," Sonya said. "It was wonderful. Truly wonderful. I'll have that song in my head for the rest of the night." *And maybe even for the rest of my days.*

"And now," Graham said, "Jazz and Shani will consult with each other to choose the winner."

Sonya walked up onto the stage and stood in front of John. "Not this time."

"What?" Kim yelled.

"The clear and *obvious* winner is . . . Arthur." She held up her arms, and John pulled her up onstage. "Give me another hug. I'm your biggest fan."

Oh, yes, this is the *hug, and, yes, it feels like love, and* he's *the one giving it to me.*

"Finally," John whispered. "The last are finally first."

"I can't wait for our date," Sonya whispered. She turned to Graham but didn't let go of John. "Where are we going on our date, Graham?"

Graham looked out at a cue card. "After an intimate lunch at Café Provençal, you'll be whisked away to a special showing of Warner Brothers' next blockbuster movie, *Goodfellas: Older but Wiser Guys,* in theaters this July. And you'll have the entire theater all to yourselves."

Dinner and a movie. Okay. "What else?"

Graham squinted. "There's nothing else on the card."

That can't be all! Sonya looked for Bob or Larry. "That's . . . it? Lunch and a movie? For what Arthur just did? He earned *much* more than that. We should be going on a jet to San Francisco or Hawaii or Tahiti or something."

John pulled her back to him. "It's okay. At least we'll be alone."

"With fifty cameras seeing us in all our aloneness," Sonya said. "Where's the justice in that?"

John put his warm lips on her ear, whispering, "Dress as if you're going hiking. Wear long sleeves and a Windbreaker and shoes you don't mind getting wet, and please don't ask why." He moved his head back and winked.

"Okay." *Yes! We are so* not *going to dinner and a movie.*

John stepped back from the embrace, but he still held Sonya's hands. "This robe is scorching hot. I need to cool off." He put his Afro back on his head. "I need a bath." He smiled. "And look — there's a big ol' bathtub right over there. Go get your suit on."

In two steps and a leap, John flew into the pool.

The Afro floated to the top.

In moments, three more Afros were floating in the pool as the rest of Earth, Wind and Fire did cannonballs into the pool.

Sonya didn't want to miss the fun.

She jumped in fully clothed . . .

And danced in the water with her Afro-less prince.

Several hours later, a towel on her head,

Sonya lay on her bed and tried not to let Kim piss her off.

"What were you two whispering?" Kim asked.

"Nothing."

"Right. What are you two planning?" Kim put her laptop on Sonya's bed. "I know you're planning something."

"I'm not planning anything," Sonya said. *John is.*

Kim looked at her screen. "The online folks think you're giving Artie Fartie a pity date."

"I'm not," Sonya said. "He earned that date. The only pity is that we haven't gone out on a date until now."

Kim sighed. "If you were playing by the rules, he wouldn't even be here."

"Good thing I don't play by the rules, then," Sonya said. *Hmm. I should be getting my clothes ready.* She went to the dresser and pulled out a blue and black flannel shirt and a pair of jeans, taking them to the bed to iron.

"Long sleeves and jeans?" Kim said. "It's supposed to be warm tomorrow."

"Movie theaters are always too cold for me," Sonya said. *And it's not an outright lie. Movie theaters are always too cold for me.*

As she ironed and Kim droned on and on about how John didn't deserve to win, Sonya tried to figure out their destination. *Maybe we're going hiking. Yosemite? Can't be. That's* at least seven hours away by car. Maybe we'll just go walking in the woods. I'd like that. Just holding hands with John in the woods. And dodging bears. Do they have bears in Southern California? John will protect me. He said to wear shoes I didn't mind getting wet. A Windbreaker.

Yes.

We're going to the beach.

To watch a sunset.

CHAPTER 51

I hope this works, John thought.

While two camera crews set up at Café Provençal, John and Sonya sat at a table looking at the menu. John slipped a simple note into his menu — "Go to BR, take exit instead, orange truck, c u in 3" — and slid his menu to Sonya.

"I think I have a different menu," he whispered.

Sonya exchanged her menu with his, opened it up, read the note, and nodded. "Yes, it certainly is different."

A few lights came on, as did the cameras.

And now, the flimflam begins.

"Jazz, what looks good to you?" John said, smiling and enunciating his words precisely.

Sonya pressed her lips together. "Well, Arthur, I think I'll go with the three-course meal. How about you?"

"Oh, Jazz, I think I shall have the same." He closed his menu.

Sonya put her menu on top of his.

John nodded.

"Oh," Sonya said, "I have to go to the little girls' room." She pushed back her chair.

"Oh, do hurry, Jazz," John said. "I hear the service here is excellent. I wouldn't want your food to get cold."

"Oh, I will hurry, Arthur." *I am about to crack up completely,* John thought. He watched Sonya moving toward the bathrooms. *And now, it's my turn.* He drummed on the table. He hummed "Already Gone" by the Eagles. He straightened his napkin.

And then he smelled his hands. "Oh my," he said to the camera. "I have forgotten to wash my hands. I must go do that. I will be back in two shakes of a lamb's tail." He stood and waved at the camera. "See you soon."

John walked casually to the bathroom, then zipped past it to an exit, slipped outside, located the orange truck — *hey, it's a Ford F-150!* — and got in, Sonya already buckled in. He pulled down the visor, and keys dropped into his hand.

"Hurry!" Sonya whispered.

John started the truck, crept out of the parking lot, and pulled out onto the Pacific Coast Highway. Neither spoke until they were five minutes away from Café Provençal.

"Where'd you get this truck?" Sonya asked.

"Rent-A-Wreck," John said. "This is the quintessential American truck."

"But how did it get there?" Sonya asked.

"As soon as I knew where we were *supposed* to be going," John said, "I called up Rent-A-Wreck and paid a little extra for them to drop it off for me."

"Where are we going?" Sonya asked.

John let out a long breath. "We're just going, Sonya. Up one-oh-one and just . . . going. A real date. No cameras. No microphones. Just two people out for an adventure."

Sonya held tightly to the armrest on the door. "Will this thing get us there?"

I hope so. He checked the gas gauge. "Yep. Full tank. We'll need it."

"A long trip, then," Sonya said.

"About three hours. Consider it an escape *to* reality."

A Volvo cut in front of him without the courtesy of a turn signal. "I hate that. I can't read your mind, sir. God bless you, sir. Yes, God bless you. No, God bless *you.* That wasn't a gang sign, was it?"

"No," Sonya said. "He's just rude. He cuts you off then flips *you* off and curses *you.* I hate that. No wonder my car insurance is so high. It's fools like that who make everyone else pay higher premiums."

John looked in all his mirrors. "Where is all this traffic coming from? Everyone seems to have the same idea today. Back home, there is no Saturday traffic."

"I'd rather take the long way home than deal with traffic any day," Sonya said. "I know all the side streets in Charlotte."

John pushed the power button on the radio. Nothing happened. "No radio."

"You can sing to me."

"I don't have much of a voice left after last night." He fiddled with the radio again, even tapping it. "I don't much like top-forty music these days anyway. It all sounds the same to me."

"I haven't heard a decent song in years," Sonya said. "Except for last night. That was wonderful."

"I was so nervous."

"You didn't look nervous," Sonya said.

"The shoes were too big," John said. "I had to stuff socks into the ends. I almost fell a few times. Until I had you up there to steady me. I hope I didn't embarrass you."

"Not at all," Sonya said. "I haven't danced with anyone since high school."

And I haven't danced since the night before Sheila died. Boo, what are you doing back in my head again? What was the song? Keith Sweat's "Nobody." And after you left me, I became one.

"Are you thinking about Sheila?" Sonya asked softly.

"Yeah. Sorry."

"Don't be."

523

"We danced the night before she died," John said. "In the dark, though, not in front of the world."

"That's sweet."

"It was so cold that night, yet . . ." *Geez, I'm about to cry, even after fifteen years. Get a grip! I finally get to be alone with Sonya, and I want to cry?* He blinked rapidly. "Your body was so hot last night."

"Was it now?"

"I mean, I was burning up in that robe and the Afro," John said. "I'm sure my head lost weight. I didn't expect your body to be as hot as mine was."

"I was flushed with the intense heat of your crooning," Sonya said.

Flushed? "Is that a good thing?"

"It's a very good thing, John."

I like very good things. "So if I dance with you again, will your body get as hot?"

"You'll have to try it and see," Sonya said. "I may burst into flames."

"Like the phoenix, huh?"

Sonya sighed. "My sister can be so snooty sometimes."

John hit the power button on the radio. *Still nothing.* "I wish we had a working radio so I could pull over and we could practice."

Sonya patted the bench seat. "We could do a front-seat-of-an-old-Ford-truck dance."

"Might be squeaky."

524

And there's that silence again. I say three words, and poof! But this silence isn't hearing-crickets silence. It's comfortable. It's easy. It's calm. He looked sideways at Sonya's left leg. *It's even sexy.*

"I have really missed talking to you, John," Sonya said. "You don't know how much. You made such an impression on me in such a short time, and then poof! Aaron's stupid rule, which we're *still* keeping though he's long gone. Why is that?"

"I don't know. Safety in numbers? Yeah. That's probably it."

"You don't feel safe around me?"

Safer than I've ever felt, actually. "It's not that. It's *your* safety I'm worried about. Widowed and alone for fifteen years. Hot woman in the house who might burst into flame the next time she dances. Both of us early risers. Darkness that early in the morning. There's no telling what I might try to do if I were alone with you again. We'd set off every smoke alarm in Malibu."

"What might you try, John?" Sonya asked.

And now arrive very carnal thoughts. "How 'bout them Lakers, huh?"

Sonya laughed. "What might you try?"

And now even more carnal thoughts involving a back rub. Should I tell her what I've been dreaming lately? Geez. "Are you going to keep asking that question until I answer it?"

"Yes."

John sighed. "That Kobe Bryant. What a ballplayer."

"Tell me," Sonya said. "What might you try?"

"Nothing . . . untoward."

"There's an ancient word," Sonya said.

"I'm an ancient guy."

"No, you're not. What would you try?"

Carnal thoughts, back off a minute, okay? "I'd try just to hold you for a while. Okay, more than just a while."

Sonya's left hand gripped the edge of the seat. "I'm suddenly not feeling so safe."

"You're in no danger." *Me? Yeah. I'm in danger. Her very presence tempts me.*

"This bench seat has a seat belt in the middle," Sonya said. "Tempting."

And to think I originally wanted a vehicle that had captain's chairs. Thank you, Rent-A-Wreck.

Sonya unbuckled her seat belt, slid over, and buckled up again. "I may rub against your thigh."

"Will you purr?" John asked.

"I'm not a cat."

"You were a stallion the first night I saw you."

Sonya slapped his thigh. "I was not!"

"Quite a mane you wore for the main event."

"Stop."

"You made me hoarse just looking at you,"

John said.

Sonya squeezed his thigh. "No more."

John smiled. "Mission accomplished."

"Pretty slick," Sonya said. She ran her palm from his upper thigh to his knee and back. "You don't have to annoy me to get me to touch you."

"Message received." *My thighs adore you. Don't stop rubbing.*

"John, can I ask you anything, anything at all, and you'll give me an answer to whatever I ask?"

This sounds dangerous. I like danger. "Sure."

"Anything? I might ask you something crazy."

I expect her to do that. "Ask away, and don't be surprised if I ask you the same question."

"Oh." Sonya removed her hand from John's thigh. "Um, do you ever . . . No, I can't ask that."

She'll ask anyway, John thought.

"Do you ever . . . dream about me?" Sonya asked.

"Yes. I've had two dreams about you, both of them very nice."

"Oh." Sonya folded her hands together. "Two dreams?"

"Yes. Want to know what I dreamed?"

"Um, no," Sonya said. "I was only curious *if* you dreamed about me. I'm not sure if I want to . . . know all the details."

Aha! She said all that while she was smiling.

She wants me to tell her. "We were on the beach in the first one and at a lake in the second one. We were outdoors, and then —"

"Um, what are some of your pet peeves, John?" Sonya interrupted.

"You don't want to know what happened to you in my dreams?"

"I can . . . imagine." She twisted her hands in her lap.

"I have a very passionate imagination. What do *you* think happened?"

Sonya looked out her window. "So . . . about those pet peeves. I don't like people who pray to hear themselves pray. God has to have a great deal of patience."

John slid his hand to Sonya's thigh. "You *really* don't want to know what I dreamed."

"I do, but I don't."

John laced his fingers into her left hand. "It was a great dream, Sonya."

Sonya squeezed his hand. "Mission accomplished."

Sneaky woman.

"Okay, what happened?" Sonya asked.

"We walked along the beach and went swimming in the lake." *Said the spider to the fly . . .*

"That's . . . all?"

John sighed. "That's all I want to tell you."

"Oh. But what if I ask you to tell me more?"

"I'll tell you."

Sonya nodded. "Okay. Tell me . . . one

thing . . . that's not too untoward."

So many things were untoward . . . "You look very nice in a bikini."

Sonya gripped his hand firmly. "I was wearing a bikini?"

"Yes. Red. Very tight. Low-cut. Had little ties on the sides and, um, in front." *Is her hand getting moist or is mine?*

"Is that how you want to see me, John?" Sonya asked.

I want to see you anyway I can, Sonya. "That's what you were wearing in the beach dream. And, yes, I wouldn't mind seeing you that way."

"I don't wear bikinis."

"In my dreams you do."

"What were you wearing?" Sonya asked.

"A smile."

"No, really."

"Really. That was all I was wearing. I have fewer clothes in my dreams than I do in real life. I'm sure that has some deep psychological significance." *Either that or I'm really horny in my dreams.*

"You were . . ." Sonya's voice faded. "But why was I dressed?"

"Who's to say you were dressed the entire time?" John said.

Sonya didn't speak.

Is she panting a little? No, that's me. "And this is making me intensely hot." He rolled down his window a few inches. "You were, um, talking about prayer. Yes, I believe that some people pray selfishly. I believe we should praise Him, thank Him, ask Him, and then say amen."

"Amen. Um, are you really hot, John?"

John rolled down his window to the bottom. "Yes. Um, you know, about those pet peeves. I can't stand people who ask, 'How ya doin'?' when they really don't care how you're doin'. I sometimes say, 'Do you really want to know how I'm doin'?' And they all say, 'Huh?' every time. They don't even listen to the answer to their question. I know they're just trying to be polite, but when I ask, 'How are you?' I *will* listen to the answer." *And now I'm babbling like an idiot.*

Sonya used both hands to hold his. "A red bikini, huh?"

Does she have to put the back of my hand on her thigh like that? "And I was just cooling off. Um, what can't you stand, Sonya?"

Sonya picked up his hand and kissed several fingers. "I can't stand people who don't speak to me when I speak to them." She set his hand on her thigh again.

"Sheila used to accuse me of that. 'You got no home training,' she'd tell me."

"Did Sheila ever wear a bikini?" Sonya asked.

I never should have mentioned the bikini. "No. She wore a one-piece, like you. I mean, she had to wear a one-piece after the Flo-rala State Park incident."

"Do I want to hear this?" She flipped his hand over, his palm on her thigh.

My hand is now squeezing that thigh on its own. I have no control over it.

"Tell me what happened," Sonya said.

"We went camping, small lake, no one around. She had this bikini that didn't exactly cover her entirely, kind of like the one Shani wears, and long story short, she lost her top. It's probably still in that little lake. That's when she vowed never to wear a bikini again. I didn't mind it, of course." *And I swear her leg is about to catch fire. No. That's my hand.*

Sonya smiled. "What . . . else . . . happened in your dreams?"

Think of something safe. Oh, that wasn't. And that was dangerous, so close to the fire, but afterward . . . "We held hands kind of like this."

"On the beach or at the lake?" Sonya asked.

"Only on the beach," John said. "We, um . . . held each other in the lake. The water was very cold, so we had to hold on to each other tightly."

"Oh. And that was when I was wearing the red bikini."

"Um, no. Not then." John tried to turn on the air-conditioner. "The AC doesn't work either. Yeah, how about them pet peeves?"

Sonya returned John's hand to his thigh. "Yeah. The pet peeves." She unbuckled her seat belt, slid over to her window, rolled it down, and slid back.

I need a new topic that will not arouse me so much. "Um, I can't stand TV sports announcers."

"Neither can I!" Sonya said. "A guy drives in for a layup, and the announcer says, 'He can do that, Norm.' It's so obvious that he just *did* it! Or the quarterback throws an interception and the announcer says, 'He shouldn't have thrown that one.' Uh, duh."

"What about the stupid phrases they say over and over. 'They're high on him.' 'The young freshman.' "

"Some of these freshmen are getting old," Sonya said. "How about 'incontrovertible visual evidence' on a replay in pro football? I don't even know what 'incontrovertible' means."

This is fun. "What about, 'He's showing a lot of athleticism out there today'?"

"Is 'athleticism' even a word?" Sonya asked.

"I think it is now." He reached for her hand.

Sonya took it.

"What about . . . 'He's shooting a three-ball!' "

Sonya nodded. "Which makes a free throw a one-ball."

"Ouch," John said.

Sonya giggled.

I like that sound.

"Um, John, how long were we in the water?" Sonya asked.

And now I'm in my dream again. "We lasted . . ." *Oops.* "I mean, we took our time in the water. And then I woke up."

"You woke up? Why?"

Because my body woke me up. "How about this one: 'Norm, he's got a hamstring.' I hope he has two! Or 'The X-rays on his head were negative.' That figures. All those concussions in football these days —"

"Why'd you wake up, John?" Sonya interrupted.

"Or 'That was a *terrible* pass, shot, swing,' as if the announcer could ever do that on his best day."

"Were you excited?" Sonya asked.

Very much so. If my pillow had hands, it would have slapped me. "These athletes today. They're all about themselves."

"I'll take that as a yes," Sonya said.

John nodded. "I couldn't sleep a wink afterward either."

Sonya picked up his hand and kissed his palm. "I can't stand athletes who think they're more important than the rest of the team. I tune in to watch a team play, not you, fool. Um, you were too excited to go back to sleep?"

She's not going to let this go! "Yes. It was an outstanding dream. Um, I don't like coaches who think they *are* the team and take credit for what the team accomplishes."

"I hate it when announcers only say an athlete is articulate if he's black," Sonya said. "They used to write that about me. 'Sonya Richardson, the articulate captain of the Houston Comets.' You never hear them saying, 'That Peyton Manning is sure articulate, isn't he?' Or, 'He's from a good family.' I've never heard someone talk about a white athlete that way."

"And what's up with always showing a black athlete's mother in the stands?" John asked. "Especially when there's clearly an older black man standing right beside her. Why don't they zoom in and identify him?"

Sonya rubbed his hand on her leg. "So I woke you up, huh?"

My hand is extremely happy. I now know that her pocket is empty. "You woke me in the nicest way, only you weren't there when I woke up so I could thank you."

Sonya's hands became still.

"I'm sorry," John said. "I've said too much."

"It's all right," Sonya said. "I was pestering you."

And now there's some cricket silence. I don't like this at all. "Um, do you have a problem with athletes who thank God in interviews but don't lead holy lives?"

"Yes," Sonya said. "I have a problem with hypocrites in general. I'm glad you're who you say you are." She slid closer to him, her thigh pressed into his. "I'm also glad you answered my question."

"You mentioned a dream, too," John said.

"I did."

"May I ask about it?" John asked.

"You may."

"Will you answer me if I ask?" John asked.

"I might."

"Did your dream end . . . happily?" John asked.

"Yes."

"Um, how happily?" John asked.

Sonya grazed his jeans with the nails on her left hand. "Uh, one thing I cannot stand is when they break into one of my favorite TV shows with some announcement that can surely wait. Last winter they broke in with weather updates when we had only had some flurries. I know it doesn't snow in Charlotte that often, but to interrupt *Law and Order* for some flurries?"

"We get hurricane and tornado warnings in Burnt Corn," John said. "I don't mind getting those kinds of warnings at all. Did you wake up, Sonya?"

"Yes."

"You, um, you only had this dream once?" John asked.

"Just last night, as a matter of fact," Sonya said. "I was too excited about our date to sleep, but when I finally fell asleep, I immediately started dreaming."

"In some cultures," John said, "a dream dreamed twice will come true."

"I hope I dream it again soon," Sonya said.

And I hope it's a reality soon. Man, now I'm heating up again. I need to steer us back to calm. "Do you, um, do you use your right or left hand to work the remote?"

"My left."

"You're left-handed?"

"No," Sonya said. "My snacks are in my right hand."

"Do you need to look at the remote anymore?" John asked.

"No. I've got that bad boy memorized. It's fused to my hand."

"Kind of like your hand is fused to mine now, huh?" John asked.

"Yeah."

This is safe. This is calm. This is cool. "I lost my remote a few years ago. I have to get up and hit the buttons."

"You need a new TV, man," Sonya said.

"Yeah." *This is safe. This is good.* "Um, what's your favorite Bible verse?"

Sonya sighed, resting her head on his shoulder. "I have so many favorite Bible verses."

"What's the verse you rely on most, the one that kick-starts you, the one that pops into your mind the most?" John asked.

"That's easy," Sonya said. "Proverbs three-five. 'Trust in the Lord with all thine heart; and lean not unto thine own understanding.' This verse has saved me thousands of hours of frustration and worry. When things go wrong, all I can do is trust in Him. What's yours?"

Psalm 43:5 has practically been my mantra for the last fifteen years. " 'Why art thou cast down, O my soul? and why art thou disquieted within me? hope in God: for I shall yet praise him, who is the health of my countenance, and my God.' For I shall *yet* praise him. I'm kind of praising Him right now. Look at that scenery!"

Sonya leaned forward and looked out John's window. "Yes, the ocean is so beautiful. I love the way it crashes on the rocks."

"I'm not talking about that kind of scenery." He glanced at Sonya's face.

"Are you farsighted, John?" Sonya asked.

"Yes. I see things near to me very well."

"Are you liking what you're seeing?" Sonya asked.

"Yes, the scenery is beautiful. I hope I don't dream of this scenery tonight, though." He slipped his hand out of hers and put his arm around her.

"You don't?" Sonya asked.

"I'd rather have . . . *you* next to me when I wake up."

Chapter 52

So . . . would . . . I, Sonya thought. *This flirta-tion is fast turning into seduction. I didn't know he had it in him. I didn't know that I had it in me. If he only waved his hand over butter right now, that butter would bubble and hiss. If he rubbed my back, I'd probably purr for real.*

"I love the smell of the ocean," Sonya said.

"It's why I wear Old Spice," John said.

"I like it. Not too strong. Just right."

A man has his arm around me while I rub his thigh in an orange and rust pick-me-up truck with no working radio or AC and we're talk-ing . . . just talking . . . Oh, and flirting . . . yeah, lots of that . . . Funny, I can't seem to flirt as much with him while I'm holding his hand. Why is that? Is it because I'm finally holding him in some way? I have to do an experiment.

"John?"

"Yes, Sonya?"

"Um, when we were in the water in your dream, were we really close?" *Whoa. His thigh is definitely heating up. It's like a lie detector.*

"I mean, *really* close?"

"We were one flesh, Sonya," John said softly.

And now I'm sweating. My own hand is on fire. My shoulders are hot. Say something! "In my dream, we, um, were one flesh, too."

"Where were we?" John asked.

Don't tell him, don't tell him . . . "On my couch at home."

John laughed. "What were we watching?"

"Each other, of course."

"Oh," John said. "I thought we'd be watching TV for some reason. *Man v. Food* or something like that."

"Is this your way of saying you're hungry?" Sonya asked.

"Yes, but not for food."

I am suddenly feeling extremely edible right now. Whoo! "Are we there yet?"

John squeezed her shoulder. "I think we're very close."

So do I.

Any closer and we'd be having puppies.

John pulled into Morro Bay State Park.

Now that is a serious rock! Sonya thought.

For the next few hours, they explored the rocks. They saw otters, sea lions, and humpback whales. They held hands as they kicked off their shoes, rolled up their pant legs, and walked along the shore.

It's as if I've been here before, Sonya thought. *It's not déjà vu but something . . . cor-*

*rect about all this, something foretold. I can't
explain it. I'm standing ankle deep in icy-cold
water looking at huge rocks and holding hands
with John. I've been here before, I just know it.*

An elderly couple approached them with a
camera.

Oh no! We've been spotted! Hide!

The man handed John a fancy digital
camera. "Would you mind taking our picture,
young man?"

John took the camera as the couple posed,
the massive rocks in the background. "Say . . .
mozzarella."

The couple laughed.

John took the picture. He turned the camera
around and showed them. "I think laughter is
better than smiles any day, don't you?" He
handed the camera to the man.

"Thank you," the woman said. "You two
take care."

Sonya watched the couple walking away
hand in hand. "They're still holding hands."

John took Sonya's hand. "And so are we."

"I meant," Sonya said, "that they've been
together for probably half a century, and
they're still holding hands."

"And recording every moment of their
journey together," John said. "We need to get
us a camera."

They got back into the truck and found a
Rite Aid pharmacy, where Sonya bought a
disposable camera. John drove them to Bay-

shore Bluffs Park, where they took silly pictures, some cheek to cheek, others of each other leaping into the air.

"You can kiss my cheek if you want to for the next picture," Sonya said.

John held out the camera, moved his cheek close to hers, and snapped the picture. "You hungry?"

"Yes." She kissed his cheek. "Very."

"For food?"

Sonya slipped her arms around his neck. "Not really."

"Me neither." John pulled her close, kissing her forehead. "But I made a reservation, so . . ."

Sonya put her nose on his. "You could kiss me." *Right now. Hard on the lips.*

"I'd rather kiss you during the sunset," John said. "If that's all right."

And that would be . . . the perfect kiss. "Yeah. That would be all right."

At The Galley just up the beach, Sonya tried to pay her half of the date, but John wouldn't have it.

"It's my treat," he said.

"But it's so expensive," Sonya said. "Please let me help."

"This is a real date, Sonya," John said. "And I am paying."

The Galley wasn't as expensive as Charlie's was, but it would still put a dent into anyone's wallet. They shared pan-seared scallops for their appetizer, ate mixed greens for their salad, and chose Naked Fish — Hawaiian Ahi for their main course. While they ate Slice of Heaven pie, apple pie with ice cream, they looked out onto Morro Bay.

"Sonya," John said, "I have a confession to make."

This pie is so good. "It wasn't a red bikini, was it?"

"No, it was red," John said, turning red. "And see-through."

And this restaurant is heating up. "Did you like what you saw?"

"Oh, yes."

I like the way he says that.

"Yeah, um, and that's what I have to confess," John said. "I have some bad habits, and I feel the need to confess them to you before we go any further. We . . . are moving further, aren't we?"

Can't you hear my heart banging in my chest from where you're sitting? "Yes."

"Good. Um, as you've noticed, I have a very active, um, dream life."

"How's that a bad habit?" *Even the crust of this pie is good!*

"It's not," John said. "I mean, I can't help having dreams, right? It's dwelling on my dreams and thinking about my dreams and, well, telling you about my dreams — that's the bad habit."

"It's not a bad habit to me," Sonya said. "I hope you can always tell me your dreams."

"I plan to."

I can't wait to hear the play-by-play.

"Um, Sonya, that's not my only bad habit," John said.

"I have plenty of bad habits, too." *Which I've never confessed to anyone. Of course, I've never had anyone to confess them to.*

"I'll bet you have three at most," John said.

Try triple digits, man. "Many more than that."

"We'll see," John said. "Um, I pick my teeth with anything handy. Edge of an envelope, my fingernail, a credit card, a key once. I can't stand to have anything stuck in my teeth."

"I suck my teeth," Sonya said, "but only when I'm agitated."

"I haven't heard you do that around me."

"You don't agitate me." *You worry my loins, however.* "Um, I pop my gum."

"I chew gum too loudly," John said. "I also sometimes wear clothes more than once. Not drawers, though. I always wear clean ones."

"I have been wearing the same pajamas for the last week. I shower before I go to bed, but still."

John smiled. "You wear pajamas?"

"Yep. SpongeBob. What do you wear?"

"Usually only my underwear and a T-shirt,

but since I live alone, and I sometimes don't get to the laundry soon enough, I, um, wear nothing."

"Oh." *And there go my loins again.* "Interesting. You, um, you haven't done that at the mansion, have you?"

"No. Justin is my roommate."

"Oh, right."

John took a sip of ice water. "I do make my bed every day, even though I don't truly see the point."

"Me too."

"Have you ever, um, gone natural to bed?" John asked.

"No. Shani's in the room with me anyway."

"Oh, right, but I meant when you're home alone in Charlotte."

What a question! "No."

"Oh. You should, um, try it once, just to see."

And I might do just that tonight . . . for a few minutes. Just to see. "Let's see. Oh. I watch entirely too much TV."

"Same here," John said.

"I just don't have . . . anyone to do things with, you know?"

"I know." John sighed. "And if you did . . . have someone . . . to . . . *do* . . . things . . . with . . ."

And now we're back to sex. Amazing how quickly we can do that. "I have had someone to do . . . I mean, if I had someone to do things with, I wouldn't be watching TV nearly as much."

"The TV might still be on," John said.

"I wouldn't be paying attention to it," Sonya said.

"Neither would I," John said. "Um, what do you eat while you're watching TV?"

"I must have pork rinds, Rolos, and peanut M and M's."

"I have to have any kind of cola and pretzels," John said.

"No chocolate?"

John leaned forward. "I love the taste of chocolate," he whispered. "I *really* like hot chocolate."

Whoo. "With the little marshmallows?"

"Yes. It's, um, frothier."

Oh . . . my.

"Sometimes I eat Peppermint Patties," John said. "They give me some extremely vivid dreams."

"Make sure you eat a couple tonight," Sonya said, "so you can tell me about your dreams tomorrow."

John leaned even closer. "I don't want to dream about it anymore, Sonya."

"Neither do I." She laughed. "Listen to us. We're talking about food while we eat." *And sex, too. There must be a connection between sex and food.*

"And we talk about TV while we're watching TV, church while we're at church," John said. "We are a peculiar people, aren't we?"

"Yes." *We're two peculiar people made for each other.* "Are you getting enough sleep, John?"

"No, not at all," John said. "Are you?"

"No. I don't get enough sleep in general."

"Me neither," John said. "I can get by on four hours' sleep most of the time."

"I sleep more in my recliner while watching TV than I do in my bed." *And there I go mentioning my bed.*

"I wake up in front of the TV at least twice a week," John said.

"You must have a comfortable couch."

"Yes." John smiled. "It could be more comfortable."

"How so?" *As if I didn't know.*

"I could be holding more than a couch pillow."

I knew he'd say something like that. "How, um, closely would you be holding this . . . someone? I'm assuming there'd be a someone."

"I'd hold her so closely that I wouldn't know where I stopped and she began."

"That's . . . that's close." *Two becoming one flesh again. I'd love to have my body get lost in his. I mean, I'd love to have his body get lost in mine. I mean . . . I am so hard up for sex!*

"You've noticed that I'm kind of quiet in church," John said.

546

"I've noticed," Sonya said. "But you sing loud."

"Yeah. But my quiet praise makes me stick out at New Hope. I don't jump and shout. I close my eyes a lot instead."

"Praise is praise," Sonya said. "I think God likes variety. Sometimes I'm quiet, sometimes I'm hyped."

"But you're always moving," John said.

"The Spirit moves me."

"And the Spirit moves you very well, Sonya. I wish I could sit in the pew behind you."

The things he says when I'm trying to steer us away from stuff like that!

"I like to watch you dance, Sonya."

"I'm dancing for the Lord, Brother John."

"And I'm jealous," John said. "I want to cut in."

"I might let you." *Why is this seat warming up again?* "Um, what's another one of your bad habits?"

"I'm trying to flirt here, Sonya."

"Tell the truth, John. You aren't flirting with me at all."

John sighed. "You got me. I'm really trying to seduce you."

And now I'm panting. "You don't have to try."

John blinked and took another sip of water. "I . . . don't?"

"No. You just . . . naturally do it." *And I just*

547

naturally fall for it.

"And you're okay with it?" John asked.

I need it! "Yes."

"Okay." John smiled. "I, um, I let the dishes sit in the sink for days even though I know I'll need a belt sander to clean them off."

Sonya laughed loud enough to upset the woman sitting closest to her. "From seducing me to doing the dishes?" she whispered.

"I sometimes dance at the sink while I wash them," John said. "And you were in front of me at the sink one time at the mansion, and you were doing a little dance, and I got to thinking how, um, fun it might be to . . . do the dishes with you. That's how I jumped from seduction to dishes. Not much of a jump actually, when you think about it."

Even doing dishes with this man will be erotic. "I sometimes dance in my kitchen, too. Linoleum floors are made for dancing. I even dance in the shower where no one can see me."

John closed his eyes and smiled. "I can see you. I can see all of you, Sonya." He snapped open his eyes, his smile turning into a frown.

"Was it that bad?" Sonya asked.

"No, Sonya, not at all." He left his side of the booth and slid in next to Sonya. "I *really* saw you." He leaned out of the booth and craned his neck side to side until their waitress saw him. "Check, please."

"Um, what was I doing?" Sonya asked.

"I saw you dancing in the shower, and your hands were . . . and the soap was . . ." He turned to look for the waitress. "I need the check now."

"Did you get in the shower with me?" Sonya asked.

John nodded. "I need to cool off, you know?"

The waitress brought the check, and John counted out seven twenties, leaving them on the table.

"Let's go cool off along the beach." He slid out of the booth and held out his hand.

I have to know what happened next! "Did we get all steamed up?"

John took Sonya's hand. "I need to hear waves crashing now. Let's go."

Do I mind being dragged by a handsome man through a fancy restaurant? Not at all.

He got in the shower with me!

They drove back to Morro Bay State Park and strolled hand in hand down a secluded stretch of brown sand as the sun began its descent into the Pacific.

"Did you really see all of me, John?" Sonya asked.

"Sonya, every time I close my eyes I see you."

"Naked in the shower?"

John shook his head. "No, I just . . . see you." He closed his eyes. "Well, *now* I see you in the shower." He smiled. "You use too much soap. Oh, so you soap *that* part a lot."

"Stop," Sonya said, but she didn't mean it.

"Don't you get ashy down there?" John asked.

She slapped playfully at his arm with her free hand. "Stop."

John opened his eyes. "I don't just see you on a couch or in the shower or . . . or in . . . our . . . bed."

Our bed. He specifically called it "our" bed.

"I see you next to me in church, Sonya," John said. "I see you next to me on the couch. In front of me on the couch. Next to me washing dishes. In front of me doing dishes. Next to me driving somewhere. Next to me shopping for groceries. And whenever we are in bed, we're watching TV and talking about food for some reason. I've been seeing you everywhere, Sonya. I even see you blocking my shot."

"I would never do that." *Are you kidding? First chance I get, I'm swatting his shot into next week.*

"I even see me taking your hand," John said, "and walking somewhere else."

"Where are we?" Sonya asked.

"Not sure," John said. "Outside. I know that."

"And . . . what am I wearing?" Sonya asked.

"A smile."

Interesting. "And what else?"

John turned to her. "A long, flowing dress. Maybe the wind is making it flow." He rested his forehead on hers. "It's a long, flowing white dress, Sonya."

Well . . . hmm. Oh . . . wow. "And did you . . . did you have a ring for me?"

John nodded and lightly brushed his lips with hers. "Want to know what you *weren't* wearing?"

"A red bikini." Sonya kissed his chin.

"You weren't wearing any shoes," John said.

Sonya's lips met his. "No shoes," she whispered.

"None."

And then John gave Sonya their first real kiss.

Oh, this is nice. He has deceptively soft lips — and a curious tongue, too! And he tastes like Slice of Heaven pie!

"Whoa," she said.

"Whoa," he said.

CHAPTER 53

John gripped both her hands and caught his breath. *That kiss was pure fire. My lips are still humming.* "The sun's going down."

"Yeah."

And I see the sun setting in your eyes, he thought. *All those beautiful colors.* "The show's about to begin. You want to watch it with me?"

"I wouldn't miss it for the world."

He slipped behind her. "And we have front row seats."

"As long as no one walks in front of us."

John put his hands on her hips. "Let's sit." He eased down to the sand, Sonya following and firmly planting her booty in his lap.

"Is that all right?" she said.

Scripturally, no. Psychically, a definite yes. "Yes." He wrapped his hands around her. "I wish we could stay here longer."

"Yeah. Think they're worried about us?"

"Probably." He kissed the back of her neck. "Thank you, Sonya."

She pulled his arms more tightly around her stomach. "For what?"

"For everything you say and do."

"Is everything I say and do in your mind, too?" Sonya asked.

Just about. "Yes. When you're in the shower, man, I am just so thankful. I'll be dreaming hallelujahs all night."

God, is this what love feels like? John thought. *Sunset, sand, warm hug, honest thoughts, and sensational body heat? You done good, God. You made love worth all the hassle.*

"I don't want to leave," Sonya whispered.

"We'll stay till the ocean swallows the sun," John said.

Sonya settled back into his chest. "Okay by me."

"I may nibble on your ears," John said. "I'm always hungry."

"Good."

He tasted an earlobe. "I may, um, also massage things."

Sonya turned her head. "Yeah? Like what?"

"Well, I can't reach your feet, but your stomach is in reach."

She lifted up her shirt. "Rub away."

John slid his hands over her one-pack, tickling her bellybutton with his index fingers. Sonya raised her hands over her head and clasped them behind John's neck.

"I'm so glad I wore this Windbreaker," Sonya said. "Feel free to . . . freely feel."

John massaged her stomach and sides, sliding his hands down her thighs, then up her thighs. He always returned to her stomach, her skin hot, and his hands rose higher, brushing against her bra.

"What you doin' to me, man?" Sonya whispered.

He slid his hands down to her belt line, teasing a finger between her jeans and panties. "I'm exploring."

"Hope you find what you're looking for," Sonya whispered.

He wormed his hands into her front pockets, letting his finger-tips wander over even hotter fabric.

"You're teasing me," she whispered.

And my loins are responding, John thought. *Thank you, loins, for still working.* He slowly slid his hands out of her pockets. "I don't want to disrespect you in any way, Sonya."

She slid her arms out of her sleeves, freeing them under the Windbreaker. She grabbed his hands and placed them on her breasts. "Squeeze, please."

John squeezed.

She guided his hands down her stomach to her beltline. "I want to turn around."

"Go ahead."

Sonya swiveled her hips and straddled him, kissing him deeply.

John rubbed her back, sliding his hands between her jeans and panties. *So firm! So*

soft! How can something so firm be so soft?
He pulled back from the kiss. "May I squeeze your booty?"

"If you do, man, I will scream." She smiled. "But in a good way."

John squeezed gently. "I didn't hear a scream."

"It was in my head," Sonya said. "Harder, please."

John squeezed harder.

"You have such big hands," Sonya said.

He moved his hands up to her shoulders, kneading soft, warm skin. "I, um, look at the sun."

Sonya turned her head. "That's better than a postcard."

"Yep."

She pushed her arms through her sleeves and rested them on John's shoulders. "Are you as excited as I am?"

"I'm probably more excited than you are," John said.

Sonya grazed his cheeks with her nails. "I doubt that." She kissed him, lips only. "If we stay here in this position for even three minutes more, you will be in danger, man."

He hugged her. "That's some danger I think I can face." He looked out over the waves. "Sun's almost gone."

"We better get going, then," Sonya said, standing and pulling him to his feet.

"Do we have any more pictures left?" John asked.

"One more." She pulled out the camera and took a picture of the sunset. "Our first sunset." She put the camera in his back pocket. "And it won't be the last."

They walked like two old lovers back to the truck, not rushing, not racing, just enjoying the feel of each other's hands, each other's shy smiles.

Once on the road back to the mansion, Sonya fell asleep, her soft cheek pressed to his chest.

This, John thought, *is the most comfortable silence I've ever known. Thank You, God. Thank for a second chance.*

Thank You for being the God of second chances.

John sat with arms around Sonya's sleeping form, the truck parked less than one hundred feet away from the driveway of the mansion. *So peaceful. So warm. Such soft hair. Such tender skin.*

Sonya stirred. "Are we home yet?"

Not yet. "We're at the mansion."

She sat up and looked out the window. "Sorry about that."

"You were tired," John said.

"First real sleep I've had since I've been here." She rubbed his chest. "You're a good pillow."

"Should I kiss you good night here or at the door?" John asked.

Sonya rubbed her eyes. "There are cameras at the door. Push the seat back."

John pulled a lever under the seat, and the entire bench seat moved back a foot.

Sonya straddled him, loosening the button of her jeans. "So your big ol' hands will have some more room to explore."

John slid his hands down to her booty.

"Wait." She unzipped her pants and wiggled a little. "Okay. Now your hands will have enough room."

John pushed her jeans down a few inches. "I have to give you room to breathe, right?"

Sonya nodded and turned her head. "Don't be shy."

"I won't be."

John's stretched his arms as far as he could, his hands cupping Sonya's booty forcefully. "You have such hot skin."

"You're making it hot," Sonya whispered. "I'm really close to screaming. We better close the windows."

With Sonya still straddling him, he bucked their bodies from one window to the other, Sonya rolling up the windows.

"Think we can make the truck rock?" Sonya asked.

"Doubt it," John said. "The suspension on these babies is —"

Sonya stole the words from John's mouth as she started a slow grind, her lips moving softly over his. "I know we can make this truck rock." She unzipped her Windbreaker and unbuttoned her shirt. "Just hold me, okay? I am really close right now."

John squeezed her booty in rhythm to her grinding, and as they kissed, Sonya sucked on his tongue until John wasn't sure he had any taste buds left.

Sonya leaned back and sighed. "Oh . . ." She lifted her hands and pressed them on the ceiling of the truck, pushing down with such force that the Ford F-150, did, indeed, move.

"You're curling my toes," Sonya said. She arched her back and fell forward. "Oh . . . whoa . . . wow." She blinked. "I will not be able to sleep tonight."

"I won't be able to either," John said. "Think we could watch some TV together, say, around four? We can just say that it's still part of the date, you know, an extension of the date."

Sonya nodded. "I'll, um, wear my pajamas."

"I'll wear a smile."

Sonya smiled. "I'll also bring a blanket. The cameras, remember?"

John kissed and hugged her. "I don't want to go back to unreality."

"Neither do I." She leaned back. "Fix me."

John took his time pulling up Sonya's jeans, zipping and buttoning them up while caressing her. He took even more time buttoning up her shirt.

"I didn't know getting dressed could be such a turn-on," Sonya said. "Don't you have to return the truck?"

"They'll come by and pick it up in the morning."

She patted the seat. "I'm so glad this didn't have bucket seats."

"Me too." He looked at the windows. "Sonya, we've fogged up the windows."

"And later," she said, "we'll be fogging up the camera."

CHAPTER 54

Why aren't I embarrassed? Sonya thought. *I just had a mostly clothed orgasm in the front seat of a Ford F-150. And now I'm holding hands with the man responsible. My whole body is buzzing!*

The front door of the mansion banged open.

Hmm. I wonder what buzz kill is approaching us now. Since I can't see who it is, it has to be Bob.

They found Bob leaning on the limo. "Where have you two been?"

Sonya held up their hands. "Y'all filming this? No. Of course not. This reality isn't right for your demographic." *Geez, we both have ashy hands.*

"You are seriously trying my patience, Miss Richardson," Bob said. "You ditched us at the restaurant, and we wasted thousands upon thousands of dollars on a crew that drove all over LA looking for you."

"Where'd you look?" John asked.

"Knowing you two," Bob said, "mostly in churches."

"Cool," John said.

"Cool?" Bob said. "I have nothing to put on the air."

Sonya kissed John's chin. "Put that on the air." She kissed his lips. "Put that on the air. Bob, I had an awesome date, and I'm sure it was awesome only because none of you were involved."

"I have nothing to show, Sonya," Bob said.

Sonya planted a longer, juicier kiss on John. *I can't get over how soft his lips are!* "We can stage a longer kiss next to the pool if you like. I know, you'll film us getting out of that truck, and we'll walk up the driveway again holding hands. At the door, we'll say seriously romantic things to each other. Oh, it will be so magical."

"That, um, that . . . won't be necessary," Bob said.

"But listen to the dialogue John and I can have." She grabbed both of John's hands. "John, let's practice." She fluttered her eyelashes. "I had a peachy keen time tonight, babe. You are so durn sexy. We really made a connection, like, OMG."

John laughed. "Yo, it was awesome, boo. You really got it goin' on, Ma. You're my honey and you got me buzzing like a bee. Yo."

Sonya giggled. "You ain't bad for a white

guy, you know what I'm sayin'? I mean, you even got a little back goin' on back there."

"I hear you, honey lamb sweetie pie," John said. "You make me want to bust a move, yo."

"You're all that and a bag of chips and the dip, man," Sonya said.

John dropped her hands and grabbed her by the hips. "Girrrl, do fries go with that shake? I hope they do, cuz I sure am hungry."

Sonya spun around, holding on to John's arms. "Oh, Bob, it will be *perfect* for the show. And then I can lead him up the stairs to my room so you can do one of your famous fadeouts."

The mansion door slammed open again.

And here's buzz kill number two. I didn't know my daughter could run so fast. I shouldn't be surprised. She has my genes.

"Hi, Shani," Sonya said.

Kim's mouth dropped open. "Where were you, Sonya?"

And where were you? I've been out here for almost five minutes messing with Bob. "Shani, John and I went to Morro Bay, three hours up the coast. We walked on the beach and on the rocks, ate too much, walked on the beach again, saw a beautiful sunset, and came back. It was a real date. There wasn't a whole lot to film anyway, Bob." *Okay, the kisses, snuggling on the beach, us making out in the truck, me*

getting my booty massaged, my orgasm —
okay, there would have been plenty to film, and
our conversations? Wow. So much seduction
and flirtation. It was all too hot for TV anyway.

"Don't blame her, Shani," John said. "It was all my idea."

"Yeah," Kim said, "you practically kidnapped her."

"I was a very willing hostage." *And I really didn't want to be found.*

"Sonya, they almost put out an Amber Alert on you," Kim said.

"What?" Sonya said. "You don't put an Amber Alert out for grown folks."

"I called you a hundred times," Kim said.

She's worried about me? Cool. "I left my phone in the room."

"I know," Kim said. "I answered it. I even said, 'Hello.' What if something had happened?"

Something did happen, and it only happened because I was free of this place. "I was in excellent hands." *The most excellent I have ever known. Parts of me are crying because his hands are not rubbing, squeezing, and gripping them. My booty wants some more love!* "And I'm back in one piece, aren't I?" *And several pieces of me are extremely happy, too.*

Kim stared at Sonya's hand holding John's. "What's this?"

Sonya felt John loosening his hand from

hers. *Don't let my scary, mixed-up daughter scare you away!*

"I'm, um, I'm pretty tired, Sonya." He gripped her hand once and let go. "I have a feeling I'll be up all night anyway."

Oh, yes. We have an extension of our date later. He'll need his rest.

John kissed her cheek. "Good night."

Sonya grabbed his face and kissed him. "Good night, John. Get some rest."

John winked. "You too."

Whoo. I think I'm going to need that rest, too. Something about the fire in those brown eyes of his. She looked down on Bob. "Anything else?"

"Just . . . don't do that again," Bob said.

"Kiss him or disappear with him?" Sonya said. "I actually plan to do both as often as I can with or without your approval or that stupid rule Aaron made."

"Just . . ." Bob shook his head. "Good night."

As Bob headed to the garage, Kim walked beside Sonya as they returned to their room.

"You could have been in trouble," Kim said, "and no one knew where you were. If I ever did such a thing, you would have had a herd of rabid cows."

Nice image. Sonya opened the front door. "Don't you do spur-of-the-moment things like that all the time?"

"That's not the point."

Sonya floated through the foyer to the stairs. "I was never in any danger, Kim."

Well, there was one moment when I wanted to tear his shirt off, and my shirt off, and then we would have created our own personal nude beach. Sorry, Lord, but I was feeling it! And feeling him, too. Oh, he would have been in danger then, not me. And in the truck, we could have made quintuplets for sure. I'll have to ask Kim where she got that bikini. I wonder if they have it in red . . .

Sonya started up the stairs.

"Did you have to kiss him right in front of everybody just now?" Kim asked.

"Yes. I did." *And I'd do it again.* "What's your point?"

"Were you making out with him the whole time?" Kim asked.

Sonya turned down the hallway to their room. "No. I slept some."

Kim tugged Sonya's arm. "You did what?"

Sonya opened their door. "What? I'm not allowed to get a leg up?"

Kim rushed into their room ahead of Sonya. "Geez, I don't want to hear about this." She sat on Sonya's bed, her arms crossed.

So angry! Sonya took off her Windbreaker. "We didn't do anything like that." *We only dreamed it and thought it, and, oh, we kind of simulated it in the truck. The ceiling of that truck sure came in handy for that final down thrust, too.*

"I don't want to know about what my mama was doing on her date," Kim said.

She said . . . "mama" . . . "my mama" . . . That's not quite mama with a capital letter, but it's progress. "Kim, we talked, we ate, we walked, we talked some more." *There was some kissing. And rubbing, and hugging, and panting, and sweating, and loins grinding.* "It was a real old-fashioned date." She unbuttoned her shirt, removed her bra, and put on her SpongeBob pajama top.

"But . . . why him?" Kim asked. "You didn't kiss on anyone else, did you?"

"Nope." Sonya unzipped her jeans, letting them drop to the floor. She stepped out of them and put on her SpongeBob pajama bottoms. "But I had no physical need to kiss them. Just John. My body is going through withdrawal already, Kim. I'm jonesing for some John."

Sonya went to the window. *He's not at the pool. Of course he's not at the pool. He's in his bed where I should be, and he's resting up for me.* "I'm even going to sneak out of this room and meet him in the great room for some snuggling later on tonight. Girl, I want this man."

Kim sighed. "Does this mean that he's

the one?"

"I know he is," Sonya said. "Yes. John is the one."

Kim fell back onto Sonya's bed. "Wow. One date."

Sonya pulled back her covers, propped up two pillows, and got into bed. "Kim, I just had the *best* date in my entire life."

"Like you've had that many dates to compare it to."

"I have had exactly ten dates in my life, one fifteen years ago, and nine here," Sonya said. "I am qualified to say that tonight was the best date I have ever had."

Kim pounded the bed with one fist. "What about Tony?"

That was random. "What about him?"

"You're not going to send him packing Monday, are you?" Kim asked.

"I don't intend to send any of them home this week."

Kim sat up. "*This* week? What about *next* week?"

Yeah. What about next week? "You know, for the first time I don't know about next week. I think I've finally found him, you know? I think I've finally found my hunk."

Kim's eyes dropped. "You're going to break up the Team?"

"I think I have to, Kim," Sonya said. "God's been working on me."

"You mean that man's been working on you."

Sonya smiled. "Him too." *And I'll let him work on me some more in a little while. Don't forget the blanket, Sonya. You know they'll be filming.*

"What's he got that the others don't have?" Kim asked.

"He has my heart, Kim," Sonya said. "And God's heart, too. That is an awesome combination in a man."

"I can't believe . . ." Kim rolled off the bed and went to the window. "It's not fair to the others. You're going to break their hearts."

"Are you kidding?" Sonya asked.

"They love you, Sonya."

"No, they don't. I'm like their cool older aunt or something." *And only John seems to love me. Whoa, I just gave myself goose bumps. At least I think he loves me.* "And if they truly love me, they'll understand that I have made my choice."

Kim stormed across the room. "Well, I don't understand." She opened the door, leaped through, and slammed it behind her.

That was overly dramatic, Sonya thought. *But I'm not concerned. She's upset and confused, and I'm going to let her be upset and confused. I can't explain how I feel about John any better except to say that I love him.*

I love him.

And if she can't understand that, she'll just have to be upset and confused.

Sonya turned off the light on the nightstand. *Okay, body, get your rest. Wait a minute.* She tiptoed to the window and saw Kim outside sitting alone at a table. *I know you don't want Tony to go, little girl, but I don't know how I can keep him after tonight.* She took a step back to the bed.

Hmm. I have a little time alone here. She took off her pajamas and panties and slipped into bed. *This is . . . odd.*

But nice.

Sonya smiled in the dark. *I actually feel . . . sexy.*

She counted to fifty, slid out of bed, put on her pajamas, and wiggled under the covers.

Hmm. I may have to retire these pajamas.

CHAPTER 55

After searching the great room, the kitchen, and the pool area, John found the rest of the Team lounging in the mini-theater watching *Friday.*

"How'd it go, Artie?" Justin asked.

Gary pointed a remote behind him, and the screen turned blue. "Yeah. How'd it go?"

John smiled. "It was amazing."

John heard three loud sighs.

"I'm real happy for you, man," Gary said.

"Me too," Tony said.

There's something . . . off about this. "Y'all are glad?"

"You love her, right?" Justin asked.

That's the ultimate question of the universe, isn't it? "Yes. With all of my heart and every other part of me. Don't y'all love her?"

No one answered his question. Instead, they gave each other some dap.

"Why are y'all so happy about this?" John asked.

"Artie, I'm in love, too," Justin said. "With

Brandy, the singer I've been talking to at Bethel. I've been waiting for Jazz to cut me loose so I could be with her. But Jazz is so special, I just can't walk out on her, you know? But now, I can. You understand?"

Not quite. "You've been waiting to get dumped."

"Yeah," Justin said. "I want to get dumped. I sang Biz Markie, dog. I didn't want to win."

It still doesn't make sense. "And you really love Brandy."

"Man, I have never felt nothing like this before," Justin said. "I don't *want* to feel anything *but* this. And now, I can go away with a clear conscience."

"I gotta get home to my kids," Gary said. "I've never been away from them this long before. I thought I could handle it, but I can't. I miss my kids."

"And his baby mama," Tony said.

"Yeah, I'm in love with her now," Gary said. "Can you believe that? I wasn't before. I *never* was before. I had to get two thousand miles away from her to realize that I can't live without her. You understand?"

"I do," John said. "I really do, Gary." *I had to get thousands of miles away from the memory of my wife to feel the love of another woman.* "Tony, why are *you* so happy?"

"I shouldn't say," Tony said.

"Go ahead, dog," Justin said. "You already

told us."

"I'm in love with Shani," Tony said.

"We tried to talk him out of it," Gary said. "The trouble he's asking for."

John couldn't think of anything to say. He wanted to say, "That woman is not lovable," but he kept his silence.

"I'm pretty sure the feeling is mutual," Tony said. "We spent a lot of time together today."

"*All* day," Justin said. "We didn't see them for long stretches at a time either."

"Like I told you, we were just . . . wandering around the mansion," Tony said.

"Uh-huh," Gary said. "You was just wandering your hands all over her."

"Really. It was just a long walk," Tony said. "Artie, I've never even dreamed of anyone like her, and I have some wild dreams. The sooner Jazz dumps me, the sooner I can hook up with Shani. But if she keeps holding on to us . . . You understand?"

"I think I do." John paced in front of the screen. "Gentlemen, this is quite a predicament."

"You're telling me," Gary said. "As long as she keeps us on the show, we can't be where we want to be. We can't be where we *need* to be."

Justin nodded and set his jaw. "I'm walking Monday night. Yep. I gotta go."

"Hold on, now, fellas," John said. "We only had one date. Yes, it was an amazing, romantic date, but in the morning, she might change her mind."

Gary stared him down. "Will she?"

John smiled. "No. I won't let her." He shook his head. "But you can't just . . . leave."

"Dude, I have to," Justin said. "I've never felt this way before. Brandy is my soul mate, I know it. I mean, we met in church. There's something holy about that. Whenever I close my eyes, I see her. Y'all, whenever I used to close my eyes, I only saw food. This is serious. Brandy is better than food to me."

"You got it bad," Gary said.

"Yeah." Justin fumbled with his fingers. "I don't even have the appetite for food like I used to have. I'm only hungry for her, you get me?"

John nodded. *My stomach is growling right now for some more Sonya.*

"I have to go, too," Gary said. "My youngest daughter has a birthday this coming Friday, her second. I can't miss it. I missed her first one cuz I was fussing with her mama."

Tony stood in front of John. "And if *they* leave, Artie, that would leave just the two of us. You get Jazz, I get Shani."

"Are you sure that Shani, um, wants you?" John asked.

"I think she wants me," Tony said. "I don't know for sure. But we, um, we held hands."

"Uh-huh," Justin said. "What else?"

"A few kisses," Tony said. "The girl can kiss."

"And what else?" Gary said. "I had to leave the pool cuz of y'all messing with each other."

"She has a great body," Tony said. "We were like . . . teenagers. I had trouble breathing."

John sighed. "But you don't really know how she feels about you."

"No." Tony returned to his seat. "I don't know anything for sure about her, but that's what I like about her. The variety, the random nature of everything about her. And I want the chance to try to figure her out. I can't be winning this thing, Artie. That would be so twisted, you know? He wins the older sister and dumps her for the younger sister the first chance he gets. I want to do right by both of them."

John faced three men. *Three friends.* "Y'all would just . . . give up like that?"

"Jazz only looks at you, dog," Justin said.

"Yeah, man," Tony said. "She only has eyes for you."

"I never seen a woman smile so much at somebody," Gary said.

John looked at the floor. "She kisses good, too."

Justin jumped out of his chair. "Ah! I *knew* you had game. You been kissin' on the princess."

John nodded. "Almost as much as she's been kissin' on me."

"Yes!" Tony shouted. "This is serious, then."

"Yeah," John said. "As serious as a walk down the aisle."

Justin dropped back into his chair. "*That* serious?"

"Yes," John said. "*That* serious. I came on this show to find a wife, fellas, and I've found her. The next logical step is to be stepping down the aisle."

Gary looked at Justin and then at Tony. "You came . . . to find a wife."

"Yes," John said. "I know it sounds crazy."

Justin laughed. "Man, I came on this show for something fun to do. Wow."

"I'm happy for you, man," Gary said. "I'm goin' down the aisle when I get home, too." He stared a hole in Justin's head. "Ain't that what you're planning, too?"

"What?" Justin looked away and sighed. "I'm working on that. Man, I haven't even gotten the chance to kiss Brandy yet with y'all around."

"You a lie," Gary said.

Justin smiled. "Yeah, I mean, I haven't been able to kiss her as *much* as I want to with y'all around. And the rest of the choir. And her mama. Nosy thing. Always checking."

"We'll block for you tomorrow, man," Tony said.

After a short silence, John smiled at the ground. "You guys are, um, . . ." *Man, I am going to miss these guys.* "Um, thank you."

"You and Jazz have been tight from the second you took off your shoes, Artie," Justin said. "I'm still not sure exactly why, but whatever you got, she wants, and she wants it bad."

"I think it was the foot rub," Tony said.

"Nah, it was when he gave her the swimming lesson," Gary said.

"Shoot," Justin said. "You're both wrong. It was the fried chicken."

"What's your secret, man?" Gary asked.

"No real secret," John said. "I've just been completely honest with her from the moment I met her. And I haven't exactly been honest with you. Fellas, I'm not thirty by a long shot."

Tony laughed loudly. "We know you're older, man. Old Spice? C'mon. Only old dudes use that stuff."

"I'm forty," John said. "Wait. I had a birthday last month. In all this excitement, I forgot. I'm forty-one now."

Gary blinked. "No kiddin'? You don't look it."

"And," John said, "I'm not a film editor."

"Cuz you're a preacher," Justin said. "All them verses you been spittin'."

John nodded. "Used to be. I just need a wife. My church believes that a pastor must be married to be a pastor."

"And I think you'll be preaching again real soon," Justin said. "Dag, I want to start packin' now instead of Monday afternoon."

Gary nodded. "One last Sunday service. And we're gonna make it a great one."

"What are y'all up to?" John asked.

"When y'all disappeared," Gary said, "we knew something was up, so Justin and I have been workin' on a song. Kind of a farewell song."

"Yes, sir, service gonna be jumpin' tomorrow," Justin said.

"This might sound strange," John said, "but I think WB should film it, don't you?" He shrugged. "Let's get the country jumpin'. What do you think?"

"We takin' America to church, yo," Justin said.

John looked up at the ceiling. "You get all that, Larry, Bob? Have a crew ready to go with us to Bethel tomorrow morning."

"There aren't any cameras in here," Tony said. "We checked."

"Don't be so sure," John said.

A little before 4 AM, John did his best to sneak out of his and Justin's room.

"You don't have to sneak, Artie," Justin said.

"Um, I'm gonna go finish our date," John said. "We're just going to watch some TV."

"Uh-huh," Justin said. "Right. Give her a kiss for me."

When John entered the great room, Sonya

already had popcorn and two bottled waters on the coffee table in front of a couch, the remote in her hand, SpongeBob's eyes staring at him from between her breasts, a blanket around her shoulders.

"What do you want to watch?" Sonya asked.

"You."

"I like the sound of that."

"I like the sound of you," John said. He slid behind her on the couch and rubbed her back. "I like the feel of you."

"I won't be able to concentrate on the show," Sonya said.

"I don't want you to."

Sonya tuned the TV to *Forensic Files*, turned down the sound, settled the blanket around them, and wormed her booty into John as they both sat facing the TV.

"What are you thinking about?" John asked.

"You."

"In a good or a bad way?"

"Both."

"The feeling is mutual." He ran his hands down her arms. "Such sexy lingerie."

"Yes. The sexiest."

He rubbed her shoulders briefly before sliding his hands down her back to her hips. "These pajamas don't leave much to the imagination, Miss Sonya. You're not wearing drawers."

"Nope."

"My hands want to explore."

Sonya took his hands and brought them all the way to SpongeBob's eyes. *Such small, hard nipples!* "I like reverse hugs, don't you?" She wiggled her booty into his lap.

"Especially when there's a frisky booty in the mix," John said.

She moved his hands slowly to her stomach, moving them in circles.

"I love your one-pack," John whispered.

"You can go lower if you want to," Sonya whispered.

"I want to."

He walked his fingers down to her waistband, found she was pulling it up to allow him to continue, and felt his way through a downy tuft of hair to —

"Right there," she whispered.

He made small circles, slow circles, firm circles, and teasing circles as Sonya arched her back.

"Faster," Sonya whispered.

He completed three fast circles when Sonya bucked back into him, her pajama bottoms sliding down as she did to reveal the most perfect booty ever created.

And this is where fifteen years of waiting —
He thrust up.

Man, I have to do some laundry. This was my last clean pair of sweats.

She turned around to straddle him. "Did you just . . ."

John nodded. "I'm a mess."

"We both are." She kissed him tenderly.

"I want to hold you until the sunrise, Sonya."

"Then hold me," Sonya said, burying her head into his chest. "Hold me and never let go."

Lord, I don't know if I can wait much longer. I mean, we almost just got seriously busy. It wouldn't have taken but a quick pull of my drawstring. I know we have to wait longer to do that, but . . . I want to be one flesh with her in the best way. I mean, Sheila and I had a reasonable engagement even though it was the longest three months of my life. I don't want to wait any longer than I absolutely have to for this woman. I know, I know, it's not about what I want. It's what You want. But I need this woman now in every sense. Help me . . . know what to say and do when the time comes, and help me remember to keep my drawstrings and belts tight.

"What are you thinking about?" Sonya whispered.

"The future."

"Me too. Is it a happy one?"

"The happiest."

"Does it involve a lot of this?"

"For the first few months," John said, "this is *all* we're gonna do."

Sonya burrowed her head deeper into his chest. "Amen."

■ ■ ■ ■

"Are we going to run any of this scene, Bob?"

"Um, this scene? Uh, no."

"We're not? Isn't this blazing-hot stuff? We may have to censor a few things, but I think we can swing it. The blanket slipping away there at the end was kind of revealing, but we can fuzz that out."

"It's, um, yeah, it's hot all right, but, no, we're not running any of this."

"May I ask why?"

"This is . . . this is far too . . . too . . ."

"Real?"

"Yes, Larry." Bob wiped the tear. "It's too real for me. You mind, um, taking over the show for a while? You've been running it more than I have anyway."

"I don't mind. Where will you be if I need you?"

"I'll, um, I'll be home with my wife and daughter. Where I should be, you know?"

"I know, Bob. I'll keep things running."

"The show won't last much longer anyway."

"So we don't run what the Team was discussing in the theater either?"

"No. A surprise ending before the . . . the only logical ending works for me. We can't give anything away in the promos, though. Just a tiny tease this time."

"A tiny tease. I'll see to it." Larry sighed. "We could never have scripted anything like this."

"No." Bob sighed. "Not that we didn't try."

"You can't script love, Bob."

"No. No, you can't. They're truly in love, aren't they, Larry?"

"Yes. They haven't said the actual words to each other yet, but, yes, they're deeply, passionately in love."

"It's, um, it's kind of beautiful, Larry."

"Yes. Yes, it is."

CHAPTER 56

"Why is a camera crew following us today?" Sonya asked Sunday morning.

"Today is going to be extra special," John said.

"What's going to happen?" Sonya said.

"It's a surprise, Jazz," Justin said.

"Do the folks at Bethel know a camera crew is coming?" Sonya asked.

John shrugged. "I hope so."

Before the service, delayed for fifteen minutes to allow the camera crew to set up, Sonya watched Justin flirting again with the singer. *They are so right for each other.* She looked down the pew. *And there's Kim flirting her skirt off with Tony. They're not exactly compatible with each other, but I want them to develop since Tony has some depth.* She smiled at Gary but only got a nod. *Gary's especially quiet, probably because he's missing home, the home he wants to reestablish.* She looked at her man sitting next to her and her hand holding his under his Bible. *This is so thrilling, and I'm not ashamed. I don't even care if the whole world notices.*

"To begin our service," Reverend Cox said, "we have a special musical selection from our television guests, Justin and Gary."

Sonya turned to John. "They're going to sing?"

John nodded. "Yep."

Gary and Justin went to two microphone stands as the choir rose.

Justin took a microphone from the stand. "If you know the Lord is good, let me hear you say my, my, my, my, my, my, my God is good!"

Oh my! Sonya thought. "God is good!" she yelled.

"All the time!" Gary shouted.

Kim slid down the pew to Sonya. "Did you know they were singing?"

"No," Sonya said. She took Kim's hand. "Get Tony down here."

Kim beckoned to Tony, Tony slid down and took Kim's hand, and then they all stood along with the rest of the congregation.

And as Justin and Gary *kilt* that Fred Hammond song, Sonya connected the lyrics to the man holding her hand beside her. *I'll never find anyone like Him . . . or the man holding my hand. And my daughter is squeezing the life out of my hand, too. God surely loves me. Does Kim love me? She seems to be work-*

ing on it. *Does John love me? I think he does. I don't want to bust out and ask him. I'm sure, but I'm afraid.*

And that makes me surely afraid.

They waved their hands above their heads.

Yes, Lord, Your love never fails, and God, I know that John's love would never fail me either.

"Do you love Him?" Justin shouted.

Yes!

"Do you know He's good?" Gary shouted.

Yes!

"All the time God is good!" Justin sang.

After their song ended and the choir began another, Sonya hugged Gary and Justin to death. "That was great!"

"God is good, Jazz," Justin said.

"All the time, Justin, all the time."

After a somewhat sweaty but spirit-filled service, Sonya saw Justin sneaking off to the choir room while Tony, Gary, and John formed a mini-wall in front of her.

"I already know where he's going," Sonya said.

"Um, he's going to the bathroom," Tony said.

"No, he isn't," Sonya said. "What's her name?"

"Whose name?" Gary asked.

Sonya frowned. "I know that Justin is in love. Now what's her name?"

"I got this," John said.

Tony, Kim, and Gary walked quickly away.

"Brandy," John said. "Her name is Brandy. And they are in love."

Lord, help me here. "Are you in love, too?"

"Nope."

Nope?

"Great service, huh?"

Nope?

John took her hand. "I'm in the mood for tacos. How about you?"

Nope? He isn't in love with me, but he wants to hold my hand? Maybe he didn't hear me correctly. "John, um, are you —" *Not now, little biddy! I'm trying to interrogate my man!*

"Hello, Jazz," the little biddy said. "Anything exciting planned for tomorrow night?" She looked at their hands. "Are you two an item now?"

"We had a date last night," John said.

The little biddy hugged John. "Well, praise the Lord! I have been praying that you'd finally win a date."

"Um," John said, "thank you, but you can't tell anyone. You're the only one who knows."

"I am?" She smiled at Sonya. "Is this true?"

Sonya nodded. "Yes." *Now go away.*

"Can I tell my sister?" the little biddy asked.

John looked at Sonya. "Um, is she a gossip?"

The little biddy frowned. "Shoot. I can't tell her. The whole world will know in five minutes. But I have to tell *someone.*"

"Pray about it," John said.

"Oh, I will," the little biddy said, and she sped to the back of the church.

"She's going to tell her sister," Sonya said.

"Yep," John said.

Sonya grabbed John by the elbows. "I asked you if you were in —" *Not now, Reverend Cox! This is a conspiracy!*

John shook Reverend Cox's hand. "Outstanding service, Reverend. The spirit of the Lord is in this place. Thank you for letting us share your church with the world."

"I don't know why you didn't get those cameras in here sooner," Reverend Cox said. "Lord knows, the world needs more of the spirit of God." He clasped Sonya's free hand. "We're having a potluck downstairs. Are you free to attend?"

"But we didn't bring anything," John said.

"We have plenty," Reverend Cox said.

Sonya smiled. "We'll be down directly, Reverend Cox." *Now, shoo!*

After Reverend Cox left, Sonya moved close to John. "I asked earlier —"

"Jazz, come on," Kim interrupted. "It's such a beautiful day. We want to go to the beach."

Sonya blinked at Tony and Kim. "We're staying for the potluck downstairs first."

Kim wrinkled up her nose. "A potluck? I don't know these people."

"Go on," Sonya said. *Shoo!*

John touched Tony's elbow. "Where's Gary?"

"He's already downstairs chowing down," Tony said. "I smell roast beef." He turned to Kim. "Let's go."

After Tony and Kim left, John rubbed his stomach. "I'm kind of hungry, too. The popcorn this morning wasn't enough to hold me."

But I haven't finished asking my question! "John, I need to know something first."

"I'm not in love with you, Sonya," John said. He held out his hand. "Come on. Let's go get our grub on."

What? How can that be? Do I take his hand? Of course I don't.

Sonya walked around John and went to the back of the church. She entered the ladies' room, walked into a stall, closed the door, and wept.

What's happening, Lord? What's going on? I'm losing control of my men and my man! Nope? I ask, "Are you in love, too?" and he says "Nope." What's that supposed to mean? Nope? And then he puts his hand out to me and says, "Let's go get our grub on." What kind of man says stuff like that?

The door to the bathroom opened. "Sonya?"

And now Kim is interrupting my pity party.

588

"Yes?" She dried her eyes with some toilet paper.

"I'm not eating any of that mess," Kim said. "You sick?"

"No." *A little heartsick maybe.*

"You dropping off the kids?" Kim asked.

"No."

"Then what are you doing in there?" Kim asked.

"Thinking." *He says "nope." Maybe that's the way they say a sarcastic "yep" in Alabama.*

"About what?"

"Life." *And all of life's little surprises, which make us run to restrooms in churches while potlucks are going on downstairs.*

"You should hear what they're talking about downstairs," Kim said. "Most people think there will be plenty of surprises tomorrow."

"There will be no surprises," Sonya said. "From me anyway."

"What's that supposed to mean?" Kim asked.

I am not going to get any peace, am I? Sonya left the stall and stood in front of the little mirror over the sink. "Nothing. I am kind of surprised at you, though."

"Me? What'd I do?"

"You fell in love with Tony."

Kim looked away. "No, I didn't."

She looked away. She's such a little liar. Her little neck is flushed, too. Oh, that's a dead giveaway. She's now wringing her hands. "How in love with Tony are you, Kim?"

"What do you mean?" Kim said. "I'm not in love with Tony. I mean, he's fine and fun to be with, but I'm definitely not in love with him. Did you know that those tattoos of his weren't real? They were henna. They've all washed off."

"I have eyes, Kim. You like him. A lot. A lot more than like. Maybe even the most intense *like* of your life." *Maybe John only likes me? I am not content with that.*

"Tony is . . . he's too normal and, well, ordinary for me," Kim said.

Sonya washed her hands. "You desperately need normal and ordinary, Kim. How do you know his tattoos weren't real?"

"They've all faded away," Kim said. "We were at the pool all day while you and John were on your date. I noticed."

Sonya dried her hands on a paper towel. "All day? Is that the longest time you've ever stayed with a man?"

"I've spent the night countless times with a man," Kim said.

"So you've told me," Sonya said. *And thank You, most almighty Father, for keeping her safe all these years.* "But this time was different."

"How so?" Kim asked.

"This time you were *awake* the whole time. Imagine that. And you obviously can't keep

590

your eyes off him. You two were down that pew trading hands the whole service."

"Like I said, he's fine," Kim said. "Looking, that's all I'm doing. I'm just looking."

"And maybe . . . touching and kissing and more, right?"

Kim nodded. "I, um, I like his shoulders. He has nice firm lips."

Sonya checked her eyes. *Bloodshot. Great.* "I think that boy is in love with you, Kim."

"Oh, I don't think he's in love with me," Kim said. "He only said he liked me a lot."

"I don't think he likes you at all."

"How can you say that, Sonya? You don't know him well enough to say that! I do! I mean, how can you say a man doesn't like me when you weren't there to hear him say, 'I like you'? He said it to me this morning. We were waiting on your late behind out by the pool, and he said, 'I like you very much, Shani.' You weren't there. How would you know?"

Now I know she's in love. "Calm down. I think it's much more than like. Much more. He's always looking at *you* when you're not paying attention, which is most of the time. Haven't you ever caught him looking hard at you?"

"No."

"You'll have to pay better attention," Sonya said. *And so will I. What did I miss? Why was I so convinced that John was in love with me?*

591

"Um, Sonya, you don't really want Tony, do you?" Kim asked.

"No, Shani. He's all yours." Sonya pushed a lock of hair off Kim's nose. "You need him. It's never wrong to go for what you need."

"I don't . . . need Tony."

"Yes, you do," Sonya said. "Like the air you breathe. Yes, you need Tony."

Kim nodded. "I've never . . . needed anyone before."

Normally, I'd be hurt, but now I only feel love for this child.

"You aren't mad at me for stealing your man, are you?" Kim asked.

"You didn't steal my man." Sonya hugged Kim, and for the first time ever, Kim hugged Sonya back. *I need to go back into that stall right now and weep.* "I want John. Only John."

Kim stepped back. "Cool." She looked at the door. "I'll, uh, I'll try a salad or something down there. You coming?"

As soon as I cry some more. "I'll be right there."

After Kim left, Sonya stared at herself in the mirror. *I still want John, only John. Even if he isn't in love with me.*

My crazy, heathen daughter just hugged me.

I am losing my mind.

Sonya sighed.

Okay, now I can go get my grub on.

CHAPTER 57

Promos stole the men away from the potluck long into the night on Sunday.

A promo for the Gap kept Sonya and Shani from the mansion Monday morning.

The Team kept their distance Monday afternoon, staying in their rooms.

Packing? Sonya thought. *It doesn't take five hours for anyone to pack. And John doesn't have to pack at all! He should be wandering around the house, watching TV, making me a ham 'n' cheese sandwich in the kitchen, taking a dip in the pool. Just like a man to leave a woman hanging after a night of bliss.*

When Sonya finally saw the Team, they sat subdued in front of the wide-screen TV in the great room, watching the first forty-five minutes. The song segment was as amazing cut and spliced as it was live. The beginning of her date with John at Café Provencal ran in its entirety — all five minutes of it — until Graham's voiceover said: "And then Arthur and Jazz disappeared for nine hours. We have no idea where they went or what they did, but both Jazz and Arthur did return with smiles on their faces."

The memory stirred Sonya's soul. *Sweaty palms, sweaty knees, racing heart, racing loins . . . I returned with more than a smile on my face. I returned thinking I had a man in love with me. I returned a new person.*

The scenes at Bethel were tastefully done, heavily focusing on Gary and Justin's song and the potluck. *At least we brought Jesus to America for a few minutes.*

"Two minutes!" Darius yelled. "Get to your marks."

The Team filed out ahead of Sonya, none of them looking back. *Why is everyone looking as pitiful as I feel?*

Sonya took her place, the lights brightened, Darius pointed at Graham . . .

Time for more of the same, Sonya thought. *Put on your plastic smile, girl.*

"Arthur finally won a date this week," Graham said.

The Team applauded.

John blushed.

Sonya pouted.

"Um, as I was saying," Graham said, "Arthur won the date this week, so he has immunity. Who else is safe, Jazz?"

Sonya took a deep breath.

"May I say something first, Graham?"

Justin asked.

Sonya exhaled. *What's going on?*

"Um, sure," Graham said. "There's obviously no script necessary on this show anymore. I don't even know why we have cue cards."

"Hush, Graham," Sonya said. "Go ahead, Justin."

"Jazz, you are the most amazing woman I've ever known," Justin said. "Next to my mama, that is. Love ya, Ma. I truly mean that, Jazz. You're amazing. You're good for my soul."

"Thank you, Justin," Sonya said. "You're pretty amazing yourself."

Justin smiled at the ground. "But I, um, I've fallen in love with somebody else."

A diva would act shocked, but I am not a diva. I'm only going to smile. "Good for you, Justin."

Justin looked up. "You're not mad?"

"No," Sonya said. "It was only a matter of time before someone else noticed how wonderful you are and stole you away from me. Of course I'm hurt and will cry myself to sleep tonight."

Justin's eyes widened. "Really?"

"No," Sonya said. "Who is she?"

"She's in the choir at Bethel," Justin said.

"I've seen you two talking an awful lot at church." She looked directly at a camera. "America, the Team and I have been attending church *every* Sunday since we've been on this show. Tonight, you got to see us in action at that church." She turned back to Justin. "She's very beautiful, Justin."

"Yeah," Justin said. "And she can really sing."

"So that's why you take so long to get to the car after church every week, right?" Sonya asked.

"Yeah," Justin said. "We were in the choir room."

"Singing, right?" Sonya asked.

"Yeah," Justin said. "Singing without making a sound."

And now I'm not pouting anymore. "I am so happy for you two."

"She's been texting me to death since the first Sunday we went to church," Justin said.

"You gave her your number the first time we attended Bethel?" Sonya said.

"She asked," Justin said. "I don't get asked that often for my number, so I gave it to her."

"Tell me about her," Sonya said.

"Tell you about Brandy?" Justin said. "Can I say hi to her?"

"Sure." *Why not?*

"Hi, Brandy. See you soon." Justin sighed. "Um, Brandy can cook, she can sang, she loves me, she's a good Christian woman like you, she laughs at all my jokes, and her kisses are real sweet. Oh, man. Now her mama knows."

Sonya laughed. "The whole world knows, Justin. I think her mama will get over it."

"You're really not mad at me, Jazz?" Justin asked.

Sonya left her mark and gave Justin a huge hug. "I could never be anything but happy for you." *And now I'm crying. Wow. I'm a leaky faucet these days.* "These are tears of joy, America. I am not sad or heartbroken or forlorn to see him go to the woman he loves. I don't want to read or hear tomorrow that I'm bipolar or on medication or drunk or crazy. Sometimes real people cry for real reasons. And this is one of them."

"And, um, y'all are invited to the wedding," Justin said.

"What?" Sonya said. "You already popped the question?"

"Well, I texted her a few minutes ago while we were watching the taped parts, and she texted back with a yes." He took out his cell phone and showed Sonya. "I'll make it official tonight. She's, um, she's waiting for me at the church, so I kinda gotta go now."

"You texted your proposal?" Kim said. "Oh my God!"

"The choir room was real crowded yesterday," Justin said. "I didn't want to make a scene."

"Trust me, Justin," Kim said. "You just made a scene."

Sonya hugged Justin again. "Don't keep her waiting."

Justin hugged Gary and Tony and towered

over John. "Artie, thanks for helping me out."

"My name is John," John said. He shook Justin's hand. "John Bond from Burnt Corn, Alabama. I want you to send me an invitation to your wedding, Justin. You won't need to know the zip code."

"I will," Justin said. "John Bond, Burnt Corn, Alabama. I may even ask you to marry us."

"I'd like to do that," John said.

But you need a wife first, man, Sonya thought, *and that should be me, but nope, you're not in love with me.*

John hugged Justin. "God bless you, Justin." He located a camera. "And you, too, Brandy."

Justin picked up his suitcases and headed for the limo. "See y'all later. Peace!" He threw his suitcases in the trunk and got into the limo. In moments, only the limo's taillights were visible.

And then there were three. John just told the world his real name. Why'd he do that? And Justin hinted at John's real profession, too. Maybe it's all supposed to come out tonight. Am I ready for it all to come out tonight? Nope!

Graham cleared his throat. "And that leaves —"

"Graham," Sonya interrupted, "please don't say anything to ruin this moment."

Graham sighed loudly. "I wasn't going to say anything. Every time I try to say something written on the cards, you interrupt me anyway, so what's the point?"

"You're learning to go with the flow, Graham," Sonya said. "But please don't say anything more."

"I won't," Graham said.

"See, you said something. Just let whatever happens happen, okay?" Sonya returned to her mark and wandered her eyes up to John. "John told me his real name the first time we talked at four in the morning the first night of the show, a scene the producers wouldn't show you. He rubbed my feet. He's a good foot rubber. The next night he taught me how to swim. He's a good swim coach." *Why are my feet moving up to him? Hey, feet! Stop!* Sonya reached out and took his hands in hers. "John, the other night was the best date I've ever had in my life, and, no, America, I am not going into any details. We spent the day together on a real date at the beach with no cameras around." Sonya kissed his cheek. "I have *never* felt so needed and wanted, John. Thank you."

"You're welcome, Jazz."

Sonya returned to her mark.

"Can I talk now?" Graham asked.

"Go ahead, Graham," Sonya said.

"Thank you," Graham said. "John, you are a hunk. I never thought I would ever say that. Jazz, who else is safe?"

"Tony, you're also safe," Sonya said.

Tony left his suitcases and joined her, smiling at Shani.

Graham took a deep breath. "Tony, you are a hunk, so that leaves —"

"Um, Jazz?" Gary interrupted. "I have something to . . . I have to go, too."

"I might as well sit down," Graham said, and he walked off the set to the pool area, sat at a table, and lit up a cigar.

Sonya smiled at Gary. "You have to go, too, Gary?"

"Yeah. I have two daughters, and they need me. The mother of my daughters needs me, too. She's been sending me two hundred texts a day since I got here. We, um, we didn't leave on the best of terms, you know? I'm gonna go home and do right by her. I'm going home to marry her like I should have already done. Jazz, I wouldn't be doing any of this if it weren't for you. You have helped me see what's really important in life. My family means everything to me. I can never thank you enough for helping me see that."

Sonya's eyes misted up. "And that Luther song you sang — you sang that song to her?"

"Yeah," Gary said. "She loves her some Luther. And she's always been the one for me. I just had to come here and meet you to see that she was. No offense."

"None taken." She held out her arms. "One last hug."

Gary came down and hugged her. "I'll

600

never forget you, Jazz. You're the lady I want my daughters to grow up to be."

The mist in Sonya's eyes turned into tears. "I'll miss you, Gary."

Gary pulled his buzzing phone from his pocket. "Sorry, Darius, I gotta check this one." He read a message and smiled. "My girl says to give you another big ol' hug from her." Gary hugged Sonya, lifting her off the ground.

I need to gain more weight, Sonya thought. *These men and their need to take a woman off her feet. How will I ever get used to it?*

Gary got some dap from Tony and John. "You mind maybe marrying us, too, John?"

"I would be honored," John said. "Send the invitation to John Bond, Burnt Corn, Alabama."

"I will," Gary said. "And John, you better get married in a hurry. You got two weddings to perform, and I know my girl ain't gonna want to wait."

Gary collected his suitcases and stood in the driveway where the limo had been parked. "C'mon, man." Gary looked back at Sonya. "I told Justin only once around the block, but y'all have pretty big blocks out here."

The limo returned. Gary tossed his suitcases into the front seat and waved.

Twice the limo leaves the mansion, Sonya thought. *We're breaking all sorts of new ground here tonight.*

Sonya looked for Graham. "Where's Graham?"

Graham sauntered out of the pool area. "You need me?"

"Yeah," Sonya said. "I need to collect myself."

Graham put the cigar in his mouth. "You mean I actually get to speak? That's amazing." He blew out a smoke ring. "Well, that only leaves John and Tony."

John laughed. "He can do that, Norm."

Sonya smiled. "Yeah, that's something he can do right there."

Graham waved his cigar in the air. "What are you talking about?"

"Graham," Sonya said, "you are the ultimate master of the obvious. The entire world can see that there are only two men left."

Graham shrugged. "Oh. Well, you asked me to say something, so I said something. I'll be by the pool if you need me." Graham returned to the pool.

Sonya looked straight ahead. "I'm all composed now." She looked at Darius, who was silently counting down. "And then," she said, "there were three."

"Commercial!" Darius yelled, and then Darius started clapping. In moments, the entire film crew, even the crew streaming out of the garage, were clapping, whistling, and stamping their feet.

We're getting a standing ovation, Sonya

thought. *I guess we done good, though I don't know how. Two men just left me without my permission! I should be furious!*

Larry appeared to her right. "That was amazing, simply amazing."

Sonya sighed. "Reality can sometimes be amazing. What happens next, Larry?"

"No more challenges," Larry said. "All that's left are the visits to Tony's hometown and John's hometown . . . and the grand finale." He took out a coin. "Tony, you call it in the air." He flipped the coin high into the air.

"Heads," Tony said.

Larry caught and uncovered the coin. "Heads it is. Jazz, you're off to New Orleans for three days first."

"Shani's going, too, right?" Sonya asked.

"Of course," Larry said. "She *has* to go to Tony's hometown, doesn't she?"

Does Larry know? He probably does. I'll bet they have cameras in my room. Where would they put them? I'll bet there's one in every laptop. "When do we have to leave?"

"Tony leaves tonight so he will have enough time to get things ready for your arrival tomorrow," Larry said. "You and Shani will fly out tomorrow. After three days in New Orleans, you're off to Burnt Corn, Alabama. John, you put your town on the map tonight."

"Yep," John said.

Oh, now *you can say "yep"!*

"And Burnt Corn is just a hop, skip, and a jump from New Orleans," Larry said. "John, you better go up and pack, hmm?"

"Yep," John said, and he trotted off toward the mansion.

Oh, right. Say "yep" twice to rub it in.

"The time will fly by in New Orleans for you Sonya, I'm sure," Larry said.

"Um, when does John have to leave?" *I have some questions for this man concerning the word "nope."*

Larry winced. "Also tonight, I'm afraid. As soon as another limousine arrives."

"What?" *Hold on, now!* "I don't want him to leave tonight."

"And leave you and John alone in that great big mansion?" Larry said. "That would give John an unfair advantage over Tony, wouldn't it?"

"What do you mean?" Sonya asked.

"Equal time must be given, Sonya," Larry said. "If Tony leaves, John must leave as well. Ah, their limousine is here."

This is happening way too fast!

Tony carried his suitcases to the limo as John shot through the front door carrying his.

They're all leaving me within half an hour! This is not fair!

John walked right past Sonya and set his

604

suitcases next to Tony's. Then he went to the back door, opened it, got inside, and shut the door behind him.

What is this? Escape Sonya Day? Uh-uh. This ain't happening.

Sonya ran to the door and knocked on the window.

The window descended.

"You're not even going to say good-bye?" Sonya asked.

"I have a problem saying that word, Sonya," John said. "I don't ever want to say that word to you."

That was . . . nice. "Well, how about a hug?" *Or a booty squeeze, geez, something to tide me over for three whole days!*

John got out, gave her a quick hug, and handed her a piece of paper. "My cell phone number. You have to call me. I don't get texts or voice mail."

"You don't?" Sonya asked.

"Nope."

There's that word again!

"Make sure you call me, especially at four in the morning," John said.

I'll set my alarm. "I'm going to miss you."

John kissed her forehead. "Try to have fun in New Orleans as the third wheel."

Sonya saw Kim making faces at Tony through the other window. "I don't know why I just can't fly out with *you* tonight. Those two will be trading hands and glands all week."

"What America doesn't know, huh?" John said.

"Yeah. How long would it take to drive from New Orleans to Burnt Corn?"

John looked up. "About four hours."

That might work. "So if I leave after midnight . . ."

John pulled Sonya close. "I would love to have you visit me, but maybe we need to step back from each other for a few days."

I don't like the sound of this. "Why?"

"We have spent, what, seventy-seven days in a row together," John said. "And I'm not asking for space or anything like that. I like the way you fill my space." He put his lips on her ear and whispered, "And I want to fill your space."

Now we're talking. Keep whispering things like that, man.

"But we need to do things decently and in order, Sonya," John said. "If you come to visit me, I know we'll be fornicatin'."

Sonya smiled. "Fornicating?"

John slid his hands dangerously close to her booty. "I believe that only married people truly make love to each other."

"We could just cuddle," Sonya said in a small voice.

"Really? *Just* cuddle? With you in your SpongeBob pajamas?"

"I don't have to wear them."

John smiled. "Then we'd be fornicating till the cows came home, cooked up some chicken, and did the dishes afterward."

Sonya dropped her head onto his chest. "I can't stand this."

John lifted her chin. "We have waited many years. We can wait a little longer."

I don't want to wait even another minute, but . . . to everything there is a season. "You're right. But before you go, I need you to explain something to me."

"C'mon, dog," Tony said from inside the limo. "We gotta go."

"Gotta go," John said. "Don't want to miss my flight, because if I miss one, I miss three." He kissed her softly on the lips. "Call me whenever. You know I don't sleep."

"I will." *And the first question I'll ask is why you said "nope"!* "This isn't fair."

John hugged her. "I think the wait will do us some good."

"There's nothing good about being away from you."

"Thank you for saying that," John said. "I will miss your smile."

"Is that all?" Sonya asked.

John nodded.

"Nothing else?"

"All I have to do is close my eyes," John said, "and I'll see the rest of you."

"Will you shout hallelujah?" Sonya asked.

"Until I'm hoarse."

"Good."

John got into the limo.

"Bye, Jazz," Tony said.

"Bye, Tony."

Sonya stuck her head in the window and kissed John's cheek. "I will call you very soon."

"Okay."

The limo pulled off.

"I'm missing him already," Kim said as they walked toward the pool.

Me too. "I thought you were more mature than that, Kim. I mean, really. You missing a man you only *like*? What's this world coming to?"

"You took a long time to say good-bye to John," Kim said.

"We weren't saying good-bye," Sonya said.

"What were you doing all that time, then?" Kim asked.

She looked at the shallow end of the pool. "I think we were saying hello."

To our future.

CHAPTER 58

John barely made his LA to San Diego flight and had only thirty minutes before his flight to Houston took off. He opened his cell, turned it on, noticed only two bars on his battery, and punched in a number from memory.

"Hello? Is that you, John?"

"Hi, Mom. Put Dad on the line, too."

"I'll get him," his mom said. "James! John is on the line!"

I'm so nervous. When did I last talk to them? "Have you, um, been watching me on TV, Mom?"

"Oh, yes, John. It's so exciting."

"Has Dad been watching, too?"

"Yes."

He has?

"At first it was a struggle. You know your father. *Monday Night Football* is so important to him. But after that ended, he was the one calling me to the TV. What's all that noise?"

"I'm in an airport in San Diego. I'm on my

way home to Alabama."

"So soon? I just watched you on TV."

"Yeah, I know. Things move faster in TV land." John heard a click. "Dad, you on?"

"Yeah."

Dad's chipper as usual. "Um, sorry I didn't tell you two that I was going on the show. It kind of happened so fast. Over a matter of a few days, really."

"Too fast to make a simple phone call?" his dad said. "We had to hear it from Mrs. Crosley, and you know how we don't like to hear anything from her."

Mrs. Crosley, professional church gossip. She has to be a hundred and ten by now. "I'm sorry. Did you watch tonight?"

"We *have* to watch now," his dad said.

"James, please," his mom said. "Yes, John, we watched. I'm so proud of you. You made it to the final two."

"Which surprises me," his dad said. "You only had one date with the girl, and you had to go running off somewhere where no one could find you."

"Yeah, Dad, story of my life, huh?" *I shouldn't have said that.* "We wanted some privacy, and I got it for us. Nothing wrong with that."

"Well, it sends the wrong message," his dad said. "It puts carnal thoughts in people's minds."

"Dad, if you had all those cameras on you

610

twenty-four hours a day, you'd try to escape, too."

"Where did you go?" his mom asked.

"To the beach for a real date," John said.

"Sounds romantic," his mom said.

"So why are you calling now?" his dad asked.

"I want you to meet Sonya."

"Who?" his dad said.

"Jazz. Sonya is her real name."

"I *told* you, Phyllis," his dad said. "No one names their kid Jazz."

I have too much of my father in me. "So could you come down to Alabama and meet her? She's visiting New Orleans, Tony's hometown, first, and then she'll be coming to Burnt Corn."

"That's not your hometown," his dad said.

"It *is* my hometown, Dad. It's where I make my home."

"You can't make a home alone, Son," his dad said.

"Which is why I want to fill my home with Sonya, Dad."

"In the same house where you and Sheila lived?" his dad said.

I'm surprised he remembered her name. "To start."

"What do you mean, to start?" his dad said. "You haven't had any income to speak of in twenty years."

"I get paid to be on this show, Dad. I have

611

about ten thousand dollars to put down on a house." *And if I win, I'll have fifty thousand more.*

"That's great, John," his mom said. "Are you two planning to have children?"

"She hasn't even picked him yet," his dad said.

"Oh, she will," his mom said. "I can see it in her eyes. And his eyes, too."

"She might choose Tony, you know," his dad said.

"He's far too immature for her," his mom said.

Should I tell them that Sonya is my age? "Um, Mom, there's something you should know about Sonya."

"No, no, John," his mom said. "Don't tell me any of her secrets."

"She has secrets?" his dad asked.

"That's how these shows work, dear," his mom said. "She's going to reveal her secrets on the last show. Isn't that right, John?"

"Yeah, Mom. She's going to reveal quite a few things."

"She is very pretty," his mom said. "And so kind. I love her smile."

"Her sister's a piece of work, though," his dad said. "Can you imagine having her visit you two?"

No. "Um, there's something . . . weird going on here."

"At the airport?" his mom said, her voice rising.

"No, Mom. This conversation. Y'all think I have a good chance of winning."

"Oh, we *know* you're going to win, John," his mom said.

"We don't know that, Phyllis," his dad said. "I think John has a sixty-forty chance. You know how women are, John. Always changing their minds. And that Tony and Shani have more in common anyway. Are her tattoos real?"

They have really *been watching.* "Yes, Dad. They're real."

"Can you see her as a grandmother holding a grandchild with that dragon on her skin?" his dad asked. "I can't."

"I can't either, Dad."

"Your mother has the whole church praying for you," his dad said.

"It sure makes Wednesday prayer meetings more interesting," his mom said.

This is . . . surreal. "Um, so do you think y'all could come down for a visit? You'll both be on TV."

"Oh, goody," his mom said.

"What's good about being on TV?" his dad asked. "I read online that it adds fifteen pounds to you."

My dad goes online? Man, has he changed.

"You don't look fat at all, John," his mom said.

"Thanks, Mom. So . . . will you . . . come down and meet her? Sonya will be in Burnt Corn Friday through Sunday."

"It's kind of short notice, Son," his dad said, "but I'll see what I can do. I'm not making any promises."

"We'll try to be there, John," his mom said.

"Y'all can do better than see what you can do and try to be there," John said angrily. "I *need* you to come down to meet her this weekend."

"And we'll *try* to get there, Son," his dad said. "I have to see if we can get a flight out on very short notice."

"You're not hearing me, Dad. I *need* you to meet her. I haven't asked either of you for anything since Sheila's funeral. I *need* you to meet my future wife."

"Have you asked her already?" his mom asked. "Will your proposal be on the next show?"

"No, Mom. I haven't asked her yet. I just know in my heart that she will be my wife."

"If she chooses you," his dad said.

"I'm positive that she will, Dad."

"You're asking a lot of us, Son," his dad said.

"No, I'm not, Dad. And I'm tired of asking. I'm *telling* you to come down and meet her."

"What'd I tell you, Phyllis?" his dad said.

"Yes, you did, dear," his mom said.

"Told her what, Dad?" John asked.

"That her attitude would rub off on you," his dad said.

"Her attitude? Sonya is a wonderful, loving woman."

"Could have fooled me," his dad said. "She orders around that announcer fellow to death. I'm surprised that *he* didn't pack his bags and leave tonight, too. He might as well have, all the good he does for the show."

John heard his flight being called. "Look, my flight is getting ready to board. Are you coming down or not?"

"Like I said," his dad said, "this is short notice. I'll have to check for available flights. Oh, yeah. And a rental car, though weekend rates will be cheaper. And a hotel."

"I'll pay you back for your expenses, Dad."

"We can stay at that nice Holiday Inn we stayed at for Sheila's funeral," his mom said. "Oh, but didn't you say those beds were too mushy for you?"

"Those beds killed my back," his dad said.

"You can stay with me somehow," John said. "Just . . . get down here, okay?"

"We'll try," his dad said. "Good hearing from you, Son."

"Yeah. Um, good to hear your voices, too. Hope to see you soon." He picked up his bag. "Gotta go."

He looked at his phone and saw his battery down to one bar. *I'll just plug it in to an outlet —*

Where's my charger
Back at the mansion.
Still plugged into the wall beside my bed.
I gave Sonya my number.
I do not have her number.
How can I call her?
He turned off his phone.
I hope she calls the next time I turn it on.

CHAPTER 59

Sonya tried to call John immediately after he left the mansion in the limo.

She let it ring twenty times.

John probably forgot to turn on his phone.

She tried to call an hour later.

She let it ring twenty-five times.

Either it's still not on or he's not turning it on while he flies.

She tried a few hours later and heard a busy signal.

Yes!

She hit redial twenty-seven times until she heard: "The number you have reached . . . is not in service."

He made a long call, then turned off his phone? What's his deal? And what kind of crappy cell phone company does he have? No text. No voice mail.

Why didn't I give him my number?

Oh, yeah. I don't give out my number to anyone.

How am I going to talk to him?

■ ■ ■ ■

The next day — between futile calls — Sonya met the entire Charpentier clan.

All thirty of them.

They swarmed her and Shani at the airport and created quite a disturbance. WB had to charter a bus to get them all to and from Louis Armstrong New Orleans International Airport.

On the short ride to the Terrytown, a suburb of New Orleans on the west bank of the Mississippi River, Sonya met all eleven of Tony's siblings, his ancient mother and father, and seventeen cousins. She found out that Tony's real name was Antonin, his nearest sister Antonette looked just like him, Mama Charpentier was Creole and black, and Père Charpentier was full Cajun. Everyone called her and Shani *"Sha"* or *"Cher"* as in, "*Sha,* you are so thin," and, "*Cher,* you have such eyes!"

They toured New Orleans in a minibus and found places still boarded up and vacant since Katrina. They ate beignets, bisque, boudin, couche-couche, dirty rice, okra, gumbo, fried oyster po' boys, tasso, and jambalaya. They spent the first night on Bourbon Street, working off all that food at the House of Blues.

These people never stay still! Sonya thought.

They don't even need sleep!

When the cameras were off and the crew finally gone from the Charpentiers' split-level house, Sonya, Mama Charpentier, and Père Charpentier sat in rockers on the patio looking out at the above-ground pool and the stars.

"I guess I better explain what's about to happen," Sonya said. "Um, Tony and Shani are going out on a date."

"No need to explain, *Sha,*" Mama Charpentier said in the most melodious accent. "I knew. You are not his type."

Sonya smiled. "I don't know whether to be relieved or hurt."

Mama Charpentier smiled. "Oh, Antonin is a good boy."

"He's canaille, sneaky," Père Charpentier said. "Good boy? No. He's got the gumbo."

"He means Antonin is too big for his britches," Mama Charpentier said. "I have never seen him so . . . focused, you know?"

"No focus," Père Charpentier said. *"Motier foux."*

"Half crazy," Mama Charpentier said. "Your half."

"Always my half," Père Charpentier said. "But, Jazz, it is really the other way around."

Tony stuck his head out of the living room, Kim hovering behind him. "Ready?" he said.

Père Charpentier stood, shaking a set of

keys from his pocket. "Do not wait up for us."

Mama Charpentier cackled. "Do I ever?"

Père Charpentier puckered up and kissed his wife loudly. "All the time. We have twelve children. She waits for me." He sauntered through the sliding glass door, shutting it behind him.

Mama Charpentier squinted. "So you tell me. How close are you to forty?"

There's no use lying about it. "Right at it."

"And John, your boo?"

"The same."

Mama Charpentier tapped her temple. "I knew. You and he are in love."

"I am. Not sure about him."

Mama Charpentier rocked a few times. "He is, too."

Do I tell her about "nope"? I've just met this woman . . . who already knows my age.

"So we play a charade for the cameras," Mama Charpentier said, "and when they leave, we live."

A fair way to put it. "Yes."

Mama Charpentier nodded. "Tony and his père will keep your daughter safe."

"It's not Shani I'm worried about. It's him." *What did she say?* "How did you know that Shani was my daughter?"

"*Sha,* it is obvious. The way you look at her. The way you speak to her. You do not lie, and your eyes do not lie. They give you away.

I had four sisters. I never look at them that way. I have many daughters. I know." She laughed. "I will not tell anyone."

"Thanks."

"You were very young."

Sonya sighed. "Yes. Too young."

"And your boo does not know."

This woman is amazing. "No. John doesn't know."

"And you are worried about this."

Just another thing to worry about. "Yes."

"This John is an amazing man. Strong. Focused. He will understand. You must call him."

"I will."

Mama Charpentier looked side to side. "The cameras are gone. You must call him now." She stood. "I am tired. You will be all right?"

Sonya nodded.

"It will be all right, too."

As soon as Mama Charpentier closed the sliding door, Sonya hit redial.

"Hello? Sonya?"

Finally. "What's up with your phone?" Sonya asked.

"I only have one bar left," John said, "and I left my charger plugged into the wall next to my bed at the mansion."

"So get another charger." *Duh.*

"I'll go out and buy one tomorrow, but we have to talk fast now. Where are the two lovebirds?"

But I don't want to talk fast! "Um, they're out on a date to Richard's in Lawtell, wherever that is, to listen to Rosie somebody play the accordion."

"And you didn't go?"

"To hear some accordion music? Really?"

"It's zydeco music, and Rosie Ledet is one of the very best," John said. "It ain't the polka. They'll be dancing all night."

"Which will give me time to sweet-talk you until your battery dies." She heard a banging noise. "What are you doing?"

"It's supposed to be in the eighties Sunday, so I'm trying to fix the church's air-conditioner."

At this time of night? "With a hammer?"

"I tried everything else."

Sonya heard a screeching sound. "What's that?"

"The sound the air-conditioner makes when it's working. The choir has to sing extra loud to drown it out."

"Are you, um, done fixing things?" Sonya asked.

"I wish I was. I was gone a long time. I've used up two rolls of duct tape and a tube of plumber's goop already."

I like a man who is dedicated to his work but not when he's supposed to be focusing on me. "Well, if you're too busy to talk to me . . ."

"I'll just come back tomorrow," John said.

"I have to keep my hands busy, Sonya."

"Why?" *Though I already know.*

"You're not here."

"I'll be there soon."

"And, um, my parents are trying to get down here."

He never talks about them. "I can't wait to meet them."

"You may have to," John said. "They said they'd try, which means they might not make it down."

"I hope to meet them."

"I hope to *see* them."

Sonya heard a crunching sound. "Where are you now?"

"I'm walking home."

"Y'all have gravel roads?"

"I'm on the side of the road, Sonya. Where are you?"

"On the Charpentiers' front porch in a red rocking chair. You almost home?"

"Almost," John said. "Red, huh?"

"Don't bring up the bikini."

"You just did."

I did, didn't I? "Is your place clean?" *Why did I ask that?*

"Sort of. The to-do list at the church was pretty long, especially when they found out the world was going to see the church on TV. New Hope folks say they don't mind cameras inside during the service, by the way. We had to take a vote, and for the first time at probably any AME in world history, the vote was unanimous. They can't wait to meet you, except for maybe Sheila's mama."

And that makes me feel nervous. She heard a door open and close. "I didn't hear any keys, man."

"I never lock the door."

Never? What section of Mayberry does he live in?

"I always leave my door open in case I get any late-night visitors," John said. "Do you have access to a car? It's almost midnight."

"Don't tease me like that."

"I'll be the guy with the big hands lying on the couch."

I miss those hands so much! "And by the time I get there, I'll be exhausted. We have been going nonstop since I got here, and the cameras just won't leave us alone. I want to talk to you nonstop with my cell plugged into something, but the cameras are everywhere. And now you're down to one bar. And why don't you have voice mail? I called you a hundred times."

"Small town," John said. "We just holler to each other. No need for voice mail. I can walk outside any night and still hear the echo."

Funny. "Promise me that when I get there we can take some escapes together."

"They're coming to rig my house tomorrow," John said. "I'll watch where they put the cameras. I doubt they'll put any outside.

The bugs are bad right now. We might be able to lose them in the woods. I'll work on it. There is an old metal shed at the church."

Sonya heard crinkling sounds. "What are you doing now?"

"Taking the plastic from the furniture downstairs. I kind of sealed this floor off after Sheila died. We had just gotten this furniture. Still looks new. Smells new, too."

"So . . . you've been living upstairs all these years?" Sonya asked.

"Yeah. There's even some outside stairs that go up there. Closer to heaven, that kind of thing. Warmer in winter, better view."

"Take me upstairs."

"Okay."

"Is your battery bar flashing?"

"Not yet."

Good. And bad. "You upstairs yet?"

"Yes."

"Give me a tour."

"You're getting heavy," John said.

"What?"

"I carried you upstairs, Sonya. You're in your SpongeBob pajamas, by the way. They have to have the thinnest material ever made."

"Well, put me down somewhere."

Sonya heard silence.

"John?"

"I put you down, but you pulled me down on top of you. We're necking, cheeking, nosing, and hipping. You're pretty insatiable."

Sonya bit her lip. "Where'd you put me down?"

"On the kitchen table. Solid oak. Built to last a lifetime."

I will love being in the kitchen with this man. "You have two kitchens?"

"It's just a kitchenette," John said. "Little cooktop, sink, and a table for two."

"Sounds cozy. Take me to the bedroom."

Sonya heard more silence.

"John?"

"You had a cramp in your foot. I had to massage it. Then I had to do the other foot since it was jealous. And then your calves got mad, and your thighs. I had to massage them, too. And then your booty started talking to me . . ."

"We may never make it to the bedroom."

"Yeah. You sure have a lot of cramps all of a sudden."

Sonya heard even more silence.

"John?"

"I set you on the bed, and now I'm taking off my shirt, pants, and drawers."

I'm talking to a naked man. And now water's running? "Are you taking a shower?"

"I have to," John said. "You smell so nice, and I smell so not nice. You know, it's going to be hard holding the phone outside the curtain while I soap myself."

"Put me on speaker, then. You do have a speaker on that phone, don't you?"

"Oh, yeah," John said. "I've never used that button."

Sonya heard a loud click.

"Can you hear me?" John asked.

"Yes. You're echoing a little. Are you using both hands?"

"Yeah."

I'm talking to a man taking a shower. What do you say to a man who's taking a shower? "You missed a spot."

"Got it."

"Almost done?" *Your battery's running out, and I need you to sweet-talk me! Oh, yeah. I also need to ask you a few questions.*

"Just need to wash my hair. Oh, hi, Sonya. You've come to help me wash it."

His imagination staggers me! "You're too tall for me to reach."

"That's why I'm kneeling in front of you. What . . . a . . . view."

Dag. I should be in my bed at the hotel.

"Wow, you *really* like that. I'm making you dance. Your legs just won't stay still."

"C'mon, man," Sonya said. "I'm on a rocking chair, and my ride to the hotel won't get here for two hours." She heard several squeaks and didn't hear the sound of water. "You done?"

"Just have to dry you off first. Slowly. I'll start with your shoulders and work my way down. Um, you can turn around now. Hallelujah!"

"John, please stop."

"But you'll still be wet when I put you on the bed."

"I am already wet," Sonya whispered. Sonya heard bedsprings. "Am I finally on the bed?"

"Yes. And you just want to snuggle with me."

That isn't what I want to do. "You're kidding."

"Wait. Um, what are you doing? You want me to do what? We are definitely not snuggling now."

I need to get to my hotel so I can enjoy myself more. "Listen, I'm going to call for my ride now, okay? I'll call you back when I get there. Turn off your phone as soon as I hang up and turn it back on in an hour, okay?"

"You're interrupting our fornication now?"

Sonya giggled. "Just . . . I'll call you back. Bye."

"Bye."

But when Sonya called him back from her hotel bed an hour later, John didn't answer. *And I'm not even wearing my pajamas! Did he forget to turn it on? Or did the battery finally run out?*

Sonya tried his number for the next hour and came up empty.

All undressed, worked up, horny, and no one to talk to.

Maybe if I just close my eyes I can see us . . .

Yeah. There we are. Oh, John, sure. You can start there . . .

John didn't answer his phone on Thursday either.

Kim, dressed in a denim miniskirt and tight frilly white blouse, looked over from her hotel bed. "What are you doing, Sonya?"

"I'm calling John, but he isn't answering his phone, and I keep getting calls from telemarketers. How did they get this number?"

Kim held out her hand. "Give it to me."

Sonya flipped her phone to Kim.

Kim scrolled through Sonya's calls. "These have three thirty-four and two fifty-one area codes, Sonya. Telemarketers usually have eight hundred or eight-eight-eight numbers. And they normally don't call back ten times." Kim smiled. "I'll bet John's been trying to call you, and you haven't been answering."

Oh no! "But three thirty-four and two fifty-one aren't John's area code."

Kim shrugged. "I'd call these back." She tossed Sonya the phone.

Sonya studied her phone. "The last call was over two hours ago. He might have tried to use a payphone or —" She groaned. "I have three voice messages waiting."

Kim rolled out of bed. "Yeah. My mama's a genius."

"C'mon, Kim. No one ever leaves me messages. I live alone, and other than you, nobody calls me. I can't remember the last time I got a voice mail."

Kim looked through the peephole in the door. "Tony's here. I'll leave you to your Alzheimer's."

"Where will you be?" Sonya asked.

"Bourbon Street."

"Again? Aren't you worried you'll be seen?"

"I love to dance with him, and those places are so packed and dark, no one will recognize me. Don't wait up." She opened the door, Tony's hand shot in, she took it, and she flew out of the room.

Sonya dialed her voice mail, put in her pass code, and listened to the oldest message first:

"Sonya, it's John. My cell phone died last night. I turned it on fifty minutes later, and it died. I should have waited the hour, right? Luckily, I wrote down your number first. I'm over in Thomasville looking for a new charger, but my phone was so old they don't have my charger in stock. They had to order me one. I'll keep calling till I get you. No, I don't want a new phone. Sorry about that. Um, I'll keep trying you. I'm really sorry about last — Yes, I'm on that show, but I'm on the phone. Can you wait a sec? Look, I know it's your phone, sir, and I'll pay you for the — Gotta go. They want autographs."

John called me just after nine AM probably just after that store opened. He tried. But why is the next call two hours later?

"Sonya, it's John again. Sorry about that first message. I'll explain later. Um, I was wondering if you were a gold or a platinum kind of woman. I'm hoping gold. Bye."

"What?" She looked in her call history and found the number, dialing it immediately.

"Tim Watts Jewelers, Tim speaking. How may I help you?"

Oh . . . man. "Um, hi. Um, this is going to be a strange question, but did a man named John Bond come into your store recently?"

"You mean the guy from that *Hunk or Punk* show?"

"Yes."

"He sure did. And he worked me for a great deal, too, and that included the long-distance phone charge."

Sonya swallowed. "What was the deal on?"

"Is this Jazz?

"Yes."

"Yeah, John thought you might call here eventually. I didn't believe him when he told me, but . . . here you are. He left you a message, too. He said, 'If Jazz calls, tell her I bought her some accessories for her red outfit.' "

Accessories for a bikini?

"He also said he's real sorry about his phone dying on you. I let him use mine, you know."

"Do you expect him to come back today?" Sonya asked.

"Nope. He completed his transaction."

"Oh." *I have to know.* "If I ask what he bought, will you tell me?"

"Nope."

I am so sick of hearing "nope" from Alabamans! "Um, thanks for the information."

A jewelry store. Gold or platinum. It has to be a ring. Or John wants me to pierce something else. I'm going with the ring.

Sonya listened to the last message, staring at her left ring finger.

"Sonya, I'll talk fast. I'm at the last payphone in Alabama that actually takes money, and I don't have any more change and your phone might not take that long of a message, so here goes . . . After I massaged your entire body for twenty minutes while you lay dripping wet on the bed, I turned you face down, and kissed and rubbed you for twenty minutes more, shouting hallelujah while you — I'll be off the phone in a minute, ma'am. One minute, that's all I ask. I don't believe it. There's a line forming beside me that begins with the oldest-living woman in

Alabama. This must be the only phone in this town. I would have called you from a neighbor's house, but you can't make this kind of call from a neighbor's house, right? I would have called you from the church, but phone sex isn't, um, biblical. I can't wait to see you. If you stop and think about it, this whole situation is the most ridiculous —"

Sonya dropped her phone on the bed. *Why didn't I answer the phone? To think that he drove all over southern Alabama looking for a way to talk to me. He always has me on his mind. God, thank You for a man who always has me on his mind.*

But why . . . didn't . . . John . . . buy . . . himself . . . a new cell phone or at least get an upgrade? Geez! Spend a little money so you can talk to your honey!

CHAPTER 60

Sonya, Kim, and their film crew arrived in Burnt Corn two hours late on Friday, the sun already setting. When their van pulled into the New Hope parking lot, there were only a few cars and a huge man in a gray three-piece suit sitting on the steps.

That would be Reverend Wilson, Sonya thought. *And he doesn't look too happy.*

Sonya stepped out of the van. "Reverend Wilson?"

Reverend Wilson's frown turned into a genuine smile. "You must be Jazz." He gave her a bear hug. "You are a sight for sore eyes."

"I'm so sorry we're late," Sonya said. "We got lost several times."

The van's driver, Marty, came over to them. "GPS doesn't function down here or something."

Reverend Wilson sighed. "Ever think of using a map? It's at most a two-hour trip down sixty-five from Montgomery."

Marty squinted. "Sixty-five?"

"Yeah," Reverend Wilson said. "Big highway. Signs all over the airport to tell you how to get on it. What route did you take?"

"Well, we rolled into Selma just fine," Marty said.

Reverend Wilson stepped back. "Selma? That's straight west from Montgomery. That van have a compass?"

"Yeah," Marty said, "but I didn't even look at it until we got to Demopolis."

Reverend Wilson shook his head. "Demopolis? Another thirty miles and you'd have been in Mississippi."

"We're so sorry, Reverend." *Now where's my man and why isn't he giving me a bear hug, too?* "Were a lot of people waiting on us?"

Reverend Wilson sighed. "Yeah. They all ate up the potluck and went home. Think there's only some three-bean salad left."

Those were some seriously hungry folks. And why is there always three-bean salad left at the end of a potluck? "Where's John?"

"It's youth night," Reverend Wilson said. "After them chaps ate everything up, they were chompin' at the bit to go play some basketball. John drove them over to Monroe County High."

"Where's that?" Marty asked.

"Monroeville," Reverend Wilson said. "Y'all had to go right through Monroeville comin' down from Demopolis. You might have even passed the church van on your way here."

Shoot! When I was trying to call him, I should have been watching the road.

"Monroeville is where the hotel is, Jazz," Marty said. "I think I can get you there."

"No," Sonya said. "You go on. I want to get there sometime this week."

Marty got back in the van.

"Reverend Wilson, can you take me there?" Sonya asked.

"Sure," Reverend Wilson said. "And I'll get you there in twenty minutes while that fool drives off to Florida. I might even play a little ball tonight myself."

Kim drifted over. "Do I have to go? I need to sleep. I'll go with the driver."

"Where you stayin'?" Reverend Wilson asked.

"The Holiday Inn Express," Sonya said.

"The hotel is just down the street from the school," Reverend Wilson said, "so you better come with us. Shani, right?"

Kim nodded.

"Both of y'all are so pretty." He pointed to a rusted white church van, NEW HOPE emblazoned on the side. "That's our chariot. It'll get us there."

They got in the van, which was roomy and clean, and followed behind the WB van until it made a wrong turn.

"They're off to Florida," Reverend Wilson said.

"Good riddance," Sonya said.

"You look just like you look on TV, Jazz," Reverend Wilson said.

"I don't know how to look any way else," Sonya said.

Reverend Wilson nodded. "Except for that first night."

"Yeah," Sonya said, "I regret wearing that blue thing."

"And the hair," Reverend Wilson said.

"And the heels." Sonya smiled. "Although those heels started something, didn't they?"

Reverend Wilson nodded. "Never watched much TV till now. I believe that God has had His almighty hand in all of this. I think God was even tugging on your feet."

"Yes, He certainly did." *Can't this thing go any faster?*

"John Bond is the best man I know," Reverend Wilson said. "He could have cut and run fifteen years ago, but he stayed, despite his sorrow."

"What sorrow?" Kim asked.

"My, um, sister doesn't know about his wife," Sonya said.

"John's married?" Kim said.

"Not anymore," Sonya said. "His wife died fifteen years ago."

"Right on this road," Reverend Wilson said.

That's . . . creepy.

"Did both her wedding and her funeral," Reverend Wilson said. "A preacher ain't *ever* supposed to do that. They're supposed to bring their kids to *my* funeral. You know, you remind me of Sheila in some ways. You got a strong, unyielding, powerful faith. Sheila was never afraid to be a Christian. She told everybody. Just like you. You told the entire world."

"What other ways, Reverend?" Kim asked.

"I, uh . . . Hmm." Reverend Wilson smiled. "I might have, um, overstepped things a little. You don't exactly favor her in the looks department."

"I've seen her picture, Reverend," Sonya said. "I know we had different body types."

"May I speak freely in your sister's presence?" Reverend Wilson asked.

Sonya nodded.

"Sheila was a flirt," Reverend Wilson said, "and so are you."

"I am not a flirt," Sonya said.

"Yes, you are, Sonya," Kim said.

Sonya turned to look at Kim. "Hush."

"Oh, Sheila wasn't a flirt in the usual sense," Reverend Wilson said. "Sheila only flirted with John. All the time. Even during service. The young lady just couldn't keep her eyes or hands off him at any time. The older and, um, wiser ladies of the church had to speak to her often about it, but she never stopped. Seemed to help their marriage, you know?" Reverend Wilson cut his eyes toward Sonya. "Seemed to make their marriage stronger."

I like this man, Sonya thought. *He gives advice without really giving it. Subtle, but effective.*

After dropping Kim off at the Holiday Inn Express, they drove a little ways to Monroe County High School.

"Good thing you're dressed for it," Reverend Wilson said.

"I only travel in sweats," Sonya said.

"Are you still representing Nike?" Reverend Wilson asked.

Sonya blinked. "Um, no."

"You still look like you did twenty years ago, Sonya Richardson," Reverend Wilson said.

"Did John tell you?" Sonya asked.

"No," Reverend Wilson said. "A woman in our church did. Researched it and everything. We all know, but we've been keeping it a secret. Who would believe anyone from Burnt Corn, Alabama, anyway?"

Sonya opened her door. "Thank you. Um, I don't want you to tell him I'm here. I just want to watch for a bit first."

Reverend Wilson raised his eyebrows. "He sees me, he'll know you're here."

"Hide."

Reverend Wilson laughed. "Woman, I was born big. I never won at hide 'n' seek. We can look in through the crack in that door over there."

639

Sonya crept up to the door and looked inside. *Hey, there he . . . is. Hmm. What kind of dribbling is that? He's practically bouncing the ball over his head! He has to jump just to dribble it again. Every kid in the gym is laughing at him! Pass the ball — that kid is open! That was a pass? Those poor bleachers! Is the ball deflated? At least he runs without tripping over the lines. Not bad on defense, but he's smiling entirely too much. I never smiled when I played defense. But at least he's having fun, and those kids seem to adore him.*

Sonya opened the door and stepped inside.

A tiny black girl no older than four immediately latched on to her leg. "It's Jazz!"

And then Sonya was surrounded by every shade of brown on planet Earth, kids of all shapes, ages, and sizes, at least a dozen smiling, laughing kids.

Sonya looked at the little girl attached to her leg. "What's your name?"

"Keisha. You're tall, Jazz."

John walked through the crowd holding the ball. "Hi. Get lost?"

"Yeah." *Hug me. Don't mind the kids.*

John looked over Sonya's head. "No cameras?"

"They're on their way to Florida."

John smiled and gave her a hug.

A chorus of "oooh" echoed in the gym.

But I didn't come here just for a hug. "Gimme

the ball. I need to teach you a few lessons."

Another chorus of "oooh" echoed in the gym.

"Give her some room, y'all," John said. "She's gonna try to school me."

The kids scattered to a set of bleachers.

John handed the ball to Sonya. "It, um, it has a little dent in it."

"From that last pass of yours." *This ball has seen many better days. Voit? They still make basketballs? Not even leather.*

John smiled at Reverend Wilson. "Reverend, you want to referee this?"

Reverend Wilson sat on the first row of the bleachers. "What's to referee? She has ball first."

"She might miss," John said.

"Didn't little Timmy get ball first last time you played him?" Reverend Wilson asked.

"Yeah," John said.

"And didn't little Timmy beat you the last time you played?" Reverend Wilson asked.

"How little is little Timmy?" Sonya asked.

"He's five," John said. "But he's big for his age. Great fade-away. Drives the lane hard. Very sharp elbows. A terror on defense."

"Check it up," Sonya said, tossing the ball to John.

John fumbled with the ball before securing it to his chest. "You said you wouldn't block my shot."

"You ain't gonna get a shot, boy."

Another chorus of "oooh" from the kids.

I like this audience. They are into our game. "Pass it — no. *Roll* it to me, John. I don't want you to put a dent in me."

John rolled the ball to Sonya and started doing jumping jacks.

This time the kids laughed.

"What are you doing?" Sonya asked.

"I call it the jumpin' John defense," John said. "It may look ridiculous, but it's designed to make my opponent laugh so hard that he, or she, in this case, can't concentrate."

Sonya smiled, shook her head, and then laughed.

"See, it's working." He pointed to the foul line. "Since you haven't warmed up, I'll give you that shot right there."

"At the foul line? No sweat." She shot, but the ball rimmed out.

John snatched the rebound. "She missed!" He faced the crowd. "What, no cheering for the home team?"

The kids were silent.

A dozen kids silent on a Friday night? And after a potluck dinner? That's creepy.

"I don't get no respect." John high-bounced the ball out to the three-point line. "You sure you don't want to warm up?"

"I'm good," Sonya said. "And why are you dribbling so high?"

John dribbled even higher. "I like to dribble this way. Easier on my back."

642

"It'll be easy to steal it from you."

John winked. "Come get it, then."

"If you insist."

Sonya jab-stepped up to John, trying to time the bounces. John bounced it even higher over her head toward the basket, slipped around her, caught the ball in midair, and shot a short jumper.

Swish.

"Hey, that's . . ." Sonya started to say.

John collected the ball. "Huh?"

Sonya blinked. *That was completely legal.* "Nothing."

"One–nuttin'," John said, and he dribbled the ball in and out of his legs back to the three-point line.

"And now you're . . . dribbling." *Exceptionally well, too.*

John dribbled the ball side to side behind his back. "Check it up." He threw a perfect chest pass to Sonya.

Sonya rolled the ball back. "You scammin' me? You can actually play?"

John spun the ball on his finger. "I had Keisha watching out the door. When she told me you had arrived, I put on a show. What took you a few years to master has taken me twenty long, hard years, thanks to these kids."

"But you told me you were terrible."

John smiled. "I told you that I *was* terrible."

"He was, yo," a tall boy in the stands said. "He flattened a ball once with a layup."

"It was a cheap ball, Jamal," John said.

"But still," Jamal said. "A layup."

Sonya moved closer. "You're full of surprises."

John turned to the bleachers. "Who da champ?"

The kids yelled, "Jazz!"

John doubled over, shaking his head. He stood. "Y'all want a ride home? Let's try that again. Who da champ?"

The kids made faces and rolled their eyes. "You are."

Sonya dropped her butt, stuck out her left arm, and bounced on the balls of her feet. "Bring it, champ."

John picked up his dribble and pointed at Sonya. "Y'all see that? *That's* how you play good defense. Look at her form. Textbook."

And I haven't done this in a while. My hamstrings are already singing the blues. "We gonna play or what?"

"Okay." John started dribbling forward, then spun and backed Sonya down into the paint.

Sonya put her hand on his hip. "You're gonna post me up?"

"Every time till you stop me," John said.

Sonya shoved a forearm into his back. "Keep talkin'."

"You're too close, too close . . ." John stepped back, jumped, squared his shoulders in midair, and made a bank shot high off the glass. "Two–nuttin'."

Sonya retrieved the ball and fired it to him. "Doin' that Tim Duncan junk."

"Tim Duncan will make the Hall of Fame doin' that junk."

True. "Come on."

John started backing her down again, faked left, spin-dribbled right, and drove the baseline.

Sonya leaped for the block, but John froze, drop-stepped under her sailing body, and did a reverse layup. "Three–nuttin'."

"That . . . that ain't right."

John snapped up the ball. "You were famous for that move, Sonya. Thought you would have seen that one coming."

Keisha ran out onto the court. "C'mon, Jazz. Please beat him. He hasn't lost in years."

Say what? Years? Sonya looked at Jamal. "Jamal, did he beat you?"

"Every time," Jamal said, "and it hurts, yo. He doesn't miss."

"He gonna miss tonight," Sonya said. "Consider the ball is checked, yo."

"Yo." John stepped behind the three-point line, rose high into the air, shot, and hit nothing but net. "Five–oh."

Sonya picked up the ball and pointed at a spot near half court. "Give you that one." She fired a pass to him.

John caught the ball and moved to the spot. He held up one finger. "Wind out of the southeast at half a mile per hour."

"Just take the shot." Sonya turned to the kids. "And, y'all, root for me or something. Y'all are too quiet."

The kids were silent.

"He gonna make it," Keisha said.

"Ahem," John said. "I call . . . bank." John shot the ball with a high arc, and it banked off the square and went in. "Seven to . . . um . . . zero." John smiled. "Jazz, how did you know that was my favorite shot?"

Sonya picked up the ball. *I need to get in this man's grill.* "Who beat you last?" she whispered.

"Reverend Wilson. He played at Auburn back in the day. I couldn't get around him. He posted me into the wall every chance he got."

"There's still a little hole in that wall, too," Reverend Wilson said.

I can't believe this. "Seven–oh is a skunk where I'm from." She handed the ball to John. "Run it back."

John sighed. "If you insist . . ."

John, indeed, could not miss. He did a Magic Johnson hook shot, the Kareem Abdul-Jabbar skyhook, the Allen Iverson running one-hander, the Sam Perkins three-point set shot, and the Bob Cousy two-hander from the elbow.

"Six–oh," he said.

Sonya moved close to him. "Please miss,"

she whispered.

John closed his eyes, lobbed it underhanded from the three-point line, and clanked it badly.

The kids cheered.

Sonya corralled the rebound and dribbled to the top of the key. "You give me this one?"

"No." He jab-stepped out to her. "You have to earn it."

Sonya tried to dribble around him, but everywhere she turned, John was there. "You can really play D."

"I'm just imagining you in that bikini," John whispered. "Have to stay real close."

Okay, old bones, at least get by him once. She tried her patented crossover, but John stole it easily. *Shoot!*

"I expected that. Game point."

Sonya crossed her arms. "Go ahead. End this thing."

John nodded. "I intend to." He dribbled to the foul line. "I think I'll use the Rick Barry granny shot." He shot a free throw under-handed, and it swished in. "Game." He smiled. "You should have warmed up first."

Sonya jabbed a finger into his chest. "I will beat you one day."

"Even if it takes you the rest of your life?" John asked.

As mad as I am for my sudden lack of skills, I have to hug him. Sonya wrapped her arms around him.

"Oooh."

"It won't take me that long," Sonya said. "Gimme a couple days."

"It might take you a few months." He waved at the kids. "Well, go on. Take the court. Play. Show's over."

The kids streamed off the bleachers and resumed play.

John led Sonya to the bleachers and a case of bottled water, handing her one.

Several little girls moved to sit near Sonya. "Sorry to let y'all down."

"But you didn't," Keisha said. "You actually got *two* shots. Most people only get the first one."

Only the first one? Man, I have really been scammed. "See, John," Sonya said. "You're already slacking."

"Yeah. Next time you might get three shots. Next year, you might get four." John smiled at the girls. "Y'all go play. I need to talk to Jazz."

The little girls scampered off.

"You aren't mad at me, are you?" John asked.

Yes. "No."

"Really?"

"Okay, a little. I was *very* good once."

John put his arm around her. "You were the best in the league, and you're still outstanding. And anyway, I had the home-court advantage. I'm sure if we were on your court in Charlotte, you'd kick my tail."

"I hardly even play in the driveway any-more. I shoot around when I'm really bored."

"I'd play with you every night."

I like the sound of that. "On or off the court?"

"Anywhere you want me to play with you," John said.

"There are a lot of places." *That you haven't kissed yet.*

"I'm game."

Sonya punched him in the arm. "But, boy, you *played* me."

John grinned. "Yeah, I did."

"I don't *like* getting played. Like when I asked if you were in love with someone and you said 'nope,' you were playing me, right?"

"Nope." John looked at the clock. "Wow. I got to get these kids back to the church. I don't wanna hear their mamas' mouths to-night."

Sonya grabbed his arm. "You're not in love with me?"

"No."

At least he didn't say "nope" this time. "But I don't understand!"

"Pray about it, Sonya. It'll come to you." He took her hand and pulled her to him.

"What?" she pouted.

"How tired are you?" John asked.

"Pretty tired. Why?" *Pray about it? Explain it*

649

to me! And then I can pray about your explanation!

"We have a big day tomorrow," John said. "Well, it's a big day for Burnt Corn anyway. There's going to be a pancake breakfast at the Masonic Lodge, the oldest building in Monroe County. Then there's going to be a parade on County Road Five right past the general store, a softball game and picnic over in Monroeville, and *another* potluck at New Hope. We like our potlucks. They're even going to set off fireworks as soon as it gets dark."

"It's not July."

"You're the biggest thing to hit Burnt Corn and Monroe County since Hurricane Katrina," John said. "It's not every day that a princess comes to Alabama."

"I was hoping for some quiet time alone with you."

"I need the same thing," John said. "But there will be plenty of time for that, right?"

I am so confused. He wants me, but he's not in love with me! He wants to spend some quiet time with me, but he's not in love with me! What gives? "I guess."

"Lean not on your own understanding, Sonya," John said.

"I'd rather lean on you for a while." *And have you get frisky all over my lean body.*

"In the dark?"

"You know a better place?"

650

"The van has a big ol' bench seat," John said. "Ride back with us. I'll make sure you get to the hotel in one piece."

"Will it be a quiet ride?"

"Nope. All that banana pudding they ate earlier ought to be kicking in soon."

"I meant . . ."

"Yes, Sonya," John said. "*We* will have a quiet ride."

CHAPTER 61

After the loudest ride in church-van history, John dropped the kids off to their doting mothers at New Hope, who just *had* to take photographs of their children standing with Sonya.

Eventually they rode to his house. John parked out front but left the engine running.

Sonya started to get out.

"Um, we're not going in," John said.

"Not even for a quick tour?" Sonya asked.

He pointed across the street. "My neighbors are watching us from their porch. They attend New Hope. And they're related to Sheila."

"Uh-*huh*. Why aren't they inside watching TV like normal people?"

"We're not on TV tonight," he said. "And it's a nice evening to sit on the porch and spy on me."

"If it isn't the cameras, it's the neighbors." Sonya sighed. "Well, I guess you should take me to the hotel, then. I like your house, though. It's big. Looks roomy."

"It is."

John drove away, flying down the road until he came to *the* curve and slowed considerably. He tried not to look at the tree, but he couldn't help himself. "Um, that's where . . . There's a cross there." *There are actually two, one just behind that one, but I don't want to think about the other one right now.*

Sonya reached over and squeezed his hand. "Is there another way to Monroeville?"

"This is the quickest way."

"You okay?"

"I'm good. You're here. That's all that matters." John put his arm around her.

Sonya snuggled against his shoulder. "I'm glad you're good."

After a few more minutes, John pulled off onto a bumpy dirt road and bounced the van around until the road ended near a large oak tree. He turned off the engine. "Is this a quiet enough place for you?"

"You want to make out with me in a church van?" Sonya asked.

He unbuckled his seat belt and her seat belt. "I just want to feel your body on mine." He pulled her toward him and slid to the right, turning her to face him.

"I'm kind of sweaty," Sonya said.

"So am I." He took off his shirt and tossed it onto the dashboard, then pulled her shirt tail from her sweats, sliding his hands up her

653

back. "I'm burning up. You burning up, too?"

Sonya nodded.

John took off her shirt. "I need some close contact, Sonya."

"So do I."

Skin to skin, their hands explored, felt, slid, and caressed. John moved to rest his head on the passenger armrest, Sonya following, her bra long gone, her chest brushing his as they kissed, his hands pulling her closer and closer —

"Sonya?"

"I want you, John."

He sat up and scooted his back against the passenger door. "I don't want our first time to be in the front seat of the New Hope AME church bus on some deserted road in Cone-cuh County, Alabama. At least I think we're in Conecuh."

Sonya laughed. "I don't either."

"I shouldn't have let it go this far."

Sonya straddled him. "It wasn't all you." She looked down at her breasts. "Did you take off my bra or did I?"

"I think we both did." He kissed each nipple. "I just can't get enough of your body."

"Now that you've seen half of it."

"It's a very nice half."

Sonya put on her shirt and stuffed her bra in her pocket. "I want to spend the night with you."

"You will."

"When?" Sonya asked.

"Soon."

"How soon?"

"Sooner than you think."

The next day John saw Burnt Corn through Sonya's eyes, and her eyes sparkled with life.

She fits in here, he thought. *She belongs here.*

They ate too many pancakes at the Masonic Lodge just after sunrise.

"I got up for this?" Shani said. "Man, I could have stayed in bed and ordered room service."

They listened to several heartfelt speeches touting the history of Monroe County and the commercial viability of Monroeville.

"Are they kidding?" Shani said. "This place is completely off the grid. No wonder GPS doesn't work down here. I'm surprised my phone even gets a signal."

Sonya and John served as grand marshals for the miniparade of pickup trucks, tractors, and horse-drawn trailers in front of the general store.

"That isn't a parade," Shani said. "That's a mini–traffic jam with a clown and some horseshit thrown in."

Sonya and John played opposing pitchers in a softball game at Alabama Southern Community College in Monroeville, a game easily won by Sonya's team because John was a "nice" pitcher while Sonya added spins and curves.

"Dag, John," Shani said, "you can't even win a pickup softball game in Alabama."

Sonya and John both decided that Shani had to go. They convinced her to return to the hotel to get some sleep.

Shani agreed.

John rejoiced.

At the evening potluck at New Hope, church members were at first hesitant to approach either John or Sonya, but once Sonya put a little dab of every pot, dish, and pan on her plate, they warmed up to her in a hurry.

"Are you going to eat all that?" John asked. *She has at least three levels of food on her plate, and that corn on the cob nearly broke the Styrofoam.*

"I will eat everything on my plate," Sonya said.

"No one, um, eats a little bit of everything at a potluck," John whispered.

"I don't want to offend anyone." Sonya cut her eyes around her. "They're watching me."

"You better clean your plate, then," John whispered.

Sonya took a deep breath . . . and inhaled what was on her plate, and then ate at least a spoonful of every dessert on the dessert table.

"I need to walk this off," Sonya said afterward. "For several years."

"We'll go walking after the fireworks," John said.

They sat in metal folding chairs arranged on New Hope's lawn and watched fireworks shoot off and scream into the sky. Sonya and John sneaked a kiss during the finale, when they thought those around them would be looking heavenward.

As people collapsed chairs, folded blankets, and said their good-byes, Sheila's mother beckoned to John.

"Is that . . ."

"Sheila's mom, Regina," John said. *And she's looking especially evil tonight. I knew she wouldn't be happy about all this. I've been doing my best to avoid her.*

"Thought so," Sonya said. "She's been grittin' on us all day but especially tonight."

John nodded. "I should have introduced you sooner, but I was afraid." He shook his head. "I haven't seen her look this evil since she found out that I took Lauren Stallworth to see *The Sixth Sense* over in Thomasville. It was our only date. I didn't know that Lauren didn't like scary movies. I'll, um, I'll go see what she wants." He took a step. "No." *Sonya and I are a team.* He took Sonya's hand. "*We* will go see what she wants."

They approached Regina, and Regina's smile faded. "Regina, I'd like you to meet Jazz," John said.

657

"Hello," Regina said.

Whoa, John thought. *That was stiff. She usually hugs the skin off visitors. I didn't expect her to hug Sonya, but only to say hello?*

"It's nice to meet you," Sonya said.

Regina nodded. "Did John tell you about my daughter, Sheila?"

No "How you like our town?" or "Did you get enough to eat?" tonight.

"Yes, ma'am," Sonya said. "He told me a great deal."

Regina looked at John. "He couldn't have told you everything."

I didn't tell it all, but I told most of it. "Regina, I told her how happy Sheila made me, how happy we were for five years, how much I miss her, the things I used to do for her, and how and where she died."

"Did you mention my grandbaby Khari?" Regina asked.

John lost feeling in his arms. "No, Regina, I didn't tell her about Khari because technically —"

"Sheila was pregnant with my grandbaby Khari when she died," Regina interrupted. "Ain't no *technically* about it, John."

"She was only a few weeks pregnant, Sonya," John said. "She didn't even —"

"And yet you let her drive herself that day, didn't you?" Regina hissed. "That rainy, nasty, windy day."

John sighed deeply. "I didn't know she was preg—"

"Oh, how you didn't know?" Regina interrupted. "You were her husband! You were supposed to know things like that!"

"I *told* you, Regina," John said, trying to stay calm. "Sheila didn't tell me because even *she* must not have known. If she knew, *you* would have been the first one to know, not me. She told you everything first all the time, didn't she, Regina?" John turned to Sonya. "I only found out that Sheila was pregnant after the autopsy." *I wish they had never told me that. They could have spared me that second bitter grief.*

"I've never believed that," Regina said. "I think you knew, and yet you let her just go on and die."

"I didn't know, Regina." He shook his head. "There's no use in arguing about this anymore, Regina. They're both gone, all right? Let it go."

"How can I let it go when you forget about Sheila and Khari by kissing this woman on the church lawn in front of everybody who knew and loved her?" Regina pointed at the camera crew. "And the cameras captured it all. It'll be all over the TV. You should be ashamed of yourself."

My heart should be hurting, John thought, *but it isn't. I should be feeling some kind of guilt, but I don't.* "I buried Sheila and Khari fifteen years ago less than two miles from this spot, Regina. Fifteen years ago. You and I stood at New Hope Cemetery for hours after everyone was gone, and we watched them put the dirt on top of their caskets. We've spent countless hours tending their graves and planting flowers. We've put in our time of grieving, Regina. Our time of grieving is over."

"It only took you ten seconds to tarnish Sheila's memory with this woman, John," Regina said. "How do you think it makes me feel to see you kissing another woman at my daughter's and my granddaughter's church? Huh?"

"Sheila would want me to be happy," John said. "Jazz makes me happy. I'm happy, Regina. Please be happy for me."

Regina turned away. "You only lost a wife and a child who you think wasn't even a child yet. I lost my only child and the only grandbaby I will ever have. You *both* should be ashamed of yourself."

"I'm not ashamed, Regina," John said. He felt Sonya's hand tighten in his. "I loved Sheila. I still love Sheila."

Regina turned back quickly. "Oh, no, you —"

"I do," John interrupted. "Love doesn't die with the person, Regina. Love *can't* die. Love is always alive. I can and I do love Sheila, maybe not as much as you do, but the love is still there. I have mourned her and Khari. I have wept for them. I have almost stopped living because of their memory. It's time I moved on. It's time I found love again." He blinked away a tear. "Jacob labored for fourteen years to win Leah's heart. I labored for *fifteen* years to keep Sheila alive for you, and I can't do it anymore."

"You mean you *won't* do it anymore," Regina said.

"We drove past the tree last night," John said.

"No," Regina said. "Don't —"

"And I slowed down like I always do," John continued. "But this time, with Jazz by my side, I felt peace, Regina. I felt hope. I didn't feel the despair that usually sweeps over me as I go around that curve and see those crosses. I felt free. You have to understand that."

"No, I don't," Regina said. "I can't see how you can even drive by there. Your wife and child died there!"

"And they're in heaven laughing their butts off at us right now because we're wasting our time on the past," John said. "I can hear Sheila saying, 'Mama, you trippin'.' "

Regina looked away. "I'm not trippin'. I just miss her."

"We all do," John said.

"You don't," Regina said.

At least she's crying and not screaming any-

661

more. "Regina, I have barely smiled for fifteen years. The first time I saw Jazz, I smiled, and I've been smiling ever since. She makes me smile, and laugh, and sing — and even dance."

"That wasn't dancing," Regina said. "I'm pushing seventy, and I can dance better than you ever will."

John nodded. "True. But whether God sent me to Jazz or her to me, I don't know. I *do* know that I'm at peace because she is in my life." He smiled at Sonya. "And it's peace that passes all understanding." He touched Regina's elbow. "It's time for a little peace, don't you think?"

"When am I gonna get peace?" Regina said. "Huh? When will I be happy again?"

"I can't answer that," John said. "All I know is that as soon as I let it all go to God, Jazz came into my life. Let go, let God, right?"

Regina nodded slightly. "You plan on marrying her here at New Hope? Where you married my daughter?"

That was the original plan, John thought. *But now?* "I don't know, Regina."

"Well, I prefer you don't," Regina said, and she walked away.

That was painful. I don't want to be in any pain today, Lord. Why'd she have to bring up Khari? She'd be turning sixteen this year, and I'd be teaching her how to drive, and we'd be tearing up the roads around here, and —

"You okay?" Sonya asked.

"Yeah, um, I want you to see my house," John said. "Now. I want you inside my house."

Sonya nodded.

And I might even weep a bit. Oh, I know I will. Who am I kidding?

John walked out of the parking lot, gripping Sonya's hand tightly, tears streaming down his face. "I guess I really haven't stopped mourning them, huh?"

"It's okay, John."

"No, it's not," John said. "I am happier than I've ever been, Sonya. Believe me when I tell you that. I am overflowing with happiness." He stopped and pulled her to him. "You make me happy." He kissed her tenderly. "I wouldn't be happy without you." He started for the house again. "But then Regina says Khari's name, and I'm flowing like a river. I didn't tell you about Khari because I never knew her, you know? I never held her, never even saw her. I only named her Khari for the headstone because Sheila once told me her first baby would be named Khari, whether she had a boy or a girl." He wiped his eyes on his shoulder. "I'm more of a mess than you bargained for, huh?"

"We all have our messes, John," Sonya said. "We all have our baggage."

"Yeah. I guess that's why I am so attracted

to you," John said. "You're, what's the word, unencumbered, not weighted down, uncomplicated. Free. You make me feel free." He laughed. "You make me feel weightless."

They reached the porch.

"Climb on my back," John said.

"I'm not exactly weightless after all the food I've eaten today," Sonya said.

"Get on."

Sonya climbed on.

John carried her inside. "Welcome home, Sonya."

Sonya slid off his back. "Are you going to turn on the lights?"

"No," John said, sliding his hands into her back pockets. "You are the light, Sonya. With you in this room, there will be no darkness."

He led her up the stairs to the apartment. "This is where I live." *Sort of.* "Test the couch. It's very comfortable."

Sonya sat and bounced on the couch. "Comfy."

John sat next to her, fumbling with his hands. "I want to drag you into the bedroom and have my way with you, but even that's not the place I want for our first time."

Sonya took his hand. "It's okay, John."

"I, um, I should have replaced the bed by now, you know?" *And now, the weeping.* "I still have Sheila's pillow in there. It smelled like her for a long time. Her Bible is still open to what she read that morning. Psalm Forty-two. 'I will say unto God my rock, Why hast thou forgotten me? why go I mourning . . .' I got stuck on verse nine. I didn't like God very much for a long time. I still went to church, though. I still went through the motions."

Sonya put her arm around him. "Isn't your favorite verse from that psalm?"

"Yeah," John said, tears spilling off his face. " 'Why art thou cast down, O my soul? and why art thou disquieted within me? hope thou in God: for I shall yet praise him, who is the health of my countenance, and my God.' It took me years to get past verse nine, and when I did, I shook off my pity party. At least I thought I did. I didn't know how miserable I was until I met you. I didn't know how alone I was until I saw your smile. I don't ever want to be alone again." He slid to the end of the couch. "Can we just cuddle for a while?"

Sonya nodded and covered him with her body. "I don't want to be alone again either."

He kissed her forehead and breathed in her hair. "Why don't we be alone together, then?"

"Deal."

CHAPTER 62

Sonya shook her head at Kim. "No, no, *no!*"

"But why, Sonya?" Kim said. "I like this outfit."

"That's not an outfit," Sonya said. "That's a gold teddy, and you're only supposed to wear something like that on your honeymoon. You're liable to bust out of that completely while you're clapping."

Kim spun around, and her breasts nearly popped out of her top. "See. They didn't pop out."

"Girl, we are going to an *old-school* AME church," Sonya said. "You can't be showing all that skin."

"But it's gonna be hot, Sonya," Kim said, "and that itchy wool skirt and I don't get along."

"*Change,* Kim. *Now.* The white blouse and the skirt. And make sure you put on that white camisole I bought you in LA. I don't want you scaring any of the biddies with your dragon."

"I am going to burn up," Kim said, snatching the blouse, camisole, and skirt from the closet.

"Better you're a little hot than you feel the flames of hell, little girl," Sonya said.

"Don't get religious on me now, Sonya," Kim said, removing the gold dress.

"I wasn't talking about the literal flames of hell, Kim," Sonya said, "though you should be afraid of them, too. I'm talking about the flames of 'hell nah!' shooting out of the eyes of the women at the church."

Kim yanked the camisole over her head. "I didn't know you were all about appearances, Sonya."

"You dressed conservatively at Bethel," Sonya said. "What's changed?"

"The weather," Kim said. "It's freaking hot."

I sure hope John has that AC working today.

"And it won't be the same without Tony there," Kim said, wriggling into the skirt. "I am not going to enjoy this."

"You'll see him tomorrow, Kim," Sonya said.

Kim buttoned up her blouse. "Well, it's not soon enough for me."

John met them at the steps of New Hope and handed them two fans from Jones Unity Funeral Home. "The AC is a bit over-whelmed today," he said. "We're standing-room only."

"Because of the cameras?" Sonya asked.

"Yep." John winked. "We're puttin' on the dog. There are only two cameras, but the folks inside seem mesmerized by them. We have the first pew on the right to ourselves. I'll lead you in."

The ushers opened the door to the sanctuary, and a somewhat cool but humid breeze wafted around Sonya's face as she walked down the aisle to the first pew, a sea of waving fans on either side of her.

A whole pew for just the three of us? "Are your parents coming?" Sonya whispered as she sat.

"I don't know," John said. "I'm saving them some space, just in case."

The organist blasted into "Have Thine Own Way, Lord," and the lights dimmed and pulsed.

"Be back in a moment," John whispered, and he disappeared through a side door.

A few moments later, the lights brightened.

John returned. "A fuse blew," he whispered. "The new one ought to hold through the rest of the service."

Sonya nodded. *I hope the organist doesn't blow out the AC.* She looked at Kim. *Maybe she should have worn that teddy.*

The organist transitioned to "It Is for Me," and a few people in the congregation softly sang, "What God has for me, it is for me . . ."

After a short prayer and a reading from Psalm 46, little Keisha led the children's choir down the aisle clapping and singing "O Happy Day." Sonya wanted to jump to her feet, but she was afraid she would be alone.

C'mon, y'all. That is the cutest children's choir on earth! Get to your feet! Give them some encouragement. Don't just tap your feet! Get up on them! At least clap your hands!

No one stood or clapped along with the music.

Just as well, Sonya thought. *It would have only added to this heat. My heels are sweating already.*

When the children finished singing, Sonya stood and clapped. "Aaa-*men!*" She glanced behind her and only saw fans. *Oops.* She sat.

Reverend Wilson rose as the children skipped out. "Amen," he said.

No one repeated it.

"I said amen," Reverend Wilson said. "It is true, it is true. Amen."

A few people said, "Amen."

"Oh, don't get all high saditty on me cuz of the cameras," Reverend Wilson said. "This Sunday ain't any different than any other Sunday. Y'all know you like to shout. It's why John has to replace the windows so often. Y'all know you like to dance. Just look at the carpet under your feet. It's almost worn clear

669

through to the wood. I'm gonna say it again. Amen!"

Everyone shouted, "Amen!"

The lights dimmed briefly, then brightened.

"That's better." Reverend Wilson smiled. "I think I want to hear the children sing that song again. Get the children back in here. This *is* a happy day, and we *gonna* be happy."

The children danced back in and took their places.

I ain't sittin' this time, Sonya thought. She stood.

The rest of the congregation stood.

"O happy day," little Keisha sang.

"O happy day," the congregation echoed.

"O happy day," Keisha sang.

"Sing it, girl!" Sonya shouted.

"When Jesus washed . . . washed my sins away . . ."

That's more like it, Sonya thought. *You want to keep children in church? Encourage them while they're in church. And here I am forgetting mine.* She pulled Kim to her feet.

Kim sighed, but she eventually clapped and sang along.

"You jump-started a church," John whispered.

Somebody had to do it.

The applause flowed over the children as they ran out the second time, and Reverend Wilson laughed his way to the pulpit. "We gonna have service now, amen?"

"Amen!"

"I'd like to thank all the folks who cooked Friday and yesterday," Reverend Wilson said. "You keep doin' that, I won't be able to button up my suit. Y'all in the front row, watch out, now. You may see a button or two flyin' your way."

Sonya laughed. *Now this is more like it. There's love and laughter in this church.*

"I'd also like to welcome Miss Jazz to our church." Reverend Wilson started clapping, and the congregation joined in. "Woman, I *never* watch TV." He turned to his wife. "Do I ever watch TV?"

His wife shook her head. "Unless Auburn's playing 'Bama."

Reverend Wilson nodded. "You got me watching TV, Jazz, and you know what, y'all? She's had America thinkin' about Jesus for three months."

"Amen!"

"She didn't have to do none of that," Reverend Wilson continued, "but she did, and sometimes the things she said were better than the sermon I gave the day before. Bless you, Sister Jazz. God bless you."

And now everyone's standing but *me, and John is clapping the loudest. Man, I don't mind this heat now.*

"Y'all be seated," Reverend Wilson said.

671

"Now the choir has been rehearsing long into the night all week. I know. I can hear them from my house." Reverend Wilson looked at Sonya. "When the Warner Brothers folks were trying to add some microphones yesterday, I had to tell them no. This choir doesn't need any help." He turned to the choir. "Y'all ready for your national debut?"

The organist played a single note.

A beat later, the choir burst into "Hallelujah Praise."

Cece Winans would be amazed! Sonya thought. *This place is rocking without drums and guitars and keyboards. And that soloist should be signed to a contract! Wow! I was expecting "Peace in the Valley" or "Take My Hand, Precious Lord" from this old-school church. Even Kim is up and dancing!*

The choir transitioned to "Lord, You Are Good."

I'm sure Florida and Mississippi hear this! They gotta at least get a drummer and a bass.

John tapped her shoulder. "My parents are here."

Sonya looked to her right and saw John's older twin and the woman who gave John his brown eyes. Sonya walked up to Mr. Bond, hugged him, and even kissed his cheek. She hugged and held on to Mrs. Bond, saying, "I'm so glad you're here."

"We wouldn't have missed this for the

world," Mrs. Bond said. "They can sing, can't they?"

"Lord, You are good and Your mercy endureth forever!" Sonya sang. *Yeah, Big Man up there, You are certainly good.*

Reverend Wilson had trouble settling himself down after the singing ended. "Y'all . . . whoo! Amen! Hallelujah! Whoo!" He drank an entire glass of water. "We were cookin', weren't we! Whoo!" He blinked. "And we're still cookin', ain't we?"

"Amen!"

Sonya looked down the pew at Mr. Bond. *So that's how John might look in, what, twenty-five, thirty years? He's a right handsome man. I see where John gets his huge hands.*

"I'd like to welcome back Brother John's parents," Reverend Wilson said. "It's been a while, hasn't it?"

"Yes," Mr. Bond said.

"First time I saw them was at a wedding," Reverend Wilson said. "Beautiful wedding. About as hot then as it is today."

Sonya saw Regina in the pew to her left dabbing at a tear. *I feel you, Regina, I really do. I lost a daughter once, too.*

"The second time I saw them was at a funeral," Reverend Wilson said. "That was beautiful, too." He stepped out from behind the pulpit. "Hmm. You're probably thinkin', 'Reverend, what's beautiful about a funeral?'

It wasn't really a funeral. It was a home-going, amen?"

"Amen."

"We sent Sheila and Khari home to Jesus. And now they're here a third time." Reverend Wilson nodded. "For a homecoming. John, we missed you. We're glad you're back home." He returned to the pulpit. "Turn with me to Song of Solomon, chapter two." He smiled. "We're gonna talk about love today. I feel it in this room. Let's see what God's word tells us about love. Starting in verse four: 'He brought me to the banqueting house, and his banner over me was love.'

"Jazz, if you didn't already know, this is a banqueting house," Reverend Wilson said. "We like to eat. But there's more to this place than food. God feeds us from His word in this place, and we have grown strong and healthy. Look at me! I have to be the healthiest man in here!"

Reverend Wilson is a wonderful preacher. There isn't anyone in here without a smile. There is love here. The man holding my hand does love me. He just can't admit it yet, but I'm okay with that, Lord. He said he still loved Sheila, and he was right — love doesn't die with the person. I still love my grandmama.

"The verse says, 'his banner over me was love.' " Reverend Wilson looked up. "I got to thinking about the word 'banner.' What's a banner? A long, skinny flag-looking thing. Businesses use them to advertise things. The big headlines in a newspaper are called banners. You may have seen a banner following an airplane. In the old days, a banner was the flag of a king — or a knight." Reverend Wilson looked at John. "You went on a quest, Sir John, and from what I've seen, you were successful, though Jazz is certainly no damsel in distress."

Laughter filled the church.

"And I can tell, Jazz," Reverend Wilson said, "that John's banner is flapping like crazy in the breeze above you even now."

John's banner over me is *love,* Sonya thought. *He makes me feel loved even if he isn't in love with me.*

"Let's read on. Verse five: 'Stay me with flagons, comfort me with apples: for I am sick of love.' " Reverend Wilson laughed. "I hope none of y'all ever think you're sick of love. If you are, tough. Why? There ain't no cure for love, amen?"

"Amen."

"Ah, but that's not what the verse means," Reverend Wilson said. "When it says 'I am sick of love,' it really means I'm lovesick. I'm infected with love. I have a bad case of love. I didn't take that love shot, and now I'm sick with it." He smiled. "Not the worst way to go, amen?"

"Amen!"

675

"Skip down to verse ten: 'My beloved spake, and said unto me, Rise up, my love, my fair one, and come away. For, lo, the winter is past, the rain is over and gone. The flowers appear on the earth; the time of the singing of birds is come, and the voice of the turtle is heard in our land. The fig tree putteth forth her green figs, and the vines with the tender grape give a good smell. Arise, my love, my fair one, and come away.' "

Reverend Wilson stepped back. "The winter is past. The rain is over and gone. The flowers are back. My yard is full of them. The birds are singing. They wake me up every morning. Even the turtle is gettin' loud. I didn't know turtles got loud." He smiled. "They're turtledoves, y'all. Birds. I went to Auburn, you know."

Lots of laughter.

"The crops are growing. It smells good outside. It smells like life." He stepped away from the pulpit, walked down to the floor, and stood in front of Regina. "And yet there are some who aren't very lively these days. Regina Mosely? The winter is past. The rain is over and gone. God's banner over you is love."

Sonya matched Regina's tears. She gripped John's hand tightly. *Lord, please take away some of her pain today. Please, somehow, replace her daughter and granddaughter.*

Reverend Wilson moved in front of Sonya's

pew. "Jazz?" He winked.

I'll bet he almost called me Sonya.

"The winter is past. The rain is over and gone. God's banner over you is love."

"Yes," Sonya whispered. *The winter is over. The past is over. All things have become new. Thank You, Lord.*

Reverend Wilson stood in front of Kim. "Shani?"

Kim wouldn't look up.

"Shani, the winter is past," Reverend Wilson said.

Sonya watched her daughter's eyes fill with tears.

"Shani, the rain is over and gone," Reverend Wilson said. "Shani, whether you believe it or not, God's banner over you is love."

Kim looked up and nodded.

Precious Lord Jesus, make Yourself real to this child. Sonya took Kim's hand.

Reverend Wilson stood in front of John's father. "Mr. Bond? The winter is past. The rain is over and gone. God's banner over you is love."

John's father nodded.

Reverend Wilson knelt in front of John. "John James Bond the second?"

Sonya smiled. *That's his full name? Cool.*

"John, the winter is past."

John nodded.

"The rain is over and gone."

"Yes," John said.

"God's banner over you is love."

"Amen," John said. "Amen."

Reverend Wilson stood and raised his hands. "New Hope? The winter is past."

"Thank You, Jesus!"

"The rain is over and gone."

"Hallelujah!"

"God's banner over you is love."

"Amen!"

"Aaaaaa-men," Reverend Wilson sang. "Aaaaaa-men! Aaaaaa-men, amen, amen. Come and sing it with me . . ."

After the song and after the benediction came the hugs. Sonya had never met such hugging, huggable folks. At one point, she faced Regina. They didn't hug each other, though Sonya wanted to. Sonya received only a nod.

I will be praying for you, Regina. You will be happy again, I just know it.

Then the entire church made a caravan down to David's Catfish House in Monroeville for all-you-can-eat catfish, coleslaw, hush puppies, and cheese grits.

There is no way I'll fit in my dress for tomorrow night! Sonya thought as she chowed down yet again. *TV certainly does add fifteen pounds to you.*

"Have you seen all of Sonya's stats?" John Senior asked.

"Dad, call her Jazz," John whispered.

A little biddy next to John slapped his forearm. "We all know already, John. And don't correct your daddy."

Sonya shrugged. "It will all be over soon anyway. So what if it leaks out."

"Well," John Senior said, "have you seen them?"

"No, Dad," John said. "I know they're good."

"Good?" John Senior said. "Son, they're great! She has some records. She had sixteen assists in a game."

"That record has been tied a few times," Sonya said.

"You were the one to do it first, though, dear," John's mother, Phyllis, said. "It's still a record in my book."

"She once had thirty-six points, nine rebounds, eight assists, and six steals in a game," John Senior said. "Those are LeBron James numbers."

The man knows my stats. Maybe they're not so boring. "We lost that game, though."

"In triple overtime," Phyllis said. "You played forty-two minutes."

Even his mother knows my stats. "And I was extremely tired afterward. And depressed. I had the best game of my entire career, including high school and college, and my team lost!"

"What impressed me the most," John Senior

said, "were your career averages. You averaged twenty-two points, seven assists, six rebounds, and two steals throughout your *entire* career. You know how many guys in the NBA did that?"

"I don't." *I really don't.*

"Only Oscar Robertson," John Senior said with a smile. "Only 'The Big O' did that in all of NBA history. Out of the thousands who have played pro basketball, only you did all that."

"No wonder you need your feet rubbed so much," John said.

"They don't know about that," Sonya whispered.

"You rubbed her feet, John?" Phyllis said.

"Yes, Mom," John said. "She just thrust them in my hands. She's so forceful sometimes."

"I did not," Sonya said.

"Yeah, you did," Kim said.

"You weren't there," Sonya said.

"I know you, Sonya," Kim said. "You're always throwing your weight around." Kim pointed at Sonya's plate. "You gonna eat those hush puppies?"

"No." She pushed her plate forward. *Go ahead, Kim. Gain some weight so your skimpy clothes won't fit anymore.* "John, I don't want to give your parents the wrong impression about me."

"She is pretty pushy," John said.

Sonya pushed on his arm.

"See?" John said.

"Really, Phyllis," Sonya said, "I'm not forceful at all."

"You sure order that Graham fella around," John Senior said. "I'm surprised he hasn't quit yet."

"He's pretty useless, if you ask me," Phyllis said. "You host that show so much better than he does." She looked side to side and leaned forward. "What's going to happen Tuesday night? Can you tell me?"

"Tuesday night?" John Senior said. "Oh, that's right. You'll be on two nights in a row."

Sonya looked at John. "We will?"

John nodded. "I thought you knew."

The princess is always the last to know. Sonya looked at Kim, John, John Senior, Phyllis, and even the little biddy. "You'll just have to tune in both nights, won't you?"

"Just one little thing," Phyllis said. "We won't tell."

"*I* might," the little biddy said, "but it would have to be something really juicy."

Sonya took a deep breath. "You'll just have to tune in."

"I already know what you're gonna do," the little biddy said.

Sonya smiled. "And what am I gonna do?"

The little biddy beamed. "You're going to follow your heart."

"Yes," Sonya said. "I am going to follow my heart."

And give John a lie detector test to make sure where his heart is.

CHAPTER 63

Kim looked out the window for the fiftieth time for Tony's arrival. She, Sonya, and John had been back in the mansion for two hours, and Tony's flight was delayed because of fog.

"What's taking him so long?" Kim asked.

"You're totally in love with him now, aren't you?" Sonya asked.

"Yes. But I don't see any fog!"

"There was fog in New Orleans, Kim."

"This is just . . . wrong."

Sonya folded and packed some more clothes. "Kim, have you and Tony . . . No, I don't have the right to ask you that."

Kim turned. "You want to know if we've made love?"

"Have you?"

"No," Kim said. "We both agreed to wait."

Hallelujah! "Who agreed more?"

Kim sighed. "He did. I would have, you know, torn him up."

She's my daughter all right. If John had whispered the word, I would have torn him up, too. "Tony is a good man, Kim."

"Yeah," Kim said. "He's the best. And somehow he's in love with me despite . . . me, you know?"

"I know." Sonya closed the first suitcase. "You know I'm completely in love with John, right?"

"I still don't see why."

"Yes, you do. You see in Tony what I see in John. A good man. A loving man. A man who will love and cherish and protect you for the rest of your life."

"Yeah," Kim said. "And you said I'd never get a good man."

I did say that. Hmm. "You want to test Tony, just in case?"

"How?" Kim asked.

"Let's get Larry to set up a lie detector test."

"Cool."

Mainly so I can get to the bottom of "nope."

In the great room in front of a roaring fire, two polygraph operators set up shop, John at one table, Tony at the other. Sonya and Kim sat behind a screen where one of the couches used to be, a TV monitor in front of them.

"Although there's not supposed to be a final challenge since we're down to two hunks," Graham said, "Jazz gets what Jazz wants. Jazz wants to give lie detector tests to John and Tony, so we're going to oblige her.

As Jazz gets the answers to her questions, only she and Shani will be able to see the results on a monitor in front of them. We will only get to see their reactions."

"Tonight we're going to see who's a liar and who's honest," Sonya said. "Tony, have you ever lied to me?"

"No," Tony said.

Sonya watched the needle jump. *Oh, yes, he has.* "Did you have a good time on each of our dates?"

"Yes," Tony said.

Hmm . . . he did. Sonya smiled.

Kim pinched Sonya's leg.

"Did you ever want to kiss me on our dates?"

"Yes," Tony said.

He did!

Kim twisted the skin on Sonya's arm.

Ow! "Why didn't you kiss me, Tony?"

"I, um . . ." Tony said.

"The test results are better," Graham said, "when you ask a simple yes-or-no question, Jazz."

"Okay, um, Tony, did you *not* kiss me because you were thinking of someone else?"

Tony hesitated. "No."

Such a liar.

Kim rubbed Sonya's leg.

"Is there someone else you're interested in?" Sonya asked.

"No."

Whew. I was worried about getting punched. This is so strange. I'm a Christian woman who is glad that a man her daughter loves is lying on national TV.

Kim patted Sonya's arm.

"Tony, are you in love with me?" Sonya asked.

"Yes."

He's so not in love with me! That machine is going to run out of ink.

Kim squeezed Sonya's hand.

"Do you want to spend the rest of your life with me?" Sonya asked.

"Yes."

That would be another "nope." That poor machine. "Do you want to marry me?"

"Yes."

Whoa. The man really doesn't want to marry me. I'm hurt. One last question to seal the deal. "Is there someone *else* you want to marry?"

"No." Tony smiled. "All done?"

Kim kissed Sonya's cheek.

I had to do a lie detector test on a TV show to get my daughter to kiss me. Ain't life grand?

"And now it's John's turn," Graham said.

Here we go. "John, have you ever lied to me?"

"No," John said.

And he hasn't. That can't be right. He said "nope"! That has to be a lie! "Did you have a good time on our only date?"

686

"Yes," John said.

He sure did. They'll definitely need more ink in his machine, too. "Did you kiss me on our date?"

"Yes."

"Did you want to kiss me more on our date?" Sonya asked.

"Yes."

I can't help this next question. "Did you want to do more than just kiss me on our date?"

"Yes."

And, sports fans, there's no doubt about it. "John, why did you come on this show?"

"Jazz," Graham said, "the test results are better when —"

"Hush," Sonya interrupted. "Why did you come on this show?"

"I came to find a wife," John said.

So true. "Have you found her?"

"Yes."

Also true. "Is there someone *else* you're interested in?"

"Yes."

And it's . . . true? She stood and peeked over the screen. *John's smiling. Duh.* She sat. "Is the someone you're interested in not on this earth and watching over us?"

John smiled. "Yes."

The man loves him some Jesus. And now it's time to really make him sweat. And me sweat. My hands are almost dripping. "John, are you in love with me?"

"No."

And . . . it's true? What? Maybe he didn't hear me. "John, are you in love with me?"

"No."

The same result? What? How can that be true? His banner over me is love! "Do you want to spend the rest of your life with me?"

"Yes."

And this is true. I am so confused! "John, do you want to marry me?"

"Yes."

Whoa. The man wants to marry me, but he's not in love with me. I know he needs a wife to be a pastor again, but . . . he's not in love with me? "Um, why aren't you in love with me?"

"Jazz, the results —"

"Go away, Graham," Sonya interrupted.

"I am so gone," Graham said. He walked through the kitchen and out to the pool.

"John, I thought you were in love with me," Sonya said.

"I can't lie and say I am," John said.

And that's true. What gives? "So you don't love me?"

"I didn't say that."

"I don't understand," Sonya said. "I'll ask it one more time. John, are you in love with me?"

"No."

And it's still true. "I don't know what to say."

"Pray about it."

"I've *been* praying about it." *Till my knees hurt!*

"Pray without ceasing, then."

Don't you quote scripture at me! "I've been praying for the last week."

"All I can say, Jazz, is for you to pray some more."

Sonya shut off the monitor, ran out of the great room, into the foyer, and up the stairs. When she got to her room, she slammed the door and locked it.

A moment later, she heard a knock.

Larry? At a time like this?

"What?" she yelled.

"It's me, Sonya," Kim said.

Sonya unlocked the door but didn't open it. She went to her bed and punched a pillow.

Kim opened the door slowly. "You okay?"

"I'm punching the crap out of a defenseless pillow, Kim," Sonya said. "What you think?"

Kim stayed by the door. "You want to talk about it?"

"I am so confused right now!" She picked up the pillow, tossed it in the air, and punched it. "I know he loves me, I know it."

"I know it, too," Kim said. "John beat the test on that question somehow. He does love you. Why would he lie?"

"But he didn't lie! You saw the results. He told the truth every time."

"He had to lie! Tony's lies must have messed up John's machine or something. Or

John's machine malfunctioned at the end. A glitch. It has to be."

Sonya sighed. "Or maybe John has the malfunction." *What am I missing?*

"You think he's playing you? Telling *you* to pray? You pray all the time."

I'm just not praying correctly.

Lord, teach me to pray.

Chapter 64

While John and Tony spent the night at the Residence Inn near the Camarillo Airport, Sonya and Kim spent their last night in the mansion.

It was a quiet night.

Sonya walked around the mansion for only a few minutes. *I think I have mansion fever,* she thought. *I have to get out of here.* She returned to her room. "Kim, want to take a walk down to the beach with me or something? I gotta get out of here, clear my head." *Get away from these memories.*

Kim struggled to close one of her suitcases. "I'm going to watch tonight's recap in front of the fire. Why don't you join me? We could pop some popcorn. Maybe make some s'mores."

And memories, Sonya thought. *Some lasting memories. What we could have done together if I had only kept her.* "Sure. I'd like that."

And while the recap ran for an hour, Sonya and her daughter spent a quiet evening in their home away from home making memories.

Michelle arrived on getaway day, surprising Kim and Sonya as they took in some sun by the pool. "How are my favorite actresses?"

"Where have you been?" Sonya asked.

"Spending money," Michelle said.

"*Our* money," Kim said. "Why are you here?"

"I called Larry, and he said it was okay," Michelle said. "I mean, you'll be on a plane to Bora Bora soon. I had to say good-bye."

"We haven't seen or heard from you in months," Sonya said. "How else have you been spending your time?"

"I've signed a few actors," Michelle said. "I got five of the first seven you dumped."

"No way," Sonya said.

"They were oh so willing," Michelle said. "And angry! They were pissed, let me tell you."

"How are they doing?" Sonya asked.

"Three are doing commercials, and two have small parts in movies," Michelle said. "I am building quite a stable of your rejects. I tried to get Aaron, but *Survivor* already snatched him up."

I hope Aaron wins. He should. "What are you really doing here now, Michelle? We're getting ready to vacate this place. We've already packed."

Michelle smiled. "I wanted to see if, after this shows ends, you or Kim wants my representation in the future."

"No," Sonya said.

Michelle pouted. "Kim?"

"No," Kim said.

"You'll make some serious coin, especially you, Kim," Michelle said. "There are several sitcoms interested in you. They're in the pilot stage already. They need you."

Wow. My daughter the TV star. "That's something to consider, Kim."

Kim shook her head. "I'm not interested, Michelle."

"They need a wisecracking, smack-talking sister for a show called *Folks,*" Michelle said, "and you are all that, Kim."

"I'm not interested at all," Kim said.

"They can also use a smooth-talking man," Michelle said. "I've tried to contact Tony. I texted him my number and all the details for the next Matt Damon movie six weeks ago, but he didn't respond."

"Tony?" Kim said. "Why'd you contact Tony?"

"You've seen him," Michelle said. "He's the hottest thing in America right now. I know he'll want to cash in on his sudden fame. He missed his chance on the Damon movie, but I have several auditions waiting for him, including that spot on *Folks.*"

"That's great," Sonya said.

"Within a year or two," Michelle said, "Tony Charpentier might get huge."

"Wait," Kim said. "You told him about a big movie six weeks ago, and he hasn't responded, texted, or called you back?"

"No," Michelle said. "Which is strange. You'd think he would jump at the chance. I expected him to respond six weeks ago. Is he slow or something?"

No, Sonya thought. *He's in love.* "He stayed for you, Kim."

Kim smiled. "Yeah. He did."

"Am I missing something here?" Michelle asked.

"No," Sonya said. "Nothing."

"You watch," Michelle said. "As soon as the show's over, he'll be calling me. At least, I hope he calls *me,* if you get my drift."

"He won't call you," Kim said.

"How would you know?" Michelle asked.

"I just know," Kim said.

Michelle turned to Sonya. "You have some pull with Tony, right?"

"I have no control over anyone but myself." *I don't even have any control over John.* "But Kim might have some pull."

"What?" Michelle said.

"We'll talk later," Sonya said. "You have anything else to say, Michelle?"

"Um, no," Michelle said. "What's really going on, Sonya?"

"Nothing," Sonya said. "Well, thank you

for putting me on this show. Now get lost."

Michelle looked from Kim to Sonya. "Okay. Have a great last show."

After Michelle left, Kim dove into the pool, then swam to the side. "Tony didn't cash in when he could have. Isn't that great?"

Sonya smiled. "Kim, you were looking for something, and maybe that something found you. Maybe acting is your thang, girl. Maybe the two of you can get on that *Folks* show."

"Maybe."

"You like LA, don't you?" Sonya asked.

"Well, yeah, but . . ."

"Just keep your options open," Sonya said. "I mean, one day the two of you could be making movies together, right?"

Kim rolled her eyes. "Right."

"At least you're getting surer about him now? Like maybe he's . . . your soul mate?"

"I think he might be."

I might be pushing this, but . . . "So Tony is husband material."

"Yeah."

Thank You, Jesus! "And how does that make you feel?"

"Special," Kim said. "Important. Loved."

Larry walked through the pool gate. "There you are." He sat across from Sonya. "I just wanted to say that I have thoroughly enjoyed working with you two."

"Thank you," Sonya said. "Where has Bob been? I haven't seen him around."

"Um, Bob has become, um, kind of a silent partner," Larry said. "He's home with his family. He seems very happy about it, too."

"Oh. I'm glad to hear that," Sonya said. "So you've been in charge the last few weeks."

"I haven't been in charge from the beginning," Larry said. "You've been in charge, Sonya. You haven't been working for me. I've been working for *you*. And all I had to do was let you loose on the world. You, too, Kim. Easiest job I've ever had."

"Any final words of advice for tonight?" Sonya asked.

"No," Larry said.

"Any ideas for how I should do the big reveal?" Sonya asked.

"No," Larry said. "You'll do it splendidly and with integrity, I'm sure."

"Thanks for . . . letting me be me," Sonya said.

Larry stood. "It is the wisest thing I have ever done."

CHAPTER 65

During the final episode of *Hunk or Punk,* the producers showed ninety minutes of *unseen* footage.

And most of it revolved around Sonya and John.

"The TV is too small," Kim said, straightening a long black skirt and pulling up her hose, the limo's TV blaring at its highest volume as she and Sonya waited inside the limo beside the hangar at Camarillo Airport.

If it weren't for all the piercings in her ears, Kim might actually be a lady, Sonya thought. *No. She's a lady no matter what she wears. I'm just glad she didn't fight me over that frilly white blouse. She actually put it on without fussing at me.*

"Sonya, I can barely see what's going on," Kim said.

"I'll narrate," Sonya said, and she gave the play-by-play for the foot rub and the swimming lesson.

"Why didn't they show that before?"

Kim asked.

They didn't expect John to win. Oh, and we were too religious. "It was too real, I guess."

When clips of John's song-and-dance rehearsal ran, Kim giggled. "He actually danced with a microphone stand. Sonya, really. You're about to hook up with a man who dances with microphone stands."

"As long as he dances last with me," Sonya said, "I don't care."

Sonya leaned in to watch the Team's discussion about leaving. "They really had it all planned out, didn't they?"

Kim sighed. "They've practically given away the ending, haven't they? I mean, there's Tony telling the world he loves me and John saying about as much about you."

About as much. He still hasn't said the words.

During the family visit scenes, camera angles made Tony and Sonya appear closer than they actually were. In one scene, Tony put his arm around Sonya's shoulders while Kim stood in the background blinking her eyes and shaking her head.

"That is a look of pure jealousy, Kim," Sonya said.

"I wasn't jealous," Kim said. "I knew he was only doing it for show."

"So I can still dance with him at your wedding?" Sonya asked.

"No," Kim said. "Tony is only ever going to dance with me."

The fireworks kiss faded into the lie detector test, and while beads of sweat formed on Tony's forehead, John appeared so cool he was almost cold.

"Maybe they didn't even have the machine turned on," Kim said. "I mean, who knows if they weren't filming another polygraph machine instead of the one in front of John to throw you off."

Larry wouldn't have done something so underhanded, Sonya thought. *Bob, maybe, but not Larry.* "No, I think those results were true."

The driver started the limo. "You're on next."

And I'm more nervous now than I was in the beginning. She grabbed Kim's hand. "Thank you for going through this with me."

"You're welcome. I had fun."

"So did I."

After several commercials, the hangar, Learjet, and their limo came into view on the TV screen. Sonya and Kim watched Tony and John get out of another limo at the other end of the hangar, both men dressed in sharp black suits, both men carrying suitcases.

They then saw their own limo parking in front of the Learjet.

"You ready?" Kim asked.

"As ready as I'll ever be," Sonya said.

The driver helped both get out of the limo, and they walked to the bottom of the stairs leading up to the jet. Sonya looked around and didn't see Graham.

She tried not to look at John, but her eyes kept drifting over to his smiling face.

At least he's smiling, Sonya thought. *I hope he's smiling in the end, too.*

And then Larry, wearing a tuxedo, walked out of the jet and down the stairs to stand between them.

"Hello," Larry said. "My name is Larry Prince, and I am one of the executive producers for this show. I want to take a few moments to make a few apologies to you, our viewers, and to Jazz and John as well. You see, we filmed Jazz and the Team twenty-four hours a day, seven days a week for over three months. As you might imagine, that's a lot of film to edit. In our zeal to present what *we* thought were the most entertaining and revealing scenes, we cut out much of what was truly romantic. You saw some of those truly romantic moments tonight. My wife, Rose, has been dead for thirty years now, and I had almost forgotten what it was like to be romantic. Jazz and John brought it all back. I wish we had shown you more." He smiled at Sonya. "Jazz, are you ready to give us your decision?"

"Yes, but I have to do something first." Sonya hugged Larry. "Thank you."

"Thank you, my princess." Larry stepped away.

Sonya faced John and Tony. "John, Tony, before I tell you my decision, I have a few things to tell you . . . and the rest of the world." Sonya took a deep breath. "I am not twenty-five. I'm forty."

"No way," Tony said.

"Way," Sonya said. "My real name is Sonya Richardson, and I used to play a lot of basketball. I have four WNBA championship rings and two Olympic gold medals. And yet John beat me soundly twice in a one-on-one basketball game in Alabama. I didn't even score a point. I still can't get over that. Anyway, Tony, I'm old enough to be your mama. Are you surprised?"

"Yes and no," Tony said. "I knew you were some kind of athlete, and I kinda knew you were older than your sister. But forty? No way."

And now for the next bombshell. Help me, Jesus. "And about my sister. Shani is not my sister." *Get ready, world. More specifically, get ready, John.* "Shani is my daughter."

Tony blinked, smiled, and laughed. "She's your . . . daughter?"

John only stared at Sonya, his smile gone.

Is that his stone face or what? Sonya thought. *Lord, help me. Make his face shine again.*

"Yes, um, Tony. She's twenty-six going on seventy." *I can't read John at all. What's he thinking? Why isn't he smiling?* "When I was barely a teenager, I did something I shouldn't have done and got pregnant. And then I did another thing I shouldn't have done. I gave up my daughter for adoption. I regretted it every day for the next twenty years until we found each other again six years ago. I love her with all my heart. Tony, her real name is —"

"Shani Neliah," Kim interrupted. "That's my real name." Kim hugged Sonya and whispered, "I love you, Mama."

That wasn't for the world, just for me. Thank You, God. What You have for me is just for me.

Sonya wiped her daughter's tears and her own. "Before I tell you two what I hope is the last decision I will ever make alone, I have a few more questions. Tony, is there anything you would like to tell me that I don't already know? You know you failed that lie detector test miserably yesterday. Start there."

Tony swayed a little, putting his hands behind his back. "I lied all through that test because I wasn't thinking about you, Jazz. I was thinking about Shani. I am in love with your daughter."

Sonya rolled her eyes. "I already knew that, Tony." She looked directly at the camera. "You see, America, we did a little flimflam on you. What happened in New Orleans really didn't happen the way you saw it happen. For three days, I hung out with Tony and his family when the cameras were rolling. After they packed up the cameras, my daughter and Tony went out on the town until sunrise." Sonya narrowed her eyes at Tony. "Why are you still standing there? I'm not your princess. Go get your princess, Tony."

Tony zipped up to Shani and lifted her high into the air. When he finally let her settle down, he said, "I love you, Shani."

"I love you, Tony," Kim said, and then they kissed. And kissed.

And . . . kissed.

"Hold up now," Sonya said. "I'm not done with your man yet. Let him go, Shani."

"Yes, Mama," Shani said.

That "mama" was for the world. I will never get tired of hearing that. "Tony, do you really, honestly, with all your heart, soul, and mind, love my daughter, Shani?"

Tony nodded. "Yes."

"And you'll protect her and care for her," Sonya said, "and keep her in line better than I ever could?"

"I'll try," Tony said, "but I'd rather let her be free."

"Good answer, Tony," Sonya said. *That's the only right answer.* "Shani, do you love Tony with all your heart, soul, and mind?"

"Yes."

Sonya smiled. "Y'all can kiss some more." They did.

Hey, bud, watch your hands. "Now get out

703

of my sight and out of my light. You're ruining my take."

Tony and Shani walked over to Larry.

Sonya addressed the camera. "America, I'm really not like this. I am so shy. You wouldn't believe how shy I am. I may have played in front of thousands, but I am so . . . shy when I'm with the right person." She smiled at John. "John?"

"Yes, Sonya?"

Oh, God, I hope that's a smile. "You passed the lie detector test with flying colors. You answered every question truthfully. Is there anything you want to tell me that I don't already know?"

"You have a beautiful daughter, Sonya," John said.

"Thank you," Sonya said. *I really needed to hear that . . . acceptance in his voice.*

"We'll have to keep praying for her, though, won't we?" John asked.

"Yes, though I think she's in good hands." *And he better keep his hands off Shani this minute! Boy, we're on live TV!*

John left his mark and sauntered over to Sonya. "There's something else you don't know, Sonya." He took Sonya's hands. "You asked me if I was in love with you, and I said nope."

Sonya nodded. "That's what he said. Nope. I hate that word."

"I'm *still* not in love with you, Sonya," John said.

And I'm crying again. "But why?"

"I'm not in love with you, Sonya, because I love you."

"But . . . what's the difference?" Sonya asked.

"People say they're *in* love or *out* of love. Love shouldn't be something to get *into* and then get *out* of. Love shouldn't be something you *fall* into or *fall* out of either. Love isn't that easy. Love is not some place you can walk into and then leave any time you want. Love is a *permanent* place to stay."

I'm trembling like a leaf, Sonya thought. *My man's preaching to the world!*

"Love is patient, kind, and endures all things, Sonya," John said. "Love *never* fails. I want to stay in that patient, kind place that endures all things and never fails *forever.* Sonya, I love you, and I want to live with *you* in that place of love forever."

"I love you," Sonya said.

They then set a record for the longest hug in reality TV history.

John pulled back first. "America, I'm forty-one, a former preacher, and a widower. My wife, Sheila, and daughter, Khari, died fifteen years ago. I came on this show to find a wife, and I have found her." John kneeled and pulled a gold ring from his pocket. "Sonya Richardson, I want to make you my wife. Will you be my wife?"

"Oh, yes." *I'm a gold woman!*

John stood and slipped the ring onto her finger. "You can wear comfortable shoes or no shoes under your dress at our wedding if you want." John looked down.

Oh no . . . John, you don't have to —

He slipped his feet out of his shoes. "I don't intend to wear any shoes at our wedding."

"What will the people at New Hope think?" Sonya asked.

"My apologies to the members of the New Hope AME in Burnt Corn, Alabama," John said. "I know some of y'all expected to see us get hitched there, but I can't wait that long. Sonya, I intend to marry you on the beach in Bora Bora . . . tomorrow."

I have lost all feeling in my body. "Tomorrow?"

"We're not getting any younger, and I know I can't wait another minute."

Oh, yes! Sonya threw herself against John. "God is good."

"All the time," John said. He kissed Sonya quickly. "Larry, how much time do we have before we wrap?"

"Two minutes, thirty seconds," Larry said.

"Let's set a record, then," John said.

"I'm game," Sonya said, and they locked lips all the way until the commercial . . .

. . . and Sonya kicked off her shoes toward the camera.

EPILOGUE

FROM THE *TAHITI PRESSE,*
APRIL 5

John James Bond and Sonya Marie Richardson were married barefoot in a sunset ceremony on the beach at the Hilton Bora Bora Nui Resort & Spa. Tony Charpentier served as the best man, and Shani Neliah Allen served as the maid of honor. The happy couple will make their home in Burnt Corn, Alabama, where John has accepted the position of youth pastor at New Hope African Methodist Episcopal.

FROM THE *COMMERCIAL APPEAL,*
MAY 5

Gary Lovett and Allison Howard were united in marriage by Pastor John James Bond, of Burnt Corn, Alabama, at the Mississippi Boulevard Christian Church in Memphis. Justin Talley and Tony Charpentier were the best men. The couple's daughters, A'isha and Bria, served as flower girls.

FROM THE *VENTURA COUNTY STAR,*
MAY 19

Justin Talley, of Philadelphia, Pennsylvania, and Brandy Baldwin, of Ventura, were united in holy matrimony at the Bethel AME in Oxnard by Pastor John James Bond of Burnt Corn, Alabama. Gary Lovett and Tony Charpentier served as the best men. The couple will make their home in Oxnard.

FROM THE *GREENVILLE ADVOCATE,*
JUNE 16

Pastor John and Sonya Bond of Burnt Corn praise God for the engagement of their daughter Shani Neliah Allen to Tony Charpentier, both of Los Angeles, California. The two will be united by Pastor Bond at the New Hope AME in Burnt Corn after filming of the Warner Bros. television series *Folks* finishes this August.

FROM THE *GREENVILLE ADVOCATE,*
MARCH 21

Pastor John and Sonya Bond are the proud parents of twins Khari Jazz Bond and John James Bond III. Godmother Regina Mosley was there to witness the blessed event.